"God, she wanted him to kiss her again."

Mateo's voice had lowered in a deep, seductive tenor. His hand reached up to brush the dusting off her cheek, then he trailed his fingers across her jaw and down her neck, sweeping her hair back over her shoulder. There was a hesitation in his touch, a flicker of uncertainty in his eyes. His gaze stayed with hers as though searching out his next move.

Everly didn't look away. It felt good to be touched, to feel her heart beating rapidly again.

"I should go to my room," he murmured, not breaking his stare.

Everly moved an inch closer to him but didn't tell him to stay. He had to decide. Judging from the heated desire pooling in his eyes, he already had.

Curiosity swirled with a tantalizing hunger. She'd almost forgotten the sensuous influence it could have on the rest of her body. It all felt so good, frightening and perfect at the same time.

Hands still at his sides, Mateo lowered his mouth to hers, barely brushing her lips as though testing her. She couldn't fight the attraction. She couldn't pretend she didn't want him to kiss her fully. The hard pound of her heart begged for it.

But he pulled back. "Tell me to go to my room."

"I can't..."

ACCLAIM FOR
SARA RICHARDSON'S
PREVIOUS NOVELS

RENEGADE COWBOY

"A beautifully honest and heartwarming tale about forgiveness and growing up that will win the hearts of fans and newcomers alike."
—*RT Book Reviews*

"Top Pick! An amazing story about finding a second chance to be with the one that you love."
—HarlequinJunkie.com

COMEBACK COWBOY

"Richardson's empathy for her protagonists shines through every page of her second Rocky Mountain Riders novel, making their long-awaited reunion into a sweet tale that will easily win readers' hearts."
—RTBookReviews.com

HOMETOWN COWBOY

"Filled with humor, heart, and love, this page-turner is one wild ride."
—Jennifer Ryan, *New York Times* bestselling author

"An emotional ride with characters that come alive on every single page. Sara brings real feelings to every scene she writes."
—**Carolyn Brown,** *New York Times* **bestselling author**

"This will satisfy Richardson's fans while welcoming new readers to a sweeping land of mountains, cowboys, and romance."
—*Publishers Weekly*

MORE THAN A FEELING

"Ruby is the kind of heroine you can't help but love and root for. Fans of Robyn Carr will undoubtedly enjoy the Heart of the Rockies series."
—*RT Book Reviews*

SOMETHING LIKE LOVE

"The author's compassion shines through her beautifully flawed and earnest characters and takes readers on an emotionally wrenching journey to the elusive goal of love."
—*Publishers Weekly*

"4½ stars! Second in Richardson's Heart of the Rockies series is a delight."
—*RT Book Reviews*

"Sizzles with sexual tension on every page. The ending was a perfect, lovely, and sigh-worthy happy-ever-after."
—*USA Today*'s **"Happily Ever After" blog**

NO BETTER MAN

Also by Sara Richardson

Heart of the Rockies Series

No Better Man
Something Like Love
One Christmas Wish (short story)
More Than a Feeling

Rocky Mountain Riders Series

Hometown Cowboy
Comeback Cowboy
Renegade Cowboy
Rocky Mountain Cowboy (short story)

True-Blue
Cowboy

SARA
RICHARDSON

FOREVER

NEW YORK BOSTON

True-Blue Cowboy copyright © 2018 by Sara Richardson
Excerpt from *Hometown Cowboy* © 2017 by Sara Richardson
Saved by the Cowboy copyright © 2018 by A.J. Pine
Cover design by Elizabeth Turner Stokes
Cover photograph by Rob Lang
Cover copyright © 2018 by Hachette Book Group, Inc.

Forever
Hachette Book Group
1290 Avenue of the Americas, New York, NY 10104
forever-romance.com
twitter.com/foreverromance

First Edition: July 2018

Forever is an imprint of Grand Central Publishing. The Forever name and logo are trademarks of Hachette Book Group, Inc.

The publisher is not responsible for websites (or their content) that are not owned by the publisher.

The Hachette Speakers Bureau provides a wide range of authors for speaking events. To find out more, go to www.hachettespeakersbureau.com or call (866) 376-6591.

ISBNs: 978-1-5387-1225-2 (mass market); 978-1-5387-1224-5 (ebook)

Printed in the United States of America

OPM

10 9 8 7 6 5 4 3 2 1

Dear Reader,

I almost can't believe *True-Blue Cowboy* is my tenth book! These last few years have been an incredible adventure, and it has been such a joy sharing it with you. I have to admit, this book has a special place in my heart. Not only is it number ten, I've also decided that Everly is living my dream life.

I based her charming little farm off a farm in the small mountain town where my parents live. We have many wonderful memories of visiting their pumpkin patch with our kids in the fall and stopping by during the summer to buy produce. There is something so appealing about the thought of simplifying your life and coming to rely on the natural world for sustenance and healing. And I love the idea of having goats and ducks and chickens as pets. (Unfortunately my husband doesn't!) I hope the scenes on the farm are as fun for you to read as they were for me to write and imagine.

I also hope you fall in love with Mateo and Everly the way I did. Like many of us, they both have a painful twist in their past, but they've learned to cope with it in two very different ways. It's amazing what happens when they realize what is holding them back and work to overcome the obstacles standing in the way of their happily ever after. It's not easy for them—just like it's not easy for any of us! But I hope you will find their journey inspiring and uplifting.

This book is the result of countless hours of work and dedication—not all of it mine. I am incredibly blessed to work with the creative, talented, and professional team at Grand Central / Forever. Specifically, I have to thank Amy Pierpont, my editor on this project, for helping me get to the heart of the tension and conflict in this story. I consider myself very lucky to have the privilege of working with you! I so appreciate the efforts of my publicist, Estelle Hallick—thank you for all of your work on my behalf. There are many others who don't get enough credit for everything they do—the sales and marketing staff, cover designers, and assistants who are so wonderful to work with. You are all my heroes. I wouldn't even be able to write more books if it wasn't for my dedicated agent, Suzie Townsend. Thank you for keeping my dream alive.

An author would never survive without writing buddies. Elaine and Kimberly, you two keep me going. I can't wait for our next retreat! I'm also so thankful to friends and family who keep me anchored. You know who you are. To my three VIPs: Will, AJ, and Kaleb—"thank you" will never be enough for all you've given me. I wouldn't know anything about love if it weren't for you. Thank you for teaching me more about it every single day.

And thank you, dear reader, for opening your heart to my stories. I love sharing this journey with you.

All the best,
Sara

True-Blue Cowboy

Chapter One

I have a surprise for you."

Everly Brooks tried not to visibly cringe, but ever since her friend had surprised her with a penis cake for her birthday last year, she happened to be a little gun shy when it came to Darla Michaels and surprises. The cake artist her friend had hired had gotten a little too carried away with the details, for Everly's taste. God, when Darla had cut the masterpiece into neat little squares revealing the red velvet cake beneath the layers of frosting, Everly had to excuse herself so she could go out and get some air.

"It's not my birthday." Thank the powers that be. This year, she would make sure to take a vacation so no one could ambush her with frosted body parts. She popped a truffle into her mouth and took a sip of the deep, rich merlot that had already warmed her stomach. "Even if it was my birthday, I don't like surprises." She'd had far too many of them in recent years, and not the good kind. Thus the reason she was sitting here at the Chocolate Therapist—Darla's incredibly successful wine and chocolate bar on Main Street—soothing the ache of past wounds before she and Darla attended an engagement party.

Though she would much rather stay here at the bar with its warm ambiance and sleek, reassuring décor, she'd promised her friend Kate Livingston she would join her and Jaden for their big celebration. Regardless of how many memories it would bring up of her own botched happily ever after, she had to be there.

"I know it's not your birthday, silly." Darla swiveled her barstool and nudged Everly's shoulder. "That's in February. Wait until you see what I have planned for you this year."

"Actually, I'm going out of town that week." Not that she had any clue how she'd be able to get away when she had a farm to run.

Her friend smirked. "Great, then I'll send the surprise wherever you are."

Wouldn't that be lovely? A penis cake showing up at the door of her hotel room? Everly wouldn't put it past her.

"Trust me, you'll like tonight's surprise." Darla bounced off the barstool and smoothed down her chic tunic. Crazy how put together the woman could look after a full day of working. Her cropped black hair still had shape and style. Though she didn't need it, her makeup still looked as fresh as if she'd put it on ten minutes ago. Her unsmudged silvery eyeliner happened to perfectly complement her indigo eyes, which always flashed with a lively energy.

Everly, on the other hand, didn't hold up so well. Her days involved cooking breakfast and lunch in the warm kitchen of her café before heading out to harvest produce and clean the animal pens on her small farm. At least she'd managed to shower and change before meeting Darla. Though she'd regretted choosing this dress the second she'd put it on. The soft red fabric swishing against her skin had sparked a flashback to when Andrew had bought it for her in Venice. He'd been so thoughtful...sneaking back into the store while she waited in line for their gelato. The next morning, she'd found the delicate package sitting on the dresser of their hotel room.

Her stomach turned. Three years later, she still couldn't seem to reconcile those good memories of him with the bad ones, with the betrayal. How could she have loved someone so corrupt?

Everly reached for the wine bottle and helped herself to a refill. One glass wasn't going to be enough to get her through tonight.

"Finally." Darla darted away in the direction of the door. "Your surprise is here."

Everly swiveled her barstool so she could see what Darla was up to. Her friend opened the door and ushered in two men off the street. Wait. Was that—

"Ty Forrester and Mateo Torres." Darla put an arm around each of them in grand presentation. "Surprise!" She prodded the two rodeo stars closer. "I knew how much tonight would suck for you, so I set us up on a double date!"

A double date? Everly knew she should say something, but her jaw seemed to be stuck open. Just when she'd thought it couldn't get worse than a penis cake...

"Ty has been begging me to go out with him for months anyway," Darla said with an affectionate roll of her eyes.

The man on her left wore the cocky grin of a decorated bull rider. "I knew you'd come around eventually."

Darla ignored him. "And Mateo here"—she patted his bicep fondly—"is always good for helping a woman take her mind off the past. Am I right?" Her elbow dug into his ribs.

"That does happen to be a specialty of mine." He eased a step closer to Everly. Everything about the bronc rider was dark—from his eyes to his clothes to the cowboy hat he wore tipped forward on his head. Mystery wrapped itself in the shadows of his face, hiding secrets he likely didn't want to share. The tattered jeans he wore gloved his lower body, but somehow he still had room to swagger. And he didn't have to try. Mateo Torres was a man who could swagger without moving a muscle.

Studying him, Everly finally understood why the women in town referred to him as Zorro. The lustrous dark hair, the tanned skin, and seductive eyes made him appear downright dangerous, but his irresistible smile fooled his prey into thinking he was harmless.

"Everly?" He reached out his hand. "I don't think we've formally met. I'm Mateo Torres. It's a pleasure."

He seemed to wait for her to offer her hand, but shock and indignation and—okay, sure, maybe a smidgeon of lust—iced her body over and she couldn't seem to move. "We have met, actually." Not that he would remember with the sheer number of women he'd likely talked to in his lifetime. "At the café. A few times." Instead of shaking his hand, she directed a searing gaze to Darla. "Can I see you for a moment?"

Uttering a long-suffering sigh, her friend trudged over. "You two can wait by the door," she said to Mateo and Ty. As soon as they sauntered away, Everly spun her stool to face the bar and took a gulp of wine.

Darla leaned in next to her. "Is there a problem?"

Problem didn't even begin to touch it. "You set me up on a pity date!"

"It's not a pity date," her friend corrected. "I didn't have to bribe Mateo at all. When I asked him if he'd go on a date with you, he said, 'You mean the hot farmer chick?'" Her friend grinned. "So there. He was dying to take you out on a date."

Everly peeked at Mateo over her shoulder. He leaned against the wall and flashed her an annoyingly confident smile.

She turned back around before he could see the blush rise to her cheeks. She hadn't dated. Not once since she'd left San Francisco. She wasn't ready. She might never be ready. "I'm not looking for a relationship."

"Trust me, honey. Neither is he." Darla eased onto the stool next to her, a familiar intensity brewing in her eyes. "That's what makes this so perfect. Instead of wallowing in sad memories, you can have a night of uncomplicated fun. You don't have enough fun in your life, Everly."

The woman had a point. Don't get her wrong; Everly loved the new life she'd built in Topaz Falls, but between keeping things up on the farm and running the Farm café, she didn't have a lot of time for fun.

"You can't tell me he's not tempting." Darla looked over to where Ty and Mateo stood, her gaze lowering. "I mean, look at that ass."

Everly already knew Mateo's ass was close to perfect. She wasn't blind. But if she was going to go through with this, she couldn't let herself develop any real attachments to the man. The less she looked at his ass, the better off she'd be. "So, what? We go to the party and hang out, have a few drinks, maybe dance, and then call it a night?" At least that would help her keep her mind off of her ex.

"What you do after the party is completely up to you."

Darla's eyebrows peaked the way they always did when she had a naughty thought. "But, darlin', this is Mateo Torres. I have a feeling he's open to pretty much anything."

Mateo had to wonder if the free chocolate Darla had promised him for this favor would be worth it. Not that she would've had to bribe him to go out with Everly Brooks. Hell, spending the evening with a sexy woman happened to be one of his favorite pastimes, but Everly sure didn't seem excited about the prospect of spending the evening with him. That could ruin his perfect track record. He'd never ended a date with an unhappy woman. He'd made sure of that. Tonight he might have his work cut out for him.

He glanced at the bar again. Surprise, surprise, Everly's back was no longer turned. In fact, she stood up and walked toward him.

"Wonder if she's gonna skip out on you." Ty seemed to be enjoying the fact that Everly hadn't exactly lit up at the prospect of going on a date with Mateo.

"She won't." At least he hoped she wouldn't. He'd never hear the end of it from Ty. Mateo moved to stand in front of the door in case she tried to make a fast escape. He did have a reputation to uphold.

Instead of pushing past, the woman stopped in front of him, her gaze unsure. "Sorry about that. Let's start over." She cleared her throat as though she was nervous. "It's nice to meet you, Mateo."

"Nice to meet you, too." He checked her out as he took her hand. Her face had that pristine look—almost untouched by age or the sun, which made sense since he'd rarely seen her without the wide-brimmed straw hat she always wore around her farm. He'd rarely seen her without that bulletproof expression either—full, curved lips frozen into a polite indifference. She wasn't unfeeling, though. Her eyes gave her away. They were gentle and perceptive, the perfect shade of brown to reflect the soft light of the dim bulbs that hung overhead. He'd noticed her around town, but had never gotten this close. From what he'd seen, not many people did get close, except for her few female friends.

Whenever he did happen to see her, she didn't look like this either. She always seemed to dress in dusty jeans and a flannel shirt, not a low-cut dress that showcased those curves he'd never noticed before. Tonight, they were on full display.

Maybe this wouldn't be so bad after all.

"We should get going." Darla flicked off the lights. "We're already late."

"Sounds good. I'll drive." Mateo opened the door and waited for Everly to go outside first. Before he could follow her, Darla snagged his elbow. "Make sure you show her a good time," she whispered. "She needs this."

"I'll do my best."

An hour later, though, it was obvious his best wasn't good enough. He'd done everything required of a good date—helped her in and out of his truck, played the charming sidekick as she mingled with her friends and congratulated Kate and Jaden. He'd gotten her a drink—vodka and tonic—and had even snagged a couple of chocolate-covered strawberries for her before they were gone. But her smile hadn't reached her eyes all night. She wasn't having fun. Everyone else seemed to be enjoying themselves. The party had taken over the main restaurant at the ski resort where Jaden worked. The place was impressive—high ceilings and log beams, an open bar and a generous-sized dance floor where a live band played country favorites. That's where Ty and Darla were, tearing up the floor with some of their other friends. That's where Mateo should be, too. Not backed up against the wall watching the action.

All right, time for plan D. He slipped the empty glass out of Everly's hand and set it on a nearby table. "You want to dance?" That was pretty much all he had left in his bag of tricks. If that didn't get her loosened up, nothing would.

"Not really." She looked around. "Actually, I could use some air." The woman slipped past him, leaving him in the dust. Mateo glanced at the dance floor again. Darla gave him a crazy-eyed glare. *Follow her*, she mouthed. He might've flipped her off and headed for the bar for another beer instead if it hadn't been for Ty's smirk. His friend was usually the one getting ditched by a woman, not Mateo.

Damn. He turned and headed for the glass doors Everly had disappeared through. When they came back in, he'd make sure she had a smile on her face just to show Ty he hadn't lost his touch.

Mateo slipped outside onto a small stone patio lit by globe lights strung overhead. Everly stood on the other side, staring at the faint outline of towering mountain peaks barely visible in the darkness.

Uh…what was he supposed to say? He wasn't good at the talking stuff. Much better at the entertaining, flirting, dancing. Fucking. He was awesome at that. Even had the testimonials to prove it. But talking to a woman who was obviously experiencing some strong emotions? That'd never been his strength.

"Mind if I join you?" He sauntered over into uncharted territory.

Everly turned to look at him. Uh-oh, were those tears in her eyes? He tried not to panic.

"You don't have to stay, Mateo." She turned back to the mountains. "I know I'm a terrible date. You should go in and have fun with everyone else."

Tempting, but then he'd have a lot of explaining to do. "I wouldn't feel right about it." He sidled up next to her. "I prefer to make sure my date is having a good time." Which he wouldn't be able to do until they got past this talking stuff. "Based on your dislike of engagement parties, I'm guessing you had a bad breakup?"

A humorless laugh slipped out. "You could say that."

"What happened?" Mateo turned to face her so she'd know he was listening. He might be out of practice, but he had grown up with three sisters. He could listen to a woman talk about her emotions.

Everly looked at him for a moment, as though deciding what to say. Finally, she sighed. "It's a long story."

"I have some time." It wasn't like she was in a hurry to get back to the party. Which meant he couldn't go back either. "Go ahead. Lay it on me. Maybe it'll make you feel better."

She shot him a doubting frown. "Okay. I found out my fiancé—who I'd dated for six years, by the way—tampered with evidence to win a trial for our firm."

"Your firm?"

"Law firm," she clarified. "Andrew paid off a doctor to change the results of a rape kit so the client, who just happens to be a star NFL player, wouldn't be convicted." She seemed to lock her jaw, but her lips still trembled. "He implicated me in the plot. Used my email to send messages to the doctor, and even though I had nothing to do with it, I got disbarred."

Whoa. So much about that sentence was fucked up, but he couldn't get past the biggest shock. "You're a lawyer?" Everly Brooks—hot farmer chick—was a lawyer?

"I *was* a lawyer," she corrected. "Back in San Francisco." Her face had paled. "Thankfully the doctor came forward and Andrew went to prison. After that...I couldn't do it anymore. I mean, I totally trusted him. I almost married a man who was trying to exonerate a rapist." Everly flattened her hand against her stomach as though the words made her sick.

They made him sick, too. There was a special place in hell for assholes like that. "Can't you fight it? Seems to me you shouldn't be punished if you didn't know."

She shrugged. "I could petition to have my license reinstated. But I moved here almost three years ago and left that life behind."

The revelation struck a nerve. Didn't sound so different from what he'd done. Minus the lawyer and getting disbarred thing. "You walked away from everything?"

"My job, my parents, my friends, my life." She counted it all off on her fingers. "I wanted to start over. Thought I could leave everything ugly behind and it wouldn't be part of my life anymore." Her eyes closed. "Obviously that didn't work."

Mateo studied her. The soft glow above their heads cast her in a different light. Before standing here, he wouldn't have said she was beautiful. Pretty, sure. Though she seemed hell-bent on hiding it behind straw hats and overalls and timidity. But her face stirred something in him. He could relate to that lost expression more than anyone would know. "I might be able to help you with that. Leaving the ugly behind."

Her eyes narrowed. Yeah, she didn't believe him. She saw

what everyone else saw—what he wanted everyone to see. The life of the party. The laid-back cowboy. "Believe it or not, I have some experience with leaving ugly things behind." He'd buried a betrayal in his past so deep, even his closest friends didn't know about it.

"What did you have to leave behind?"

"See, that's rule number one." Mateo eased a step closer. "You don't talk about it. Talking about the past makes you dwell on it. And dwelling on the past makes you miss out on the party."

She shot him an amused smile. "What's rule number two?"

"When there's a live band playing, you dance. Nothing makes you forget the shitty parts of life like dancing."

"I don't know how to dance."

He gaped at her, letting his expression speak for itself.

Everly raised her shoulders defensively. "I've danced at weddings and stuff. But I don't know how to dance to country songs. That wasn't exactly big back in San Francisco."

"Lucky for you, I've gotten pretty damn good at it." On the circuit, he'd spent his fair share of time in country music bars all over the good ol' U.S. of A., and he'd learned real quick women like a man who can dance.

Mateo walked back to the door and propped it open so they could hear the music. "Let's Go to Vegas." Yeah, he could work with that. "We'll start with the two-step. It's pretty simple. All you have to do is follow my lead." He slipped his hand onto her waist, curving his fingers around her hip, and clasped her right hand into his left.

Everly's shoulders went rigid, and she leaned back as though trying to keep space between them. But space didn't work when you were dancing the two-step.

"Rule number one for dancing." Mateo guided her body closer to his, not so they were touching, but so that she could at least feel his movements. "Relax."

"You have a lot of rules," Everly muttered. If you asked him, she sounded a little breathless. Of course, he wasn't much better off. The feel of her body under his fingertips had his heart drumming.

"Trust me." He tightened his grip on her. "The only thing you need to know right now is quick, quick, slow, slow."

"Quick, quick, slow, slow," she repeated, inching closer. Her eyes were focused on his.

"On the first step, I move my left foot forward and yours goes back." He demonstrated, his hip grazing hers. "Then I move my right forward and your right goes back." He completed the step, keeping his hand firm on her hip to show her how to move.

"Got it." Her face had flushed.

"Then we do the whole thing again, just slower." He turned her and did it again, holding the steps a beat longer.

"That's it?" Everly gazed up at him with a smirk. "That's not so hard."

"It'll go a lot faster when you're actually moving with the music. Think you're ready for that?"

"Oh, I'm ready."

Grinning, he waited for the beat then launched into the dance, holding her against him, breathing in the scent of cinnamon and something sweet. "Quick, quick, slow, slow," he murmured, whirling her around before doing it again.

Everly clung to him, laughing as he danced her across the patio. He watched her face while they moved, watched it come alive with a happiness that brightened her eyes and electrified him with the desire to give her more.

* * *

Mateo was right—dancing did have some kind of magical power. Everly couldn't stop laughing as her whirled her and spun her and dipped her low. She was breathless and warm—so very warm against his body. Even the chill of the fall night couldn't touch her.

"Quick, quick, slow, slow," he murmured against her hair, keeping their movements perfectly aligned with the music. God, that rhythm. It wrapped her up, took her away, made her lightheaded and giddy. Had she ever been giddy?

The music ended abruptly, and Mateo pulled her even closer before dipping her grandly, his strong arm supporting her back. His forehead glistened and those magic eyes of his flashed with sparks of mischief. He was exotic and playful, so different from any man she'd ever met.

"Not bad for your first two-step," he said, raising her back up. The second his hands fell away, disappointment washed over her. *Don't stop touching me.* It had been too long since she'd been touched. Held. And it felt so good that she could've danced with him all night. But the band must've been taking five. The only sounds coming from inside the party were laughter and chatter.

"You want another drink?" Mateo asked, rolling up his shirtsleeves. His forearms were as rock-solid as the rest of him.

"I'm fine. Good." She *was* good. For the first time in what seemed like forever, she couldn't stop smiling.

"We could get some food." Mateo moved away from her and headed for the door, but going in would break the spell.

"Wait." Her heart refused to settle.

He turned, one corner of his mouth lifted in a sexy smirk.

"You haven't told me rule number three yet," Everly murmured. It was all she could manage with the way her heart pounded. Crazy how alive it made her feel.

Mateo glanced at her, his gaze darker than it had been minutes before. "I'm not sure you're ready for rule number three."

She marched over to him, not stopping until the tips of her ballet flats touched his boots. "Try me." She stared into his eyes, a smile still tugging on her lips. "I need the full three-step program." Especially since something told her the third rule involved more physical contact than his hand on her hip. She needed more. More energy, more color, more passion, more courage. Those parts of her had been crushed, but they were still there in pieces. When Mateo touched her, somehow she could feel them coming back together, strengthening to raise her up. Darla was right. She needed this—to feel something again, something exhilarating and carnal. And uncomplicated. Mateo wouldn't love her, which meant he couldn't hurt her either.

"Rule number three"—Mateo's intense stare lowered to her mouth—"can't be explained. It has to be shown."

Everly slid her hands up his broad shoulders. "Then show me." *All of it.* "Make me feel something." The words came out in a whispered plea.

Eyes steady on hers, Mateo brushed his palm against her jaw and gently tilted up her head, guiding her lips to his. The light touch of his mouth made her knees tremble. Energy expanded through her—bright and scorching. Mateo teased her with small kisses, slight scrapes of his mouth against hers. Her breath hitched painfully under her ribs, dislodging the months of loneliness that had made her heart feel so heavy.

He pulled away too soon, gazing at her as though wondering what she thought.

"I haven't quite got it yet," she murmured, stunned by the power of her body's response to him. "More." She ached for more.

Without hesitating, Mateo wrapped her up in his arms and pressed her in close enough that she could feel the hard bulge at his crotch. His mouth was more commanding this time, almost urgent. God, he was soft and hard at the same time. And his tongue... it wound around hers, seeking, exploring, igniting something deep within her. A moan trembled in her throat.

Mateo backed her up until he had her pinned against the brick wall, and she couldn't stop her hands, couldn't hold them still. She reached around and grabbed his perfect ass, urging him to grind against her.

"Fuck, Everly," he growled out as he kissed her jaw. "You taste like cinnamon."

"I bake a lot," she gasped, letting her head rest against the bricks. Mateo moved his hot mouth down her neck, licking and nibbling until her thighs were pressed tightly together, quivering like they'd forgotten how to behave. Good grief, she was out of practice...

Mateo traced his lips up to her ear. "You want to go somewhere else?"

"Yes." Lordy, she sounded pathetic. Desperate. But seriously. Where had Mateo been all her life? He could make her laugh and pant and dance and grab his ass. There was no telling what else he could make her do.

"They have rooms to rent in the lodge." He gazed into her eyes.

Yes. A room. A bed. Anticipation gripped her throat. "Let's go." She broke away from him and went for the door, but it flew open.

Three women came stumbling onto the patio in a giggling huddle. They were young, so pretty and made up that even Everly did a double take.

"Oh, hi, Mateo," the one with the long blond hair purred.

"Hey, Chrissy." Mateo shot her the same grin he'd been using on Everly all night.

It didn't matter. This was Mateo Torres. She knew his reputation. Like Darla had said, he provided uncomplicated fun. To a lot of women.

The blonde gave him a perfect sex-kitten glance. "I didn't know you were here tonight. I would've saved you a dance."

"I'm here with Everly," Mateo said, not glancing at her. "Her friend set us up."

The unnecessary explanation recoiled through her. *Her friend set us up.* Right. Because he wouldn't be here with someone like her by choice. Seriously. Look at those women. They were gorgeous, dressed to seduce, the kind of women Mateo preferred. And she was simply on a pity date. "It was a blind date," she informed them, with a cold look directed at Mateo. "He had no choice in the matter."

He winced. "That's not what I—"

"You go on a date with someone you don't even know before calling me?" The blonde gave him a pout. "You know I'm always available for you, Mateo. It's been a while."

"I've been busy," he said, having the decency to look uncomfortable. "Out of town a lot."

"Well, now that you're back in town, call me sometime." Blondie ran a hand up his arm. "I've missed you."

"Uh. Right. Sure." His hand gripped the back of his neck like he'd suddenly gotten too hot.

Funny, because Everly's whole body had frozen. So much

for the hot ache of desire. A pity date was one thing, but she drew the line at pity sex.

With a little wave, the trio headed back into the party, taking the trail of Chanel No. 5 with them.

Silence pounded in Everly's ears. See? This was exactly why she didn't go out. Why she didn't dance. Dwelling on the past was far less humiliating than becoming someone's charity project. She'd agreed to get a hotel room with him, for God's sake! All because he felt bad for her? No. She'd prove she wasn't that desperate.

"Sorry about that." Mateo's eyes still wouldn't meet hers. "They hang out at the Tumble Inn a lot." He stuffed his hands into his pockets. Shockingly, Mateo the badass bronc rider could look seriously awkward and guilty when he wanted to.

Except he had nothing to feel guilty about. In fact, she was glad they'd been interrupted. For a brief few moments, when she'd confessed her deepest hurts to him, she'd thought she saw a flicker of recognition in his eyes, like he understood something about those wounds. But she'd been seriously mistaken. He'd only been fulfilling a promise to her friend.

"Don't worry about it." Everly slipped past him. "You don't owe me an explanation. I know Darla talked you into this." She stepped inside, but peered back over her shoulder. "Thanks, Mateo. Your three-step program was a huge help. But I think I'll get a ride home with someone else tonight."

Chapter Two

Everly had to admit, when she'd marched her Jimmy Choo shoes out of the Ivy League halls of Stanford University with her law degree in hand five years ago, this wasn't quite what she'd pictured for her future.

Dried mud caked her red rubber boots—and her jeans, for that matter. From the feel of it, she even had a smear of mud on her cheek. But it was hard to complain too much with that view staring her in the face.

From anywhere on the small farm she leased, she could see some of the tallest mountains in Colorado. They stretched out on all sides, surrounding the valley of Topaz Falls, sealing it into its own beautiful haven. Back in San Francisco, she'd never really noticed the sky. But here that royal blue sea above the mountain peaks stunned her every single time. Being covered in mud was a small price to pay for living in a place she loved and finally following her passion.

Though she was starting to feel less and less passionate about waterfowl.

Reaching up, she swiped the mud off her face and stomped across the pen that housed the resident chickens and ducks.

Ducks. Why had she wanted ducks anyway? Sure, their eggs were rich and made her cakes and scones extra fluffy, but had she known what kind of trouble Walter would cause her, she would've left his cute, fuzzy little duckling ass at the feed store last year instead of paying three dollars for him. Now she understood why he'd been marked down in the half-price sale.

"You were so adorable when you were a baby," she muttered as she eased toward the harebrained mallard who'd cornered a squawking hen against the fence. It seemed that Walter was in one of his lusty moods again and Henrietta— who was supposed to be his mate—had wedged herself behind the coop to hide from him. Everly got it. A woman could only take so much.

"I don't have time for this," she informed the duck, moving slowly toward him so she wouldn't set off a foot chase. At seven o'clock on the nose, she had to open the café and serve breakfast to her regulars, which gave her, she glanced at her watch, fifteen minutes to get Walter into lockdown so he couldn't put the moves on any more of her innocent fowl.

"You can't mate with a chicken, you dope. You have to stick to your own kind." She made a stealthy grab for Walter, but the most recent object of his affection chose that moment to bolt away in a wing-flapping whorl of chaos. Feathers flew as Walter tore after Dixie 1 (one of the three "Dixie Chicks" she'd picked up in the same sale as Walter).

Everly started after him, but the mud slurped her boot and

held her foot in a rut. The rest of her body pitched forward, landing her face-first into the muck. "I'm adding a special to the menu," she called, mopping the slop off of her face. "Duck confit!"

"Need some help in there?" Owen Gotthard stood on the outside of the fence, his arms draped casually over the top rail.

"Nope. I'm good." Uttering a rib-shaking groan, Everly eased to her feet. If it had been anyone else, she would've been embarrassed about getting outwitted by a duck, but her landlord had once been a farmer himself, so he got the whole struggle with animals that misbehaved.

Besides that, he had a kind, grandfatherly look about him—thinning hair as white as the glaciers on Colorado's highest peaks, quirked lips that hinted at a sense of humor, eyes lined with a lengthy history of hearty laughter.

Even though she was covered in mud, Everly couldn't help but smile at him. "You're early for breakfast," she said, making her way to the fence. Behind her, the squabble between Walter and Dixie 1 moved into the chicken coop.

"Uh, yeah." For once, Owen's sooty dark eyes didn't smile. "I gotta talk to you. Thought I'd best do it before you open up for the day."

She ducked under the fence, her own smile evening out. It wasn't unusual to see Owen hanging around the farm. He loved his land, but being in his late seventies, he couldn't work it the way he once had. After leasing Everly the farm plot, he and his wife had moved into a patio home in town. If you asked her, that twelve hundred square feet of confinement seemed to make him stir crazy.

She faced him. "What can I do for you? Besides serve you a warm coconut scone with your breakfast?"

Owen stared at a rock next to his boot as though he wished he could crawl under it. "I sold the land, Everly," he muttered. "I had to. I got an offer I couldn't refuse."

Her lungs strained to hold back the surprised gasp that split her chest in two. In the courtroom, she'd learned to be prepared for anything, to never let her surprise show, and she grasped at that practiced composure now. "Wow." She stripped the sudden surge of emotion from her tone. "That's, um…definitely a surprise."

Owen's face scrunched with such concern she might as well have been sobbing. "The guy offered me cash," he blurted. "More than I would've ever asked. Me and the missus have been talking about a move to Florida for a while now. You know how bad her COPD is."

"Of course." The shock of Owen's news tied her throat in knots, but Everly adopted her courtroom voice. "I understand." Her hands didn't seem to, though. They trembled. "I know you've been concerned about her." And he owned the land. He had every right to sell it. She'd just hoped he'd be selling it to her one day.

"You don't have to worry about the farm, though." Owen gave her hand a squeeze as though desperate to offer her reassurance. "I told the guy all about it. That it's a fixture in this town. That it's important for the community. Hopefully he'll leave it alone."

Hopefully? She drew in a long, purifying breath so her voice wouldn't break. "Who did you tell? Who bought it?" Who was sneaking up on her to take away everything she'd dreamed of having for herself?

"Mateo Torres, that new bronc rider in town."

"No. That's not possible." A mere two weeks ago, she'd spent the evening with Mateo. She'd danced with him. She'd *kissed* him. She would've done a lot more with him, too, if she hadn't come to her senses. "Mateo would've told me." He hadn't mentioned anything about purchasing Owen's land that night.

"He signed the papers right in front of my eyes. Gave me a check for the full amount like it was nothin'," Owen marveled, but Everly was not impressed. She'd known plenty of men who threw their money around to get what they wanted. Her ex-fiancé, for example. Her own father. She'd grown up with men like that. The only difference was, Mateo wore a cowboy hat and brass belt buckle instead of a tailor-made suit. But she guessed he was still a liar just like the rest of them.

"What does he want with it?" she asked, glancing at her watch. Her regulars would have to wait for their coffee this morning. "Why would he need this much land?" As far as she knew, he still traveled the circuit, which meant he wouldn't be in Topaz Falls full-time anyway.

Owen's shoulders shrugged in an arthritic hunch. "Don't know. He didn't say much. I'm sure he won't bother you about the farm, though. I told him you were a good tenant, always pay on time."

Now she'd have to pay Mateo. God, he'd be her landlord. The man she couldn't seem to stop fantasizing about would be the one controlling her future. "I wish I could've bought it." The words slipped out unchecked. It had only been a few years since she'd left the courtroom and she'd already lost her touch.

"Could you?" Owen almost looked hopeful. Obvious guilt bore down on the poor man's forehead. "Maybe it's not too late…"

The slightest hesitation flickered in her heart. She could.

She could call up her parents and tell them she needed money, and they'd send it right away. It didn't matter what amount. But the day her life fell apart, she'd decided. She had to be done with that life. She wanted to be done with the money that brought secrets and lies with it, that covered things up, that had given her a false sense of security in the world.

She'd left so fast she didn't give her parents a chance to try and convince her to stay. Her whole life they'd chosen everything for her—her prep school, her friends, boyfriends, her college, grad school—and it hadn't worked out so well. Now she was on her own. Or at least she had been until Mateo had gone and bought her dream property. She wasn't stupid. Mateo wouldn't want the farm with its old decrepit buildings and lack of a steady profit.

"I definitely can't buy it. Especially not with cash," she told Owen. "You did the right thing taking Mateo's offer. I'm happy for you, Owen. Really." She'd already learned it was possible to be happy and devastated at the same time. Tears pinched at the corners of her eyes. Before they fell, she prodded Owen toward the entrance to the café. "Now, why don't you go on in and claim your table? I'll bring out your coffee as soon as I deal with Walter."

"Okay." His head still bowed slightly, as though he couldn't quite look her in the eyes. "I'm sorry, Everly. Really."

"You have nothing to be sorry for." All of the forced smiling had started to hurt her cheeks. "You two will love Florida. It'll be great for you both."

"Yeah, I really think we will." He turned and glanced over his shoulder as he walked away. "Let me know if you want to meet with Mateo and me before we leave."

"Not necessary," she sang, as chipper as a chickadee. "I'll meet with him myself." After the anger stopped boiling up in her chest. It wasn't like she could scream and yell at her new landlord. He had the power to kick her out of her own damn home.

Would he? Would Mateo come in and ruin everything she'd built on the farm? She couldn't let him. The community needed this place as much as she did. She taught cooking classes and delivered meals to people who were struggling, and invited the kids from the school over to learn about the animals. He couldn't take that away. From her or from the town.

Everly slogged over to the chicken coop. The squawking had quieted, and when she ducked inside she saw why. All of the hens had turned on Walter, pecking the air madly in his direction. Being the wuss that he was, he'd cowered in a corner. "All right, all right." She shooed the irate hens away. "Come here, mister." Leaning down, she snatched the duck into her arms. He honked irritably, but didn't fight her. Before he could change his mind, she crept out of the coop and back into the sunlight.

God, it was beautiful. A perfect fall day. The cragged mountain peaks were still frosted with powdery snow from an early storm two weeks ago. And the changing golden aspen leaves only seemed to make all of the other colors more vibrant—the deep greens of the pine forests slanting the mountainsides, the tall browning grasses that had started to wilt under morning frosts. After hearing Owen's news, she appreciated the view even more.

The little farm sat on the edge of town, a humble operation that included a small stone summer house—which she'd turned into a farm-to-table café—and the main two-bedroom farmhouse where she lived. For the past year and a half, she'd put everything into this place. Her heart and soul. She'd refinished the entire interior of that house with her own two hands and on her own dime. She'd resurrected the garden plots that Owen had let go to ruin. She'd lovingly made it hers. Now it might be taken away.

"What am I going to do?" she asked Walter as she carted him over to his own enclosed pen. Solitary confinement, she liked to call it. "I guess I could find another place to live." Maybe use the MBA she'd earned along with her law degree. But the thing was...she'd fallen in love with the farm. The animals, the gardens, the green hills and valleys that stretched over to the mountainside. She'd even fallen in love with the mud. And yes, with Walter, too. She set him down and gave him an affectionate pat as he waddled away from her.

When she'd left San Francisco, a friend of a friend had told her that Owen's farm was for lease in Colorado. At the time, she'd needed a refuge so she'd figured, what the heck? She'd check it out, maybe stay while she figured out what she wanted to do with the rest of her life.

Well, she'd figured it out, but it wasn't exactly a profitable vocation. For the first time in her life, she could barely pay her bills each month.

Everly locked Walter's pen and glanced around the farm. The facilities themselves weren't much to look at. She'd mended the fences and kept the garden plots weeded and neat. But everything else was still old and rustic.

Mateo might've seemed like a good guy that night they'd gone to the party, but it was obviously all part of his act. He would do whatever benefited him. Which meant she had to convince him that the farm had value.

Everything had been taken away from her once, and she wasn't about to let it happen again.

"Easy, Amigo." Mateo slid onto the bronc's back, holding the reins in a firm hand.

The sleek, coppery gelding tossed its head, those bulging muscles twitching in a show of agitation. Amigo loathed being confined by the bucking chute's metal gate. Fences made the horse restless.

Mateo could relate, though the fences that threatened to confine him weren't exactly the literal sort. Nope. They came more in the form of responsibilities and expectations and promises he'd made to himself a long time ago. Those were the burdens he tried to buck when he rode.

Anticipation boiled up from that unreachable place inside of him. He didn't know where it had come from, only that it had always been there—the need to battle, to conquer, to win. But the bronc's will happened to be as strong as his own, which meant both of them always put up one hell of a fight. Even when they were only training.

"Ready?" Levi Cortez stood outside the chute, poised to unlatch the gate and turn Amigo loose into the corral. Tucker, Cortez's stable manager, stood on the other side, untying the tethers that kept the horse in place. Tightening his grip, Mateo gave his friend a nod and braced his upper body into position. Truth was, he never felt ready. Maybe that's why he loved it so much. You couldn't prepare yourself for getting flung around by a pissed-off, two-ton horse. Once they were in that arena, it was all instinct and adrenaline, baby. His two favorite things.

The gate flew open and Amigo hurled himself out of the chute, already kicking his entire back end high into the air. The force was like going from zero to eighty in two seconds. Mateo welcomed the adrenaline rush. His whole body locked into Amigo's momentum, tensed into position while the bronc thrashed its way across the corral. The effort grated on Mateo's joints.

"Not today, you fucking son of a bitch." Trash-talking the horse had become part of his routine. Not that anyone could hear it over Amigo's grunts and snorts. Almost sounded like that damn horse was laughing at him. Which only made him dig his heels in harder.

At the pressure, Amigo jackknifed left and jarred Mateo's grip loose. Before he could correct, the bronc arched his back and gave a flying kick, sending Mateo head over ass above the horse's mane.

The sensation of sailing through the air always gave his stomach that nauseating sting. When he finally hit the dirt, the thud echoed back in his ears. "Damn." The winded groan punched through his mouth. He was lucky the impact had only knocked the wind out of him and nothing else. Just to be sure, he lay there a minute sucking air and moving his limbs to see if they still worked.

Tucker lured Amigo into the other corral while Mateo ripped off his helmet and stared up at the sky.

"Six seconds." Levi sauntered over and held out his phone so Mateo could see the timer. "But it might be a record for somersaults. Looked to me like you got in three good rotations." His friend reached out a hand to help him up. Levi was a bull rider; he knew something about pain.

"You don't win purses for somersaults." Mateo spit out the metallic blood that had flooded his mouth and tossed his helmet to the ground. Must've bit the inside of his cheek when he'd hit. "Seems Amigo is in a mood today." The ride always ended up with him off the horse, but usually he managed to stay on longer than six seconds. And sometimes he was even able to land on his feet. Pain needled between his shoulder blades. Not today.

"Damn shame they don't pay you for somersaults." Levi stuffed his phone back into his pocket. "We'd both be rich."

Mateo ducked the fence and leaned against it, his ears still ringing. "I'm not gonna rely on my acrobatic abilities to give me long-term security." Didn't have to be a genius to figure out this gig wasn't going to last forever. Every year that passed, it seemed he fell harder, and his body had started to feel every buck well into the next day. "Is it just me or does it hurt worse every time?"

Levi's laugh was dull. "I wish it was just you." The two of them had grown up together on the circuit—training under the famed all-around rodeo champion Gunner Raines. Along with bull rider Ty Forrester and barrel racer Charity Stone, they'd become known as Raines' Renegades. They'd had a lot of success, and even a sponsorship with a denim company. Back then, Mateo would hit the ground and bounce right back up. These days it had turned into more of a stagger. Not that he'd admit it to Levi, but lately he'd started to think more about the future. Which was why he'd gone and sunk most of his savings into Owen Gotthard's land.

"You want me to pen up Amigo for the day?" Tucker handed Mateo and Levi each a water bottle.

The horse was still trotting along the arena's fence, winding himself down.

"Nah. He needs a good run." Mateo hadn't been riding him as much since he'd had his horses bunking up at Levi's family ranch. It'd been a couple of months since he'd moved his favorite training broncs to Topaz Falls, and he didn't have a place to keep them. *Yet.* "I'll put him back when he's settled—"

"Mateo! There you are!" Charity Stone stomped out from behind the stables.

"Uh-oh." Levi assessed their colleague with a smirk. "Someone's got their panties in a tangle. What the hell did you do now?"

"No idea." He'd hardly seen Charity the last few days. He'd been too busy finalizing the purchase of his land. "It's been a while since she's punched me. Maybe she's going through withdrawals." Out of the four Raine's Renegades, he and Charity sparred the most. They had that brother/sister thing happening. Seeing as how he missed his three sisters, it made him feel more at home. Though Charity looked nothing like Inez, María Luisa, and Ana Sofia. With that long blond hair and angelic face, he'd seen many a man mistake Charity for a sweet, charming rodeo queen. Until she opened her big mouth, that was. "Hey there, Calamity Jane." He greeted her with a smile meant to set her off.

Sure enough, her crystalline blue eyes blazed. "I can't believe you bought Owen's farm."

Mateo stretched, trying to work a new kink out of his lower back. "What's wrong with that?" Everyone knew he'd been looking for property to buy. The last few months, when he was in town, he'd parked his fifth-wheel on Levi's property, but he didn't want to camp out forever. Sixty-five acres would give him plenty of room to build his own place and then section off the rest to put up an investment property. Freedom. That's what Owen's land would give him. Free rein over his future—his family's future.

Charity bolted her hands to her hips as though she was trying to make herself look taller. Not that she needed to.

She'd already perfected the art of intimidating glares. "Everly's my friend."

Couldn't resist a setup like that. Mateo shared a look with Levi. "The poor woman." They both cracked up.

Her glare could've sent two-ton Amigo running scared. "What about the farm?" Calamity Jane demanded. "What's gonna happen to Everly's home?"

Ohhhh. That's what had her all riled up. Mateo shrugged. "Not sure yet." Though he doubted he'd have to worry much about it. He'd spent less than an hour with Everly on their mandatory date, but he'd seen enough to know she was still hung up on her life back in San Francisco. She might look the part of the country girl now, but she'd also been a lawyer, which meant she'd likely come from money. And yet she was only leasing the farm. She hadn't bought it. That was one reason he'd finally approached Owen. He fully expected her to go running back home eventually, and that'd be just fine with him.

Somehow, Everly had gotten to him that night. Most of the time he could walk away from a date and forget the woman's name, but he couldn't seem to stop thinking about her. Couldn't seem to forget how it'd made him feel when she'd moaned and grabbed his ass. She was definitely a complication he did not need.

"What do you mean, you're not sure?" Charity got that look about her, the one that warned she wanted to punch him in the shoulder. Mateo backed up just in case.

Levi frowned, too. "I assumed you'd leave the farm alone."

Then they were both thicker in the head than he'd thought. That land was in a prime location—right between town and the mountains. It had killer views. And it was a huge acreage full of untapped potential. Why would he simply sit on a gold mine? "I'm exploring some options."

He wouldn't be a bronc rider forever. Hell, he already had to support his younger sister in Seattle, his mom, and his other two married sisters who barely scraped by back in Mexico. He'd seen what kind of decisions you had to make when you were broke. Decisions like marrying off your daughters young. Then there were the decisions his brother had made. He would never be in that position. He'd never let anyone in his family be in that position again.

"Everyone in town loves the farm," Levi said. "That's where half the town eats breakfast on a regular basis."

"Everly's not going to stick around Topaz Falls anyway." If she left on her own, it wouldn't be an issue. He wouldn't have to be the asshole who'd bulldozed the town's favorite breakfast spot.

"Why would you say that?" A familiar indignation colored Charity's face.

"She's still hung up on the past." She might've forgotten for the ten minutes they were dancing and making out, but that didn't change who she was. "Her whole life is back in San Francisco. She told me herself."

Levi's face took on that pensive expression he'd started to wear a lot more often since he'd gotten married. Man, he used to be fun. "I don't know. She seems pretty happy here. Her and Cass keep in touch."

Of course they did. All the women in this town seemed to keep in touch. It was a conspiracy meant to make the men dance like monkeys.

"You'll have a riot on your hands if people in this town lose their favorite breakfast spot," Charity informed him, raising her eyebrows in victory. "And I can tell you for a fact. Everly is not leaving Topaz Falls."

Mateo raised his hands in a defensive stance. "I'm just saying...she's young, single..." Sexy in an unobvious sort of way. "Hard to believe she'll want to be a farmer forever." It seemed more likely to him that she'd wanted a vacation from her life. Once it got old, she'd go back. And that would make his life a hell of a lot easier in more ways than one.

"Last week she told me she wanted to expand her fruit orchard for her preserves," Charity said with a contradictory smirk.

"Expand the orchard?" Owen hadn't said anything about the orchard. "She can't do that without asking me first." He had plans for the land, and they didn't include more fruit trees.

Charity assumed a fighter's stance. "You can't run Everly off the farm."

"I won't run her off." But he might be able to convince her to move on. He grinned at Charity. "You have nothing to worry about." He wouldn't send Everly packing. Yet. But if she left on her own, well...no one could fault him for that.

Chapter Three

In Everly's world, happy hour used to mean a little black dress, strappy heels, sapphire martinis, and schmoozing with the firm's wealthiest clients in a private room at Saison. But she wasn't in San Francisco anymore, Toto.

As she walked into the Tumble Inn, the heels of her worn, thrift-store cowgirl boots crunched against the peanut shells you weren't supposed to throw on the floor. She paused inside the door. Instead of the clean lines and sleek modern decor of her past, the place was a hodgepodge. Battered metal covered the bar. Concrete floors glistened with a generous coat of sealant. The heavy wooden pub tables bore the scars of endless games of beer pong, and maybe the occasional bar fight.

The place even sounded different from her old life. Instead of glittery laughs and muted tones of classical music and hushed murmurs of gossip, this place was as loud and rowdy as an off-color great-uncle. Country music blared from the speakers, and seeing as how happy hour had already started, it was accompanied by echoing laughs and loud chatter.

Okay. Deep breath. She raised her head with a shaky confidence and waded into the crowd, keeping an eye out for Mateo. He'd definitely be here tonight. Probably surrounded by his harem. Not that she'd admit that's why she'd actually showered and put on a sundress. Nope. That wasn't for him. Everyone else would be here, too. Darla had set up a get-together, since their friend Cassidy was in town. Now that she was a pediatric nurse in Denver, they didn't get to see her much.

Everly made her way closer to the bar, clinging to the outskirts of the crowd along the wall. From the shadows she spied Cassidy with her husband, Levi. They were kissing, of course. Not far away, Darla stood in a small huddle with some man Everly didn't recognize, Ty Forrester, Charity Stone, and yes, ladies and gentlemen, Mateo Torres.

Nerves rolled through her before settling heavily in her stomach. Her new landlord had one elbow leaned onto the bar top. That enticing smile of his was on full display. He looked just as good as he had at the engagement party. Maybe even better now that she knew how that hard body felt against hers.

She smoothed her hands down her dress, wiping off the clammy feel of nerves, and raised her shoulders the same way she always had before she'd walked into the courtroom. She'd have to forget about the dancing and that kiss. From now on, this would be a business relationship. Whatever she did, she had to show him a capable, savvy professional who could be an asset to him instead of a burden. Maybe she wasn't yet, but she would be. Eventually.

Smiling like she believed it, she strode across the room to her friends.

"You're here!" Cassidy untangled herself from her husband's arms and caught Everly in a hug. "I didn't know if you'd make it."

"I wouldn't have missed a chance to say hello." Everly returned the embrace, grateful that she'd connected with Cassidy and her book club friends. Along with Cass, Darla and Jessa and Naomi Cortez had taken Everly into their little group, giving her a place to belong. She wouldn't have survived the past few years without them.

She pulled back and gave Cass a once-over. "You look amazing." Nowadays Cass spent half her time in Denver, and every time the woman came home for a visit she looked even rosier, especially when Levi happened to be nearby.

It only convinced Everly she'd done the right thing in walking away from her old life and an upcoming marriage that had seemed more like a business arrangement than a romantic escapade.

"How's work been?" Her smile came more easily with the warmth beaming from her friend.

"Crazy," Cassidy said. "And wonderful, too. I'm busy and running all day, but instead of being exhausted, taking care of those kids energizes me, you know?"

Everly nodded. For the first time in her life, she did know. She knew how it felt to wake up every day and find a significant purpose in what she was doing. "I'm so glad you love it."

"What about you?" Concern shadowed her friend's pristine blue eyes. "I can't believe Owen sold his land. He was such a fixture in this town."

"Yeah." And he was pretty much the only one who cared

about the farm as much as she did. "I'm sure it'll be okay." She kept that chipper harmony in her voice. "I mean, once he sees how important the farm is, I think Mateo will leave it alone."

"Of course he will." Cass leaned in. "And even if he doesn't, Levi is one of his best friends, so I may have some influence in that department." She winked. "You let me know if you have any issues, you hear?"

Relief smothered the nerves stirring in Everly's stomach. "Thank you. I might have to take you up on that." She glanced over at Mateo again. The three women from Kate's engagement party had officially invaded his personal space and were giggling with the force of high school cheerleaders at whatever he was saying.

"Oh, there's my mom. I'll be right back." Cassidy slipped away, but Everly didn't have time to feel lonely before the rest of her friends crowded in.

"Everly!" Darla, Jessa, and Naomi drew her attention away from the spectacle currently taking place around Mateo. Seriously, he stood in the center of those women like some mythical god...

"Here. I already ordered your drink." Darla handed her a dirty martini from the bar. Everly thanked her and threw back a sip while all of her friends took a drink from their colorful frozen cocktails. Okay, so maybe she hadn't left San Francisco behind completely.

"I thought you were going to be here an hour ago," Darla said.

"Leave her alone," Naomi butted in. "She's a busy lady. Running a farm, serving breakfast and lunch. It's not like she has a lot of free time."

"And yet she still looks like that." Jessa appraised her

with a look of mock jealousy. "Seriously. You look gorgeous."

"So do you." Her friends were all beautiful, strong women in their own ways. Darla with her sassy black pixie cut and chic clothes. Naomi with her long red hair and friendly girl-next-door manner. And then there was Jessa, with her blond hair and adorably round innocent face. Lately, Jessa seemed to be even more radiant than usual, too, though no official announcements had been made.

"Well, I'm glad you're here." Darla leaned in and linked their arms together. "I've been dying to hear if you've seen your new landlord in his underwear yet." Her eyebrows wiggled with hints of dirty thoughts. "Or better yet, without it."

Everly's face burned hotter than it had when Mateo had kissed her. A kiss she'd neglected to mention to any of her friends. "He just parked his trailer on the property a few hours ago," Everly told Darla. "When could I have possibly seen him in his underwear? Or without it, for that matter?"

Darla directed her gaze over Everly's shoulder. "I'm guessing he's the kind of man who isn't shy about showing off the goods."

"Definitely not," Jessa agreed, openly staring in Mateo's direction.

"I bet he walks around naked all the time," Naomi added, suddenly as rapt as everyone else.

As if he needed more attention. If the flirty touching was any indication, he had his hands full at the moment. "I haven't seen him at all," Everly said to land their focus back on her. "Clothed or naked." Not for lack of trying. To see him clothed, that was. All afternoon she'd found excuses to zip past his trailer, but he hadn't been around.

"Well, you can see him right now." Darla slid her glance sideways, but Everly refrained from looking.

"Mateo doesn't do it for me," she lied. Oh, he'd done it for her all right. She simply couldn't *let* him do it for her.

"Well, he sure seems to be watching you," Naomi murmured into her margarita glass.

Jessa's eyes popped open wider. "Totally. Wait...he's coming over here!"

"What?" Suddenly panicked, Everly whirled and lost her grip on the martini glass. It flew from her hand, and sailed right toward Mateo, hitting him square in the forehead before it fell and shattered on the floor.

A collective hush smothered the room.

Shock appeared to ice over Mateo's gaze. He slowly raised his hand to his head.

"Oh my God! I'm so sorry!" Glass crunched underneath her boots as she rushed over to him, vaguely aware of the stares and whispers following behind her. "The glass flew out of my hand and..." God, she'd hit her new landlord in the head with a martini glass. "You're bleeding." She snatched a napkin off the table next to her and went to wipe the trickle of blood from his forehead, but he quickly stepped out of reach, his expression stony.

"What the hell was that for?" His eyes looked even darker than normal. And the trail of blood had now streaked down over his left eyebrow.

Her mouth fell open. "Seriously? You think I did that on purpose?" Unbelievable. "It was an accident," she ground out. "I'm sorry. It's not like I'm one of your young, high-drama admirers looking for attention." As soon as the words flew out of her mouth, she wanted them back. The crowd had fallen silent, all eyes on her. *Shit.* She ducked to pick up the glass and deflect the stares, doing her best to collect herself. Calm. She had to stay calm so they could talk like two grown adults. But when she rose to her feet Mateo was already gone.

Well, that was a first.

Mateo leaned closer to the mirror over the men's room sink and dabbed at the small cut on his forehead with a paper towel. He'd been the deserving recipient of a few drinks splashed in his face. Hell, he'd even been slapped a couple of times back in his younger days. Again, well deserved. But he'd never had a woman throw her martini glass at his head.

Seemed Everly was still bitter about Chrissy interrupting their kiss a few weeks ago. Must not be too happy about having a new landlord, either.

Satisfied that the bleeding had stopped, he tossed the paper towel into the trashcan and reached for the door, but it flew open before he could touch it.

Everly stormed in all bold and brassy, as if it didn't faze her to walk straight into the men's room. "When someone apologizes for *accidentally* hitting you in the head with a martini glass, the polite thing to do is acknowledge them."

Mateo simply gazed at the woman. Though her guarded posture made her seem rigid and untouchable, the silky golden-brown braids that fell along each of her delicate shoulders hinted at the carefree spirit he'd seen when he'd taught her how to dance. The memory of her body pressed against his heated him right up. Without meaning to, he dropped his gaze to her lips.

"And when someone tracks you down in the men's room," she went on in a frosted tenor, "the polite thing to do is say, 'Thank you for coming to check on me. I accept your apology.'"

He quirked his mouth and stared directly into her eyes. Anger looked good on her. It brought a flush to her face and a fire to her eyes.

Everly glared right back at him, her gaze not shying away once. What a pleasant surprise. The woman who'd turned tail and run out early on their date actually had some grit. "Thank you for coming into the men's room to check on me," he repeated almost verbatim. He'd never been one to resist an opportunity to be a smart-ass. "I accept your apology."

Her expression didn't change, but the reddish hue lighting her delicate skin deepened. He couldn't tell if she was embarrassed or downright mad.

"I'm fine, by the way," he added, gauging her reaction. If she was embarrassed, she'd likely bail out on the conversation as soon as possible.

The fact that she stood her ground made her even more appealing.

"Good. I'm glad you're fine." Her gaze flickered up to his forehead where the welt still throbbed. "And again, I'm sorry. It's been a while since I've had a martini. I'm not usually so careless."

And he wasn't usually so aroused from a two-minute conversation. He wouldn't be if she wasn't standing close enough that she could grab his ass again. "Like I said, it's fine." He kept his voice as cool as hers. Flirting with his new tenant could get him into serious trouble. Especially because he kept wondering where that kiss could have led them if they hadn't been interrupted. Now that he was her landlord he wouldn't ever know. "Owen said he told you the news."

"Yes. He did." She gave him a tight smile. Yeah, she wasn't thrilled about this new arrangement. Maybe that alone would be enough to send her packing. "You really should have told me when we—" Her face suddenly turned red. "I mean, at the engagement party. You should've said something about purchasing Owen's land."

"I hadn't bought it yet." He'd had his eyes on it for a long time, but it was only in the last week he'd decided to do something about it. "I ran into Owen at the gas station the other day. He was talking about his wife's health. Said he didn't know if they could do another winter here. So I offered to take the property off his hands." Surely if Everly had planned to stick around, she would've bought the place off Owen a long time ago. Why rent if she wanted to put down roots?

"Well, congratulations." The sentiment had a hollow ring.

He ignored her obvious resentment. "Thanks," he said cheerfully. "From everything I've heard, it's going to be one hell of an investment." Especially once he put up a few high-end condo buildings.

"It's a beautiful piece of property." Something that sounded suspiciously like yearning weighted her words. "I've put a lot of work into it over the last year."

Work? Far as he could tell, the place hadn't been upgraded since Owen Gotthard was a boy.

"Of course, I have tons of ideas about how to continue making improvements and growing the operation."

Mateo did his best not to wince, but he'd never been good at pretending. "Do you, now?"

Everly didn't appear to detect his lack of enthusiasm. "I'd like to start a food co-op. And there are tons of opportunities to add more community education programs with the crops and animals," she went on, as though she didn't want to give him time to get in a word.

Those all sounded suspiciously like nonprofit activities to him.

"I've also thought about expanding the orchards, planting a few more fruit trees, and maybe a vineyard as well."

The hopefulness in her expression shot down the *hell no* that had been teetering on the tip of his tongue. He would have to find a better way to tell her none of that was going to happen on his land.

"Why don't you come down for a tour tomorrow morning?" she rushed on. "I can make you breakfast at the café and show you around."

Breakfast. That was all he heard. Coffee and one of Everly's buttery cinnamon rolls drowning in a puddle of cream cheese frosting? Shit, he'd agree to anything. "Sure. That sounds good—"

The door opened, sending in a *whoosh* of popcorn-scented air.

Everly startled as Ty Forrester sauntered in. When he saw them standing near the sinks, his friend stopped and did a double take. A smile rose to his lips. "Pardon. Didn't mean to interrupt anything." He shot Mateo an impressed look.

"You didn't interrupt anything," Everly said, nearly as breathless as she'd been right after Mateo had kissed her two weeks ago. Damn, he needed to stop thinking about that kiss.

"I was just checking to make sure he didn't need a doctor or anything." She quickly spun and headed for the door. "Glad you're okay. I'll see you tomorrow."

Before he could return the sentiment, she disappeared.

"You and Everly, huh?" Ty clapped Mateo on the shoulder. " I thought she hated you after she skipped out early on that date."

She likely did hate him. And if she didn't now, he'd give her a few weeks. "She only came in here to make sure I wasn't passed out on the floor. Nothing was happening." Nothing was going to happen between them, either.

"Why not?" Ty cozied up to the urinal while Mateo checked the cut on his forehead again. "Seems like it'd be nice and convenient with her living right next door and everything."

"Convenient? Try complicated." Especially since he had to find a way to tell her he wasn't planning to renew her lease.

Chapter Four

It wasn't personal, it was business. Mateo had to keep telling himself that.

He led Blake Wilder away from the Tumble Inn's lingering happy hour crowd to a quiet table where the glares and gossip buzz couldn't interrupt their meeting. They both sat down with their beers. It probably hadn't been the smartest move to invite Blake to the bar to propose his idea. That might make his intentions more public than he would've liked at the moment. But at least Everly and most of her friends had already gone home.

It's a beautiful piece of property. That statement bothered him more than anything she'd said about expanding the farm. It wasn't so much the words as what hid behind them. A sense of longing that made him wonder if he'd completely miscalculated her intentions about staying in Topaz Falls. What if she really loved it here? What if she didn't go back to her old life?

"So what is it you wanted to discuss?" Blake was one of those men who seemed to check his fancy smart watch about every thirty seconds. He also might've been the only man to ever walk into the Tumble Inn wearing a tailored suit. In contrast, Mateo had holes in his jeans, and his boots weren't just for looks.

Despite their differences, Mateo needed someone like Blake—an executive at the ski resort—to partner with him on his new venture. "I bought Owen Gotthard's land." As expected, Blake's eyebrows shot up. Rumor had it that the Wilder family had been trying to get their hands on Owen's land for years, but the old man wouldn't even talk to them.

"Interesting." Based on Blakes's sudden total focus on Mateo and not his watch, he found the news more than interesting.

"I'm hoping to develop an investment property. Maybe some kind of condo resort." Something that would bring in more high-end tourists and make him a lot of money. "And I'm looking for a business partner."

"You definitely came to the right place." Blake flashed a schmoozing grin. "That's my business. No one around here knows resorts like I do."

And no one had Blake's capital, either. "That's why I called. I figure I can supply the land. And you can supply the resources and investors."

"I like the way you think." Blake pulled a tablet out of his overpriced briefcase. "Wilder Incorporated would be more than happy to explore a partnership. What about the tenant who currently occupies the land?"

Damn. He'd had to go and mention Everly. Mateo did his best to shut out the memory of the hope in her eyes earlier. "The lease is up in two months." Guilt crowded in, encroaching on his logic. "Sixty-five acres is a lot of land. Maybe we should consider keeping the farm." He almost couldn't believe that came out of his mouth. *Keep the farm?* What the fuck was wrong with him? One conversation with the woman and he was going soft.

Blake glanced at him like he was thinking the same thing. "I'll level with you here, Torres." He leaned over the table in the practiced pose of a skilled negotiator. "The kind of clientele we'd need to attract won't want chickens and goats running around. They won't want to look out their windows and see some shitty house circa 1955. They want modern and sleek, rustic elegance. That's what the Wilder name promises." He leaned back. "If that's not what you're after, you need to tell me right now."

"Of course that's what I'm after." The Wilder name also promised money. That's what Mateo had to stay focused on. New houses for his mom and sisters. Paying for Ana Sofia's college education so she didn't come out of school with debt. A steady income that would offer them all the security they'd never had, even after he retired from the rodeo world.

"We've been trying to purchase Owen's land for years," Blake went on. "But I don't want to be jerked around. If you partner with us, you'll have to make some concessions." He paused and folded his hands on the table as though he wanted to give Mateo time to consider that.

He didn't have to consider it. "Why don't you come up with a proposal?" Mateo wanted everything laid out—the breakdown of ownership, the projected income, the building plans. "Then maybe we can talk in terms of actual details."

"Sure. We can work on that." Blake fired up his tablet and sent off a text to one of his minions. *New development proposal for the farm. Now.* He turned his attention back to Mateo. "But you have to understand, we need every square foot of this land for the kind of project we're talking about. Which means we'll have to the level the farm."

"Sure. Not a problem." He ignored the guilt that tugged at his heart. He was better at using his head.

A crash ripped Everly from sleep. At least, it sounded like a crash. She glanced at her clock. The alarm wasn't supposed to go off for another twenty minutes. Maybe she'd been dreaming—

Outside her window, the noise thundered again—a clatter of metal and wood followed by the terror-stricken squawk of eight chickens.

Not a dream! She clawed her way out from under the cozy down comforter and dashed to the window. It was too dark to see anything, but she'd be willing to bet the mountain lion that had been prowling around lately had come back.

Shit! She felt her way down the hall and veered into the living room where she stored the old rifle Owen had forced her to keep. That had been part of his agreement when she'd leased the farm. He'd told her that he'd spotted those big cats on the property more than once, and he wouldn't let her sign the lease until she'd agreed to keep the gun and take a class so she would know how to use it when the time came.

Since she'd moved in, she hadn't had to pull out the rifle once. There'd been evidence that mountain lions had come around—prints, claw marks on the fences, scat. So she'd bought extra locks for the pens and coops and made sure to keep the animals locked up at night, but from the sound of things outside, a simple lock wasn't going to keep this cat out.

Her hands shook as she unlocked the gun safe that

doubled as a coffee table. Initially, she never would've agreed to having a gun in her house, but all it had taken was ten minutes of online research on mountain lions to convince her that keeping the rifle might be a good idea.

They were big and powerful—fierce. She'd rather die than shoot a living thing, even a mountain lion, but at least she could fire a warning shot into the air and scare it away.

The gun sat heavy in her hands. Big and clunky. Cold metal. Making sure the safety was on, she lugged it to the front door, stepped into her rubber boots, and quietly slipped outside. Everything was dimmed into the kind of surreal darkness that catches the world just before the sun comes up. The sky stretched above her, gray and colorless, wrapping everything in eerie shadows. Chilled morning air washed over her bare arms but the continuous flow of adrenaline heated her from the inside as she crept across the porch and into the dew-laden grass.

The fences were down. One whole wall of the chicken coop had fallen over, and all of her fowl had scattered, flapping across the lawn in a frenzy.

But where was the lion?

Inside what was left of the coop, there were more clatters. More squawks. Easing closer, she watched for the predator to emerge. "Go on!" she yelled as loud as she could manage. "Get!"

One of the chickens screeched.

No, no, no. God, she couldn't let it eat her chickens. Arms shaking, Everly took off the safety and raised the barrel of the rifle toward the sky, bracing herself for the kickback. She squeezed the trigger and a shot rang out, jolting through her, silencing the noise. Her breath caught and held as she waited, waited, waited.

A dog barked.

A dog?

Sure enough, a bulky form emerged from behind the rubble of the chicken coop's wall and came barreling straight at her, woofing happily.

It was a damn dog?

"Dante!"

Oh. Hell. No. That was Mateo's gruff, manly voice behind her. He'd called the dog by name. Which meant the dog that had been terrorizing her chickens belonged to him.

The adrenaline vanished, but there was still plenty of anger to keep her warm.

Dante raced past her in a blur, presumably sprinting to enthusiastically greet his master. She, however, was not enthusiastic. Especially given the fact that she was only wearing an old John Deere T-shirt that barely touched the tops of her thighs.

"What the hell happened out here?" Mateo asked from behind her. "Did you just shoot at my *dog*?"

Irritation joined the jumbled emotions that boiled through her. "Your dog was terrorizing my chickens." Still unbalanced, she whirled and nearly dropped the gun.

"Whoa! Easy..." Eyes on the rifle, Mateo raised his hands. The white towel he'd been holding around his waist fell to the ground and left him standing there naked in the predawn light.

Whoa nelly. Once again, she lost her grip on the rifle, this time dropping it to the ground. Another shot rang out, ricocheting sideways in the direction of the dilapidated coop.

"What the hell?" Mateo covered his head with his arms. "Do you even know how to use that thing?"

Did he know he was still standing there stark naked except

for his cowboy boots? The pinkish light of the sunrise had now started to fringe the sky, which meant she could see more than a shadowy outline of his body. *Mmm-hmmm.* She could see every hard and muscular plane and angle.

Geez Louise, he should pose for a painting.

"I'm coming to pick up the rifle," he informed her in the same tone he might have used on a lunatic.

Okay, sure. She could see how she might look a little crazy right now. She'd been staring at him. Really staring, but could he blame her? This wasn't the time or place for him to do a striptease. Not with her coop in ruins and her poor chickens still flailing around in chaos and her running around with a rifle. "I can get the gun." She could handle a rifle. Just not when a sexy cowboy decided to flash her, apparently. "Why don't you focus on putting your towel back on?" She did her best to sound annoyed instead of awed.

While she picked up the gun and put on the safety, Mateo snatched his towel off the ground and secured it around his hips again. "I was in the shower when I heard a gunshot." Talk about annoyed. His jaw had cranked so tight she was surprised it didn't snap right off. "So excuse me if I didn't have time to get fully dressed." He approached her and took the rifle out of her hands as though he didn't trust her with it.

Probably for the best.

"What're you doing out here with a rifle anyway?" Mateo demanded, standing close enough now that she could see scars slashed into his rock-solid pecs.

"I thought it was a mountain lion," she muttered, dragging her gaze to his face. His black hair was still wet, slicked back and a little curly. "But I didn't shoot at your dog. I fired a warning shot into the air."

The criminal dog in question trotted over and sat right next to Mateo's leg, on his best behavior.

"Well, it scared the hell out of me." He leaned the rifle up against the fence and stood in front of it like a guard.

"Scared the hell out of you?" she shot back. "I thought there was a one-hundred-fifty-pound cat with lethal claws tearing down my chicken coop."

For the first time, Mateo looked toward the mess. His jaw finally softened. "Right. Sorry about that. I let Dante out before I got in the shower. Didn't even think about it."

"Well, you're going to have to start thinking about it now that we're neighbors." Of course, at the moment Dante looked perfectly innocent and sweet. He wasn't as big as she'd originally thought. Even sitting up like that, his head only reached the middle of Mateo's thigh. And the dog was actually adorable. He had that mutt look, brown fur with white socks and one ear that stuck up all the time. She resisted the urge to sink to her knees and fawn over him. That wouldn't do when she had to set some boundaries with her new neighbors. "Will he be trying to eat my animals on a regular basis?" she asked.

"Nah." Mateo gave the dog a hearty scrub behind the ears. Dante leaned into the attention, his hind leg thumping the ground. "He never eats anything. He likes the thrill of the chase."

"I see." Everly narrowed her eyes against Mateo's sinful little grin. Oh, she saw, all right. Dante took after his owner.

Chapter Five

Everly glared at him, her shoulders pulled back straight and proud, the way she used to hold herself when she'd stood in a courtroom, he imagined. Except instead of wearing some fancy sharklike suit, she had on an old John Deere T-shirt that was frayed around the edges, the loose threads brushing the very tops of her five-star thighs. Those legs weren't her only award-winning feature, either.

He never would've dreamed that John Deere could beat out sexy lingerie for the win, but it was a good thing he had a towel around his waist right now or she'd see a whole lot more of him than he wanted her to.

"Maybe it would be best if you keep Dante on a leash," Everly said stiffly. She seemed to be doing her best to not look directly at him. Funny, since she hadn't looked away once when his towel had been on the ground.

"Dante hates leashes." Couldn't blame the dog. He liked to roam free. Mateo had rescued him from a shelter in

Oklahoma where the dog had been housed in a four-by-four cell for six months. So no, he wasn't about to keep the dog leashed. "I'll keep a better eye on him." Or maybe he wouldn't. Maybe Dante would actually help his cause and encourage his tenant to vacate the property when her lease was up. That same guilt she'd embedded in his conscience last night at the Tumble Inn kicked him in the chest again. Damn it. He had to find a way to kill it for good. It shouldn't be that hard.

"Yes, well, I would appreciate it if you kept a better eye on him." Everly turned and stomped away. "Before he causes any more damage."

Mateo had been so focused on her that he'd hardly noticed the fact that chickens still ran loose all over the yard. For the first time he assessed the destruction Dante had inflicted on her property. One wall of the coop had been laid out flat and feed and scraps of wood were scattered everywhere. "You're trouble, you know that?" he muttered to his dog. Then he started after Everly. "Wait. Where are you going?"

She stopped and turned, her cheeks as rosy as they'd been in the men's room last night. "I have to get dressed so I can chase my chickens all over the farm." Her eyes lowered to the towel around his waist. "You should get dressed, too."

"Sure." Mateo backtracked a couple of yards to the pair of jeans he'd managed to grab on his way out of the trailer. Once he'd seen Everly wielding that gun, however, he'd dropped the pants and run over to make sure she wouldn't murder his dog.

The jeans lay in a heap right where he'd left them. After kicking off his boots, he tossed the towel aside and picked up his pants.

"What're you doing?" Everly threw a hand over her eyes and turned away as if she'd never seen a naked man before.

"I'm getting dressed. Like you asked."

"What about underwear?" Her hand still covered her eyes as he buttoned up.

"That would mean going all the way back to my trailer." He stepped into his boots. "I'll take care of that later. First let's get your chickens situated."

"Fine. You can work on propping up the fence while I go get dressed." She'd already made it halfway to the farmhouse porch.

"Sounds like a plan." Mateo headed toward the downed fence. It was a damn shame Everly wasn't willing to work in that John Deere T-shirt. It'd make the manual labor a lot more fun.

As he approached the chickens, Dante went spastic again, growling and barking. "No," Mateo said firmly. "Leave it." He pointed at the ground. "You lay down and stay."

The dog obeyed with a pathetic whimper. "You've already caused enough trouble," Mateo reminded him. "Stay."

Dante rested his jaw on his paws the same way he did when Mateo got ready to go off somewhere and leave him for a few hours.

Satisfied his dog wouldn't go after the chickens again, he inspected the fence posts that had been pulled out of the ground in the commotion. They hadn't even been cemented in. And he had a feeling that was just the beginning of the shoddy work around this place. But he'd best save that topic for another day.

He easily shoved the posts back into the holes and packed dirt around them, so at least they were standing. Just as he started to untangle the chicken wire, Everly hurried over.

She'd only thrown on jeans and a different T-shirt, but somehow the sight of her still dropped his jaw. She'd pulled her soft hair back into a loose braid, exposing her neck. Damn, her skin was so silky...perfectly lickable.

"What a good boy, Dante," she crooned. "I guess we won't have to worry about him enjoying the thrill of the chase when you're around." Her face still glowed and she wouldn't look directly at Mateo.

"He listens when I'm the one talking." He held off a grin and went back to examining the chicken wire. "Do you have a hammer and nails?" He did someplace, but it would take hours to find his toolbox in the storage under his fifth wheel.

"Oh sure."

While she ran off again, he bent and stretched the chicken wire to fit against the fence posts. By the time she got back, he'd already managed to get it into place.

"Here you go." She handed him a pink hammer. Pink.

He stared at it with a smirk.

"It works the same as all the other ones. I promise." A smile opened up her face, making her appear less guarded, bringing back some of that spark she'd shown him when they'd danced on the patio at the party.

"We'll see about that," he teased, wanting her to hold onto that smile. It changed her face, made her seem so carefree in comparison to the subdued expression she usually wore.

He took a nail from the box she held out and got to work pounding the chicken wire into place. "The posts aren't very secure, but I can pick up some cement at the hardware store later." *Wait.* Had he really just offered to make a special trip to fix her fence? The fence that would be demolished in a few short months, along with the rest of her farm? Man, he never should've kissed her. It was seriously messing with his head. For the next two months she was his tenant. That's it. They had no other connection besides her lease.

"I don't need you to do that." Her expression hardened again. "I can handle it."

"Suit yourself," he said, handing her hammer back. Everly took it from him and walked away. She obviously didn't want to rely on him for anything. But he was still her landlord. It was his job to fix things when they were broken, especially when his dog was responsible.

So whether she liked it or not, he would take care of the damn fence posts.

Just her luck she had to teach a cooking class on a morning when she couldn't seem to get it together.

Luckily, Hector, Charlie, and Gus hadn't seemed to pick up on her flustered incompetence. The widowed retirees were currently too busy managing their own challenges. Working in the kitchen wasn't exactly their forte. They were content to let her make their breakfasts at the café, but she figured they needed a few easy, healthy recipes they could make at home.

She'd never dreamed teaching three over-eighty-year-olds how to make whole grain pancakes could be so complicated. So far, they'd been at it over a half hour and they still weren't done mixing the batter.

"What is this, birdseed?" Gus held up the bag of flaxseed.

"No, that's a healthy grain," Everly said patiently. "It adds lots of fiber. You can all add two tablespoons into your batter."

"Is the batter supposed to be lumpy?" Hector leaned

closer to the mixing bowl on the counter in front of him, squinting through his Coke-bottle glasses. "That looks too lumpy."

Everly hurried over, taking a glance at his concoction, which had the consistency of bread dough. *Huh.* "Um. Are you sure you measured the oats right?"

"Well, I think so. Two cups, you said, wasn't it?"

"No, she didn't say two cups," Gus muttered. "A *half-cup.*" He raised his voice. "Turn up your hearing aid."

Charlie dropped his mixing spoon with a sigh. "Great; now we're gonna have to wait for him to start all over."

"No, no. It's fine." Everly took Hector's bowl and replaced it with hers, her hands fumbling clumsily like they had since she'd come in. Dear God, she had to get it together and stop thinking about Mateo. There were some things that couldn't be unseen, and Mateo Torres standing naked in the morning light happened to be one of them.

In her defense, it'd been a while since she'd seen a man naked. And even then, the men from her previous life in Yuppie Ville tended to have a different body type. Fit, sure. But not so...hard. Athletic. Broad and strong. Her ex-fiancé had run five miles a day and took a weight-lifting class, but the sight of him naked hadn't completely mesmerized her quite the way the sight of Mateo had when his towel dropped to the ground...

"You got any more coffee?" Hector asked. He'd already downed three cups.

Everly shook herself and smiled sweetly. "Didn't your doctor say you needed to cut back?" If it wasn't for her, these three wouldn't mind their health at all. "Here. I'll get you some water." She grabbed the pitcher she'd put out, but the handle slipped out of her hand and water went everywhere.

"I'll get that cleaned up for you." Charlie shuffled past in his arthritic gait, and even though she could've found a towel and sopped up the mess much faster, she let him. These men were always trying to do small things to help her out—tightening the doorknob for her when it got loose, refilling the salt and pepper shakers on the tables when they got low. She smiled as he mopped up the water. Everyone needed to feel useful sometimes.

When he stood, she laid a hand on his shoulder. "Thank you, Charlie."

"Anything for you, my dear." He tossed the towel aside, gave her a wink, and swaggered back to his station at the stainless steel island.

"Okay." Everly blew her bangs out of her eyes. "We've got approximately twenty minutes to finish these pancakes before I have to open up the café. Think we can do it?"

"You bet we can." Gus straightened the apron she'd lent him. He hadn't wanted to stain his best sweater vest. It took a real man to proudly wear polka dots.

"Come on, men." He led the charge over to the commercial gas range where Everly had set up the cast-iron griddles.

"This next step is really simple." Everly squeezed in closer to the stove with the men surrounding her. "All you have to do is pour a little batter onto the griddle and wait for the steam to rise." She demonstrated with the perfect plate-sized pancake. "Once the bubbles form, it's time to flip it." She waited an extra few seconds to get that golden brown color, then used her spatula to turn it over.

The men *ohh*ed and *ahh*ed.

"Would you look at that? It's perfect." Hector patted her on the back. "You're so talented, Everly."

"Aww. Thanks." She gave him a quick hug. Every girl

should have a support group of elderly men to tell her how wonderful she was. "Okay, Gus. You're up."

The man retrieved his mixing bowl and carted it over to the stove. "Just pour it on?" He seemed doubtful it would work.

"Yep. Exactly like I showed you." She tried to boost his confidence with a smile. "You can totally handle it." But just in case he couldn't, she moved closer.

Gus raised the bowl and started to pour batter onto the griddle.

"Hold it straighter, you oaf," Charlie grumbled. "You're making a mess."

The comment seemed to fluster poor Gus. "Mind your own business," he shot back, turning to scowl at his oldest friend. Everly swore those two were like an old married couple.

"Pay attention, Gus." Hector could never seem to stay out of the fray.

All of the commentary distracted Gus and he dropped the bowl onto the stove. Batter oozed everywhere. "Now look what you made me do, you blunderbuss."

"It's okay! It's fine!" Everly rubbed at her temples. "I can clean it up."

"No, I got it." Charlie swiped a towel off the shelf and waved it toward the stovetop.

"Wait! Stop!" She dashed over but it was too late. The gas burner ignited the edge of the cloth.

"Jumpin' Jehosaphat!" Charlie threw the towel, which happened to land on the counter where Everly had set the newspaper earlier. The whole thing went up in flames.

"Shit!" Everly lunged for the cabinet where she kept the fire extinguisher, but before she could get there the back door opened.

The *whoosh* of air sent the flames higher until they reached the very edge of her lace curtains.

Mateo walked in. "What the hell?"

"Fire!" Gus ran to the sink and got the sprayer, but instead of aiming it at the flames, he misjudged and sprayed Hector right in the face.

"Get the extinguisher!" Everly growled, pointing to the cabinet behind Mateo. He jumped into action, opened the cabinet door, and had the fire out before Gus could douse it.

A layer of white covered the countertop, wall, and curtains. Smoke clouded the ceiling. Everyone seemed to be in a state of shock, including Mateo.

"Okay. Well. I think class is over for today." Easing in deep, cleansing breaths, Everly went to the window and pulled it open. The fresh breeze swooped in, clearing the air. Well, clearing the smoke from the air. Everly could feel Mateo watching her. She could practically hear the unspoken questions firing from his brain.

Way to look competent in front of your new landlord. At least he didn't say anything in front of the guys.

"I'm so sorry." Gus's shoulders drooped even more than they usually did.

"Me too." Concern deepened the lines around Charlie's mouth.

"We can help you clean up," Hector offered.

"That's okay. I can handle it." She had to handle Mateo, too. She gave Gus's hand a squeeze. "No harm done. Actually it was a great lesson in why you always want to have a fire extinguisher in your kitchen. Do any of you have one?" She looked at each of the men in turn.

One by one they shook their heads.

"Then go out and buy one. Today." She put her arms around Gus and Charlie, nudging them toward the dining room. Hector followed along behind. "Now I want you three to go claim your table and start your crossword puzzles. I'll bring out your breakfast as soon as I get this cleaned up."

At the doorway, Gus paused and placed his hand on her cheek affectionately. "Don't know what we'd do without you, doll."

The words warmed her through. Who cared about a small fire? "I don't know what I'd do without you three, either." She gave them each a pat. "We're still on for class next week, right?"

"We'll be here," Charlie assured her.

"Great. Maybe we'll try something that doesn't involve the stove." Smoothies, perhaps? Or she had a great oatmeal dish they could make in the microwave. "Give me a half hour to get your eggs made," she said as they lumbered to their table.

When she turned back around, Mateo stood in front of her. "What the hell happened in here?"

"It was...nothing." She slipped past him and went to the towel cabinet. Hopefully she had enough to clean up the mess from the fire extinguisher.

"Nothing? Really?" He followed right behind her. "Because it looked to me like your kitchen was on fire."

Everly pulled out an armload of towels. "It was a small fire. Minor. No one was hurt."

"They could've been." Mateo shadowed her as she went back to the counter and started to mop up the debris. "What were those three doing back here anyway?"

She dragged over the trash can and peeled the charred

newspaper off the counter to throw it away. "I was teaching them how to cook."

"Why?" he asked as though that were the stupidest thing he'd ever heard.

Everly swallowed an exasperated sigh. "Because their wives used to do it for them, but they passed away." As if this was any of Mateo's business. He might be her landlord, but he didn't get to come in here and run her café. "I thought it would be nice for them to have a few recipes they could make at home." She reached up and unlatched the curtain rod so she could toss the charred fabric into the trash.

"I don't think it's a good idea to invite those guys back into the kitchen." Mateo had crossed his arms into an unyielding stance. It was all Everly could do not to roll her eyes.

"Why are you here?" she asked, retrieving a spray bottle from under the sink. She'd have to scrub the whole area before she could do any cooking.

"You invited me for breakfast. Remember? Last night?"

Oh, right. She'd invited him for breakfast and a tour so he could bear witness to how skillfully she ran her business. There went all of her credibility. "I won't be ready to make breakfast for a while. So how about you leave and I bring you something later?"

Mateo's seductive eyes narrowed. "Are you kicking me out?"

"Yes." She stared him down. They had to have boundaries. Maybe she wouldn't have been so distracted all morning if he hadn't started her day with a private peepshow. She'd never look at him the same way now, never be able to stand within ten feet of him without picturing that exquisite physique. Between that and memories of their kiss, it would be a miracle if she could get anything done when he was around. "I'll bring you a cinnamon roll as soon as I can," she promised. With a hand on his shoulder, she directed him to the door. "I'll even add extra frosting." As long as he stayed out of her hair.

Chapter Six

It'd been years since he'd gone duck hunting back in Oklahoma, but this crazy mallard hadn't given him much of a choice.

Mateo pushed open the creaky door to a run-down stable where the duck had fled when he and Dante finally had it cornered near the front porch. Since Everly had banned him from the kitchen, he had more time on his hands. Figured he could round up the animals that were still scattered so they could avoid another possible catastrophe in the form of a fox or a hungry coyote.

Crazy that rounding up the animals had been the most difficult task he'd tackled today. Especially considering he'd literally put out a fire. He'd been starving after he'd finished fixing Everly's fences, and figured he'd make good on her breakfast offer. When he'd opened the kitchen door and smelled the smoke, he'd been ready to rush in and pull her out of there. What if something would've exploded? What if Everly had been hurt?

He forced the thought out of his head. He was getting good at that, at forcing thoughts of her out of his head. It didn't mean anything that his heart had taken a nosedive when he thought she might be in danger.

Somewhere at the back of the stable, the damn duck quacked. The outbuilding was dark and musty, like every other structure on this farm. Didn't look like Everly used it for much except storage. Rakes and shovels leaned against the warped walls, and a covered ATV took up all the space in the center. "Let's go, Dante." His dog followed behind him as he maneuvered his way between an ATV and another pile of gardening tools. "Come on, duck. I know you're in here."

Dante put his nose to the ground, sniffing and wagging his tail as though he was hot on the duck's trail.

"I should let you eat the damn thing," Mateo mumbled. And yet he knew he wouldn't because he didn't want to have to explain that to Everly.

A clatter drew him to the other side of the shed.

Barking, Dante tore to the back wall, and sure enough, the duck cowered behind a lawn mower.

"Off, Dante. Leave it."

The dog whined, but backed up. Mateo eased toward the duck a few steps, then lunged and captured it in his arms. The thing squawked and tried to flap its wings, beating Mateo in the face. He held it tighter against him, smoothing down its wings while he carted it out of the shed.

The duck seemed to give in to its fate, calming some as Mateo lugged it over to the pens where the chickens pecked at the ground.

Dante paced on the outside of the newly secured fence, eyeing the animals as though he could come up with a few good uses for a duck.

"Sorry, boy. Not today." Mateo glanced his watch. He should probably get cleaned up. With any luck, Everly would bring him that cinnamon roll she'd promised before he got hungry enough to break down and make something himself.

"Let's go, Dante." He checked to make sure the gate to the animal pen was secure, then headed in the direction of his trailer. He needed a shower. Desperately. He had sweat more when he thought Everly might be in danger than he had the whole time he'd been cementing in her fence posts. Sure it was nice of her to try and help those old guys, but she didn't have to do that. It didn't benefit her business.

Shaking his head, Mateo looked down. A trail of water dribbled past his feet on the way up the hill. Water? *Uhh…* He shot a glance up at the sky. All clear. Mind-numbingly blue. No rain. And as far as he knew, there was no irrigation system up here. Just his trailer.

His trailer…

Fuuuuuuck. Mateo's steps turned into a jog when he crested the top of the hill. "No way." Water oozed from the sides of his fifth wheel, dripping down to the ground where it formed a steady stream that trickled under his feet.

It was flooded. The whole damn thing. He sprinted the rest of the way and tore open the door. Water gushed out, running over his boots, and when he stepped inside, there still had to be a good four inches standing on the expensive hickory floors.

Mateo sloshed through the mess, all the way back to the bathroom. It was worse in there. When he'd heard that gunshot, he'd bolted out of there so fast he must've forgotten to turn off the shower. That meant the entire fresh-water tank had flooded the interior of his trailer, ruining the floors, the carpet, and probably everything he had stored underneath. He grunted in frustration, tore down the shower curtain, and threw it; then he splashed back down the narrow hallway through the small kitchen and bolted outside.

Dante whined and crouched on a patch of dry ground. The dog had never been a fan of water.

Damn it. How could he have been so careless? He jogged to the storage door at the back of the trailer and ripped it open, hoping like hell that the bin of pictures and souvenirs from his childhood had survived. Funny how he didn't care about his clothes or his possessions or even the bin of his rodeo accolades. Instead he dug around until he found the plastic bin that held the scraps of the past he never wanted to face. He shimmied it out of the small space and dried the top with his shirt before popping the lid open.

Relief ached in his lungs. Everything seemed dry. All of the pictures, the notes from his sisters, the small trinkets they used to give each other at Christmas, most of which were scavenged from other people's trash. He dug through, making sure there was no damage, carefully lifting out the pictures he hadn't bothered to look at in years. The one of him and Andres stopped his heart. It had been taken only a few months before his brother had walked out on them. On him. Mateo had been eight—a scrawny kid, especially compared to his older brother. In the image, he looked up at Andres the way he would've looked at a father. That was how he'd seen his brother—as his protector, his provider.

A familiar rage swelled through him, tightening his grip on the flimsy picture. He should rip it up, tear apart the last piece he had of his brother. But for some reason he couldn't seem to make himself do it. Instead, he tossed the photograph back into the bin and shoved the container aside.

"The pancakes are burning!" Hilda, Everly's lovely and affordable sous chef, lumbered over and hip-checked her out of the way. It didn't take much. The woman had hips the size of a barge. Not surprising when you considered she'd birthed seven children. Now Hilda had thirty-one grandchildren, which made her the most efficient force in the kitchen that Everly had ever seen. She wouldn't be able to run the café without her.

"You're as flaky as a hand-rolled piecrust today," Hilda muttered, scraping the burnt pancakes off the griddle before tossing them into the trash.

"Sorry." Everly stood back. Ever since she'd hired Hilda, she didn't have to do nearly as much work in the kitchen as she used to. Sometimes she missed it. Not today, though. She was still reeling from the morning's events—shooting the rifle, naked Mateo, the fire in the kitchen…good lord, was it only ten o'clock? She was about ready for bed.

"Why don't you go on out to the dining room and make the rounds?" Hilda may as well have told her to get out of her way. "It's so packed out there this morning, there ain't no room for an apple to fall."

It sure was, and it couldn't be a coincidence. Something told her this morning's rush had little to do with luck and more to do with the fact that Mateo Torres now shared land with her little café.

Everly wandered to the crowded room and skirted past three tables of women who were dressed like they'd just walked out of a dance club. Ah, yes. There was her old friend Chrissy. The woman who had interrupted her and

Mateo at Kate's engagement party. Today she looked especially eager in an off-the-shoulder sweater that glistened with sequins.

She swore that ever since those rodeo stars had moved into town, the female tourist population had more than doubled. Of course, she shouldn't be complaining. The café was never this busy during the fall season, and right now she needed the money. So she put on her sweetest smile and served them all the sunrise smoothies and egg-white omelets they'd ordered in record time. When she'd finally set down the last plate, she'd broken a sweat.

A "thank you" came from Chrissy. She apparently didn't recognize Everly from the night of the party. No surprise there.

"You're welcome," Everly said as warmly as she could. In her opinion, it was way too early for sequins, but that was just her. "Can I get you anything else?"

"Actually..." The woman glanced around. "Does Mateo Torres ever eat breakfast here?"

"I heard he lives here," another woman chimed in.

"Is he around?" a made-up brunette asked.

"Nope." The lie slipped out easily. "I mean, yes, he does own the land," she quickly explained. "But I hardly ever see him." Another blush fired up. She'd seen a whole lot of him just that morning. "He's so busy. Training and traveling to competitions." At least she hoped he'd be. Then he wouldn't keep barging in on her life like he had earlier that morning.

Chrissy cut her omelet into neat little squares. "Well, if you do happen to see him, tell him Chrissy, Michelle, and Aimee stopped by. We know him from the Tumble Inn."

The same irritation that had lit her fuse when they'd fallen all over Mateo at the party zinged again, and there was no stopping the words that came out of her mouth. "Yes, well, it's definitely hard to keep track of all the women he meets at the Tumble Inn."

Three pairs of painted lips parted with shock, but Everly kept her candied smile intact. "Let me know if I can get you anything else," she said before quickly scurrying away. There went her tip, but it was totally worth it.

Smiling to herself, Everly checked on a few more customers, refilled some coffee, and then went back to the kitchen. Hilda was humming while she stirred scrambled eggs and kept a watchful eye on the blueberry pancakes.

"Everything seems to be under control. Mind if I step out for a minute?" She still had to deliver that cinnamon roll to Mateo, and she'd like to get it over with before the lunch crowd came in.

"Of course not." Hilda waved her away. "I can hold down the fort. Take your time."

Hopefully it wouldn't take any time at all. Everly boxed up the cinnamon roll and even slathered it with extra frosting, as promised. He did put out the fire in her kitchen, after all.

Relief washed over her the second she stepped outside. The sun warmed her face and the cool fall-scented breeze reinvigorated her. Sure, her morning had gotten off to a rocky start, but things could only get better from here, right?

She traipsed down the path toward the farm, but stopped cold when she reached the animal pens.

The fences had all been repaired, the coop had been patched up, and the animals were each where they were supposed to be. Even Walter and Henrietta waddled around inside the fence, quacking irritably at each other.

Tears caught her off guard. Mateo had fixed it. Everything. And from the look of things, he'd done a solid job. Much better than what she could've done herself. She swiped at her eyes, annoyed at the emotion. She'd told him she would take care of it. Didn't he think she was capable?

Everly veered off the path and stomped up the hill toward Mateo's trailer. He had no idea what she was capable of. He hadn't seen the inside of the farmhouse yet. She'd redone the whole thing herself, from the floors to the kitchen cabinets to replacing the plumbing in the bathroom. She hadn't needed his help with that, had she? Nope. And she didn't need his help with the farm either—

Ummm…was Mateo having a yard sale or something? The area around his trailer was a mess. Boxes and plastic tubs were stacked everywhere.

The door opened and Mateo stomped out, hauling more crap. He was shirtless again, the showoff. And she was staring again. The sun's heat seemed to intensify on her face.

Mateo dropped a heap of rugs on the ground and looked up as though she'd startled him. "Hey."

"Hi." Despite her most angelic intentions, her gaze immediately dropped to where his jeans sat low on his hips. The display of his tensed lower abs made her heart flutter. *Ahem.* "Doing some fall cleaning?" she asked, distracting herself with a glance at the mess. It looked like he'd dragged out everything—clothes and dishes and food…

"Not by choice." For once he wasn't wearing that cocky grin. "My trailer flooded. I left the shower running when I came down this morning and now everything's soaked."

"Ohhhh." It came out in a dread-filled groan. So maybe now wasn't the time to lay into him for taking care of the fences when she'd asked him not to. She looked around. "Wow. That sucks." *Way to state the obvious.* After all he'd done for her that morning—while his own home was flooding—you'd think she could come up with something a little sympathetic. "I mean…is there anything I can do? I have a Shop-Vac back at the house." She'd used it to suck up all the water when her bathroom had flooded last year.

A trace of amusement raised Mateo's dark eyes. "Thanks, but I don't think a Shop-Vac is gonna cut it." He posted his hands on those chiseled hips and surveyed the clutter scattered around them. "The floors are shot. I'll have to have it towed to a shop in Denver so they can gut the inside."

Guilt recoiled through her like the kickback of her rifle. "I'm so sorry. This is all my fault."

"It's not your fault." Was it just her or did his jaw soften every time his eyes met hers? "I shouldn't have let Dante out so early."

As if he'd heard his name, the dog came trotting out from the trees and greeted her with a lick on her ankle, then stretched his nose toward the box in her hands.

"I almost forgot." She held out the container to Mateo. "I brought you that cinnamon roll I promised." At the moment, the offering seemed wholly inadequate, but the man had to be starving.

"Thank God." He opened the lid, picked up the roll, and took a huge bite. "Mmmmm." He closed his eyes and chewed slowly, which was really kinda hot. "I love your cinnamon rolls, Everly Brooks."

There was no battling the blush that rose high on her cheeks. She cleared her throat so her voice wouldn't purr. "It's the least I can do." She should bake them fresh every morning as penance for forcing him to run out on his shower. "So, if you have the trailer towed, where will you stay?" Everly asked, unable to resist patting Dante's head.

Mateo bit off another hunk of the cinnamon roll, taking his time to chew before he answered. "Not sure yet. The guy at the shop said he thought they could have it done in a month."

A month? Mateo would be homeless for a month?

"I'm sure I could bunk up at Levi's house. Not that I want to crash the newlywed party. Those two should have their own space when Cass is in town."

"You could stay here. At the farm." The words tumbled out before she could process what they meant. Heat flashed to her face. Had she really just invited Mateo Torres to move in with her?

He seemed just as surprised as she was. "You mean at your house?"

Well, technically it was *his* house. Not that she wanted to admit that to him. But this could actually be perfect. She didn't have much time to convince him that the farm had value. It might not make a huge profit, but it brought the community together in so many ways. If he stayed with her, he'd see that. He'd see how much this place mattered.

"There's an extra bedroom. Plenty of space." It wasn't like she was around the house much anyway. When she wasn't at the café she was out weeding garden plots or feeding animals or taking walks in the afternoon sun. And she hung out with Darla and her book club friends a few evenings a week. So, really, it shouldn't be a big deal to have him there. "It's nothing fancy, but the guestroom is pretty much empty except for a queen-sized bed. And you could store your stuff in the cellar until your trailer is fixed."

Mateo gawked at her, his head tilted. He set down the half-eaten cinnamon roll on a box. "You want me to move into your house? With you?"

Well, not when he said it like that. "I don't care if you stay for a month," she rephrased for clarity's sake.

"You don't?" A look of suspicion pulled his mouth into a frown.

"Nope." She squared her shoulders to prove it. "I'm hardly ever around." And she could be around even less if she wanted. The café had a small office in the back. She always had a ton of work she could catch up on. "Besides, it'd be a good chance for you to get to know the property since you own it now." It would be a good chance for him to fall in love with the farm so he would keep it around.

"I guess it would be."

Well, that was it, then. Everything was settled. Mateo Torres was moving in with her. They would be living in the same house. Sharing a bathroom...

"You're sure you're okay with this?" he asked in the same soft voice he might use on a toddler.

Nope. Not even a little bit. "Of course," Everly bluffed with a sturdy smile. "In fact, I'll even help you get all of this stuff loaded in your truck." That would give her a chance to work out the nervous energy that suddenly pinged between her pulse points. She stooped to pick up a plastic bin. "Then you can drive down and move everything in." Because he was going to live with her. For a month. He was going to sleep right across the hall from her every night. For a month...

Whew boy, the box suddenly felt heavy in her hands. She went to set it back down, but accidentally tipped it over. The lid popped off and sent pictures and papers cascading across the ground. "I'm so sorry!" She quickly scrambled to collect them, and carefully restacked them in the box. "Is this your family?" She couldn't resist taking one out to get a closer look. The five of them were posed in front of one of those cheesy blue backdrops from the nineties. The older woman—his mother presumably—was a good foot shorter than Mateo, but her genuine smile gave her a larger-than-life presence, even in the photograph. Her daughters all resembled her with their lovely dark hair and beautiful thick-lashed eyes. Mateo looked so different. A lot scrawnier and a little angry.

"That was taken right before I left for the States," he said, looking over her shoulder.

"Wow," she marveled. "You had a lot of women in your life."

"Have," he corrected. "I still have them all in my life." He said it with conviction, strong and protective.

Everly had never heard him sound so serious. She didn't even know he had it in him. "When did your family move to the States?"

He hesitated as though he didn't want to talk about it. "My family didn't. I came to live on Gunner Raines's ranch when I was sixteen." Mateo turned away and started to stack some of the boxes lying around in an obvious effort to end the conversation, but there had to be more to his story.

She thought back to the night they'd danced. He'd said he had to leave ugly things behind and move on. That was hard to believe when she looked at the charismatic cowboy who charmed women into dancing and kissing. Nothing seemed to get to him. But there was obviously another side to Mateo. "You left your family at sixteen?" she asked, moving to stand across from him.

He set down the crate in his arms rather impatiently. "Didn't have a choice. My dad passed away when I was six.

In an accident while he was working at Gunner's ranch. His truck collided with a semi on some country road."

The words came out matter-of-factly, but Everly didn't miss the flash of pain in his eyes. "Oh, Mateo..."

"Gunner always felt responsible," he interrupted, pushing aside her sympathy. "He knew my mom struggled to provide for us with my father gone. So once I was old enough to help out on the ranch Gunner took me in, spent years helping me become a citizen, and gave me a career to make sure I could take care of my family."

Everly glanced at the picture again. God, what a contrast to her privileged life. "They're lucky to have you." She set the photograph back in the bin. "Do you see them much?"

"It's hard to get home." He picked up another crate and carted it over to his truck. "I can't take too much time off from training. Mom comes every once in a while, but my oldest sisters are too busy with their families to travel."

Everly followed him and set the bin of photographs on the tailgate. "What about your youngest sister?" The one who was holding Mateo's hand in the picture.

"That's Ana Sofia. She's in Seattle on a student visa. At the University of Washington." His chin lifted in a show of pride, much like a father's would. "She got a late start, but she's killing it up there. I see her the most. Once in a while, she'll come to competitions, and I make it up there a few times a year."

She smiled. It was sweet how he talked about Ana with so much affection. It seemed the man had a heart after all. She went to glance at the picture again, but a different photograph caught her eye. A tattered snapshot of a young Mateo with an older boy. She picked it up. "Who's this?"

Mateo looked over. "No one." His jaw tightened as he

swiped it out of her hand and buried it in the bin before replacing the lid. "We should get everything loaded." He moved swiftly away from her.

Everly watched him haul more boxes to his truck. His movements were tense. Almost angry. Which proved one thing. Whatever ugly memories Mateo had buried in his past, it seemed he hadn't quite left them behind after all.

Chapter Seven

Before standing directly in front of it, Mateo hadn't paid much attention to the farmhouse on Owen's property. Hadn't seen the point since he had other plans for the land. But now that he saw it up close, he couldn't seem to stop noticing the many imperfections.

The white paint had started to peel back in more than one place. The siding closest to the ground had rotted. And don't get him started on the roof. It had been compiled of shake shingles, which were a serious fire hazard, by the way. Maybe it wouldn't have been so bad if someone had kept up with it, but the shingles were warped and weathered from who knew how many years of wind and snow and sun. Then there was the pitiful front porch made up of a concrete slab, which was sloped and crumbling.

"Wow," he couldn't help but mutter as he followed Everly to the front door. "Owen sure didn't keep this place up, did he?"

"What d'you mean?" Her expression tightened.

"Uh..." Surely she'd noticed the house had gone to ruin. That couldn't be news to her. "It needs a new roof, new siding, and new concrete work." He could've kept going, but decided to stop when she peered over her shoulder with a frown. She'd obviously tried to dress up the porch with a colorful bench and pots of various flowers, but you couldn't hide the facts.

"It's fine for now," she snapped as she unlocked the door. "I haven't had time to do much work on the outside."

He didn't see any point in reminding her that the work was actually the landlord's responsibility. His responsibility, in other words. Yet another reason to bring in the bulldozers. A roof alone would set him back at least ten thousand dollars.

Everly scooted on ahead of him into the house, but Mateo hesitated. If the outside looked this bad, he'd better brace himself for what he'd find on the other side of that door.

Turned out, he didn't have to. When he finally did step inside his jaw dropped. The place was immaculate. Small, but seriously impressive. A kitchen was nestled into one corner of the open room, and it looked like everything had been replaced. Gray cabinets gleamed with a fresh coat of gloss and the butcher-block countertops were in pristine condition. Even the farmhouse sink seemed to sparkle. Then there were the oak floors. They'd obviously recently been sanded back to perfection and coated with a dark stain, which really made the white shiplap on the walls stand out.

Opposite the kitchen sat a small family room, hallmarked by a brick hearth with an understated leather couch, armchair, and the same coffee table he'd seen at Owen's house, which he happened to know doubled as a gun safe. Rustic accents were tastefully scattered around the room—an antique pitcher along with dried plants on the mantel, paintings of chickens and tractors, and an old pallet sign that said, *Life is Better on the Farm.*

"Wow," he said again. "Looks a little different on the inside."

"Yeah." Everly quickly straightened the shoes that were piled next to the door as though she was embarrassed by that tiny display of disorganization. "It was a lot of work. Which is why I haven't had time to fix up the outside."

Mateo whirled to face her. "You did all this yourself?" She had to be pulling his leg. There was no way. The cabinets had been completely refinished. And then there were the floors...

"Sure." She shrugged like it was nothing more than a simple weekend project. "It's amazing what a little elbow grease can do for a space."

Judging from the house's rough exterior, this had taken a hell of a lot more than *a little* elbow grease. "The floors look incredible." Yes, he was fishing, but he never would've guessed a lawyer from San Francisco knew anything about refinishing oak floors.

Everly drifted over to the kitchen, where she started to rinse the few dishes that sat in the sink, carefully placing them in the stainless dishwasher. "I rented a sander, then watched a YouTube video on how to stain them."

A YouTube video? He happened to know that refinishing and staining floors was not an easy job. He'd helped Gunner do the same thing at his place. "What about the cabinets?" Mateo wandered through the kitchen, examining the perfect paint job.

"Stripped them and painted them myself." A hint of pride

spoke through the words, as though she knew he doubted her. But she didn't gloat. She wouldn't even look at him while she wiped up the counter. Which was funny considering he couldn't stop staring at her. All of these new revelations cast her in a different light.

It seemed he'd misjudged Everly Brooks.

"You know that's not your job as a renter, right?" She shouldn't have to pay to renovate a house she didn't own. It didn't make sense. It wasn't like she'd get anything out of the investment. "That's the landlord's responsibility."

"Owen told me I could do whatever I wanted. He didn't have the time or money. And since I planned to—" That guarded expression took over her face again. "Never mind. It's no big deal. I loved doing it."

"Since you planned to what?" Mateo strode over to her, searching her eyes. He had a feeling he already knew. She'd planned to buy the place. Obviously. Why else would she have put all this work into it? A sudden tension pulled at his temples, signaling the beginning of a nasty headache. He'd misjudged more than Everly's talents. He'd also misjudged her commitment to the farm. She'd already started to make it her home.

Leaving his question unanswered, Everly moved briskly down the short hallway that opened up between the kitchen and living room. "The guestroom is back here."

Mateo trudged behind her, wading through a quicksand of complications. He was moving into Everly's cozy little house at the same time he was talking with Blake Wilder about demolishing it. *Shit.* He shouldn't stay here. He couldn't.

"This will be your room." She gestured to the door on the left and reached in to turn on the light, which flickered weakly over their heads before brightening.

"Do the lights always do that?" More dollar signs danced around his head. Rewiring the place would take another ten grand.

"Only once in a while." She shrugged with a smile. "It's charming, really."

Sure, charming. Or faulty, outdated wiring...

"I haven't had time to do much with this room yet." Everly seemed to watch his face for a reaction.

Mateo pulled his attention away from the light and glanced around. The room was bare except for a plain oak dresser and a queen-sized bed. "It's fine." At least, the room was fine. But staying in it for the next month while he made plans to demolish it? That didn't feel right. "I don't want to intrude on your space though. I should stay with Levi."

"You don't like the room?"

Great. Now he'd offended her. "No. It's not that. The room is nice." He didn't need much. Just the basics. But... "This is your house." And it was small. Living room, kitchen, two bedrooms, probably one bathroom. So he wouldn't be able to avoid her. They'd see each other all the time. He'd already proven once he couldn't keep his head straight when she was around, and he hadn't even slept across the hall from her or run into her in her pajamas yet. *Mamacita*, her pajamas. Did she wear that John Deere T-shirt and nothing else to bed every night? Would she wear it around the kitchen in the morning? A sensual curiosity drew his gaze back to her body. So damn perfect. What would it feel like to touch her? He let himself imagine it, just for a second, running his hand from the curve of her waist up her shirt, feeling that soft skin under his fingers...

"You're staying here," Everly informed him. "Really. It's

no trouble at all. It makes zero sense for you to take everything over to Levi's house when I have a perfectly good room for you here." Her resolute tone left no room for him to disagree. In addition to her handyman skills, the woman also had developed a talent for winning arguments.

"Fine. I'll stay." What else could he say? "I appreciate it." He'd appreciate it a lot more if that attraction between them didn't spark every time she stood close. He knew how soft her lips were, how it felt when her hands worked their way over his shoulders. They'd ended that kiss with things unfinished, and every time he was around her, he couldn't help but wonder what it would feel like to take it further.

And from the way she kept sneaking looks at him, he had to wonder if she was thinking the same thing. It was going to be mighty hard to keep his hands to himself for the next month. Hopefully the repairs on his trailer wouldn't take that long. He'd only spent ten minutes in this house with Everly and already he was feeling conflicted about things. He hated feeling conflicted. He'd always been a black-and-white sort of person. Practical. Especially when it came to finances.

"The bathroom is right here." Everly slipped out of the guestroom and opened the door at the end of the hall, leaving the third one closed. That must be her room. Yeah, he definitely didn't belong in there, but, again, his mind wandered. Was the bed soft and feminine? He had no business finding out, and he'd best remember that.

"The plumbing is a little finicky," Everly said, drawing his attention back to the bathroom. This room had been updated, too. One pedestal sink, a new toilet, and a claw foot tub with a rain showerhead and a white gauzy shower curtain that would hide absolutely nothing if, say, he happened to walk in on her in the shower...

"Just an FYI, the hot and cold faucets are mixed up." Everly's gaze hesitated against his as though she was trying to hear his thoughts. "It's not so bad once you get used to it."

"Doesn't bother me." None of this bothered him. He'd keep telling himself that. "The trailer doesn't have the best shower, either."

Everly nodded quickly then zipped past as though she couldn't stand to be trapped in such close quarters with him. "I can clean out a few cabinets in the kitchen so you'll have room for your groceries. And I'm sure all of your boxes and tubs will fit in the cellar. There's access on the outside of the house."

"Sounds good." Mateo followed her at a safe distance. At least it should've been safe, but the back of her looked just as good as the front in those skinny jeans she was wearing. He quickly dropped his gaze to the floor.

Once they reached the living room again, Everly went to slip on her boots by the door. "I guess we should unload your truck, huh?"

"That's okay." Hopefully she didn't pick up on the panic that had edged into his voice. "I'm sure you have stuff to do. I can handle the unpacking." What he didn't know how to handle were the feelings she stirred in him.

Even after a week, being alone in Everly's house still felt...wrong. And yet it was better than the alternative—being here with her on a cozy evening, that light rain tapping the windowpanes while the cold air begged for a fire in the hearth.

Mateo rinsed his soup bowl and assessed where to put it in the dishwasher. Everly seemed to be one of those people who had a system for keeping the dishes organized. When he'd lived in his trailer he'd tossed them in wherever they fit, but for the last week he'd been walking on eggshells. So far, he'd managed to miss seeing her in the mornings. He'd wait to come out of his room until he heard her leave the house. Then he'd rush through a shower and take off for Levi's place, where he'd spend the day training. Everly hadn't been around much in the evenings, so he'd heat up a quick dinner for himself before going out to the Tumble Inn or to Levi's house for poker. Every night when he came home her door was already closed. He had no idea if she was sleeping or just avoiding him the way he was avoiding her. Didn't matter either way. So far it had worked. Now, if they could only keep it up for another three weeks.

Mateo went back to inspecting the top shelf of the dishwasher. Guess you couldn't go wrong wedging the bowl in with the other bowls, right? He made it fit, then closed up the dishwasher and went back to the kitchen table.

Dante had been lying at his feet while he'd eaten his dinner, but now his dog was gone. That couldn't be good. He called in his most authoritative voice, but Dante didn't come running the way he usually did when he knew he might get in trouble. "Hey, pup, where'd you go?" He lightened up on the sternness and rounded the corner into the hallway. Everly's bedroom door stood wide open.

That definitely wasn't good. He hadn't seen her bedroom door left open once. "Dante, come."

The dog did not obey, so he had no choice but to step into the room. It looked like a page from one of those magazines Charity was always looking at—*Country Style* or some shit like that. The walls were painted a calming gray, as pale as the clouds that misted over the mountaintops outside. A massive four-poster bed dominated the small space.

Mateo studied the intricate carving on each of the posts. Looked like it'd been handmade. Knowing what he knew about Everly now, he wouldn't be surprised if she'd carved the damn thing herself.

The bed linens were a crisp white and had that soft look like they were stuffed with downy feathers. It seemed to be a bed made for two—a place to lounge around on late Sunday mornings or a place to hunker down and make love on a cold rainy night.

Over the last week Mateo had gotten better at ignoring thoughts like that, but a seductive scent in the air played with his head. It was something subtle but sexy, more spice than floral. The kind of scent that would catch his attention, even in a crowded room. The kind of scent that had distracted him from searching for his delinquent dog.

"Dante." Mateo strode to the other side of the bed, noting the absence of any personal touches. There were no pictures of Everly, no pictures of anyone, which didn't seem right.

But anyway...his dog. Everly's personal life was none of his business.

"Dante?" He finally made it to the closet. It was bigger than he'd anticipated, a full walk-in, which must've been added after the house was built based on the way the wall seams didn't line up. Way back in the corner, his dog had stretched out and was lazily gnawing on what looked to be a very expensive stiletto.

"Leave it." Mateo's voice bordered on a growl, and the dog immediately heeded the warning, dropping the shoe before he took off like a shot, bounding over Mateo's boots and out of reach.

"Come on, man." He knelt and picked up the shoe, inspecting the damage. Everly would never be wearing the sparkly silver heel again. Not with all of those teeth marks. "Why do you have to make trouble, Dante?" The dog was likely already out of earshot, hiding under the kitchen table or something. It was probably because Mateo had kept him on lockdown in his room whenever he wasn't around to keep the dog in line. This was his punishment. Now he'd be forced to have a conversation with Everly while holding what could only be described as a *fuck me* shoe. And damn, if she had these things on he'd be more than glad to.

He set the shoe back on the low shelf next to its match. There were a lot of shoes in the closet. Nice ones. Shiny heels in just about every color. The clothes were nice, too. Along one wall, Everly had hung tattered jeans and flannel shirts and ragged worktops, but all along the other wall were the clothes she must've worn in her other life—suits and sexy low-cut dresses and swanky silk blouses. A grin pulled at his mouth. She hadn't ditched her lawyer wardrobe when she'd moved to Topaz Falls. She'd lived here for over two years, and she still hadn't gotten rid of her old clothes. Maybe there was a part of her that didn't want to. Maybe she still wondered about going back...

His phone rang, sending a shot of panic through him that made him flail out of the closet. Luckily it was only his sister Ana's number.

He quickly strode out of Everly's room and firmly closed the door behind him. He'd have to talk to her about the shoe later. And maybe take his troublemaker dog over to Levi's for an extended stay. Back in his own room, he clicked on the phone and brought it to his ear. "Hey, *hermanita*."

"Mateo?" Static blipped through the line. "Is that you? You sound out of breath."

That's because I was snooping around my hot tenant's

closet. He almost laughed. Ana would murder him. "Of course it's me. I was just...lifting." Not a complete lie. He and Ty and Levi had gone to the gym earlier.

"Well, go take a shower. I'm coming through town in about two hours. Can you meet for dinner?"

"I'm sorry, what?" The phone must've cut out. "You're coming through town?" His sister had always been impulsive, but why the hell would she drive all the way down from Seattle without a phone call? Wasn't it the middle of her semester?

"I need to talk to you," she said impatiently. "In person."

That might as well have pulled the rug right out from under his feet. Everything around him seemed to spin. "Jesus, what's wrong? Are you okay? Is everything okay? Is it Mamá?"

"*Buen Dios*, Mateo." That kind of mutter always came with an eye roll. "Get a grip. Everything is fine. Where can I meet you?"

He sank to the bed. If everything were fine, she wouldn't be driving through Topaz Falls on some unannounced trip, but Ana's stubbornness rivaled his bronc's. She wouldn't tell him what was up until she wanted to. "How about on Main Street? There's a mediocre Italian restaurant." Which he couldn't even remember the name of. "You can't miss it."

"Sounds perfect," Ana said. "I'll see you soon."

Chapter Eight

If Everly could take one picture that communicated exactly why Topaz Falls needed the farm, this would be it.

She stood back and watched little Benny and Jake Hart toddle around the potato patch and dig up the yams that were ready to harvest. Kenna, their mom, followed behind them reminding them they couldn't eat the potatoes until they were cooked. The two towheaded young boys were covered in dirt, which only seemed to make them happier. They used Everly's small spade shovels to dig up the yams, and every time they uncovered one, they cheered and hugged like they'd found a buried treasure.

She almost wished Mateo would come outside so he could see this. So he could see that this place made a difference. The Hart family had been through hell over the last month after Kenna's husband had been indicted for insurance fraud. He'd been quite the successful agent in town until people realized he was stealing from them. In one day,

Kenna had lost her marriage and most of her friends in Topaz Falls.

Everly didn't know her well, but when the three of them had come to the café for lunch, she'd invited them to stay for the afternoon and help her with some work on the farm. So far, the boys had helped her weed the gardens, pick what was left of the winter squash, and clean out the goat pens. All in between rides in the wheelbarrow, of course. The boys seemed so much more exuberant than they had when they'd walked into the café. And even Kenna had laughed and smiled watching them transform into little farmers.

Everly glanced toward the farmhouse, where Mateo's truck was parked. *See?* she wanted to yell. This place matters. Broken hearts could more easily be mended under the sun, with your hands in the dirt while you worked in the shadow of the beautiful mountains. It had definitely helped her heal.

"Don't think there's any more whams," Benny said, stomping over to where Everly stood. Clumps of mud weighed down his shoes.

Grunting, Jake dragged over the basket they'd filled. "But we found lots."

"You sure did." Everly crouched and picked up a yam, carefully inspecting it. "In fact, you might've found the magic yams."

Benny's eyes went wide. "Magic whams?"

"Yep." She set the vegetable back in the basket and stood. "These ones are special. They have so many vitamins that they'll make you grow big and strong."

The boys looked into the basket with awe.

"How about you take half of them home?" Everly shared a smile with Kenna. "Then your mom can cook them for you."

Benny's nose wrinkled. "I don't think I like whams."

"I didn't either," Everly admitted. "Until I started putting butter and brown sugar on them."

"Sugar?" The boys said it at the same time.

"You can eat yams with sugar," Everly confirmed. "That's why it's my favorite vegetable."

"Can we, Mom?" Jake tugged on Kenna's jacket. "Please? Can we take them home?"

"Sure." She smiled at Everly again, but there was a deep sadness in her lovely hazel eyes. "That would be wonderful. Thank you." She ruffled her son's blond hair. "I think we should probably get going now."

"Aw, Mom. No." Benny's lips curled into an automatic pout.

"We haven't finished helping Miss Brooks yet," Jake insisted.

Everly glanced at her watch. "Well, I have to be somewhere soon, but I need help with one more thing." She shot a questioning look to Kenna, who nodded. "We need to round up the chickens and ducks and put them in their pens for the night."

Jake frowned. "You mean you lock them up?"

"Only to keep them safe. Sometimes predators come around after dark, so they're much safer in the coop." Everly waved them over to the chicken yard. "You guys want to try shooing them in there for me?"

"Yeah we do!" The boys went after the chickens, raising their arms and giggling. "Here, chicky chickies! Time to go to bed!"

The chickens, of course, did not listen. They scattered, running circles around the boys. Benny and Jake thought that was hilarious.

Laughing, Everly stood with Kenna and watched the joyful chaos unfold.

"Thank you so much for doing this." The young mom turned to Everly. "We haven't gotten out much lately." Her eyes reddened. "This has been so good for them."

"It's been good for me, too." She could live for this, for helping kids fall in love with the farm the same way she had.

Not far away, Jake and Benny had changed their approach. They got real quiet and were trying to sneak up on the chickens from behind. That seemed to work much better. The slower and quieter the boys were, the more the chickens calmed.

Everly didn't miss the tears on Kenna's cheeks. She gave the woman's shoulder a squeeze. "How are you doing?"

"I think I'm still in shock." She dug a Kleenex out of her coat pocket and dabbed at her eyes. "I'm trying to be strong for the boys, but I'm not doing a very good job. It kills me to see their world falling apart. They didn't deserve this."

"Neither did you," Everly pointed out. No one had ever told her that after her world fell apart. No one had said much of anything to her, except for the judge who took away her license. He'd harshly told her he didn't believe she hadn't been aware that her fiancé was a criminal. It seemed everyone else thought the same thing. How had she not known? The silence from her old community of friends and colleagues had shamed her the same way she suspected Kenna was being shamed by most of the town.

"I should've known." Kenna's fair skin flushed, and Everly recognized that potent combination of anger and humiliation. "Or at least had some idea. I never asked any questions. I simply trusted that everything was fine."

The words brought an onslaught of her own buried pain.

Those same questions still plagued her. *How could I have been so stupid? How did I not know that Andrew was capable of something so disgusting?* It had been almost three years and she still went back over her relationship with him, analyzing whether there were hints, things she should've picked up on.

Why did she still find it so hard to talk about? Why couldn't she tell Kenna she'd fallen for lies, too? It was the shame. That ugly shame bearing down on her with all of the negative things she'd told herself. That she was weak and gullible. Even after all this time, she still worried it was true.

"I'm sorry," Kenna said with a sigh. "I didn't mean to dump all of that on you."

"Don't apologize. I—"

A black Escalade turned onto the driveway and parked next to the fence a good thirty feet away. Everly's stomach rolled the way it always did when she got on an airplane. The last time she'd seen a car like that drive onto her property, her parents had come for a visit.

"Looks like you have company." Kenna collected the boys and herded them toward her car, which was still parked at the café. "Thanks for having us here, Everly. This was so good for them."

"Of course." She picked up the basket of yams and followed Kenna, keeping a wary eye on the Escalade. "You and the boys are welcome anytime." She had to make it a point to invite the woman over again. When they had more time to talk. When Everly could find a way to share her own story so Kenna wouldn't feel so alone.

"Bye, Miss Brooks!" Just before getting into the car, Jake threw his arms around her waist for a hug. "This has been the best day ever."

Everly squeezed him back. "You have to come again real soon. Maybe next time you can play with the goats." She winked at Benny, who happened to be a bit shier than his brother.

"You think they'd let us pet them?" Jake immediately looked at his mom with pleading puppy dog eyes. It was a wonder that Kenna could ever say no to anything.

"We can't stay today, but we'll come back soon," Kenna promised. She helped the boys into the car and thanked Everly once more before driving away.

It was tempting to go on in and hide in the café's back office where she had a mountain of paperwork waiting, but instead Everly soldiered on down the driveway to where the Escalade sat idling.

Sure enough, her father got out of the SUV. He must've left her mother at home this time. During the last visit, all Sherri Brooks had done was cry and plead with her to come home. Knowing her dear old dad, he'd decided to change strategies.

"This is a surprise." She stopped a few feet away. The little girl in her wanted to rush into her daddy's arms the way she used to when he would come home from work. He'd pick her up and swing her around, and even toss her into the air if her mother wasn't watching. He'd always been fun and charming and energetic. It stunned her how he looked the same except for a little more silver on the fringes of his dark hair. His deep brown eyes had sharpened, too. Or maybe it only seemed like they got sharper when they looked at her. "You could've called."

"This isn't really a phone conversation." Her father walked a few steps closer, his loafers out of step with the muddy, rutted driveway. He was dressed nicely—in gray

slacks and a starched button-up shirt. Casual by his stan-
dards. His typical travel wear. He also had a manila folder
tucked under his arm, which couldn't be good.

"I have some business in Denver so I thought I would stop
by."

"Sure. Great." She didn't mention that this was a few
hours out of his way. He had a reason for *stopping by*, and
she had a feeling it wasn't simply to say hi. "Would you
like to come into the café for some coffee?" The last time
she'd offered that, her parents had refused. It was as if they
couldn't bear to see how she was wasting her life, but the last
thing she needed was for Mateo to walk outside and interrupt. Her dad would lose it if he found out she was suddenly
living with some random cowboy.

"I can't stay long." Her father's features were solemn. "I
just came to tell you it's time to stop hiding. You have to face
things, Everly. It's time to come home where you belong."

And there it was. They still wanted to control her, to make
all of her decisions for her. God, she loved her parents, but
they didn't even know her. "I belong here," she said, the conviction much stronger since Kenna and the boys had visited.

Her father was a master at remaining stoic, but she'd
learned to detect the signs of anger in his features, the twitch
of his left jaw, the slight narrowing of his eyes. "You don't
have to live like this. I mean, look at you. You're a mess."

Well, she couldn't deny that. Her jeans had gotten muddy
in all of the shenanigans with the boys. "Gee, thanks, Dad."

He ignored the sarcasm. "Come on, Everly. What happened with Andrew was a small setback in your plans. But
you can get your license back. I've already talked to Harold
about representing you." He held out the folder. "We've done
all the research. I have the paperwork right here. We'll fight

until they give in. You can be practicing law again within six months."

"I don't want to be a lawyer anymore." It didn't matter how many times she said it; he still couldn't hear it.

"But you worked so hard." His composure started to melt away. "All those years. All that school. You were at the top of your class. How can you give up on your dream?"

She couldn't. She could never give up on her dream. Not now that she knew how it felt to live it. "Being a lawyer was never *my* dream. You pushed me in that direction. You chose for me. Now I'm choosing for myself." And she refused to be sad about it. She refused to let him guilt her away from what she loved.

"It won't last," he barked. "You can't make ends meet here. What about your future? Your retirement? You think being a farmer is going to provide for all of your needs?"

"I don't know." She had to admit there was some freedom in not really caring at the moment. "This makes me happy." Not that he would understand. Her father wouldn't be happy without money and prestige. Yes, he loved his career, loved it so much he wanted it to be hers, too, but it wasn't.

"Happy?" Her stoic father threw up his hands, waving the folder. "That's your long-term plan? Being happy? I'll tell you what you're being." He pointed at her, resorting to courtroom theatrics. "Irresponsible. You're throwing away your money every month renting this dump. You need to get your head on straight, Everly. This venture of yours will fail. You come back now, I can get you a legal team, and, eventually, a job. If you keep waiting, that will be much harder to do."

Was that a threat? She looked into his eyes, needing to believe that his anger was motivated by love. He'd always called her his princess, but that was back when she'd done everything her parents had asked of her. When she'd let them choose for her. And yes, it made her sad to see his heart breaking, but she couldn't go back to that life. She wouldn't.

She walked over to him and squeezed his strong hand. "I love you and Mom. But I'm not coming back. Even if this venture fails." Which would kill her. She couldn't picture her future without the farm. But if she lost it... "I'd find something else here." Surrounded by the mountains and the people who let her be who she was. "I can never go back. So you need to stop asking."

Her father ripped his hand away from hers. "Don't come running to me when it doesn't work out." He stalked to the SUV and leveled her with a final glare. "I've tried to help you, but I'm done." Without giving her a chance to respond, he got into the car and drove away.

Inside the door of the Chocolate Therapist, Darla had placed a coatrack with a sign that read HANG YOUR COATS, CARES, WORRIES, BURDENS, DOUBTS, AND REGRETS AND LEAVE THEM BY THE DOOR.

Everly was pretty sure she could fill that coatrack with each of those things right about now. Well, everything except for a coat. But worries, burdens, regrets, and doubts? She had plenty of those to offer. Nothing like a pep talk from your father to make you suddenly recognize all of your inadequacies.

The scent of rich dark chocolate seemed to take the edge off her sadness. Walking into her friend's wine bar/chocolate confectionery always seemed to minimize life's biggest complications. It wasn't only the smell. It was also the ambiance and sleek, modern décor—simple but elegant with stained concrete floors, dark accent walls, and wooden pub tables strewn through the large space. A stone-clad bar ran the entire length of one wall, and it never sat vacant unless the place was closed.

The combination of chocolate and wine attracted an assortment of people—tourists and locals alike. Everyone seemed to smile as they chatted and laughed and caught up and celebrated. The world needed more places like this. Happy hubs of community that provided a momentary refuge from the uncertainties and hardships of everyday life. And family. Family provided plenty of hardships.

Everly claimed a stool at the edge of the bar. Amazing how someone else's lack of faith in you could nibble away at your confidence.

"Everly!" Kate Livingston rushed over and wrapped her up in a hug. "How are you?" She pulled back, her dark eyes sparkling with friendly excitement. "I hardly got to talk to you at the party."

Ah, yes, the party. She hadn't had time to talk to many people at the party since she'd left early to get away from Mateo. Funny how a few weeks later she couldn't seem to get away from him at all. "I was so bummed I had to leave early. It was such a beautiful party." Everly couldn't smile as big as Kate if she tried.

"You okay?" Her friend perched on the stool next to her. "You don't look so good. I mean, you look lovely, of course, but you seem upset."

"Upset" wasn't the right word. Tired. Demoralized. "It's been a long week." Made longer still by her father's impromptu visit. Then there was the sexy cowboy living in her house. He'd made himself scarce over the last week, which meant he hadn't witnessed any of the wonderful things happening at the farm. How would she ever convince him it was worth keeping if he was never paying attention?

"Long weeks always call for a full glass of petit syrah and our dark French roast truffles filled with a velvety ganache." Kate took the liberty of marking down Everly's order on the customer card.

"I'll take two boxes." Maybe she could use the other one to lure Mateo out of hiding.

"Coming right up." With a wink, Kate bustled over to the bartender and rushed Everly's order to the top.

Ahhhh. She inhaled the dark chocolaty scent and rested her forearms on the bar, letting her shoulders sag. Coming here had been the right decision. She'd started to feel more relaxed already.

"If I didn't know better, I'd think you were hiding from someone." Darla pulled up a stool next to Everly's and grilled her with a glare. Despite having recently hired Kate to run the place, Darla still seemed to hang around a lot.

Everly knew enough to avoid her friend's gaze when Darla was on the hunt for information. She did not need any questions about Mateo living in her house. All week, she'd done her best to downplay it, so no one would read too much into her offer to let him stay. Too many questions would only fluster her, and that was exactly why she'd avoided Darla all week. No one needed to know that, while Mateo irritated her, she also thought he was sexy and tempting. And an incredibly good kisser.

"Why would you think I'm hiding?" she asked innocently.

"You're two hours early for book club."

"I needed chocolate." Mateo had left the house right after her father, so she'd gone in to change and then decided she didn't want to sit alone and wallow in her heartache. "It's been a hell of a week."

"I'll bet it has." Her friend grinned. "Have you seen your new roommate naked yet?"

Uh-oh. A swallow stuck in Everly's throat. "No." She dragged the word out too long to be believable.

"You have too!"

Thankfully the bartender came over and set down Everly's wineglass with two small boxes of perfect, delectable truffles.

"Those are on the house, Miguel," Darla said with a wink.

The young bartender nodded and bowed in Everly's direction. "Enjoy, *la chica bella.*"

He probably thought she was blushing on account of his charm, but it had more to do with the way Darla looked at her. "I trade truffles for secrets," her friend said. "So spill yours, sister."

"I don't have secrets." Lies. So many lies.

Darla knew it, too. She always knew. "Tell me or I'm going to start asking more detailed questions in a much louder voice."

"Fine." Everly sighed. Darla never made empty threats. "There was a little incident where Mateo's dog got into my coop early one morning. I thought it was a mountain lion so I fired a warning shot and he came running out in his towel." There she went again, recalling every detail of his body. The image had been seared into her brain.

"I knew it." Darla stole one of the truffles from the box and popped it into her mouth. "So? What'd you think? Does his body look as good without clothes as it does with those sexy jeans he wears?"

Better. So much better. "I didn't stand there and evaluate

him." God, if Mateo could hear her right now, he'd probably laugh. When he'd dropped that towel, time had stopped. She had no idea how long she'd stared at him.

"I wonder if he'd be willing to do a reenactment," Darla said with a wicked grin. "Why don't you ask him—?"

"Hey, Everly." Charity Stone waved from across the room.

Thank God. The perfect person to distract Darla from all her questions about Mateo's goods. Everly had seen Charity put Mateo in his place more than once. She wouldn't want to talk about him getting naked.

"Hey." She waved Charity over and pulled up another stool.

The woman happened to be the kind of gorgeous that made other women roll their eyes when she walked past. Long blondish hair, high cheekbones, and dark intense blue eyes. She looked so sweet, but that mouth of hers could put even the gruffest cowboy to shame.

"Is it true that you let Mateo move in with you?" Charity blurted before she'd made it to the bar.

Heads turned.

Well, damn. It would be in the newspaper tomorrow.

"Oh, it's true," Darla answered for her.

Charity slid onto the stool next to them. "When Levi told me that, I told him he had to be shitting me. Everly's not that stupid. She wouldn't let Mateo move into her house."

"It *is* rather interesting," Darla mused. "Why would Everly invite a sexy cowboy to live with her? Hmmm."

Both women—along with a few strangers—stared as though demanding an explanation.

"His trailer flooded. What was I supposed to do?"

"I don't know." Charity's eyes seemed to search the

ceiling for an answer. "Make him move in with Levi maybe?"

"You could've sent him to my place," Darla offered. "I wouldn't mind having a hot, bronc-riding roomie for a few weeks."

Right. That's exactly what she should've done. Except then she wouldn't be able to make her case for the farm. "I figured it would be a good chance for him to get familiar with the land since it's his now." And yes, she also felt bad about being the reason his trailer had flooded.

Inviting him to stay had made so much sense in her head. But that was before she'd stood with Mateo in her hallway and realized there would only be about twenty feet separating them every night. Which might not have mattered if it hadn't been for that stupid, sensual, intoxicating mistake of a kiss they'd shared. Her memory of that kiss always seemed to flare and retract like the flames of a tantalizing fire between them.

"What's going on over here?" Kate asked, butting back into the conversation. There must've been a lull in new customers. "I heard you guys squealing about something all the way from the back."

"Oh, haven't you heard? Everly invited Mateo to move in with her." Darla thrived on making shocking announcements.

"He's using her shower," Charity added with a grossed-out look.

"Really?" Kate pulled over a stool, too. "So you and Mateo, huh?"

"No, no. There's no me and Mateo," she assured them all.

"That's good," Kate said, her eyes wide with relief. "Because I just saw him walk by outside with a woman."

"A woman?" Darla shot to her feet.

"Yeah. And she was gorgeous." As if she realized how that sounded, Kate patted Everly's knee. "Not nearly as gorgeous as you or anything, but pretty. Sort of."

"It's fine," Everly said quickly. "And thanks for the compliment. I'm well aware that I'm not exactly Mateo's type."

"Thank God for that. Who was he with, though?" Charity demanded like an overprotective sister. "Did you recognize her? Is she a local?"

"I didn't get a good enough look." Kate almost seemed sorry she'd brought it up. "But I think he had his arm around her."

"Of course he did." Charity rolled her eyes. "That's how he works, Everly. You mark my words. He'll be trying his damnedest to get into your bed before you even know what's happening."

He hadn't yet, and he'd already lived there for a week. She sat up straighter to keep the subtle disappointment closeted where it belonged. "I'm not interested." That classified more as a fib than an outright lie.

"Well, I am," Darla said. "In fact..." She tugged Everly to her feet. "Let's follow him. See where he's taking this mystery woman."

"No thanks." Everly pulled away. She'd learned enough to steer clear of Darla and her wild schemes. "I don't care who he's with." At least she shouldn't. Mateo's Don Juan ways only gave her one more reason to stay away from him. As illustrated the night he'd almost had her naked in a hotel room.

"Aren't you a little curious?" Charity's sly grin taunted. "Don't you want to know who might be showing up in your guest room tonight? Or who you might see at the breakfast table tomorrow morning?"

"He wouldn't bring her back to my house... would he?" She'd told him to make himself at home at the farm, but surely he wouldn't go that far.

Charity's deadpan expression answered the question. "If he thinks he has a shot at getting laid?" Her face scrunched with disgust. "He'd pretty much do anything."

Everly pictured herself lying in bed tonight listening to the extracurricular activities going on in the room across the hall. *Ew.* She really should've thought this through before she'd insisted he move in.

"I saw them go into that Italian restaurant across the street," Kate said helpfully. "I wish I could join you, but I have wine and truffles to serve."

"The Italian restaurant?" Darla gagged. "Why would he bring a date there?"

"Maybe because he knew we'd all be here," Charity reminded her. "I can guaran-fucking-tee he's not gonna bring a potential girlfriend anywhere near me. I have too much dirt on him."

"So what do you say?" Darla asked, her eyes sparkling with telltale excitement.

Everly hesitated. Darla's escapades rarely ended well. "I guess we can take a peek." That would at least give her the chance to see if he looked serious enough about this woman to bring her home tonight. "But no making a scene. He can't know we're spying on him."

Chapter Nine

Good evening, Mr. Torres." The hostess at Cibo per Favore batted long, fake eyelashes in Mateo's direction, which immediately drew a dramatic eye roll from his sister.

"Seriously? They greet you by name around here?"

"It's not my fault." Could he help it that he was something of a local celebrity? Not like it was hard to achieve star status in a town the size of Topaz Falls.

"Can we get a table in the corner?" Ana asked the hostess, still giving him an irritated glare. "Preferably something out of the way so I don't have to watch women flirt with him all night?"

"Oh yes, of course. It must be hard dating someone famous." The young woman snatched two menus from the hostess stand and beckoned Mateo to follow her.

This time, Ana uttered an audible groan. "We're not dating," she announced loud enough for the entire restaurant to hear. "He's my brother."

"Oh." Perky Hostess stopped and glanced back at him with a little quirk of the lips likely reserved for eligible bachelors. "Are you dating anyone?" she asked, using those eyelashes again.

Mateo opened his mouth, but Ana stepped between them. "Yes. As a matter of fact, Mateo is in a relationship with someone. His name is Amigo and he weighs about fifteen hundred pounds. Now, if you'll show us to our table..."

Perky Hostess didn't seem to know what to do with Ana. Most of the time, Mateo didn't, either. After an awkward silence, she turned back around. "Right this way."

Grinning at his sister, Mateo followed the hostess like a good little celebrity. The woman had a certain appeal—long dark hair, a seductive smile, and some tempting curves— but she was way too young for him. Probably only a few years past eighteen. He'd already been down that road, and he'd learned real quick that he liked his women more experienced.

"Here we are." Perky Hostess stopped at a booth that was literally stuck in the very corner of the restaurant. "I hope this will work."

"Looks good to me." Ana sat down.

"Wonderful. Your waiter will be with you in a moment," the woman purred, casting a long, sultry look at Mateo before she drifted away.

"If she could've seen you fifteen years ago, she wouldn't be interested." His sister opened her menu.

Mateo couldn't help but laugh as he slid into the booth across from Ana. "You got that right."

Fifteen years ago, he was a scrawny kid who'd been too afraid to talk to girls. Ana, on the other hand, had inherited most of the looks in the family. He'd always had to watch out for her with the boys in grade school. Of course, before he'd taken up bull riding, he'd gotten his ass kicked by kids two years younger than him, and Ana Sofia would never let him forget it.

But she hadn't driven all the way out to Topaz Falls to reminisce. "What're you doing here, sis?" he asked, not bothering to peruse the menu. He wasn't hungry. His imagination had spent a whole hour designing several worst-case scenarios. Maybe she was pregnant, which meant he'd soon be arrested for murder. Or maybe she'd gotten kicked out of school for something she hadn't done. Because Ana was brilliant and determined and careful. She didn't screw up.

Ana seemed to ignore his obvious worry. "We'll both take the spaghetti and a glass of the house merlot," his sister called to a passing waiter.

The kid stopped. "Actually, I'm not your waiter, but—"

"Oh, sorry." She offered up her most charming smile. "It's just that I've been driving all day and I'm so hungry. Do you happen to know our waiter?" she asked sweetly. Mateo wouldn't be surprised if she started to bat her eyelashes like the hostess had. "I mean, if you see him, you could surely put in the order for us, right?"

"Sure. I can let him know." The kid hurried away under Ana's spell.

Mateo shook his head. "And you got mad at the hostess for flirting."

"Yeah, yeah, yeah," she mumbled. "I'm temperamental. I've been driving all day. And you know how angry I get when I'm hungry."

Or tired, or stressed, or hormonal. He kept his mouth shut since she was in the perfect position to kick him in the shin.

"Which brings us back to my original question. What are you doing here?"

Ana inhaled deeply and raised her shoulders, somehow looking older than he liked to think she was. "I'm going home."

"Home," he repeated. "As in back to Chihuahua?" She was driving all the way back to Mexico?

"Of course Chihuahua, dumbass. Things are not good there, Mateo. Which you would know if you paid attention."

The jab got him underneath the ribs. "I call Mamá every week." He sent money every month just like he had since he was sixteen years old.

"I know, I know." His sister's shoulders slouched. "I'm not supposed to say anything, but she's spent all of the money on private detectives. Trying to find Andres."

Anger ignited in the hollow of his stomach. "*All* of it?"

"He sent her a letter a while ago. And now she's obsessed with finding him."

Mateo rested his head against the back of the booth. He closed his eyes. Of course Andres wrote their mom a letter. He should've known his brother would come back to haunt his family eventually. "Why hasn't she told me?" He raised his head. If his mother had told him right away, he would've taken care of it. He could've found his brother and told him to go to hell.

"Because she knew you took it the hardest when he disappeared," Ana murmured. "And she didn't want to get your hopes up until she knew more."

His mother didn't want to know more. "What did the letter say?"

"That he missed her." She rolled her eyes like she didn't

believe it. "And that he was sorry he had been gone for so long, but that's the way it had to be."

Damn right that was the way it had to be. Especially considering Andres had walked away from the family to join a cartel. Mateo was the only one who knew. He'd woken up early the morning his older brother had packed up his stuff. He'd only been eight at the time, but he'd seen Andres make some runs. He'd seen him sell drugs.

That morning, Andres had told him to go back to bed, but Mateo had followed him outside. He'd begged his brother not to leave. He'd heard what happened to people who joined the cartels. They disappeared. Never came back.

"You can't tell Mamá," Andres had said. "It would kill her."

"Then stay," Mateo had begged. He feared his brother's disappearance would kill their mother anyway, especially after they'd already lost Papá.

"I can't. This is my only chance to get out of here." His brother had hugged him one last time.

That had been eighteen years ago, and Mateo had never told anyone. Not Mamá, not Ana Sofia, not his older sisters. He couldn't tell them the truth. He couldn't destroy their love for him. So he'd kept it a secret. Even at eight, he'd known it was better for his mother to think Andres had disappeared than to know her son had left her behind to work for a drug lord.

Mateo had never seen Andres again, but he would come home to find envelopes of money stashed under his pillow, and he knew where it had come from. Andres must've meant for him to give it to Mamá or use it for the family, but Mateo couldn't stomach the thought of using drug money. He'd always taken it down to the local parish to donate it instead.

Ana folded her hands on the table. "I thought you should know what's going on. I'm going to stay down with Mamá for a while. To help her get her finances in order and to convince her to let this go. He's been gone too long. He shouldn't be allowed to come back now." Based on the sudden coldness in her eyes, she must've suspected Andres hadn't up and joined the Peace Corps.

It had been so many years, but Mateo still couldn't tell her. He couldn't admit that he'd kept a secret from her all this time. What good would it do his sister to find out the truth now? It would only hurt her. It would only hurt their mom. "You can't go home right now." Not until he took care of this. Not until he made sure Andres would stay away. "What about school? It's the middle of the semester. You can't leave." She only had a year left until she'd graduate.

"I already have left." She glowered the same way she always did when someone told her she couldn't do something. "I've made arrangements to finish the semester through their remote program. I'll go back to Seattle in the spring, but Mamá needs me down there, Mateo."

And what was he supposed to do? He couldn't go. He had a competition coming up, though he hadn't won any cash on his last couple of rides. "I don't want her to worry about money. I've got plenty." Enough to keep things afloat for a while, anyway. "And I just bought a huge acreage, too. I'm planning to partner with the ski resort to build a new condo development." Guilt clawed at his throat. And there was Everly again, haunting the dark corners of his mind. He pushed the image away. He didn't have a choice. He needed the money to take care of his family now more than ever.

"I know Mom appreciates all you do," Ana said, almost smiling. "You're good to her. You're good to all of us."

"I can do more." He could call in a few favors with Gutiérrez, an old friend from grade school who was now a cop back in Chihuahua. Maybe he could ask around and see if anyone had ever dealt with his brother. "I'll find him," he told Ana. "And I'll make sure he doesn't contact Mamá again."

This had been a terrible idea.

Everly tried to put on the brakes, but Charity and Darla had positioned themselves on either side of her and they were now marching her past the storefront windows of Cibo per Favore.

"I don't see him." Charity paused and peered through the tinted windows.

"Kate said that's where he went, so we'll just have to go in and get something to eat." Darla eyed the entrance as though it were the gates of hell. "Or maybe something to drink. Not that they'll have any quality wines."

Spoken like a true wine snob. Everly weaseled her way out from between them. "We don't have to go in." This was exactly what she'd wanted to avoid—turning this into some big scene that would end with Mateo seeing them.

"Yes we do." Darla linked her arm through Everly's. "I'm not going back until we get a good look at Mateo Torres on a date."

What if she didn't want to see him on a date? It was probably with one of those women who'd come into her café looking for him last week. A buckle bunny who had no use for his loyalty or thoughtfulness or perseverance. Not that Everly had any use for them, either. Nope. Her attraction to him was purely physical. All because of that damn kiss. So what if he obviously took care of his family? Who cared that her heart had given a hard tug when she saw his face soften as he'd looked at the picture of his mom and sisters? Sure, he might've fixed up her chicken coop and put out the fire in her kitchen, but she would not fall for Mateo. Those flutters in her chest were driven by lust, not feelings. No way would she be stupid enough to let herself develop real feelings for someone like Mateo.

"I can't believe he'd take a woman to this dive," Charity muttered as they ducked inside the restaurant.

"I'm sure it's a fine establishment." Everly tried to smile at a couple who was leaving.

She stepped into the small foyer, which was wallpapered with old Italian news clippings.

"It's not like there's an overabundance of good date spots in Topaz Falls." At least Darla had tried to whisper so the hostess wouldn't hear.

"Welcome to Cibo per Favore." The hostess pronounced the name with a bad Italian accent.

"Thank you." Darla peered past the woman's shoulder, already on the hunt for her mark. Everly elbowed her. Did she have to be so obvious?

"We'll take a table for three," Charity said.

"Of course. Right this way." The hostess grabbed three menus and led the way into the dining room.

Darla and Charity nudged Everly along, both of them squinting and panning their gazes all around the room like two not-so-secret spies.

"I don't see him," Darla whispered as they passed the doorway to the kitchen.

"Me neither." Charity only had one volume. So much for being inconspicuous. People were already starting to stare at them, and they hadn't even been in here five minutes.

Luckily, Everly didn't see anyone they knew. Most people in Topaz Falls avoided Cibo per Favore, but the tourists weren't aware of its reputation.

"How is this?" The hostess stopped at a table near the windows at the front of the restaurant.

"Ummmm..." Darla wrinkled her nose with distaste. "Do you have anything a little quieter, maybe? More toward the back?"

Everly shot her a look. Did they really have to case the whole restaurant?

"Of course." Everly recognized the hostess's smile. It was the same one she gave to Hank Green when he complained about his eggs.

"Right this way." This time the woman led them to a table along the back wall. "Will this work?"

"Actually—" Darla started, but Everly prodded her to sit.

"This is perfect." She wasn't going to let Darla's nosy curiosity drag them all over the restaurant.

"I guess this works," Charity muttered, scooting in across from them.

"Wonderful." The hostess handed out menus and briskly told them their waiter would be right with them.

"We could've had her bring us to the other side so we could see if Mateo is over there." Darla opened her menu and immediately frowned. "Oh my God. They spelled alfredo wrong."

Yeah, the food didn't look so appetizing, but that was fine with Everly. She wasn't hungry. "Let's just drop this whole thing. Please." What if Mateo caught them stalking him? He'd probably assume she was one of his groupies, and it was already awkward enough between them at home.

"Oh!" Charity gasped. "There he is! I see him!" Even the

people sitting at the next table looked in the direction she pointed.

"Will you take it down a few notches?" Everly hid her face behind a menu.

"That's definitely him," Darla confirmed. "But I can't see the woman he's with."

Using the menu as a shield, Everly peered around the side to where they were pointing. Sure enough, Mateo sat in a booth that was tucked into the opposite corner of the restaurant.

"We're too far away." Charity craned her neck and nearly fell out of her chair. "We won't be able to hear anything from here."

Everly set down her menu. "We don't need to hear anything." If they could hear something, that would mean Mateo would hear them. She was surprised he hadn't recognized Charity's voice already.

"I just saw her," Darla whispered. "She leaned forward for a second. She's definitely pretty."

"Damn," Charity grumbled. "I can't get a good look at her."

The two of them openly stared while they squirmed around trying to get a better view. Everly, on the other hand, sat with her back edged up against the chair. "Let's just go—"

"Good evening, ladies." A waiter swooped in. "I'm Jeffery and I'll be taking care of you tonight."

"We'll start with the garlic bread," Darla informed him dismissively. "Oh, and three beers. Any IPA will do." As soon as the waiter left to put in their order, she glanced at the wine list. "My God, their house merlot is made in Indiana."

"Did you have to order food?" Everly wanted to lay her

head down on the table and cover her eyes until this whole thing was over.

"Come on." Darla squeezed her hand. "Where's your sense of adventure? Don't you want to know who the man you saw naked is on a date with?"

"She saw him naked?" Once again, Charity managed to draw the attention of a crowd.

Everly slumped lower in her seat. "Accidentally. And only for a second."

"That makes me want to throw up," Charity said, but it must've only been an expression because when a food server dropped their drinks and a bowl of garlic bread on the table a minute later, she dove right in.

"Oh, I just caught another glimpse of her." Darla leaned halfway over the table. "Only for a second. She looks young."

"He's dated a lot of young girls." While Charity recited a list of the women Mateo had "dated," Everly nibbled on a piece of garlic bread and planned the rest of her evenings for the week: tomorrow, go to bed early and read. Actually, she'd pencil that in for the rest of the month.

"Uh-oh." Darla suddenly grabbed her shoulder. "He's coming this way!"

What? Everly stopped chewing and jerked her head, her eyes searching.

"Shit." Charity gathered up her purse. "He's gonna see us. Abort mission! Abort mission! Meet in the bathroom." Since they were on the outside of the table, Charity and Darla managed to scamper away, but Everly clumsily knocked her knee into the table on her way out of the chair. The half-chewed piece of garlic bread lodged into her throat. She tried to clear it, but—

"Everly?"

The sound of Mateo's voice behind her brought a full-on gasp, securing that bread into her windpipe. Her entire chest suspended in a painful convulsion. Oh, God, she couldn't breathe...Hands grasping at her throat, she looked wide-eyed at Mateo.

"Are you okay?"

Gagging sounds came from her throat as she fought to get air...

"You're choking!" He positioned his body behind hers, locking his arms beneath her ribs. One hard jab ejected the bread out of her mouth like a soggy projectile missile that landed in the center of the table.

All around them applause broke out while Everly wheezed and desperately refilled her lungs with air.

"Are you okay?" Mateo asked again, his arms still around her. "Did I hurt you?"

"No," she rasped. "I'm fine." All she could feel at the moment was the familiar burn of humiliation.

"Great. Now he's a celebrity and a hero." The woman who had walked over with Mateo was the only person in the room who wasn't crowding him.

"Oh my God!" The hostess ran over, and Mateo finally released Everly.

She slumped into her chair.

"That was amazing!" the hostess gushed, not even glancing in Everly's direction. "You just saved her life!"

More people crowded around, moving in to congratulate Mateo on such an impressive display of heroism.

"Oh for the love of God." Mateo's companion grabbed the seat across from Everly and propped her chin on her fist. "We'll never get out of here now," she said sullenly.

Well, she sure as hell would get out of there. Everly had finally started to breathe normally again. She quickly collected her purse. Hot coals burned in her throat, stinging all the way to her eyes, and her ribs ached like she'd done too many sit-ups. But, as Mateo accepted all of the accolades from his many admirers, she managed to slip out of the chair and escape unnoticed.

Chapter Ten

Where'd she go?" The crowd around Mateo had finally thinned, giving him a clear view of the table where Everly had been sitting. Now Ana sat there alone.

"Where'd who go?" she asked, studying her phone.

"Everly." He turned in a circle searching for her, his heart still rattling in his chest. "Where'd she go? She was just here." Choking. Jesus, she hadn't been able to breathe. The terror in her eyes had about done him in.

"I think she left." Ana stood and slipped her phone back into her purse. "I should go, too. I have to get on the road again."

Mateo blew out a breath, trying to think past the pulse of adrenaline. If Everly left, she must be okay. "You could stay here tonight," he said to Ana. Maybe not with him, but he could try to find her a room somewhere.

"No thanks." As usual, his sister charged past, already five steps ahead of him. "I'll stay somewhere in New Mexico. I want to get across the border tomorrow."

Mateo held open the door for her, returning the hostess's fluttering wave.

"Hope to see you here again soon," she called. He made no promises. That hadn't exactly been a stellar dining experience.

Out on the sidewalk, he and Ana walked side by side. "It's not safe to drive late at night," he told her. He didn't know why he bothered. She would drive down to New Mexico tonight no matter what he said.

She eyed him with disbelief. "Sheesh. You really do have some kind of hero complex, don't you?"

"Apparently." Maybe it came from taking care of four women his whole life. Just a guess. Maybe that was also why he couldn't wrangle his pulse back into a normal rhythm. When he'd put his arms around Everly and squeezed, he'd felt her ribs give. Had he hurt her? He'd never physically hurt a woman before. He scanned the deserted streets looking for her truck, but there was no sign of her anywhere. "Did Everly seem okay when she left?" He should've been paying attention, but the whole thing had happened so fast, and all those people swarmed him...

"Well, she bolted pretty quick, so I'm guessing she's fine." They crossed Main Street and headed for the parking lot a block down. "She was probably just embarrassed," Ana said. Then she stopped abruptly. "You seem awfully concerned about her. Who is she anyway?"

"She's my..." Tenant? Roommate? Fantasy? "It's complicated."

"Ah, one of those." Ana stopped at her car. At least she had reliable transportation for the drive. He'd helped her purchase the sedan when she'd first moved to the States.

"She leases the property I just bought," he clarified, for

Ana and for himself. That's why he felt some responsibility for her. That was *all* he felt for her. Responsibility. Not intrigue, or desire, or deeper things he couldn't seem to name.

His little sister peered up at him with the same skepticism that made her such a good student. "She didn't look like your type."

"What's that supposed to mean?"

"You know exactly what it means." Her lips pinched into a smirk. "She has a wholesome look. Almost innocent. The jeans, the T-shirt, the lack of makeup. She definitely doesn't try as hard as the women you usually date."

"That's because she doesn't have to." He could say that to Ana. She was leaving town. It would never get back to Everly.

"Wow, *hermano mayor.*" Her eyes did their twinkling thing. "I've never heard you offer such a big compliment. And I've never seen you this worked up about a woman. She must be special."

"No, it's not that." He couldn't let it be that. It didn't matter how special Everly was. In seven weeks, he had to send her packing. "I'm worked up because she could've died." Right there in his arms. His stomach heaved, and he immediately shot down the thought.

"Whatever you say." Ana mocked him in the same singsongy voice she'd had when they were little.

He ignored her obvious doubt. Ignored it all—the way Everly's face kept flashing in his mind, the way his fear still simmered. "I'll wire more money," he told Ana. "To *your* account." That way their mother wouldn't hire any more private detectives who saw an opportunity to take advantage of a woman who missed her son.

"Thank you." Ana planted a quick kiss on his cheek.

The gesture made him feel even worse. He usually told Ana everything, but he couldn't this time. Not until he knew more about what Andres was up to. "Text me every once in a while until you make it home. So I won't worry." They both knew he would anyway.

"I will. Promise." She got into the car.

"And try to convince Mamá that she needs to move here. With us. We could work on getting her a visa." He'd been trying to get her to move to the States for years.

"You know she'll never do that. She'll stay there forever waiting for Andres to come home."

"I'm not so sure that'd be a good thing." If Andres came home now, he'd bring a whole lot of trouble with him. Mateo had kept an eye on the news about the cartels back home. And things always seemed to be escalating. "I might do a little investigating of my own. See if I can track him down, figure out what he's been up to." And find a way to get him a message: Stay the hell away from the family.

"I think that's a good idea." In another rare show of affection, Ana squeezed his hand. "I'll let you know what I find out, too."

"Sounds good." He backed away from the car. "Be safe," he called as she started the engine. She simply shook her head at him and waved as she drove on past.

Sure he might've been overreacting—overprotective—but could she blame him after what had happened in the restaurant? Damn, he still couldn't get himself together. Wouldn't be able to calm down until he made sure Everly was okay. He'd promised Levi he'd stop by the Tumble Inn after dinner, but instead, Mateo drove straight to the farm.

When he pulled up in front of her house a soft yellowish light brightened the windows. He climbed out of the truck and jogged up the porch steps, then halted. Should he knock? Even though he happened to live here at the moment, she probably didn't want him barging in with no warning.

He settled for rapping his fist lightly against the door. A good two minutes passed before it opened.

Everly stepped back as though he'd caught her off guard. "You don't have to knock." She moved aside, giving him room to walk in. "You're free to come and go whenever you want. You have your key, right?"

"Oh. Yeah." To his relief, she looked fine. Her cheeks were rosier than normal, but she seemed to be breathing and moving around okay.

"I was worried about you." He walked past her and shed his jacket, hanging it on the coatrack next to hers.

"I don't need you to worry about me." Everly hastily retreated into the kitchen, where she had some kind of baking project going on. The countertops were covered with bowls and measuring cups and ingredients like flour and sugar. That would explain the ruffled apron she wore.

"I'm fine," she insisted.

Was she fine? He may have detected a rasp in her voice. Mateo walked over and pulled out a stool on the other side of the counter, positioning himself where he could get a good look at her. "You sure I didn't hurt you? I didn't break your ribs or anything, did I?"

"No. I said I'm fine." Everly turned her back to him and started to whisk something in a bowl. Something that would bake up fluffy and sweet. If you asked him, she seemed to move more stiffly than normal. He watched her carefully. "When I saw you choking, I panicked. I probably squeezed too hard."

"Well, it worked, didn't it?" She still didn't turn around.

Whatever she was making must've required some thorough mixing because she kept right on whisking. "I didn't mean to ruin your date, though."

"My date?"

"Yes. Your date." She turned back to him and set the bowl on the counter. Instead of looking in his direction, she focused on uncapping a bottle of vanilla extract. "The woman you were with didn't seem too happy about the interruption."

Mateo laughed. Okay, that was just wrong. "Yeah, my little sister isn't a very patient person."

Everly paused from pouring drops of vanilla into the bowl. "That was your sister?"

"Yeah." Couldn't she tell? Ana was much better looking than him, but there was a definite family resemblance. "Ana Sofia. The one in the picture you saw."

"Wow." Everly added a few more drops of vanilla to the bowl. "She looks so different."

"She grew up." Unfortunately. That meant she got to do things like drive down to Mexico all by herself. Which reminded him, he needed to track her cell phone later so he could monitor her progress. He'd keep an eye on her whether she liked it or not. "Ana was driving through town and wanted to have dinner. What made you think I was on a date?"

"Nothing made me think anything," Everly said quickly. "It was all Darla and Charity. Oh, and by the way..." Everly went to the kitchen table and held up a familiar silver stiletto. "I found my shoe on the floor in my closet. I'm assuming Dante had something to do with the teeth marks?"

"Right." His gaze bounced back and forth between her and the sexy heel. Damn, she would look good in those. "I was going to tell you about that."

She raised her eyebrows as though awaiting an explanation.

"Uh..." He had to stop picturing her legs in a short skirt and those heels so he could actually form a coherent sentence. "I swear I didn't realize Dante snuck into your closet until it was too late. Sorry. I took him over to Levi's. He can stay there until the trailer is back."

"That's not necessary." She opened a cabinet and tossed the shoe into the trash can. "I never wear them anymore, anyway."

His gaze slowly moved down her body. That was a shame. She definitely had the legs for it. Though he couldn't deny she also looked incredibly sexy in her tight jeans and that T-shirt. Then there was the John Deere shirt she wore to bed...

And those were the exact thoughts he had to avoid. After talking with Ana about their mother's situation, he was going to need this partnership with Blake more than ever. So he needed Everly out. Preferably by her choice and not his. Instead of helping her forget the past like he had at the party, he should be trying to remind her of the things she might've loved about San Francisco. Her ex-fiancé might've been a complete tool, but surely she missed her family and friends. "You probably wore shoes like that a lot back in your old life, huh?"

Everly picked up the bowl and started to whisk again. "I guess."

"Don't you miss it?"

She paused and glared at him. "What d'you mean?"

He held her gaze. "It seems like you have a lot of connections back home. Isn't your family there?"

Her eyes narrowed. "What does that have to do with anything?"

"I don't know." Obviously family wasn't the right card to play. There had to be something else that would tempt her to go back. "It's nice to have family around." Yeah, right. He was one to talk. "And I bet you could get your law license reinstated. Sounds to me like you didn't do anything wrong. Maybe you should fight it."

Everly slammed the bowl down onto the counter. "Don't even start."

Whoa. That seemed to appeal to her even less than family. But it made no sense. Why not redeem herself if she didn't deserve the punishment? "I'm just saying...becoming a lawyer is no easy task. How long were you in school? Eight years? That's a huge invest—"

"You sound exactly like my father," she interrupted, beating the batter in the bowl so hard some of it splattered onto the floor. She didn't seem to notice, though. She was too busy melting him with an incinerating glare. "He came for a visit earlier this evening. Told me all of the reasons I can't stay in Topaz Falls and why I'm going to fail at whatever I try to do with the farm." More batter went flying. "Well, you know what, Mateo? I'm sick of people telling me I can't do this. That I can't do what I love and still find a way to support myself."

"That's not what I was saying." She just couldn't do it here. At the farm. Now might not be the best time to tell her that, however.

"Do you know what he had the nerve to say to me?" Everly asked, pointing the whisk in Mateo's direction. Another blob of batter fell to the floor.

He shook his head. Seemed safer than talking.

"He told me I was a mess. That I don't have to live like this." She marched closer, stirring again. "I mean, can you believe that? He was talking to me like I've been a complete failure here."

A fiery anger glowed on her face, but it was her eyes that filled him with sympathy. They were doubting and sad. Her dad had wounded her, and damn if it didn't tempt him to wrap her up in his arms so he could make her smile again. "You're not a mess." Mateo stood and took the bowl from her hands. He set it on the counter out of her reach. "And you're definitely not a failure."

Everly turned away from him and closed her eyes as though she didn't want him to see her emotion, but it was too late. It drew him to her the same way it had the night he'd kissed her. There was something so genuine about her. Something wholesome and innocent—worth protecting— but something strong, too.

"It takes a lot of courage to do what you did. To start over somewhere else." He gently pulled on her arm to bring her closer, but she winced and stepped back.

"I knew I hurt you." He dropped his gaze to her hand, which had protectively covered the lower side of her left rib cage.

"It's fine. Just sore." She smiled a little. "Small price to pay for being able to breathe."

Funny, he hadn't choked on anything, and yet breathing had suddenly gotten more difficult for him. She stood close enough to trigger the memories of holding her against him, of kissing her lips. They were soft and full. So rich and sweet and tempting. "Where does it hurt?" He placed his hand where hers had been. Warmth from her body seeped into his palm through that sexy apron and sent a charge of arousal all through him. This time he couldn't shoot down the thoughts, the fantasies, the desires she stirred in him.

Touching her made him want them all.

Chapter Eleven

Mateo's touch brought a soothing rush to the sore muscles beneath her ribs. Sparks pinged through her in heated flashes that struck every erogenous area of her body. "The pain's not so bad. I hardly feel it." At the moment she only felt him, touching her, charging the air around her.

When she looked up, she saw much more than detached concern in his eyes. They were darker, so focused on her, as though he was trying to read the feelings hidden in her heart. They couldn't have been difficult to decipher. Every emotion rose straight to her face—hope and desire and want. God, she wanted him to kiss her again.

"You have flour on your face." Mateo's voice had lowered in a deep, seductive tenor. He reached up to brush the dusting off her cheek, and then trailed his fingers across her jaw and down her neck, sweeping her hair back over her shoulder. There was a hesitation in his touch, a flicker of uncertainty in his eyes. His gaze stayed with hers as though searching out his next move.

Everly didn't look away. It felt good to be touched, to feel her heart beating again.

"I should go to my room," he murmured, not breaking his stare.

"No." Everly moved an inch closer. He didn't want to go to his room. His voice was as ragged as hers. "Don't walk away." She had to know if his mouth would taste as good as she remembered—rich and spicy like sandalwood and cloves.

A smile twitched on Mateo's mouth right before he kissed her, his lips moving against hers in a seductive overture. Shivers rippled through her when his tongue skimmed her bottom lip. Her hands moved over his shoulders, gripping tightly to maintain her balance. She was falling, spinning, reeling from the intensity of his hot mouth against hers. She kissed him back eagerly, seeking his tongue, pressing her body against his, grasping at his shirt, letting the release of passion sweep her away.

Mateo's breaths came as heavy and fast as hers. He pulled away to gaze at her face, to flash her that sexy grin before bringing his mouth back to hers at a different angle. "*Quiero besarte para siempre*," he whispered.

She didn't know what it meant, only that it sounded beautiful and intimate.

Mateo lifted her to the counter and she straddled his waist as he skimmed his lips to the base of her jaw, then her neck, then her collarbone, kissing and murmuring about how good she tasted.

There was another sound, too. A sound that didn't fit. Knocking. Pounding...

"The door!" She pushed Mateo away and sprang off the counter, flailing to catch herself before she fell.

"Do you really have to answer—"

Another round of knocking drowned him out. "Everly! Are you in there?" Charity's voice could've easily made it through a steel vault.

Oh God. "Hold on," she croaked, straightening her shirt. Her legs teetered, but somehow she made it to the door and managed to get it open.

"Where have you been?" Darla barged in, followed by Charity. "We looked everywhere! We thought you would meet us back at my place, but you never came. We were so worried about you."

"Someone at the restaurant said you choked." Charity looked her over as though searching for visible damage.

"Uh..." Everly's body still smoldered in the afterglow of Mateo's breathtaking kiss. She gulped down a hard swallow. "Yeah. I choked on the garlic bread." Hopefully they assumed her spastic breathing was from the earlier trauma.

"And Mateo saved your life?" Darla hadn't seemed to notice him standing off in the corner of the kitchen yet. She was too focused on Everly.

"Don't know about that, but I definitely bruised her ribs." He sauntered over and gave Everly a small private smile.

"Well, well, well." Charity looked back and forth between the two of them like she knew exactly what they'd just been up to. "You look a little flushed, Everly. Are you sure you're all right?"

"I'm...great." Unsteady and shaky and still dizzy in a really fun way.

"And what about you, Mateo?" Charity addressed him like a mother talking to her little boy. "Are you okay? Because you look a little sweaty."

"Never been better." He didn't look away from Everly even for a second.

She quickly whirled and traipsed back to the kitchen as buoyant as if she were hopping from one cloud to the next.

"Did we interrupt something?" Darla asked, slapping her hands on her hips.

"No." Everly couldn't look at Mateo. Couldn't even look in the vicinity of Mateo. That kiss . . . wow. She peered into the bowl at the dough for her scones. She'd definitely over-mixed it. "Why do you ask?"

"Because it took you a while to answer the door." Darla marched across the room, suspicion still lurking in her eyes.

"She spilled some of that dough on the floor and we were trying to clean it up." The lie flowed so easily from Mateo. Not one blip in his voice. Not one flicker in his easy gaze. He was probably used to getting caught in compromising positions.

Her friends both glanced around the kitchen as though looking to confirm the story. Thankfully, there were still blobs of dough all over the place from her mixing tirade.

Both women seemed satisfied enough to let the inquisition go.

"Well, now that we found you, are you coming to book club with us?" Charity asked.

"Can't." Everly busied herself with rinsing the dishes that were piled in the sink. "I'm in the middle of baking." Actually, she'd have to start over now.

"Then maybe we should move book club here," Darla suggested. Without waiting for permission, she dug her phone out of her purse and started typing away. "I'll just let Naomi and Jessa know we're changing locations."

Well, crap. That wouldn't be good. They'd definitely find out she'd kissed Mateo if they stayed. She couldn't even look in his direction without her cheeks getting all warm. Everly shut off the water. "Actually—"

"Sounds good to me." Charity went straight for the refrigerator. "I'll search for some snacks."

"Guess that means I'll go hang out in my room. I still have some unpacking to do anyway." Mateo gave Everly a look that made it very tempting to follow him, but where would that put her? Mateo might know exactly how to make her feel good with those hot kisses and his strong hands caressing her body, but that didn't change the fact that he got to do whatever he wanted with *her* farm.

He was in a position to screw her over, and she had to stop forgetting that.

The only good thing about old farmhouses was that the walls happened to be paper-thin. That, combined with the fact that Darla and Charity seemed to have no volume control, meant Mateo could listen in on the cross-examination currently taking place in Everly's living room.

So far, Everly hadn't said much. He wouldn't know what to say, either. He shouldn't have kissed her, but the moment she'd told him she didn't want him to go to his room, he'd lost control. Couldn't stop himself. Couldn't hold back. The woman completely undid him.

The trouble had started when he'd walked into the house and saw that ruffled apron she had on. His body ignited just thinking about that damn apron. It had been tied tight around her waist, emphasizing the shape of her body, hitting him with an instant fantasy about how she would look in that apron and nothing else.

It wasn't only her body, though. It was that sadness in her. He wanted to take it away, to make her feel good, to give her a reason to smile. Mateo slumped to the bed. What was he thinking? Kissing her like that might give her a reason to smile, but he'd only take it away from her when she found out about his plans for the farm.

"So you're telling me that you and Mateo were simply hanging out in the kitchen together?" The wall hardly muffled Charity's pointed question.

"Yes. That's what I'm telling you." Everly's voice was too rigid to be believable. Charity would never buy it. The woman had a sixth sense for sniffing out bullshit.

"Hanging out can mean a lot of different things," Darla said.

"Actually, we weren't hanging out. I was baking and he was telling me about his dinner with his sister."

He had to strain to hear her. She obviously didn't want him listening in. Nice recovery, though.

"His sister?" Darla repeated. "You're telling me we followed him on a date with his *sister*?"

"Shhhh, be quiet," Everly hissed.

They'd followed him to the restaurant? Mateo almost laughed, but that would've been bad. They would've heard him, and he didn't want to miss this.

"His sister was passing through town and wanted to have dinner with him," she said in a lower voice. "So yes. Because of you two geniuses, we followed him on a date with his sister. And then you ditched me when our cover was blown."

Mateo pressed a fist against his mouth. He was going to hell for this. Eavesdropping and laughing at a woman who was clearly not amused by any of the evening's events. He happened to be very amused. Not to mention still aroused. Damn it all, why'd Everly have to be his tenant?

"So you two are getting along, then?" Darla asked, the words as sharp as a probe.

"Of course." Everly's nonchalance shrugged off any insinuations that they were doing more than getting along. "We're getting along fine. I actually wish he would spend more time around here so he can understand why the farm is so important. That's the only reason I invited him to stay. I don't want him to change anything around here now that he owns the place."

Ohhhh. He'd been shocked when Everly invited him to move in with her, but now it made sense. She wanted him to leave the farm alone. Yeah, that wasn't going to happen. Mateo lay back on the bed and stared up at the ceiling. Like the rest of the drywall, there were cracks everywhere. Because it was an old, run-down farmhouse that would drain his savings account instead of growing it.

"He won't change anything around here," Darla insisted, twisting the blade of guilt stuck between his ribs. "Actually, I think he has a thing for you. He sure doesn't look at me the way he looks at you."

No. He didn't look at Darla the way he looked at Everly. He didn't even look at Chrissy, his Tumble Inn groupie, like that. It did seem he'd developed a thing for Everly, but that was about to become irrelevant. He had to tell her the truth. Had to tell her about Blake and the resort. She deserved to know. He couldn't wait anymore.

Groaning, he dragged himself off the bed and trudged to the door. Dread crammed his stomach as he cracked it open. "Hey, Everly," he called. "Can I talk to you for a minute?"

There was a long silence. He could picture those three women staring at each other, wondering what he could possibly have to say to her right now. He wished he could say something else. Something about how much he admired her strength and the depth of her emotions. He'd always thought feelings made you weak, but that wasn't true for her. She was driven by her heart, and something in him envied that. Of course, she wouldn't want to hear those things from him after he told her about the farm.

This was going to suck.

"Uh, I'll be right there." Footsteps hurried down the hall and she slipped inside his room, her face so lovely and rosy that he was tempted to continue avoiding the truth so he could kiss her again.

"Is everything okay?" Everly looked around the room awkwardly.

"There's something you need to know." Buying time, Mateo closed the door behind her, but no matter how long or hard he thought about it, there would be no easy way to say the words. He forced himself to look directly into her eyes and braced for the fallout. "I'm not planning to renew your lease."

"What?"

He shifted his gaze to the floor, couldn't stand to see the heartbreak in her eyes. "When I bought the property from Owen, I thought you'd go back to your life in San Francisco." After their date, he'd been so sure. She'd told him straight up that she could petition to get her license back. It wasn't like she'd shot down the idea. He'd assumed she'd go for it eventually.

Everly crossed her arms tightly over her chest. "But I'm not going back. I'm *never* going back."

"I get that now, but I bought this place as an investment property." He said it as gently as he could. "I have to take care of my family. They depend on me, and I don't know how much longer I can keep competing."

Everly seemed to teeter. She steadied a hand against the wall. "What are you saying?"

Truth. He had to tell her all of it. "I've been talking with Blake Wilder about developing a condo resort here."

"And the farm?" Her voice had hollowed.

Mateo ignored his own surge of emotion—guilt and regret and anger at himself for stringing her along. "I can't keep it. It's too run-down. You have to see that. This place is way past its prime. Financially, it doesn't make sense to restore it."

A breath of pain escaped from her lips. He went to touch her shoulder but she shrank out of reach.

"I'm sorry." He should've told her the day when she'd hit him with that martini glass. "I won't do anything until your lease is up. That should give you time to find—"

"Get out."

Aw, hell, she was about to cry. "Everly—"

"Get out of my house." She marched closer and got in his face. "Right now, this is still my home and I want you out."

He backed up, raised his hands. "Sure. Okay." She had every right to be pissed. "That's fine. I'll pack up my stuff and—"

"No." She pushed his shoulder toward the door. "You can get your stuff tomorrow. When I'm not here. Right now, you're going to get the hell away from me." She pushed him again. "Get out!"

"I'm going." He swiped his keys off the dresser. "I'm sorry. I didn't mean to hurt you."

"Screw you, Mateo." She'd officially started to cry.

He deserved that. Deserved worse probably. He bolted out the door, but Charity and Darla were ready to intercept him in the hallway.

"What the hell, Mateo?" Charity smacked him on the arm.

He kept right on walking.

"If I weighed more, I'd kick your ass for this," Darla called after him.

This time he stopped. Turned around to face them. "I'll be the first to admit I didn't handle this whole thing the way I should've." He shouldn't have kissed her ten minutes ago. That was on him. "But I won't apologize for doing what I can to take care of my mom and sisters. When's the last time either of you have had to ask someone for money on the street?"

Neither one of them said anything.

Yeah, he didn't think so. "I had to do it all the time. We had nothing. I tried to make things better, but I couldn't. Not when I was kid. I had to watch my mom work twelve hours a day so she could struggle to feed us, and I couldn't help her. But I can now."

Charity stared at him, wide-eyed. "I had no idea. You never said anything."

"That's because I knew you wouldn't understand." None of them understood. They had no idea where he'd come from. As much as he'd like to forget, he couldn't. "Take care of Everly," he said, turning around so he could get out of there. "Make sure she has the support she needs to find another place." They would. These women took care of each other.

God knew Everly would be a lot better off with them than she would be with someone like him.

Chapter Twelve

Lucky for Mateo, the lights were on at Levi's house. He parked the truck and waded through the muck of lingering guilt on his way up to the porch. It might not seem like it right now, but he knew things were better this way. He'd told Everly the truth, and now he could get on with making plans. His first order of business was finding a place to stay until he had his trailer back.

He knocked on the door. Somewhere inside, his dog went crazy. Dante had probably assumed it was only a matter of time until Mateo screwed up and had to join him over at Levi's. At least someone would be thrilled to have him.

His friend answered the door with a confused look. "What're you doing here? Poker night's tomorrow."

Mateo stepped inside and took a knee to accept slobbery kisses from his favorite mutt. "Looks like every night might be poker night for a while." Not that either one of them could afford it, the way Ty repeatedly kicked their asses. He stood and kicked off his boots. Compared to the farmhouse, Levi and Cassidy had a rustic mountain castle. It was at least four times the size of Everly's place, and all new. No flickering lights here. No mixed-up water faucets. Levi had built it with the help of his brothers. The wood floors gleamed with polish, and the open concept living area and kitchen could have easily accommodated a hundred people. There was a grand stone fireplace that went all the way up to the vaulted ceiling and enough picture windows that you wouldn't want to walk around naked. "I don't think I'll be going back to the farm for a while." Until Everly's lease was up, most likely.

"Uh-oh. That doesn't sound good." His friend drifted into the kitchen and paused in front of the subzero refrigerator. "Do we need beer for this conversation? Or whiskey?"

"Neither." Didn't matter how much he drank; he wouldn't be able to forget that shattered look on Everly's face.

"Whoa. Maybe I should sit down for this." Levi went into the expansive living room and claimed the recliner by the fireplace.

Mateo walked over to the couch. Damn, he was tired. Dante followed and curled up on his feet as if he was afraid Mateo would leave him. "Don't worry, buddy. I'm bunking up with you tonight." That's what he should've done in the first place. He should've moved in with Levi for a while. Then he wouldn't have kissed Everly right before breaking her heart.

"I'm guessing the unannounced visit means Everly finally kicked you out of her house." Levi obviously wasn't about to let him keep the story to himself. No matter how much Mateo would like to.

"She didn't even give me time to pack up my stuff."

Amusement flickered in his friend's eyes. "She must've had a good reason."

"I told her I'm not renewing her lease."

Shock tinged his friend's expression. "Wow. Yeah, I'd say that's a good reason."

Mateo hunched over and kneaded his forehead. "Don't give me shit about it. I already feel bad enough."

"I won't give you shit. The rest of the town, on the other hand . . . Whew, man. You might want to take a vacation."

"I can handle it." He didn't care what the town thought of him. Their opinion wouldn't get to him nearly as much as Everly's did. "I should've told her right when I bought the place."

"Why didn't you?"

"I like her. Didn't want to upset her." This was the first time he'd admitted it, even to himself. "But we won't be able to compete forever. You know it as well as I do. I need this condo development. My *family* needs it."

Levi acknowledged the truth with a grim frown.

"This deal with the Wilders is my safety net." Not that Levi would understand any better than Charity and Darla had. His whole life Levi'd had someone to take care of him. It had never been the other way around. He'd never had to provide for his siblings or his dad. "We didn't have the opportunities you guys had growing up. My nieces and nephews back in Mexico won't have them either, if I can't help." And then there was his mom. She had no health insurance, no long-term care plan if something happened to her. Mateo was it.

"It makes sense you want to take care of your family," Levi said. "But I feel like it's my responsibility as your friend to mention that I've never heard you say you like a woman."

Mateo shot him a doubting look. Out of all his friends, he talked to Levi the most. "Sure you have."

"No, I haven't." His friend smirked with an irritating surety. "I've heard you compliment plenty of women. But appreciating their physical appearance is a hell of a lot different than liking who they are as people."

He had nothing to say to that. Usually, he didn't make time to get to know the woman behind the appearance. But living at the farm had meant he'd seen glimpses of Everly's heart, whether he'd wanted to or not. Like the morning she'd done that class with those three old guys. She'd been kind and patient, even when they were burning down her kitchen. And a few days after that, he'd looked out the farmhouse window and saw her pushing the two little Hart boys around in a wheelbarrow. It had put a pang in his chest to see her entertaining two little kids who were going through a tough time.

Mateo dropped his focus back to Dante so his friend couldn't read his face. "I didn't mean I *like* Everly. I meant she's a good person." A much better person than him.

"Whatever you say."

Mateo nudged Dante off his boots and stood. "I didn't come here to talk about Everly anyway. I came to see if I could stay with you until the trailer is done." But he'd be glad to go find another place—hell, maybe even sleep in his truck—if Levi insisted on analyzing his feelings for Everly. They didn't change anything—not his situation, not hers.

"Lucky for you, Cass is working in Denver this week." His friend still had that smug expression. "But I can't promise you a room when she gets back."

"Got it." Based on Charity's and Darla's reactions to the news, he'd be on Everly's friends' shit list for a good long while.

* * *

Sometimes life was all about small victories. Like when you didn't burst into tears the moment you let your goats out of their stable in the morning.

Today, instead of a snotty deluge, the tears came out in more of a trickle when Everly patted Matilda, Honey, Wormwood, and Trunchbull affectionately on their furry little heads. "You've been such good friends," she said through a sigh. She'd acquired the four goats from a ranch about an hour away, and they were the first pets she'd ever had. She'd named them after characters in *Matilda*, her favorite childhood book. Now she'd likely have to give them up along with the ducks and chickens, her gardens, and the café. "What're we going to do?"

Two days had passed since Mateo had kissed her, right before telling her he planned to kick her out, and she still didn't have a plan. She'd looked at properties on the Internet, but none had the facilities to set up both a farm and a café, and she didn't have money to build or renovate.

She had only about six weeks. It felt like someone had lit a fuse on her life and the minutes were ticking past too quickly, barreling toward a full implosion.

Everly walked down the worn path through the goat pens, hardly letting her gaze skim the mountains on the horizon. It hurt her heart to look. She couldn't imagine living anywhere else, couldn't imagine being anyone else, but it didn't seem like she'd have much of a choice other than to reinvent herself once again.

Right as she came around the side of the chicken coops, Mateo's truck turned onto her driveway and parked in front of the house. Emotions clashed inside her—anger and embarrassment, but also a scrap of tenderness that had somehow survived the immense disappointment he'd leveled on her.

The truth was, she couldn't despise him. Not after what he'd said to Charity and Darla about his family. She could be mad, but she couldn't hate him. No matter how much she wanted to. Mateo was driven by years of feeling helpless, and she couldn't even begin to imagine how that had impacted him. God, she'd grown up in a Pacific Heights town home with a chef to cook meals and a live-in housekeeper to do her laundry. Every time her anger at Mateo surged, she got an image in her mind—a little boy with thick black hair and dark expressive eyes standing on a street corner holding out his hand while people walked by. He might know how to have fun and be the life of the party now, but his past had shaped him. It still haunted him, too. The difference was, he didn't let anyone see it.

She waited for him to get out of his truck, which seemed to take an awfully long time. When he finally did, he stuffed his hands into his jeans pockets, hunched his shoulders, and walked over. That small scrap of tenderness buzzed like a flickering light bulb low in her stomach. It wouldn't be there at all if he hadn't tried to comfort her after her dad's visit, if he hadn't kissed her lips with such a convincing fire. It wouldn't be there if she didn't admire something about his desire to protect the people he loved.

"Sorry for showing up like this." His gaze met hers then quickly darted away. "I thought you'd be out feeding the animals."

"I just finished." She did her best to look through him, but her voice wobbled. Anger. She had to harness the anger so he wouldn't realize she felt something deeper for him. Mateo probably didn't feel anything. Except for guilt, maybe. He did look pretty guilt-ridden.

"I came to get some of my things. But I can come back another time."

"It's fine," she said as stiffly as she could manage. "I'm leaving soon, anyway. I just have to grab a couple of meals from the freezer and I'll be out of your way."

"Meals?"

Did he really have to ask? To prolong this conversation and torture her? "Today's delivery day. I'm bringing a few dinners over to Kenna Hart." Then she'd swing by Jessa's house and drop off a few meals, too. At book club the other night, her friend had mentioned she hadn't been feeling well. So far, no official announcements had been made, but Everly had her fingers crossed. Jessa and Lance had been trying to get pregnant for a few years, and she couldn't wait for those two to be parents.

Smiling a little, she turned her attention back to Mateo. "I'll be gone a good hour or so. That should give you plenty of time to pack up."

He didn't move. "Why are you bringing her meals?"

Everly shrugged. "I do that sometimes. For people who are sick or going through a tough time." Shortly after she'd opened the café, she'd discovered it was a hub for sharing news. People would come in and tell her about friends or family members who were struggling with illness or financial burdens or serious family crises.

At first, hearing the barrage of challenges and difficulties that so many wonderful people were facing had overwhelmed her. Then one day, she'd gotten an idea. Why not make extra dishes she could use to help people who were hurting? Food couldn't fix problems but it could bring comfort. It couldn't take away pain but it could reduce stress. It was one small way she could give back to the community that had given so much to her.

Tears banged at the backs of her eyes. The dinner delivery

rounds had become a highlight of her week. She loved seeing the looks of hopeful surprise when she showed up on
someone's doorstep. She cherished the hugs and the friend-
ships and the neighborly interactions her rounds brought.
Yet another thing she might have to let go of if she didn't
have the farm. So far, the only way she could see supporting
herself would be to get a full-time job somewhere. And there
weren't exactly a ton of openings in Topaz Falls.

Somehow, she zapped the threatening tears with a hard
blink. When she opened her eyes, Mateo was staring at her.
"Um. So you can go in and get whatever you need." She
cleared her throat and turned to head into the house. "Just
lock the door when you leave."

"Right." Mateo's footsteps thudded behind her. "I only
have time to grab a few things. I'll have to come back for the
rest later."

"Sure. Whenever." She didn't look back as she made her
way up the porch steps and into the house. Why did he have
to make her heart pound so hard?

"And the stuff I stored in the cellar—"

"You can leave that." She marched herself to the freezer
and stacked all of the premade meals into a box she had
waiting on the counter. "It won't be in my way. I'll be moving out soon, so it doesn't make sense for you to do anything
with it." She lifted the box and cruised to the door.

Mateo stepped in front of her. "Did you find a place yet?"

"No. Haven't had much time to look." Everly sidestepped
him and tried to shift the box so she could free up a hand to
open the front door.

Mateo ended up opening it for her. "I can take that to your
truck for you."

She wanted to laugh. A little late for him to become her

white knight now. "I've got it." Without a good-bye, she moved swiftly down the porch steps and practically jogged to her vintage pickup. Owen had sold it to her for next to nothing so she'd have a way to haul things around on the farm. It was a joke compared to her Beemer back in San Francisco, but she loved how it sputtered and bounced along as though it was never in a hurry.

Today, though, she was in a hurry. After she loaded the box into the passenger's side, she scrambled to climb into the driver's seat. Mateo stood on the porch watching her. *Leave me alone,* she wanted to yell out the window. Instead, she kept her posture tall and straight as she drove past.

Once the farm disappeared from the rearview mirror, she let her shoulders slump, but she couldn't let herself wallow. Compared to what Kenna was going through right now, Everly didn't have problems.

The Harts lived on a street that was part of the newer neighborhood in town. Instead of old craftsman and bungalow-style homes that had been built when the town was settled, the street was lined with cookie-cutter style homes. Nice, but also redundant and obviously controlled by one of those neighborhood covenants that ensured houses would each be a slightly different shade of beige.

She pulled up in front of the one on the corner, where Halloween decorations already covered the front yard—cute little ghosts and scarecrows that were more lovable than frightening. It was your average family home, a place where little kids ran in and out, judging from the bikes and scooters parked at the front door. It seemed impossible that a criminal lived here. Even a white-collar criminal. God, these poor kids. How in the world would they ever understand what their father had done?

Everly cut the engine and got out of the truck, somehow maneuvering the large box off the seat. Teetering under the extra weight, she managed to slam the door shut with her foot and then carefully made her way to the front door, stepping over and around the children's toys as if she was navigating an obstacle course. When she finally made it to the porch, she had to lean over a Batman bike to knock.

The sounds of trampling, skidding feet and giggling little boys brought a smile to her face.

"Don't answer it!" The door muffled Kenna's voice, but Everly still caught the panic.

Despite the command, the door swung open. "Oopsie." Jake stared up at Everly with a bashful grin.

"Hi there," she said cheerfully.

"Hi." He drew the word out into a grand announcement.

Good lord, what a little cherub.

Kenna came scurrying around a corner and into the foyer. "Jake, I told you not to answer the door." She looked up. "Oh. Everly." A relieved sigh slipped out. "Hi. What are you doing here?"

"I'm making a special delivery from the Farm café. I figured maybe you could use a couple of ready-made dinners this week."

"What kind of dinners?" Jake asked as if suspicious that there might be vegetables involved.

"Good dinners," Everly assured him. "Really good. Lasagna and a yummy roast with sweet potatoes and a quiche." The kid did not look convinced, so she went on. "And special brownies with chocolate chunks."

That did it. He jumped and squealed. "Brownies! Brownies!"

She turned her attention back to Kenna, who stood frozen

behind her son, gaping at Everly with watery eyes. "You...brought us food?" That last word broke apart into a sob.

Wow, yeah. Today must be one of the rough days when sadness made every muscle drag. She remembered them well. "Hey, Jake." Everly knelt to the boy's level. "I have an idea. Why don't you and your brother go pick up some of the bikes and scooters outside and organize them real nice for your mom? Then maybe you can have a brownie for being such a big helper."

"Really?" Jake's eyes went as wide as the scarecrow's outside. "A brownie for *breakfast*?"

"Maybe." Was that against the rules? She'd forgotten that it wasn't even nine o'clock. On a normal day, the boys probably didn't get chocolate for breakfast, but it seemed that Kenna was in no state to answer the question. She'd turned away from the door, but Everly could hear her crying.

"Yes! A brownie for breakfast!" Jake shot down the hall and disappeared. "Come on, Benny! We'll go out the garage!" he yelled seconds before a door slammed.

Kenna didn't move. She'd lodged her shoulder against the wall, her upper body hunched and her face hidden in her hands.

God, this poor woman. "Um...can I bring the food to the kitchen for you?" Everly asked quietly.

Kenna nodded, drying her eyes with the backs of her hands. "Of course. I'm sorry, it's just..." The words dissolved into more tears. "No one has come by to bring me anything. Only to yell at me or question me." She moved away from the wall and led Everly to the kitchen. "I think this is maybe the nicest thing anyone has ever done for me."

Everly doubted that, but she accepted the gratitude with

a smile. She set the box on a decent-sized island covered in granite. "I've made it a habit to bring food to people who are going through tough times," she said. "Then dinner is one less thing they have to worry about. I figure it's one small way I can help."

Kenna started to cry again. "It's not small. Not at all." She snatched a tissue and blew her nose while Everly took a quick look around. Both the woman and her house epitomized grade-school teacher. There were chore charts with stickers hanging on the stainless refrigerator and canisters of markers, scissors, and colored pencils organized neatly on the counter.

"I'm sorry I'm such a mess." The woman blotted her face with the Kleenex.

Everly had said the same thing repeatedly after she'd learned the truth about what Andrew had done. *I'm sorry I'm such a mess. I'm sorry I didn't know. I'm sorry I didn't stop him.* Now that she heard Kenna say it, she realized how ridiculous it sounded. "You need to stop apologizing."

Kenna's eyes widened, but Everly didn't regret the sternness in her tone. "You did nothing wrong."

"But I should've noticed something." Kenna slumped onto a stool. "I should've figured it out."

Everly had said those exact same words to herself. She still said them sometimes. But truthfully, her only mistake had been loving someone—trusting someone—who took advantage of it. Andrew had been the perfect boyfriend for six years—thoughtful and attentive and supportive. Those were the only sides of him he'd let her see. "You are not responsible for another person's shitty choices. Not even your husband's." The force in the words drew Kenna's eyes to hers. "My ex-fiancé did some terrible things." The admission came with a shudder. "Things I never dreamed he was capable of."

Kenna stared at her in disbelief. "I...didn't know."

"Not many people here do," Everly admitted. "I've always been too ashamed to talk about it." And yet somehow, she'd been able to tell Mateo...

"It's humiliating." Kenna dabbed at her eyes and looked down at the counter. "The worst part is that I still love him." Her lips trembled. "I don't want to, but that's the truth. He lied to me. He hurt people. And I still want him to walk through the door and pick up his boys like he always did."

"You're not a bad person for loving someone." Everly unpacked the box of meals and carefully placed each one in the freezer before coming back to the island. "His bad choices won't destroy you." Andrew's hadn't destroyed her. "Trust me. I'm speaking from experience." Since leaving San Francisco, Everly had risen into a stronger, truer version of herself. And now, even though it would hurt to leave the farm, she could do it again. She could rise stronger and truer. She could still love. Maybe even more so because of what she'd been through.

Kenna didn't look convinced. "I have no idea what I'm going to do."

"It'll take time, but you're going to heal. I can promise you that." She squeezed the woman's hand. "In the meantime, you're going to pick yourself up and keep going. Day by day, figuring it out along the way." That's what she would do, too. Just like she had three years ago.

At first when she'd moved to Topaz Falls, she'd felt so alone. But then she'd met Jessa and Darla and Naomi and Cassidy, and she'd realized there was another life for her. People would love her again and she would love them. There was pain but also glimpses of light—and life—everywhere if you cared to notice them. "Whatever you do, don't give up on feeling things." She had for a while, and in numbing herself to the pain, she'd also overlooked the beauty. "Let yourself feel the sadness, but feel the joy, too." Everly had found it on the farm—nestled in the shadows of the mountains, hidden in the lush, wildflower-dappled meadows.

She glanced at the refrigerator and smiled at the silly pictures of Jake and Benny. "Those boys of yours bring so much joy."

Nodding, Kenna pressed her fist against her lips while more tears slipped down her cheeks.

"Joy will be enough." It would sustain her, give her hope for the future. Just like it would for Everly.

Chapter Thirteen

He never should've gone to Everly's house that morning. Mateo pulled up in front of the ski lodge and parked near the grand entrance, but he couldn't seem to make himself get out of the damn truck.

His gut hadn't stopped churning since he'd asked Everly if she'd found a place yet. She'd brushed him off, but devastation had shown up in her eyes, in her swift movements, in the way she avoided looking at him. It was as if she knew she was too fragile to face him, so she hadn't.

Then there was the whole meal delivery thing. Everly was spending her day distributing comfort food like some kind of culinary angel, and he was spending his day meeting with Blake Wilder to negotiate the terms of their lucrative partnership. If that didn't highlight the differences between them, he didn't know what did.

There were so many reasons he didn't belong anywhere near Everly. And yet when he kissed her, none of them seemed to matter. In those moments when he'd held her close, losing himself in the warmth of her lips, he'd felt...connected. Anchored. With any other woman, he could take kissing or leave it, but with Everly...well, he'd take it as much as he could get it if the circumstances were different.

Circumstances weren't different, though. The damage was already done. She hated him, and things were better that way. They could both move on and figure out what was next. For him, it would be the condo development. A new source of income to make sure he could take care of his family the way he needed to.

Mateo got out of the truck and strode along the cobblestone sidewalk that led to the lodge's main entrance. It was a relatively new facility, built like a castle, all stone and steeply pitched rooflines against the backdrop of the ski hill. Double glass doors parted when he stepped in front of them, leading him into a reception area that resembled that of a swanky hotel.

No going back now.

"Good afternoon." The receptionist behind the desk greeted him with one of those smiles they likely taught in Hospitality 101. "How can I help you?"

"I'm here to meet with Blake." Or Mr. Wilder? Hell, he didn't know. He had no experience negotiating business deals.

"Oh, of course." The receptionist's face brightened. "Mateo Torres. I'm a big fan." Most women around this town were. Though he suspected that had more to do with his single status than with his bronc-riding abilities.

"Can I get you anything? Coffee? Water?" *A roll in the hay*, her flirtatious little smirk seemed to ask.

"Nah, I'm fine." And not nearly as charming as all of these women fantasized him to be. Just ask Everly.

"Okay then. You can head through that door on your right and Mr. Wilder's office is the last one at the end of the hall." The woman pushed some button that must've unlocked the door.

"Thanks," Mateo called as he went through.

Blake waited for him at the end of the hallway. "Torres." He offered a firm, take-no-prisoners handshake. "I'm glad you're here. My investors are fully on board. They're anxious to get it hashed out."

"So am I." The faster they worked out the details, the less time he'd have to second-guess his decision.

"Why don't you come on in and have a seat?" Blake led the way into an office that appeared to have the same square footage as Everly's entire house. One corner had the typical office setup, with a large desk and bookshelves, while the other had a massive conference table with seating for sixteen. In the middle of the room, plush couches were clustered around a stone fireplace that had somehow been built into the glass wall that looked out on the slopes.

"Wow." Mateo couldn't take his eyes off the view.

"We upgraded our offices last spring," Blake said. "Business is good, Mateo. Really good. And it will only get better with more development. Trust me, there's never been a better time to partner with Wilder Enterprises."

Ha. Mateo didn't trust him. Not at all. That's why he wouldn't sign until he'd had a lawyer look over every word of the contract. "I've heard things have picked up around here." He knew they were planning to open a new terrain park for the upcoming season, which would draw more snowboarders. "But I have some questions."

"Sure." Blake went to a refrigerator and pulled out two bottled waters. "I can promise you right now I'll have all the answers." He handed Mateo a water and gestured for him to take a seat in a leather chair by the fireplace.

Of course he'd have all the answers. If he didn't, he'd likely pull them out of his ass. "First, I'm curious why the ownership percentage went down from the last time we talked." Mateo unzipped his backpack and pulled out the informal proposal Blake had emailed, opening to page four. "Originally, we discussed twenty percent and now it's down to ten."

"Right," Blake said as though he'd anticipated Mateo's concern. "We've decided to add more investors so we can add more amenities. Things like a rec center for our patrons, some restaurants, and a couple of outdoor gathering places where we can host concerts in the summer and special events in the winter."

More opportunities for year-round income. Sounded good to him. "So you're trying to spread out the upfront development costs more."

"Exactly. We'll bring in ten investors instead of five, and then we'll have some room to dream bigger."

Mateo was trying—really trying—to dream bigger, but that damn guilt kept right on churning. "And there's no room for the farm? Even if we scaled it back?" He had to ask one more time. For his own conscience.

"I thought we already talked about this." Funny how Blake could go from mellow to irritated jackass in the span of one question.

Mateo could speak jackass. "This is someone's life we're talking about. Someone's home. So, if there's any way to figure it out, I have to consider it." She'd done so much work on the place. And she had all of those animals...

Blake sat forward in the leather chair, a certain audacity in his posture. "There's no room for the farm. Period." The man shook his head like he couldn't believe Mateo cared. "It's a dump. You know that, right? You keep that place going and you'll be throwing money into a sinking ship."

Yeah, he knew. He'd already racked up the list of the pricey repairs in his head. "Point taken." He turned to the next page in the proposal. "What about the zoning—"

His phone rang from his back pocket. "Hang on. Sorry." He dug it out and checked the screen. *Gutierrez.* Finally. Two days ago, he'd put in a call to his old friend back in Chihuahua to see if he could find out anything about Andres. "I have to take this." He shot to his feet. "Probably best if I go outside." Blake didn't need to know he had a delinquent brother. No one needed to know.

"Sure thing." Blake stood, too, and walked him to the door. "I have a meeting to prep for anyway. Just come on back whenever you're done."

Mateo gave him a nod and ducked out of the office to answer the phone before he lost the call. "Hey, Miguel."

"Yeah. Listen, Torres, I finally have some news."

"Give me a second." He trucked down the hallway past the receptionist's desk and stepped outside. "Okay. Did you find anything? Location? Phone number?" Anything that would get him in touch with his brother so he could tell him to stay the hell away from the family?

"It's not good," Gutierrez warned. "I wish I had a better report."

"I wasn't expecting it to be good." His brother was part of a fucking cartel. "I don't care about the details. I just need to know where he is."

"I talked to a few guys who've worked undercover." The

man spoke in a low voice, as if he didn't want anyone else to hear. "Andres was an informant."

An informant. Mateo steadied a hand against the truck. "Like . . . for the cops?" That couldn't be right.

"He spent years working his way up and got in with the cartel's top leadership. But according to my source, your brother must've had a change of heart. A couple of our guys turned him a year ago and he fed us information."

Everything the man was saying was in the past tense. Mateo's mouth went bone dry. "He's not an informant anymore?"

"They found out he was ratting on them, Mateo. They executed him two months ago."

The news hit him in the backs of the knees. He grabbed the edge of the pickup to steady himself. This was the one thing he hadn't prepared himself to hear. Because he couldn't imagine it. Couldn't imagine that Andres was dead. A sharp-edged grief sliced through him. That's why he'd written their mother a letter. He'd known he would die.

"I'm sorry," Miguel said. "I know it's not what you were hoping to hear. But in the end, you can be proud that he did what was right."

No. Mateo tipped his head back, staring at the cloudy sky. He couldn't be anything. Not proud or sad or even angry. He was too numb. Andres was dead. The brother who'd been like a father to him. The brother who had abandoned him. He was gone. Really gone now.

Before Gutierrez had said those words, Mateo hadn't even realized he'd been holding on to hope. Hope that he might see his brother again. That maybe there could be reconciliation, forgiveness. He squeezed his eyes shut. "Is there any way to . . . get his body?" His throat tightened around the words. "So we can give him a proper burial?" So his family could have the closure they deserved.

"No." There was a pause, as though Gutierrez was trying to figure out the best way to give him more bad news. "Another informant told us about Andres, but those guys make sure the body is never found."

Nausea washed over him, pricking his face with sweat. "Right. Okay." He tried not to picture what those last moments had been like for his brother. What they'd done to him. He'd heard things about the cartels, about how they tortured and killed...

"Do you want me to tell your family?" his old friend asked solemnly.

"No." That responsibility rested solely on his shoulders. "I'll take care of it. Thank you, Miguel." He disconnected the call and sank to the curb, hunching over with his head between his knees. Pain pounded in his chest. Maybe it was the heartbreak he'd never let himself accept. Jesus, Andres. Why'd he waste his life like that? Why'd he waste a perfectly good life? Anger dulled the grief.

Mateo stood up and dusted off his jeans. He had to tell his mom. In person. But he couldn't leave now. He had to train. Couldn't back out of his upcoming competition. Couldn't or wouldn't? The truth was, he couldn't face going home, or the memories that he'd left behind. So he'd bring his mom here, and give her the opportunity to grieve away from the home where she'd raised—and loved—Andres.

Right now, he had to get back to the meeting with Blake. Later he might grieve. He might go back to Everly's so he could go down to the cellar and find the picture of Andres. But now he had to focus on the next thing. Look forward instead of back. That had always been his salvation.

* * *

Evening happened to be Everly's favorite time of day on the farm, especially in the fall. When the sun started to sink beyond Topaz Mountain, the day's chaos would soften in a gentle quiet made even more enchanting by the golden aspen leaves that dangled from scarred white branches and the clusters of fiery-red scrub oak that dotted the hills. Shadows crept slowly down the mountainside, bringing with them a chill that would bite at the tip of her nose.

And, oh God, the sky... It still shocked her even though she admired it every evening. The colors swirled above her head—reds, oranges, and pinks fusing with the fading blue. In the mountains, the sky seemed so much closer, like Heaven was breathing down, not nearly as far away as everyone thought.

Since this place would soon no longer be hers, she took her time with the evening rounds, soaking up the serenity, the beauty, so she could take the memory of it with her.

"Come on, Walter and Henrietta." Everly leisurely coaxed the ducks along with vegetable peels she'd brought home from the café. The two of them waddled behind her, quacking out pleas and stretching their necks in pursuit of the special treats, but she kept them out of reach until the ducks were safely stashed in the coop with the hens. "There you go." She tossed the scraps into the far corner and hurried to lock the door before Walter got any fancy ideas about a jailbreak. None of the animals loved being caged up at night, but, as she'd tried explaining to them on numerous occasions, spending the night in the coop was better than being devoured by a hungry predator.

On her way to the goat pens, she practiced the mindfulness breathing technique that the book club had read about in last month's selection. The scent of dried leaves and cold air and hints of animal manure charged through her senses before coming to sit heavily in her lungs. It was perfection. Out here among the mountains and the trees and the animals, she felt an overwhelming sense of belonging.

"Matilda, Honey, Wormwood, Trunchbull." She called each of the goats by name. The monikers fit the goats' personalities perfectly. Matilda came trotting right over, always friendly and spry, albeit a bit mischievous. Honey ambled along behind Matilda, never far from her side. Those two were by far Everly's favorites, so easygoing and even affectionate sometimes. Well, as affectionate as a goat could be, anyway. After frolicking past her, Tilda and Honey went right into the small stable as though they were ready to call it a night.

Then there were Trunchbull and Wormwood, still grazing lazily on the opposite side of the pen as though they hadn't heard her. Stubborn, haughty, ill-mannered goats. Those two knew how to ruin a good sunset. "Don't make me get out the leads." Everly eased toward them. "You know very well when I come out here that means it's time for bed."

Trunchbull eyed her as she approached, and then let out a disgruntled bleat when she got too close. As usual, Wormwood mimicked his boss.

"Go on now." Everly waved her arms, ushering them in the direction of the stable. "It's bedtime, you ingrates." They obeyed, but took their sweet time with it, pausing every couple of steps to munch on whatever they could get their teeth on—remnants of hay and thistle growing alongside the fence. As if they didn't have enough time to eat during the day.

Everly followed behind them, muttering and sighing

until finally they marched their hairy little butts into the stable where they belonged. "You two are worse than toddlers," she informed them as she knelt to set the padlock. "Did you see how nice Tilda and Honey went in? Why can't you be more like—?"

An eerie feeling fell over her. A disturbance in the air. The second she stopped talking, everything else went suddenly quiet, too. The swallows that had been noisily scouting for worms nearby. The squirrels that had been chattering. Even the squawking from the chicken coop had hushed. Everly slowly straightened, still facing the stable. An unsteady tremor worked through her legs before spreading over her chest and then prickling up her neck. Something was watching her.

Inch by inch, she turned around, her eyes scanning the empty pens, the garden plots, the thick stand of scrub oak on the hill.

A flash of movement drew her gaze to the gate on the other side of the goat pens. Something was there. In the bushes.

God, let it be a rabbit. Or maybe a fox. Something small and furry and cute. But she'd seen both of those creatures during her walks on the farm, and none of them had managed to suck the air out of the atmosphere, silencing even the natural world.

Everly moved cautiously in the direction of the house, but before she'd taken three steps a mountain lion crept out into the open, its lithe, powerful body crouched as it paced the perimeter of the fence.

Dear God. A hollow coldness shivered through her, sinking into her bones, weighting her legs with an overpowering heaviness.

The animal glided closer, graceful and intent, its haunting yellowish eyes locked on her.

Everly couldn't look away. She'd had no idea a cat could look so frightening. It wasn't only those luminous eyes; it was the broad, hunched shoulders, the giant, oversized paws. She'd seen pictures of what those paws could do with one swipe.

An awed fear overflowed her lungs, until all she could manage were short, shallow breaths. Her eyes followed the big cat as it paced back and forth outside of the fence, but she didn't dare move. She had nowhere to go. That Goliath cat stood between her and the house—her and the rifle she'd never wanted to need.

They don't usually attack, she told herself. Unless there was something they wanted. Like a small herd of goats locked away in a stable, maybe?

A humming disrupted the ghostly quiet. A diesel engine that sounded a lot like Mateo's truck. Hadn't he said he would be back later? *Oh, please let him be back.* Everly looked in that direction but couldn't see the driveway. He wouldn't be able to see her from this angle either.

The mountain lion stilled, its head turned toward the noise near the front of the house.

Everly inhaled. She couldn't scream, couldn't provoke it or spook it into attacking, but she had to get Mateo's attention. She had to tell him to get the rifle.

A car door slammed, and she braced herself for the worst, but the lion didn't react. It didn't even move. Yet.

She closed her eyes. "Mateo." It almost sounded like the beginning of a song the way his name came out—loud but soothing and melodious instead of terrified. "Mateo. Rifle."

Goliath cat turned its attention back to her, stretching

its body out to slide under the fence and into the farmyard where she still stood frozen in fear. The animal seemed to assess her, slinking closer until it stopped maybe twenty feet away. It was even bigger than all of those pictures she'd seen online. Big and muscular and the most frightening thing she'd ever seen.

"Easy," Everly whispered, savoring each breath. How many more would she get to take? Hadn't Mateo heard her? She'd been loud enough. "Easy." She slowly shuffled her feet, moving back to the stable. Would she have time to get in before it attacked? Her eyes frantically searched the ground for something to fight back with if the lion lunged.

"Everly? Did you say something?" Mateo came around the chicken coop and stopped cold. For an eternal second, he looked back and forth between her and the lion, and then muttered something low and inaudible. Likely the same expletives that were on repeat in her brain.

"The rifle," Everly murmured in a soothing tone. "It's hidden in the coffee table." Which now seemed like the absolute worst place to keep it. Mateo could get to it, though. He could carefully back himself right up and out of sight on the side of the house.

The lion still seemed focused on her, as though it knew she would be the easier target.

"Go get the gun," Everly hissed. Before it attacked them both. Why was Mateo just standing there? "You have to fire a warning shot."

The man still didn't budge. "That would mean leaving you here."

She broke the showdown stare with the lion to glare at Mateo. *So?* she silently asked with a flare of her eyes. Normally she wouldn't want to be left alone with a hungry mountain lion either, but they had no other choice.

"I'm not leaving you out here with that thing." The words were almost a growl. "Hey." Mateo waved his arms at the mountain lion. "Over here. Come over here."

"What're you doing?" Everly's teeth started to chatter, even though fear burned through her. Every tendon in her body strung itself so tight that her joints ached.

The mountain lion was on the move again. It ducked lower and came at her cautiously, ignoring Mateo's efforts to lure it his way.

"The gun," Everly wheezed. Or she could just pass out? Yes, she wanted to pass out. She didn't want to feel anything when Goliath cat sank its teeth into her.

"Get out of here!" Mateo marched directly toward her and the lion, waving a dead tree branch in the air. "Go on! Get!" He stooped to pick up a big rock and chucked it in the cat's direction, missing but also making the beast jump back. "Get the hell out of here!" His shout echoed around them, seeming to bounce off the distant peaks. He found another rock and launched it close enough to the lion that dirt sprayed up in its face.

Goliath cat spewed a horrifying hiss and bared its teeth, but then darted for the fence, clearing the five-foot posts in an effortless leap before tearing up the hill and disappearing into the scrub oak.

Air whooshed out of her, emptying Everly's strength. Her legs faltered, causing her to collapse against the stable.

"You okay?" Mateo jogged over as calmly as if he took on colossal, crazy-eyed felines every day.

"No, I'm not okay." Her lungs sputtered as the rush of relief met a rise of anger. "You should've gotten the rifle!" What the hell had he been thinking confronting a mountain lion? "It could've charged you!" What she'd meant as an angry shout came out a squeak instead. It couldn't be helped. What would she have done if the cat had gone after Mateo? She couldn't have gotten the rifle...It would've been too late.

Mateo didn't react to her terror, which only pissed her off more.

"Oh my God." Trembles wracked her body. "It could've killed you." She thrust her palms into his chest to push him, but he caught her wrists and pulled her close.

"It's okay," he murmured, wrapping her up in his arms. "You're okay. There's no way I would've let it hurt you." He pressed his lips to her forehead and held them there in a long, gentle kiss. Warmth seeped into her again, persuading her to stay there in the shelter of his arms. She rested her forehead against his chest, breathing, breathing, breathing. The sandalwood scent of him soothed away the anger. Her hands fisted his shirt, clinging to him.

"We'd better get inside." His gaze drifted back to the hill as if he was worried the lion might be lurking somewhere nearby.

Jesus. Of course it was lurking somewhere nearby. It had probably hunkered down in the bushes and was waiting to get her alone again. But she didn't move. Couldn't step away from his body. He was warmth and safety and strength.

"The animals all locked up safe?" he asked, smoothing his hand over her hair.

Everly nodded, her forehead still against his chest.

"Then let's get you inside." Mateo swept her up into his arms, cradling her with a careful tenderness before walking out of the farmyard, past the chicken coop, and into the house.

Chapter Fourteen

Before taking Everly into his arms, Mateo hadn't known there was a difference between carrying someone and holding them. But as he stepped through Everly's front door, he felt it. His arms kept a firm grip on her yet they softened around her, too, nestling her closer into his chest, trying to soothe away the trembling in her shoulders.

He couldn't help himself. When he'd come around the corner and seen her frozen in fear—and then that lion stalking her like prey—instinct had taken over. Maybe it would've been smarter to go after the rifle, but if that cat had attacked her while he'd been in the house, Mateo never would've forgiven himself. She might've been tough and determined, but the cat would've easily overpowered her.

Relief washed over him as he carried her across the living room. She was shaken, but whole. And beautiful. So fucking beautiful and perfect in his arms. He gently lowered Everly to the couch, not letting go until he'd positioned her back against the soft cushion. A blank look had emptied her eyes of emotion as though she were replaying the scene over in her mind, as if she were wondering if it had really happened. He'd worn that same look before. The wondering look of someone who'd seen death coming at them, but had somehow walked away from it.

The ghosts he'd been seeing all afternoon crowded in again, haunting him with yet another memory. The memories of his brother were so much closer now. Somehow, learning about his brother's death had unlocked the vault.

He lowered to his knees in front of the couch. "Hey." He touched her am. "You're safe."

Her head cranked slowly, turning to Mateo's face. "I thought...it would've attacked me. If you hadn't come—"

"But I did come," he interrupted. He couldn't stand to hear her say what might've happened. He'd only come back to the house to get the rest of his things. Instead, he was kneeling in front of Everly, feeling every damn emotion he'd ever suppressed. The second he'd seen her standing there vulnerable, those feelings had broken through to the surface—helplessness and fear and a devastating need to be close to her. "Everything's fine now," he said, almost afraid to touch her again. He wouldn't want to stop. Not until she understood what he felt for her. "Are you cold?" He pushed to his feet and went to the fireplace. Luckily, it had been replaced with a gas insert so all he had to do was flip a switch and flames ignited the realistic pile of logs.

"A little." She didn't look at him.

Mateo unfolded the blanket that lay over the back of the couch and tucked it in around her. "I'll call Dev and let him know what happened." At least he figured they should call the police. Dev Jenkins was a deputy who lived in town.

Mateo had hung out with him a few times at Levi's house. On his own, Mateo wasn't qualified to deal with a mountain lion. He sure as hell didn't want Everly out wandering around on the property until that thing was gone.

Everly tipped her head back and closed her eyes, looking so small and weary that Mateo wanted to slide in next to her and hold her again. Instead, he dug his phone out of his pocket and dialed Dev's cell.

The line clicked. "What's up, Torres? You in some kind of trouble?"

"No." He made sure to sound offended. Why would the man assume that? It's not like the deputy had ever had to arrest him. "I'm staying at Everly's and—"

"Oh yeah. I heard you two were shacking up."

Mateo glanced at Everly. Her eyes were still closed. He moved farther into the kitchen area and lowered his voice. "It's not like that." Everly didn't want him. And anyway, she deserved better. He decided to spare Dev the details. "When I pulled up at the house a while ago, I found Everly facing off with a mountain lion." What if he hadn't pulled up when he did? What if he hadn't heard her call to him? He wouldn't have gone around back...

"Shit. Wasn't expecting to hear that." Dev's voice sobered and immediately went into professional cop mode. "She okay?"

"Physically she's fine. I was able to scare it off." This time. "But I'm not convinced it would've left her alone without some hefty encouragement."

"Probably not," the deputy agreed. "There was an attack last week. On a trail a couple miles west of the farm. A big cat confronted a jogger but the guy fought it off."

Mateo didn't like the sound of that. "You think it's the same one?"

"Most likely. They don't usually hang out around populated areas unless they're weak or sick. Sounds like this one's looking for an easy food source."

"Like goats." And chickens and ducks. And petite farmers...

"Exactly." Dev paused. "The parks and wildlife guys are already on the lookout, but until they have him, Everly shouldn't be out on the property alone. Especially in the morning and evenings. Guess it's a good thing you're staying there."

"Yep." He'd be moving back in now. Whether she liked it or not.

He switched the phone to his other ear. "I've got a competition this weekend, but I can keep an eye on things until then. I'll let you know if we see it again."

"Sounds good," Dev said. "I'll put in the report and keep you posted on any news."

After he'd stowed the phone back in his pocket, Mateo moved around the kitchen collecting everything he needed to make her a cup of hot chocolate—milk, chocolate chips, vanilla, cinnamon, and cayenne. Everly's cabinets and refrigerator were organized with a baker's precision, though he did have to dig to find a saucepan.

"What're you doing?" Everly lifted her head slowly, as though she had just remembered he was there.

"Making you a hot drink," he said matter-of-factly.

She pulled the blanket tighter around her shoulders. "What did Dev say?"

"He'll put in a report with parks and wildlife." Mateo poured some milk into a saucepan and turned on the burner, trying to decide how much to tell her so he wouldn't freak her out. "There was an incident on a trail not too far from here last week. He thinks it's the same cat." When steam rose, he whisked in the vanilla, cinnamon, and cayenne, and then dumped in enough chocolate chips to make it extra rich.

"What kind of incident?" Everly sat up straighter, pale and wide-eyed again.

Mateo hesitated, watching the chocolate chips melt, but he couldn't keep it from her. She'd likely find out about it anyway. "They think the same lion attacked a man who was jogging on a trail last week."

"Oh God." She wilted back into the cushions.

"The guy was able to fight it off, though." He poured the hot chocolate into a mug. "Dev said it's not a good idea for you to be out on the property alone until it's taken care of." *If* it was taken care of. He'd heard how hard it could be to track those animals. They tended to stay hidden unless they wanted to be seen. There were plenty of tales about how they stalked their prey in hiding, and then pounced without warning. A shudder ran through him as he walked across the room and handed her the mug.

A grateful smile softened the worry in her features when she accepted the drink. In fact, everything about her looked soft and delicate in the fire's muted glow. Especially her lips. Those lips had felt so silky against his own...

"I can't go out alone? Like, at all?" She curled her hands around the mug, holding it tightly. "How am I supposed to take care of my animals?"

Awareness pounded through him as he settled in beside her on the couch. That alluring scent of her. So sweet. "Dev seems to think our friend is looking for an easy food source. Not to worry, though. I'm happy to move back in and help out with the chores until they can track him down."

"Really?" She shot him a skeptical look.

"Sure." That's what a landlord should do. Take responsibility for his tenant. Yeah, that's all he felt for her. Responsibility. Mateo inhaled cinnamon, could almost taste it on his tongue. Sitting so close to her made it harder to lie to himself.

"You know I go out and do the chores every morning at five thirty and again around six thirty in the evening, right?"

"Yes. I can make that work." Then he could go off and train while she was at the café during the day. "I've got a competition this weekend, but I'll only be gone for a few days. I'm sure Dev wouldn't mind coming by to keep an eye on things."

Those enticing lips of hers formed a stubborn pout. "I don't need someone here all the time. I've been fine on my own for over two years. I think I can handle a few days."

Even so, he'd inform Dev that he should swing by around feeding times for the animals so she'd have backup if necessary. She wouldn't run off a cop. "You need to keep the rifle handy when you do go out alone." It didn't seem to do her much good locked away in the coffee table.

Everly didn't appear to warm up to the suggestion. "I'll be fine," she said with a feeble confidence. Then she brought the mug to her lips and took her first sip of the hot chocolate. Her eyes closed with rapture. "Wow. What is this?" She held the mug closer to her nose and inhaled deeply.

Mateo didn't know if it was the romantic glow of the fire, or the vulnerability that still lurked in her eyes, or the fact that he so badly wanted to forget the news he'd gotten only hours ago, but that telltale lazy heat wound through him, coiling itself tightly in his belly. "It's hot chocolate," he said, eyeing her lips again. They had power, those lips. He'd already tasted them twice. They had the power to take away his thoughts, to bring him outside of himself.

"It's way better than hot chocolate." The woman took another sip and seemed to savor the taste. "Where did you get the recipe?"

He almost lied and said he'd found it online. But his brother was dead and he could no longer deny his existence. In his life or in his memories. "My brother used to make it for me." The words were shaky. Unsure. His brother. Before the last couple of days, he hadn't uttered that phrase in years.

"You never mentioned a brother." Everly turned her body to his and pulled her legs up on the couch. So comfortable and open. Such a contrast to him. His body felt locked and rigid. So damn tense.

"My brother is..." Why did he find it so hard to say? "Gone. Dead." Yet somehow more alive to Mateo than he had been for eighteen years.

"I had no idea. I'm sorry." Everly got that startled look again, her gentle brown eyes wide, her mouth drawn as though the revelation made her genuinely sad.

"I didn't know, either." He hadn't meant to mutter, but his throat had gone raw.

Everly's head tilted in a question. She could say so much without using a single word.

Mateo stared into the fire. He'd never told anyone about his brother. Not even Levi. Some of it was shame, but mostly it had been too easy to live in denial so far away from who he had been, so separated from his family. He'd become who he wanted to be. A strong, undamaged man. As if that even existed in the world. For a while it had worked, but now—today—he couldn't stop seeing Andres's face. "My brother left the family when I was eight. To join a cartel."

"Like, a *drug* cartel?" Everly asked as though that were completely outside the realm of possibility. Around here, it was.

"Yeah. We didn't have much. Mom always struggled. So Andres took care of us. He was eight years older than me. I looked up to him." He could've said more—that his brother had been like a surrogate father to him—but Everly already seemed to understand that, given the sympathy that welled in her eyes.

"You never saw him after he left?" she asked as though grasping for a glimpse of hope in the midst of a tragic story.

"No." Sometimes a tragedy was just a tragedy. Sometimes there was no hope to grasp. So what was the point in reliving it?

"How did he...pass away?" The words were nearly a whisper. "And how did you find out?"

"He sent a letter to my mom a while back. First communication since he left. So I called a buddy who works on the police force down there. Asked him to check around." Maybe he shouldn't have. Maybe it would have been better never knowing. "My buddy told me Andres turned a year ago and was working as an informant."

"So they killed him?"

He had a feeling that was putting it mildly. Gutierrez had said executed. "Yeah."

Everly brushed tears from her cheeks. How did she do that? Feel things so deeply? Once again her tender heart stunned him. "God, Mateo. I'm sorry. That's heartbreaking. Your poor mom."

"She doesn't know. I never told her I watched him leave. I never told her where he went."

"What?" The woman gasped. "Why?"

"It seemed better that way." Everly didn't know what the cartels were like. How evil they were. She didn't want to know. "My mom raised us to be good people. I thought it would kill her if she knew."

"That must've been so hard for you. To keep the truth from her all those years."

"It was, but then Gunner brought me to his ranch and it got easier." The distance had made everything easier. Living at Gunner's ranch and competing and signing sponsorship deals with the Renegades had kept him busy enough that he didn't have to think about it. He hadn't wanted to. He'd continued to take care of his mom and sisters as much as he could, but he'd moved on. Made himself forget. He was good at that.

"You look like you could use a drink, too," Everly murmured, shedding the blanket. "Can I get you a beer? Or I have some scotch."

"That's okay." He turned his face to hers. "I've got a big training day tomorrow. A competition this weekend." And he wasn't craving a drink nearly as much as he was craving her lips, her hands grasping at him again. God, his body ached for her. Did she feel it, too? He stared into her eyes so he could see the truth. "Can I ask you something?"

She stared back, her cheeks flushed. "Sure."

"Why did you let me kiss you?" Why had she kissed him back with so much longing?

"What d'you mean, why?" One eyebrow quirked. "I don't know. Mostly because I wanted you to kiss me." Her eyes shied away. "It felt good to be kissed."

"That's it? It wasn't because I'm your landlord and you felt like you had to let me?"

"Of course not." Her eyes were wide when they found his again, like she couldn't believe he didn't know. "I like you. I'm attracted to you. Isn't it obvious?"

He let his gaze drift over her, taking in the casual flannel shirt she wore, the way her hair had been pulled back loosely, exposing her neck, the color that had risen high on her cheeks. "You are *increíblemente hermosa*." He couldn't keep the observation to himself. Everly was nothing like the women he typically dated out on the circuit. She was too good for him. Too sweet. Too delicate, and yet here he was sitting by her side trying once again to convince himself he was not allowed to have her, to kiss her, to touch her.

"I took French, so I only know a little Spanish," she said, but judging from the way her eyes wouldn't quite meet his, he assumed she'd gotten the gist of it.

"Amazingly beautiful," he translated for her. "Stunning. Too good to be true." She didn't need fancy clothes or makeup or the fake flirty laugh so many women approached him with. "You're radiant." Beauty shined through every part of her.

Her head lowered as though she wanted to look away or deflect the compliment, but then a smile sparked. "And you are *un bel homme*."

"A big stinky goat?" he guessed.

The self-deprecation earned him a laugh. "No." Everly scooted closer to him.

"You are a very good-looking man, Mateo." She stopped just short of his lap.

He held back the want that growled through him. "Tell me to go to my room." He would. If she didn't want him, he would walk away.

But Everly bit into her bottom lip seductively. "You already know I won't."

The words had barely escaped her mouth when he covered it with his.

Chapter Fifteen

She'd forgotten the power of a kiss. Or maybe she'd simply never felt power like this.

Mateo's lips were hot and heady, moving against hers while his tongue teased with long, tantalizing strokes. She opened her mouth to him, inching forward until she straddled his lap, and matched his obvious greed with her own.

Mateo swept her hair over her shoulder and uttered lovely Spanish phrases while he kissed his way down her neck. *"Tu piel es tan suave."*

She had no idea what he'd said, but it sounded passionate. "I like hearing you speak Spanish," she murmured, cupping her hands around his jaw to guide his lips back to hers.

"Hueles tan bien." The words growled from his throat.

"Mmm-hmmm," she sighed against his mouth.

"Puedo tener suficiente de ti, bebé." He slid his hands down her back and under her butt, centering her on his lap. He was hard and strong—all muscle and brawn—but his

hands were tender on her body, moving up over her thighs to caress her lower back. "That means I can't get enough of you, baby," he whispered hotly in her ear.

"I can't get enough of you, either." Desire flooded through her, swift and scorching and fierce enough to silence her inhibitions and carry her away. God, it had been so long since she'd gotten carried away. She moved her lips along his jaw, and then let her tongue trail down his neck until his breaths came heavier, louder. Mateo moaned into her hair. His hands worked at the top button of her shirt, but then he paused and focused his dark, dilated eyes on hers. "Tell me if you want to stop."

"Don't stop." She needed this as much as he did, to let go, to be held and caressed and intimate with someone who could rouse her desires, coax her passion back to life. "We don't have to stop. I don't *want* to stop," she said, making sure he got it.

"You sure your friends won't show up again?" A smile reached the corners of his eyes, crinkling them with a mischievous tenderness.

"If my friends show up this time, I'll ignore them," Everly promised, bringing Mateo's hands back to the buttons on her shirt. He worked them slowly, one by one, fascination in his gaze as each button revealed more of her colorful polka-dotted bra.

"It's like a party happening under here." He slipped the shirt off her shoulders.

"I have a thing for buying pretty undergarments." It was one of only a few habits she'd salvaged from her old life.

"And I have a thing for admiring you in pretty undergarments." He lowered her back to the couch and unbuttoned her jeans before slowly working them off her hips to reveal her underwear. "They match."

Everly propped herself up on her elbows, feeling sexier

than she had in…well…ever. "Of course they match." She couldn't say why it was so important to her to wear good underwear, but now she was damn glad she did. The mesmerized look on Mateo's face made it worth every penny.

"Stand up so I can see more." He reached out a hand and she gladly took it, emboldened by the way he stared at her.

Mateo remained seated while she pushed off the couch and stood in front of him, offering him a profile view, and then turning to show off the G-string.

"*Mamacita.*"

Everly had never heard such a manly whimper. She turned to face him fully, hands on her hips. "And what does that mean, exactly?" She had a pretty good idea, but she wanted to hear him say it.

"Hot mama. It can mean all kinds of other sexy things, too." He shifted to the edge of the couch and traced his finger from the very center of her bra down over her bellybutton all the way to the lace edge of her underwear. "You, Everly Brooks, are all kinds of sexy."

Everly moved closer and straddled his lap again. "And how do you say, 'make love to me'?" she asked, between wet kisses right below his ear.

"*Hazme el amor.*" His hand played with her hair as she continued kissing different spots on his neck.

"*Hazme el amor,*" she whispered into his ear, drawing out the last syllable as she shimmied his T-shirt up and pulled it off over his head. Muscles rippled in his chest. She leaned back for a better view and ran her hand over them, reading the tight bends and curves, tracing the few scars that dented his tanned skin. "*Tu es exquis.*"

"You are a hairy donkey?" he asked, flashing that playful grin.

God, she loved how he made her laugh. "No." Everly bent her head to kiss each scar. "You are exquisite." Deep and passionate and wounded and real. She kissed the left side of his chest, letting her lips linger there, feeling the rapid thumping of his heart.

"I'm just a cowboy." Ragged breaths punched through the words. "Not nearly good enough for you."

"I'll be the judge of that." Her hands frantically worked at the button fly of his jeans.

Mateo lifted her off his lap and set her on the couch. Then he stood and lowered his jeans one inch at a time, his lower abs and hips tensed into rock-hard perfection. The more she saw, the wider her eyes got. Everly imagined her expression told him everything.

Finally, his jeans lay pooled next to him on the floor.

Everly stood and wrapped her arms around him, drawing his body to hers.

Mateo reached around and popped the clasp of her bra with one hand. He slid the satiny straps down her shoulders and dropped it on the floor, never taking his eyes off her body. She inhaled deeply when his lips brushed her skin, drifting lightly over her left breast then her right. He took his time exploring and tasting, his tongue toying with her skin as though he had all night to arouse her.

She pushed down his boxer briefs and teased her hand up the hard length of him.

He growled against her chest, the sound resonating in her ribs. Everly glided her hands up the front of him and pressed her palms against his shoulders, pushing him to sit back on the couch. He paused on the way and searched his jeans for his wallet, where he found a condom.

While he put it on, Everly flashed him a naughty grin and

worked her underwear down her hips, then slowly over her legs until the G-string drifted to the ground and she could kick it aside.

"*Sí, bebe. Ven aca.*" Mateo hooked his hand onto her thigh and prodded her closer.

"Yes, baby." She'd understood that much.

"Come here," he finished for her. His fingers threaded through hers, entwining their hands intimately as she lowered to the couch and straddled his lap, making sure her breasts were level with his mouth. He took full advantage of the position, kissing and nibbling and sucking while his hands urged her to rock against him. His hard length grazed her most sensitive spots, coiling cords of pleasure torturously tight, making her heart beat faster, her lungs work harder. The sensations built so fast she lost control, breaking apart under the rhythm of his hands moving her body over his, the delectable feel of his mouth on her skin. The orgasm jarred her with electrical currents and she could only hold onto him, riding it out while she incoherently expressed how good it felt.

Once her body stilled, she rested her forehead on his shoulder, still breathless. "Sorry," she murmured, unwilling to look at his face. "I should've at least tried to wait for you."

"Oh, no, *niña bonita*." Mateo ran his strong hands up and down her back. "You should never apologize for enjoying yourself." He raised her face to his. "I have no problem making that happen again. And again."

Smiling at him, Everly balanced her elbows on his shoulders and ran her hands through his thick dark hair. "This time no one gets left out." She lifted her hips and came down on him, burying him deep inside of her.

Mateo's lips parted, a long, groaning breath easing out of

him. His hands grasped at the small of her back, bringing her in closer, tighter, as though he thought she had the power to save him.

The connection eclipsed their bodies and reached something deeper in her. Maybe because he had been betrayed, too. Abandoned. She wanted to take away the sadness that had stolen the light out of his eyes earlier. She wanted to leave no room for it to hold him captive. *"Vous avez une belle âme,"* she murmured against his lips. "You are a beautiful soul."

"Not me." He shook his head slowly, those sorrowful eyes aligning with hers. "Your soul is far more beautiful than mine." His voice lowered with a solemn intensity. Everly kissed away his doubts, moving her hips, sliding up his body and back down, taking him as deep as he could go. Mateo's head fell back as he thrust up to meet her movements, again and again, faster until that stimulating pressure built inside of her again. She tightened her legs around his waist and clawed his back with her fingers every time his hips lifted her. He was waiting for her—she felt his strain—so she embraced the convulsions, turning herself over fully to the explosion of passion, letting it claim her. Mateo let go, too, murmuring her name and more beautiful Spanish words, holding her tightly against him as his body shook with release beneath her.

Quiet settled over them, interrupted only by the sound of their breathing. Everly let her upper body drape over his. "Wow. I'm tired. In a very good way. Very, very good." She turned her cheek so she could peek at his face. "So relaxed. And…happy." Strangely happy. Like in this moment every piece of her fit together perfectly.

"Me too." Mateo brushed a kiss across her temple.

"But tired." She laughed. "Did I already mention that? I'm so tired I don't know if I can move."

"Then let's go to bed." He stood, lifted her into his arms, and carried her back to the bedroom.

Movement shook the mattress, jolting Mateo awake. By the time he managed to get his eyes open Everly was standing next to the bed, pulling a shirt on over her head.

"What're you doing?" He propped himself up on his elbow, letting his eyes feast on her bare legs. Damn those legs, that body of hers…

"I didn't realize it was so late!" She snatched a pair of jeans off her dresser and shook them out. "I have to get to the café. Gus and Hector and Charlie are probably already waiting for me. I'm teaching them how to make oatmeal today."

"The old guys?" Mateo scooted to the edge of the bed and pulled her against him, bringing her to lie down on the soft mattress all wrapped up tight in his arms. "They can wait. Stay in bed. With me." As far as he was concerned, they could stay in bed all day doing the same things they'd done last night. He slid his hand down her hip, savoring the feel of her silky skin.

But Everly wriggled away from him. "They'll be at the café at six. They're never late—"

Mateo silenced her with a lingering kiss that seemed to leach the tension from her body. When he pulled away, she was leaning into him, relaxed and lazy again. "I really shouldn't make them wait…" She dragged her hand down his bare chest and seemed to lose her train of thought.

"Te ves tan hermosa por la mañana," Mateo murmured. "That means you look so beautiful in the morning." The word "beautiful" didn't do her justice. Her golden hair had

mostly escaped from her ponytail, flowing down over her shoulders. Sleepiness made her eyes droop in the corners in the sexiest way. "Just call your gentleman admirers," he whispered in her ear. "And tell them you're sick. I promise we'll have fun."

"I can't." Everly's face sobered. She wriggled away from him and got out of bed. "This might be my last chance to teach them something."

"Your last chance?" He knew her friends were old, but that was a little pessimistic, wasn't it?

Everly turned away so he couldn't see her face. She hastily pulled on the pair of jeans she'd dropped only a few minutes ago. "I won't have the café anymore. So, no. I'm not going to tell them I'm sick. And I'm not going to stay in bed with you, Mateo."

Fuck. He let his head fall back to the pillow and stared up at the ceiling. "Everly..." What could he say? How could he make her stay when he'd already kicked her out? "I'm sorry—"

"Stop." She undid her ponytail and snatched a brush from the dresser, pulling it through her long hair. "This never should've happened. I never should've slept with you. Things were crazy last night. I was too emotional."

"Wait." He sat up. "Hold on. I thought...you wanted it to happen."

"I did." She tossed the brush onto the dresser with a loud clang. "But I don't do this, Mateo. I don't roll out of bed after a night like that and move on the way you do. It actually meant something to me. Which might sound pathetic to you, but I want intimate moments to mean something."

"It doesn't sound pathetic. It meant something to me, too. I know things are complicated, but—"

"It's not complicated." Her voice raised. "Not for me. I can't turn off my feelings the way you do. Or maybe I could, but I don't want to because even though sometimes they make my heart hurt, they also make my life more meaningful." She pulled on a sweatshirt, her movements frantic. "Sleeping with someone occasionally won't be enough for me. I want someone to know me in a way you never could."

"That's not fair." He threw off the covers and scrambled out of bed. "Maybe I could know you." Maybe he wanted to.

Everly shook her head, backing toward the door. "Rule number one—don't dwell on the past," she said, her voice quivering. "Rule number two—when a live band is playing, you dance." Everly swallowed hard. "Then you showed me rule number three. Mess around because it makes you forget." She closed her eyes. "It did. Last night made me forget all my problems. But they're not gone. Just like your grief over your brother isn't gone." Tears brightened her eyes. "Everything you do is about avoiding reality. And that won't be enough for me. I want something real." She turned and ran out on him before he could stop her.

Chapter Sixteen

Everly shoved her feet into her rubber boots—which were unfortunately the only shoes by the door.

"Wait," Mateo called behind her.

"I have to go." She tromped outside and down the steps on shaky legs. Tears pounded at the backs of her eyes, but she refused to let them fall. Damn her heart. Damn it for being so open and naïve. Damn it for letting her develop a connection to a man whose whole life revolved around avoiding connections that might take away from his fun.

She hurried down the path to the café, determined that Mateo would not catch her. She'd said everything she needed to say. Last night, he'd let her see a glimpse of him, of his pain, but then he'd turned back into the charming cowboy determined to show her a good time. And he had. It had been a very good time. But when she woke up this morning, she'd realized nothing had changed. He wanted to use her as a distraction, but she refused to be one of his groupies from the Tumble Inn.

Everly rushed around the back side of the restaurant. Gus, Charlie, and Hector were all gathered by the door wearing concerned frowns.

"Sorry I'm late!" She jogged the rest of the way, fumbling to get the keys out of her pocket.

"We were about to call out the search party," Hector said, looking her over as though he wanted to make sure she was okay.

"Especially when we saw that bastard cowboy's truck parked outside your house," Charlie grumbled. "I thought you told him to leave because he kicked you out of your own home."

"He didn't kick me out." At least not yet. "I'm staying until my lease is up." Everly scooted past them to unlock the door. The ache in her heart deepened into more of a throb, but she kept a smile on her face. "Who's ready to learn how to make oatmeal?"

"He's gonna flatten this place, isn't he?" Gus asked, following her inside.

"Over my dead body," Hector muttered.

"He still at your house right now?" Charlie went to peer out the window. "'Cause I'll go on over there and give him a stern talkin' to."

While she would've liked to see that, it wouldn't make any difference. "All right, fellas. It's not worth getting all worked up about. Mateo owns the land. He can do whatever he wants with it." She'd known that from the beginning. She'd been foolish to think he'd want to keep the farm around. "This just means it's even more important for you three to learn some skills in the kitchen since I won't be around to make your breakfast anymore."

Those sneaky tears heated her eyes again. She'd miss it—greeting Gus and Hector and Charlie each morning, chatting while she poured their coffee and served their eggs. She'd miss helping them with their crossword puzzles and hearing them poke fun at each other. But if she started to focus on everything she'd miss, it would be a very long day.

"Let me get organized." She slipped her apron over her head and tied it around her waist.

While she rummaged through the pantry, Hector walked over and covered her hand with his. "What're you gonna do, doll?"

"I'm not sure yet," she admitted. She'd have to find a job; that was for sure. At least she wouldn't be homeless, though. Darla had already told her she could stay at her place as long as she needed to.

"I heard that diner off the highway is looking for a cook," Gus offered. "It's only about twenty miles outside of town."

"Thanks. I'll look into it." Though she had a feeling her cooking style might not fit in at a highway diner. She had a thing against grease. "I appreciate all of your concern. Really. It's so sweet. But we need to get this class going." So she could block out the sadness, the thoughts of last night. At least for now.

She finally located the old-fashioned oats, cinnamon, and brown sugar and lined them up on the counter. "I was running late this morning and didn't have time to take care of the animals. So, I'll get you three started on the oatmeal, then I'll have to sneak out for a few minutes." Leaving them on their own might be borderline dangerous, but at least there were no open flames involved. "The recipe we're making today is called apple pie oatmeal in a mug."

The men seemed to perk up.

"Apple pie?" Charlie asked with sudden enthusiasm.

"Yes." Everly dug some apples out of the refrigerator. "It's just as good as real pie, but a whole lot healthier." Especially for their hearts. "First, you're each going to chop up half an apple." She set out three mugs and cutting boards, and then selected semi-dull knives. "Then you're going to mix a half cup of rolled oats with one cup of water, a teaspoon of cinnamon, and three teaspoons of brown sugar." She jotted it all down on a pad of paper. "Add in the apples, then pop it in the microwave for two minutes, and violà! Apple pie oatmeal in a mug."

"Two minutes? That's it?" Gus picked up the mug and inspected it as though he suspected it might have magic powers.

"Two minutes," Everly confirmed. "You guys have got this." She headed for the door. "When I get back, I want to see three mugs of perfect apple pie oatmeal."

"You got it, boss." Charlie had already started to chop.

"We'll be fine," Hector assured her.

"I know you will." Even so, she moved extra fast through the restaurant and out the door. If she hurried, she could probably have the animals fed and situated in ten minutes. She darted down the path and veered to the left to get to the chicken coop. Halfway there she stumbled to a stop.

Mateo was scattering handfuls of chicken feed across the grass, all of her hens following behind him, pecking at the ground.

Her heartbeat picked up at the sight of him dressed in his worn jeans and a tattered T-shirt. He was so beautiful it tempted her to question whether she really did want something real. Or maybe she just wanted Mateo every night...

No, no. She'd already had a superficial relationship, and

look at how that had ended. With deception and heartbreak. Things would be no different with Mateo. Eventually she wouldn't be a good enough distraction anymore and he would have to find something else. The thought helped to curb the sudden flutter in her heart. "What're you doing?" She marched over to him.

Mateo seemed startled. He dropped the bag of feed on the ground. "I took care of the animals for you. Since you didn't have time." Everly tried not to notice how sad his eyes seemed. "They're all fed. Then I checked around to make sure there was no sign of our friend from last night."

Awww. That was actually thoughtful of him. But no, she couldn't let his thoughtfulness tempt her into a swoon. Boundaries. She had to set healthy boundaries so she wouldn't want him more than she already did. "Thanks, but I could've taken care of it."

Those dark magic eyes seemed to droop lower. "You shouldn't be out here alone. Especially in the mornings."

"Yeah... about that." She leaned over to right the feed sack so she didn't have to look at him. "I don't think it's a good idea for you to move in again." Then she'd end up right back where she'd been last night. In bed with him. On a regular basis. Boundaries had never been one of her strengths.

"Okay." Mateo's jaw tightened. "Then I'll have Dev come out here every morning and evening to do the rounds with you."

There was that thoughtfulness again. Or maybe he simply didn't want her to die on his property. "It's not necessary. I can—"

"It's not up for discussion," Mateo interrupted gruffly. "I'm not willing to take a chance with your life. So it's Dev or me."

Whoa. He looked pissed. "Fine," Everly muttered. "You can talk to Dev." That would be much safer than spending more time with Mateo. "I should get back to the café." She made the mistake of glancing at him. God, those sad eyes of his. She had to get away. "Thank you for taking care of the animals."

"No problem," he said as she walked away. "Everly?"

Her heart clenched at the sound of her name on his lips. She turned.

"I'm sorry I hurt you. I didn't mean to."

"I know you didn't." But he had all the same.

Word had definitely gotten out that the café would soon be closing. The place was so packed that Everly hadn't sat down for a full two hours. All morning, she'd served pancakes and omelets and cinnamon rolls, all while accepting people's condolences that she was being forced out by an outsider cowboy who obviously didn't understand the significance of a small-town business.

While she appreciated the support, the whole dance had started to exhaust her. Once again, she drifted back to the dining room, her tray piled with plates and mugs of black coffee, which she served with a smile. She refilled waters and chatted about the warm fall weather and the fact that snow probably wasn't too far off.

When Everly turned to head back to the kitchen for a few minutes of quiet, the door opened, sending dried leaves swirling along the wood floor. Darla and Charity sashayed through, looking a little too conspiratorial with their heads tilted together.

Everly hurried to intercept them. "You two are in early." It was a rare occasion for Darla to leave her house before noon.

"We thought we should do some investigating," her friend said with a clandestine look at Charity.

Everly hustled them to a table in the corner. Far away from the rest of the town's listening ears. "What are we investigating?" she asked when they were out of earshot.

Charity removed her cowgirl hat and set it on the table as if she wanted a full view of Everly's face. "Mateo didn't show up for our training session at six this morning. And Levi said he didn't come home last night."

Uh-oh. Everly clasped her hands in front of her waist, wringing them together nervously. He hadn't said anything about a training session with his friends that morning. Of course he hadn't. He'd been too busy enticing her to stay in bed.

"We thought that was odd," Darla commented blithely, scooting into the chair across from Charity. "You know what else is odd?" Her eyes did a quick appraisal of Everly's attire. "You look like you just rolled out of bed."

Cold thoughts. She had to think cold thoughts so her face wouldn't go molten. *Icicles and igloos.* Yeah, that didn't work. "I woke up late," she finally said.

"Why'd you wake up late?" Charity propped her chin on a fist and stared her down.

"What d'you mean, why? I just did." That sort of thing happened to people all the time, right?

Darla's peaked eyebrows channeled the all-seeing Maleficent. "Did Mateo happen to wake up late, too? Because—and this is just a stab in the dark—if he didn't sleep at Levi's house last night, I'm guessing he was at your place."

There was no denying it. Her friends weren't stupid. "Fine. He was at my place." That didn't prove anything, though.

Darla pointed an accusatory finger at her. "You slept with him." At least she said it quietly.

Everly neither confirmed nor denied the allegation.

"You've got to be kidding me." Charity's nose wrinkled with a look of disgust. "Mateo? Really?"

"It was a one-time thing," Everly whispered, reminding them to keep it down. "And it wasn't my fault. He saved me from a mountain lion out on the property." That was how it had started, anyway. He'd been so comforting when he'd carried her inside, and then he'd taken care of everything— calling Dev, getting her warmed up, making her that insanely delicious hot chocolate.

"Oh my God!" Darla's gasp commanded the attention of the entire restaurant. "You got attacked by a mountain lion?"

"A mountain lion?" Hank Green, the uncontested mayor of Topaz Falls, looked up from his newspaper. "When did you get attacked by a mountain lion?"

"I never said it *attacked* me." Her jaw tightened at the same time her glare admonished Darla and Charity to shut the hell up. They did not need to bring the entire town into this conversation. "I ran into it when I was out feeding the goats and Mateo scared it away." Best to end the story there. "Don't worry, we called Dev," she added for Hank's benefit. "He's on it."

"No one told me we had a rabid mountain lion on the loose," Hank grumbled, digging out his phone. "I'm only the mayor of this town, but no one sees fit to tell me a damn thing."

"That's because you're a numbskull," Hector called. He and Charlie were in their corner booth. They snickered like two junior high boys.

Hank tossed aside his newspaper as though ready for a fight. "No one asked you."

While the old men traded insults, Everly sat down across from Darla. "Anyway," she whispered. "Mateo was really sweet to me. I was terrified, obviously, so when we got inside he called Dev to put in the report and then made me hot chocolate."

"Hot chocolate," Charity scoffed. "What a ploy."

"It was good hot chocolate." As smooth and indulgent as Mateo himself. "Then we talked for a long time. One thing led to another and next thing I knew clothes were coming off."

Darla shook her head, pouting with a resentful frown. "It's not fair. You don't even like hookups. That's supposed to be my thing."

"You can have it back," Everly said. "They're definitely not my thing, and I told him as much this morning."

"I'm going to kick his ass," Charity muttered.

"No." Everly shut down their grumbles with a dirty look. Why did everyone assume that he'd taken advantage of her? "I wanted it." Two minutes into kissing him, she'd practically been begging him to keep going. If she remembered right, she'd specifically told him not to stop—never to stop—multiple times. "It's been a long time. And it was . . . really great."

"Oh God." Darla shared a concerned look with Charity. "Don't start falling for him, Everly. You're so sweet. And he's a cowboy."

Yes, well, it was a little late for that.

"He's a cowboy who takes full advantage of his star status on the circuit," Charity added. "Trust me. He gets as excited about commitment as he does about fancy three-piece suits. Have you ever seen him wear anything except for jeans?"

No. She hadn't. "I know." She wasn't stupid. Too emotional and caring and impulsive, maybe, but not stupid. "He's afraid of commitment. It's because of his brother..." The abandonment, the betrayal. Not that Mateo would acknowledge it. Hence the reason he was incapable of having the kind of relationship she wanted.

"He doesn't have a brother," Charity informed her. "Only sisters."

"Oh. Right." She studied the wood grain pattern on the tabletop, remembering how solemn his face had been when he'd told her about Andres. At least he'd been telling the truth about no one else knowing his secret.

"If you want to date someone, what about Dev?" Darla suggested.

"Yeah," Charity agreed. "He's pretty sexy. For a cop."

"I don't want to date Dev." And did those words really just come out of Charity's mouth? Everly had never heard the woman call anyone sexy. She decided to save that conversation for another day. Right now she had to shut down this one. "Mateo and I aren't dating. And don't worry about me. I'm completely over last night. It meant nothing." She'd keep telling herself that until it was true.

Chapter Seventeen

Mateo climbed down the ladder and stood back to inspect his work. The crack in the farmhouse's foundation appeared to be patched for the moment, but the bigger concern was why it had cracked in the first place.

When he'd come down to the cellar to find the picture of Andres, he'd noticed some moisture buildup on the walls. Then he'd moved his boxes and found a squirrel's nest, which led him to investigate where they might be coming in. The crack in the far corner of the basement was a couple of inches wide. At least Owen had left some good caulking behind. That'd saved Mateo a trip to the hardware store.

He folded up the ladder and put it back where he'd found it. There were so many things he should be doing right now—getting everything ready to head out for their competition in Wyoming—but he didn't want to leave things unsettled with Everly. So he'd spent hours cleaning and fixing up her basement because he'd been too chickenshit to follow her to the café. Everything she'd said about him was true. He'd never wanted any relationship to be more meaningful than a one-night stand. And she was right. She deserved more.

He rearranged the boxes and bins, moving them away from the walls so he could get to his old photographs. The picture of him and Andres was still buried at the bottom of the bin where he'd stashed it after Everly had found it. He picked it up and went to sit on the stairs. Crazy that he had no clue what his brother would've looked like now. In the picture, he still had a boyish face, an easy grin. He'd still been a kid when he'd walked out. Older than Mateo but not much wiser. And Andres would've turned thirty-six this year. He would've looked so different Mateo probably wouldn't have even recognized him on the street.

His phone rang, sending in a rush of hope. It was too late to fix things with Andres, but maybe he could fix things with Everly. Maybe she was calling because she'd come back from the café and saw that his truck was still here. Maybe she wondered where he was. He pulled it out of his pocket knowing that was wishful thinking. She wouldn't call him. She wanted nothing to do with him.

Sure enough, Ana's smiling picture lit up the screen instead. "It's about time you called to check in," he scolded without a greeting. They'd texted a few times, but Ana hadn't answered any of his calls since she'd arrived in Mexico.

"Sorry," she said, sounding somewhat sincere. "Mamá's been running me all over to reintroduce me to all of her friends. She's making such a fuss, you'd think I'd risen from the dead."

The statement landed a punch, folding him over to ease

the rise of pain. She was joking but he couldn't laugh, couldn't say anything. Their mother loved her children. Even Andres. Maybe especially Andres, since he was the one she'd lost. How was he supposed to tell her that her son would never come back?

"Anyway," Ana went on when he didn't respond, "I finally snuck away for a few minutes so I could call and read you the letter Andres wrote."

He looked at the picture again, at the smiles, at the hope on young faces. *He's dead.* Mateo almost said the words to Ana because they were eating him up on the inside. Everly was right. He'd used her to cover the grief last night, to alleviate the pain, but it had come again, raw and exposed. Stronger because he carried it alone. But he couldn't tell Ana over the phone. He couldn't tell Mamá from thousands of miles away. He had to be there so she could lean on him, so he could hold her up. "I'm listening." He might be shaky and queasy but he was listening.

"Okay." Ana paused. "It's kind of weird. The letter isn't addressed only to mom. There's no greeting. She thinks he meant it for the whole family. Not just for her." Silence loomed as though Ana expected him to react.

"Maybe," was all he could manage. He tried to picture it—his brother sitting down to write them a letter, but all he could see was Andres as a kid. Not a man who'd been down a road Mateo couldn't imagine traveling.

"So he starts out with an apology." Ana cleared her throat. " 'I'm sorry. I've wanted to tell you that all these years.' " Her voice quieted.

Mateo's head fell forward as he slowly exhaled. Why didn't he? Why didn't Andres write that letter years ago? Before it was too late? Probably because he knew. Before

Mateo had found out he was dead, he was going to tell him to go to hell.

"'When I left, I always thought I would come back some-day,'" Ana read. "'I always planned to make something of myself so I could change everything for us. For all of us.'" His sister paused. "Do you think that means he left for a job or something?"

"Not sure." The lie put a crack in his composure. But he would tell the truth. He would bring them out here as soon as he could and tell them everything.

"'I know I failed you,'" Ana continued. "'Eventually, I knew it was better if I didn't come home. It's not because I didn't want to. I just couldn't face you after what I put you through. I don't have much to offer. But I wanted you to know I'm sorry. I hope you understand I didn't leave because I didn't care. I was too young to know how much I would regret it later. I know it's too late. My words proba-bly don't mean much to you now, but I had to tell you I love you. I have no right to ask for your forgiveness, but I hope for it.'"

Silence expanded between him and Ana. For once, Mateo didn't try to fill it. He couldn't. He'd never thought about how similar he and Andres were. Always prided himself in being the better man. But his brother had wanted more for the family, too. At sixteen, he just hadn't known how to help.

"It doesn't make sense," Ana finally said. "I thought maybe he wrote because he needed money, or he wanted to see us, but this letter makes it sound like he's never coming back."

Anguish caught Mateo by the throat. He wasn't. Andres was never coming back. And from the sound of his words in the letter, his brother had known that. It was a last plea. A final request for forgiveness.

"Have you been looking for him?" An echo of fear hid in Ana's question. She'd always been intuitive, but he couldn't answer her over the phone.

"I'm working on it." Mateo folded the picture in half and stuck it in his wallet. "In the meantime, do you think you could get Mom to come out here with you in a few days? I can book the tickets."

"Why?" He was glad Ana couldn't look at his face. She'd see the grief his voice disguised.

"It's been a long time since I've seen her," he said. "I know the letter shook her up. I want to make sure she's okay." And he wanted to be able to comfort her when she found out her oldest child was dead.

"*Is* everything okay, Mateo?"

Gritting his teeth, he forced himself to lie. "Sure. Everything's great." He only had to pretend a while longer. "I just want to see Mom. Spend some time with her."

Ana sighed. She didn't believe him. "Fine. I'll get her to come."

"Thanks, sis," he said, emotion thick in his throat. "I'll text over the info as soon as I book the tickets."

Outdoor venues had always been Mateo's favorite place to ride for a crowd. There was nothing like walking out into the arena, the blinding lights buzzing overhead, the smell of beer and peanuts and fried fair-style foods drifting on the air, the crowd noise rising all the way up to the night sky.

Mateo knew full well the crowds mainly cheered for him because he'd been one of Renegade Jean Company's golden boys. Without that endorsement, no one likely would even know his name. Sure, he was a decent rider—always placed in the top fourth—but he wouldn't call himself decorated by any means. Early on, Gunner had taught him that this sport was about showmanship as much as anything else, so, as he made his way to the bucking chute on the south side of the arena, he whooped it up, waving to the stands while he flashed his well-honed smile and stopped to sign little kids' felt cowboy hats and the programs they had open to his bio page.

Adrenaline simmered beneath the wild-man persona he'd perfected, and truth be told, that's why he rode. Not for the crowds or the cheers or even the money. It was the adrenaline, the high. Until the other night with Everly, no feeling in his life had ever come close to it.

His thoughts drifted away from him again, and he wondered what she was doing now.

Was Dev keeping an eye on her like Mateo had asked? Someone had to, and she hadn't wanted him there. Not that he blamed her.

"Up next, Mateo Torres riding Major!"

Hearing his name echo over the loudspeaker ripped him away from his regrets about how things had ended between them. He jogged the rest of the way to the chute and hopped the fence. By the time he slid onto Major's back, the crowds were chanting his name.

Major's handlers held the bronc in place while Mateo waved and secured his grip on the lifeline that would ensure his success or failure.

"Give 'em hell," Ty called from the other side of the fence. He stood with Charity and Levi, who were watching the ride from the gate like they always did. Even Gunner had shown up for this competition. He tried to come and support the four of them as often as he could, which seemed to be less frequently these days.

Mateo gave his old mentor a nod. The horse stood eerily still, his dark coat still slicked with sweat from the warm-ups. Major Dick, as Mateo liked to call him, was fifteen hundred pounds of pure rippling muscle, from his thick neck all the way to his hindquarters—beautiful from a distance, lethal when you found yourself sitting on his back.

The countdown always went too fast, but that was good because it didn't give him time to think. He liked to ride with a clear head. Nothing about bronc riding was logical. It was all instinct, nerve, and grit, and he had plenty of that.

Right as the gate swung open, he strengthened his grip. *Here we go.*

Major Dick launched into the arena, arching his back end into the air with a kick. Seemed the horse was in a mood today. Mateo clenched his fist on the rope and raised his other arm over his head, moving with the bronc's momentum instead of fighting it. The violent bucks rocked his body, whipping his head forward and back, giving him fleeting glimpses of sky, then dirt, then the blurred-out crowd.

Major Dick whirled an airborne 180, wrenching Mateo's elbow. Pain shot through the joint, hot and fast, locking it up. His grip weakened. *Fuck.* He fought to steady himself on the horse's back but his elbow refused to cooperate. Major Dick arched and kicked, twice, three times and it felt like his arm was being ripped off. One more buck knocked him loose and sent him rolling across the dirt.

Mateo gritted his teeth and bit down on the pain. His other hand felt around the injured joint and his stomach gave a hard lurch. It was dislocated. The angle of his arm was all wrong. A groan punched through his lips as he sat up, cradling the damaged elbow to his chest. Pain sent waves of nausea crashing over him, threatening to push him back to the ground. *No*. He wouldn't stay down, wouldn't be forced into the ambulance. Holding his breath, he locked his hand onto the forearm just below his elbow and gave a hard tug, snapping the joint back into place. Sweat rolled down his temples and his stomach heaved, but he somehow staggered to his feet, even with the ground shifting beneath them.

The crowd had quieted the way it always did when there was a potential injury, but now that he stood tall again, the cheers rang out even louder. Mateo waved with his good arm, pretending he'd come through the failure just fine. That's what you had to do, Gunner had told him. When things went south, you rose as the victor who'd beat out the pain and still claimed the crowd's respect. Mateo waved a few more times, doing his best not to stare at the Jumbotron where his pathetic time had been advertised in lights. He hadn't held out long enough to even qualify for a score.

The cheering continued as he made his way to the fence, arm throbbing and hanging limply at his side. The fans liked him. Probably figured it was one bad ride and he'd recover. But Mateo was starting to wonder. Without stopping to sign autographs, he continued to the staging area, where he did his best to pace off the pain between the horse trailers where no one would find him.

Charity, Ty, and Levi knew enough to leave him alone after a ride like that, but not Gunner. The old man ambled over and eyed the bruising that had started to spread down Mateo's arm. "Need a medic?"

"Nope. I'm good."

Gunner called him out with a look. "You just snapped your elbow back into place. Might want to have a professional take a look."

"If I did that, they'd only tell me things I don't want to

hear." Mateo fisted and unfisted his hand to stop the throbbing. They'd likely tell him his riding days were numbered, and then what would he do? Right now, riding was all he had.

Gunner chuckled. "You're more like my son than my own flesh and blood." That was true. Somehow Gunner's son had left home at age eighteen to become a stockbroker in New York. He was already gone by the time Mateo went to live there, but he'd heard plenty of stories from Gunner. "How is Ryder, anyway?"

"He's good." Even though his son had gone about as far away as he could from the rodeo world, Gunner still looked proud. "A real yuppie now. But he's happy and I guess that's all that matters."

"Yeah." Mateo leaned against a horse trailer and forced his elbow to bend. At least it still worked. "I guess so."

"Are you happy?" The old man had a knowing look in his eyes.

"Sure." The word came out too fast to sound convincing. He had been happy. Before that night with Everly, he'd thought he knew what happy was, but her words had gotten to him. *Everything you do is about avoiding reality.*

"How's your family?"

That question hit him below the belt. "They're okay. Mom and Ana are coming to visit in a few days." He wished he was looking forward to it, but he still hadn't figured out how to tell them about Andres.

"What aren't you telling me, Torres?" Gunner's patience had apparently started to wane. The older he got, the less he seemed to have. "You lived with me for four years before you went out on the road full-time. I can tell when you're hiding something."

Yeah, for some reason he wasn't as good at hiding things as he had been a few weeks ago. Maybe that was progress. He hadn't been able to talk to anyone else about what he'd learned. Except for Everly, but she wasn't exactly speaking to him at the moment. None of his friends even knew he had a brother. Ana didn't know their brother was dead. He guessed Gunner was as good a person as any to help him work it all out in his head. "Andres is dead. I had a buddy on the force back home check up on him. After he left home, he joined a cartel. But he recently started working for the cops and someone found out."

The old man nodded as though the news didn't surprise him. He'd known of Andres, knew he'd left the family and that they'd never heard from him. "Your mom know?"

"Not yet. I have to tell her when she comes." He'd have to stand there and watch her heart break all over again, helpless to do anything about it.

"Sorry, kid." Gunner rested his hand on Mateo's shoulder. "I know how much it hurt you when he left."

For once he didn't try to deny it. "I'll never understand. How he could've chosen that life over his family."

"Sometimes when you're young, a certain life chooses you. He must've regretted it or he wouldn't have helped the police. I'm sure he knew the risks."

He must've known, but he hadn't cared. That might've bothered Mateo more than anything else. His brother likely didn't have much to live for. No family. No one who'd cared about him. How was that any different than Mateo's life? He had his mom and his sisters, but beyond that, he'd avoided any significant relationships.

"I should've found him earlier." Everly was right. He was too busy running from the past instead of dealing with it.

"I could've convinced him to come home a long time ago. Or to move to the States." He could've helped him run from the cartel. Instead, he'd let the anger hold him back. "I don't know what to do with it. After all these years." A dooming sense of *too late* ripped through him. "I guess there's not much I can do now."

"That's a cop-out." Gunner edged closer, his face as stern as it'd been when he'd caught Mateo sneaking out of the house the night before a competition. "Things like this'll put you at a crossroads in life. Trust me, I've found myself standing there more times than I'd care to admit. Best you can do is accept your regrets and let 'em make you a better person."

"I have plenty of regrets right now." Letting his brother continue on a path Mateo had known would one day lead to his death, for instance. What other end was there for someone in a cartel? Then there were his regrets about how he'd treated Everly, about how careless he'd been with her heart.

"Then it's time to face things, son," Gunner said quietly. "Avoiding the medics ain't gonna change a damn thing. You won't be able to compete forever. That part of your life is gonna fade—the fame, the parties, the women. No more distractions to keep your mind off things. You need to figure out who you want to be when it's all gone."

Don't get Everly wrong; she liked Deputy Dev Jenkins, all right, but over these last few days, he'd turned into her constant shadow whenever she was out doing chores.

"Bet you didn't know this one," Dev said, following her around to the goat pens. For the last twenty minutes, he'd been informing her of all the strange laws in Colorado that no one knew about. "Riding a horse while you're drunk can get you a DUI."

"Wow." She dredged up an interested smile as she locked the padlock on the stable door. Inside, Trunchbull and Wormwood were stomping around and whining about the confinement. "I had no idea." She turned and started the trek back to the chicken coop.

Dev ambled along by her side. "And in Colorado Springs, it's only illegal to wear a holstered six-gun on Sundays, holidays, and election days."

Everly glanced at his boyish face. "But it's fine on Wednesdays?"

"I know, right?" Dev shook his head with disbelief.

She had to laugh. He might be awkward when it came to chitchat with women, but he really was a nice guy. Good-looking, too. Tall and broad, shy hazel eyes and decent hair—soft brown and neatly trimmed. And then there were the muscles that filled out his uniform nicely. But none of that did much for her. In the last two years, only one man had done it for her, with his dark eyes and thick black hair and sinful grin—but she wasn't supposed to be thinking about Mateo.

"Well, I'm about done here, so you can go if you want. You don't have to hang out anymore." The chickens were all bedded down for the night, but she checked the lock once again just in case.

Dev didn't budge. "Mateo said you shouldn't be out here alone. And I agree. The parks and wildlife guys still haven't tracked the lion. Until they do, you'd best use the buddy system."

And he was her new best buddy. Fighting the temptation to sigh, she glanced at her watch. "I'll only be a few more minutes out here, so it's okay if you have other things to do."

Dev gave a stubborn shake of his head. "I'm stayin' until you walk into that house. I promised Mateo."

In that case…Everly grabbed a rake that was leaning up against the fence. If he insisted on sticking around, she might as well use the opportunity to get all the leaves up before the snow came. "Really, Dev. I'm fine. Maybe you should go on patrol or something. I heard there's been some shoplifting at the market lately." Hank had muttered something about it at the café a few days ago.

"Carla Holden's toddler accidentally walked out with a pack of gum." Dev grabbed the other rake that was leaning against the coop. "I'd hardly call that a crime wave." He started to rake a few feet away, scraping up a huge pile of leaves in no time. "Besides, I wouldn't feel right about leaving you. Did I mention Mateo has texted me at least four times to make sure I'm checking in on you?"

That made her smile in a wistful sort of way. It had been a long time since anyone had been so concerned about her. Then there was all the work he'd done in her cellar. She'd gone down to look for the sealant she'd used on the floor and noticed that the crack she'd been meaning to fix had been all patched up.

"Speaking of Mateo." The deputy's gaze suddenly fell to the pile of leaves. "You think anything ever happened between him and Charity?"

Everly almost dropped her rake. *Oh God.* Charity would die if she heard him say that. "No. Nothing has happened between them." Other than the occasional bar fight, maybe. She took in the bashful flush on his face. "Why do you ask?"

"Just curious," he muttered, still focused on the ground as he raked. "She's pretty. Seems nice."

Nice? That wasn't on the list of adjectives she'd use to describe her friend. Strong. Independent. Willful. Generous. Determined. Those all fit. But nice? "I wasn't aware you two knew each other well."

"We don't. I mean...she doesn't. Know me." He moved swiftly past Everly and went to work on the other side of the fence. "We'd better get moving on this raking business. It'll be dark soon."

Tempering her smile, Everly raked her way across the pen to him. She couldn't get over it. Charity had an admirer. Who would've thought? "Maybe you should ask her out," Everly suggested innocently.

Dev fumbled with the handle of the rake and ended up dropping it in the pile of leaves. "I don't think so." He snatched the handle, but dropped it again. The redness on his face had spread to his neck.

"Why not? As far I as I know, she's not dating anyone." Had Charity ever dated anyone? Not that Everly could remember hearing about, but the woman had called Dev sexy just the other day. What would it hurt to tell him that? "She's mentioned you to me."

"Really?" He froze. "When? What'd she say?"

"Can't remember exactly," Everly lied. "But it was something about how good-looking you are." Maybe if she didn't give him specifics, Charity wouldn't hunt her down.

"Good-looking, huh?" From the way his mouth mumbled the words, it was obvious he was trying not to smile.

They raked in silence, but she could see the wheels in his head spinning fast. He worked the rake double time. At that rate, he'd have the whole yard done in twenty minutes.

They didn't need to do the whole yard, though. And Dev had nothing to be nervous about. He'd be a catch for the right woman. Everly leaned her rake against the fence. "She'd be lucky to go out with you, Dev." From everything she'd heard and seen about him, he was a true gentleman. Of course, Charity's language and manner sometimes reminded her of the trucker who often delivered her farm supplies, but she supposed stranger matches had been made. "I can talk to her, if you want—"

"Uh-oh." Dev hadn't heard her. He was looking down at the ground. Everly walked over to see what had him so concerned.

"Prints. Mountain lion." He pointed to the soft dirt at the edge of the chicken yard.

Unease rippled through her stomach. "Maybe it was just a dog."

"Too big to be a dog." Dev knelt and inspected the print. "And it's not the right shape." He stood back up. "This is definitely a mountain lion. Fresh, too. Probably made when the grass still had dew on it this morning."

"This morning?" Everly scanned the scrub oak on the hill. A shiver skittered across her shoulders. "But you were out on the rounds with me this morning. We didn't see anything."

"We wouldn't. He probably came around before we were even up. That's the thing with mountain lions. They're good at hiding." Dev wore that grim cop expression again. "Mateo's back in town tonight, right?"

"Um, I think so." At least she knew Charity would be back from their rodeo event tonight, and they were likely traveling together. "But he's not staying here anymore."

"How come?"

Because he's too attractive, okay? That, combined with her inability to keep her heart out of things. Not that she needed to get Dev's perspective on her and Mateo. "He's staying with Levi." That seemed like the simplest answer.

"I'd feel better if he stayed with you," Dev said. "Just in case. This print is awfully close to the house." The deputy pulled out his phone. "I can call him and let him know."

Before she could argue, he had the phone against his ear. "Hey, Mateo. Everly and I found a print near the chicken coop. Looks like the cat made an appearance sometime today." He paused. "Yeah. I was here this morning, but we didn't see anything. Since it's still around, I think it'd be best if you stayed here for the next few nights."

Everly leaned closer, but couldn't hear Mateo's response.

"Of course she's fine with it." Dev shot her a questioning look.

She shrugged as though she had no idea why Mateo would be concerned. She was not about to explain their situation to Dev.

"Sounds good. I'll tell her." The deputy pocketed his phone. "He's only about an hour away. Says he'll come straight over."

"Great." That was just great.

Chapter Eighteen

Less than a month ago, when Mateo had driven up to this same little farmhouse, it had looked so different. Small and decrepit, a landlord's worst nightmare.

It was still the same house, with the shabby siding and the worn roof, but Mateo saw it differently now. Everly had treated the place with the same care she treated her customers, her friends, and him. She had this restorative touch, nurturing and steadfast.

He parked behind Everly's truck and stared at the little house, which glowed with the soft lights on inside. The whole trip home, he'd thought about Gunner's take on his situation. The man was right. When you took away his riding career he didn't have much of an identity, no roots, nothing to ground him. He'd left all of that behind. Or at least he thought he had. Maybe it wasn't possible to deny who you were and where you came from. Maybe that would always be part of you no matter how hard you tried to reinvent yourself. Everly had a completely different life than she'd had back in San Francisco, but she didn't hide from her past. Maybe he could learn her secret.

Nerves rolled through his gut. He'd almost dropped his phone when Dev had told him Everly didn't mind if he stayed at her house. Of course, she likely had no other option but to agree, and now he had no other option but to go in there and face her disappointment with him.

When he pushed out of the truck, nerves simmered into anticipation at seeing her again. Maybe he would tell her more about Andres, about his childhood. Maybe that would help him figure out who he wanted to be, what he should take with him from the past and what he should leave behind. He took the porch steps two at a time, knocked, and waited.

Everly didn't answer the door. "Hello?" He tried again, straining to hear noise inside, but only silence answered. "Everly?" The door wasn't locked. He pushed it open and stepped inside. The kitchen and living room sat empty, but all of the lights were on. "Anyone home?" For a brief moment, he wondered if she was in the shower. Maybe she would come out in a towel and greet him with that soft smile of hers. Not very likely after she'd run out on him the other morning, but that didn't stop him from hoping.

Mateo listened carefully and made his way down the hall. No water running. The bathroom was empty and dark. He rapped his fist against her bedroom door. "Everly?"

No answer. "Hello?" He pushed it open. A look at the bed they'd shared tortured him with a surge of want. God, he wanted to feel her skin against his again, wanted to hear her quick breaths and sexy little moans as he slid into her, bringing their bodies together.

Mateo backed out of the empty room, an urgency pounding through him. Where was she? Why wasn't she in the house?

The café. Maybe she had some work to finish up. Though he didn't like the thought of her walking back and forth from the house to the café alone at night with a mountain lion on the loose. He left the house and followed the path she would've taken, shining the light from his phone around to look for any sign of her.

Up ahead, the café sat dark. He peered in the windows, worry settling heavily in his chest. Where was she? "Everly?" he yelled, taking off for the house again. When he reached the porch he tried her cell, but it went right to voicemail. "Damn it." Helplessness washed over him. He had no idea where she would go, why the door would be unlocked and all of the lights left lights on. Unless she'd stepped outside for something...

The possibility ignited the worry into panic. It was a known fact that mountain lions would drag away their prey after a kill. Sweat broke out on his forehead. His hand shook as he dialed Dev.

"Hey, Mateo, what's—"

"Where'd Everly go?" His body felt like it was on fire.

"I thought she was with you."

"I just got here, and I can't find her anywhere." Mateo lifted his head and surveyed all of those acres stretching into the dark night.

"Maybe she went out with friends," Dev suggested with a yawn.

Mateo wanted to throttle him through the phone. "Her truck's here. The door was unlocked and all of the lights are on."

"Well, shit." The deputy finally sounded concerned. "That's not good."

Tell him something he didn't know. Mateo stepped back inside the house. "Did she say anything before you left? Did she have more work to do outside?"

"Not that she told me about." Dev was out of breath. "I stayed until she finished raking up the leaves, but then she went inside. I thought she'd be there for the night."

"Well, she's not." Bracing the phone against his shoulder, Mateo started to search the kitchen drawers for a flashlight. "I'm going out to look for her." He moved his search to the front coat closet and finally found a flashlight big enough to make a dent in the moonless night.

"I'll be there in a few minutes," Dev said. "Hang tight."

Not a chance. Mateo hung up and ducked back outside. He couldn't wait around for help. Everly was out there somewhere, and he had to find her.

"I have a surprise for you." The glimmer in Darla's eyes struck fear into Everly's heart.

"Can we just agree to no more surprises?" She sipped her spiked mocha cocktail and gave Kate, Jessa, and Naomi a look. "I'm still recovering from her last surprise," she informed them. "AKA the double date to Kate's engagement party." Otherwise known as the night she'd climbed onto the Mateo Torres roller coaster.

Well, technically, she hadn't climbed onto him until last week, but still. It had all started with the date. Since the party, Everly had pretty much experienced the full gamut of emotions—she'd been elated, disappointed, excited, sad, and scared out of her mind that she'd never find a way off the ride. Seriously. She'd slept with the man who was kicking her out of her house, and now she couldn't seem to get her mind or her heart off of him.

That's why she'd texted her friends to ask for an impromptu book club meeting at the Chocolate Therapist. Hiding in Darla's comfy back room had sounded like a much smarter choice than sitting around in her living room with him all evening.

"I still can't believe you set her up like that," Kate said to Darla.

"Especially with Mateo Torres," Jessa added. "Geez, talk about throwing her to the wolves."

"This surprise is different," Darla insisted, waving them off. "I promise. You'll love it."

"You will," Kate agreed.

"It's a good one." Naomi shot a conspiratorial grin to the others. If they were all in on it, it must not be too terrible.

"All right. What is it? Lay it on me." Everly was feeling especially open to anything after finishing one of Darla's specialty cocktails. It had been warm and chocolaty and calming. *Mmmm*. She sighed and let her back sink against the couch cushions.

"Well…" Darla drew out the word excitedly. She hopped out of her chair and zipped over to a row of filing cabinets along the wall. "The girls and I were talking about the farm."

"About how we can't stand to see it go," Jessa clarified.

"Right." Darla opened a drawer and pulled out a jar. "So we took up a collection." She brought the jar over and handed it to Everly. It was stuffed full of cash and checks…

"Oh my God." Everly sat up straighter, holding it in her hands, staring wide-eyed at a whole bunch of money.

"That's just over two thousand dollars," Naomi said,

beaming. "Darla kept the jar here and we spread the word around town."

"You guys…" She sniffled but couldn't hold back the steady flow of tears. "I can't believe this."

"We know it's not enough to pay off Mateo and save the farm," Kate said. "But we're hoping it'll start the fund for a new farm. Somewhere nearby. Eventually."

Everly couldn't speak. She could only nod. And blubber. No one had ever done something like this for her before. Something so generous and unexpected.

"That's not all," Darla said, starting to sound like a game show host.

Everly dried her eyes. "But it's enough." She didn't care if it was only $20; the gesture alone was enough.

Naomi dug in her messenger bag and pulled out a flyer. "We've also planned a Farewell to the Farm fund-raiser. For next week."

Everly took the flyer and did her best to read it through bleary eyes. "Come and celebrate everything the farm and café has meant to the community. There will be food, drinks—"

"Provided courtesy of the Chocolate Therapist," Kate interjected.

"Music and activities for the whole family," Everly continued.

"Including some entertainment that Charity is working on with some of the rodeo stars in town." Darla looked quite pleased with herself. "It'll be an epic party with donations strongly encouraged."

"This is amazing." Everly looked at each of her friends, hoping they could see the gratitude that welled up in her. "I don't think you understand how much this means to me."

With their acts of kindness, her friends were helping keep her dream alive.

"You've done so much for the town, Everly." Jessa gave her hand a squeeze. "People were practically begging to contribute."

"And you don't have to worry about a thing," Naomi assured her. "We're taking care of all the details for the event. All you have to do is show up and enjoy it."

"I will." Everly finally got a handle on the tears. "I'll enjoy every minute of it."

There was more talk about the details, and Darla gave them a quick overview of the refreshments, but after a few minutes Jessa stood. "Sorry, girls. I have to get home." She yawned. "I've been so tired lately."

Everly shared a smiley, hopeful look with Darla. They'd regularly discussed how their friend had seemed a little plumper lately. In a good way.

"I should go, too." Naomi gathered up her bag. "The inn has been so crazy lately that Lucas has had to be on toddler duty a lot." Naomi and Lucas's daughter Charlotte was just over a year old and one of the cutest little sweethearts Everly had ever seen.

"Thank you." She rose and gave each of her friends a hug, which wasn't nearly enough. "I've been so depressed about moving, but this helps." She would still grieve over the farm—her sanctuary, her place of healing. She'd likely never be able to drive past it without a wrench in her heart, but she was also learning that life was about new beginnings. When one thing was taken away, something else was given in its place.

"Come on, girl." Darla slung an arm around her. "Let's get you home."

Everly sighed. "I suppose it's time." She did her best to appear calm. She'd neglected to mention to her friends that Mateo was moving back in for a while. Mainly because she hadn't even wanted to think about it.

While Kate stayed behind to catch up on paperwork, the rest of them paraded out to the street. Everly said good-bye to Jessa and Naomi and then crawled into Darla's sleek little Mercedes.

"We need some tunes." Darla dug around in her purse and pulled out her phone. "Oh. Wait. That's weird. I have three missed calls from Mateo."

"Really?" That couldn't be good. Since Darla had offered to pick her up, she'd neglected to bring her phone. "Maybe he wondered where I was," she muttered. "He's staying at my house again because Dev spotted another mountain lion print nearby."

"Ooohhh." Darla's eyes lit as she sped away from the curb. "Then I guess I don't need to call him back. I'm surprised you didn't want to go home earlier. If I had Mateo Torres as my houseguest, I'd never leave."

And that was the difference between them. With Mateo there, she never wanted to go home. "Maybe we should switch places. You can stay at my house until they find the lion and I'll stay at yours." Darla and Mateo would probably have all kinds of great, unattached sex.

"Nah, he's too hung up on you." Her friend sped down the side streets, probably hoping for an opportunity to bait Dev into pulling her over so she could flirt.

"He's not hung up on me. Mateo doesn't get hung up on any—" The sentence ended in a gasp. There were three cop cars parked in front of the farmhouse, their lights flashing.

"Holy shit." Darla turned the car onto the driveway. "What's going on?"

"I have no idea." Everly fumbled to get her seat belt off and had the door open before the car had even stopped.

"Everly?" Dev stood by his cruiser holding a flashlight and a radio.

"Did you find the mountain lion?" she asked, running over to him. "Where's Mateo?" God, he hadn't been hurt, had he?

"No mountain lion." The deputy almost looked amused. "And Mateo is out searching for you."

"Wait. What?"

"He couldn't find you when he got here, so he called out a search party." Wearing a huge grin, Dev brought his phone to his ear. "Hey, Torres, she just came back."

"Nope. Not hung up on you at all," Darla muttered behind her with a laugh.

Dev laughed, too. "I told him it was possible you'd gone out, but he was convinced you were on the property some-where. Scared the shit out of him, if you ask me." Dev slid into the driver's seat of his car. "I've gotta call my deputies back. They were searching the other perimeter."

Dear lord, a search party? Embarrassment flooded her face. "I was just at book club." Wasn't she allowed to hang out with her friends without someone calling the cops on her?

"Next time you may want to leave him a note," Dev said with another chuckle.

Really, a note? It wasn't like Mateo was her roommate. Or her dad. She had a right to come and go whenever she wanted. "Sorry, Dev. I didn't mean to cause such a fuss." Or waste police resources. Not that this was her fault.

"No problem. At least it wasn't a boring night."

Next to Everly, Darla zipped up her coat. "Can't wait to see Mateo's face when he gets back. This ought to be good."

Not really. Everly had had enough of a scene for one night. "Actually, I'm cold. I think I'll go inside." Which would hopefully encourage Darla to leave. She gave her friend a quick hug. "I'll call you tomorrow."

"Okay," her friend sang, retreating to her car. "Can't wait to hear all about this one."

Everly ignored her and marched into the house, where she and Mateo could have some privacy for the impending confrontation. Whatever she did, she couldn't let it end with kissing. *No. Kissing.* Heat flooded her body. She could really go for another one of those chocolate cocktails right about now.

Everly took a break from pacing and peered out the window. Two of the police cars were driving away, but Dev and Mateo stood near his cruiser talking. Judging from the wild arm waving, Mateo wasn't too happy.

He turned and started toward the house. Everly darted away from the window. Mateo hadn't even made it fully inside before he started in. "What the hell, Everly? Where have you been?" He stopped just short of slamming the door behind him.

"I was at book club." She matched his irritation. "I went out with my friends like I do all the time." God, did he have any idea how ridiculous this was? "I can't believe you called the police."

He threw up his hands. "Your truck was here. You left your door unlocked and your lights on."

"So you thought I went for a nighttime stroll with a mountain lion on the loose?" She reined in her tone. "I knew you'd be here soon. That's why I left the door open and all of the lights on."

"You knew I would be here soon so you left," he accused.

"Does that really surprise you?" What did he expect after the other night? "I don't know what you want from me." Other than to be around when he needed a distraction or when he wanted to play the hero. "What *do* you want from me, Mateo?" She held her breath, waiting for the answer, still hoping he had one even after all of the disappointment.

"I don't know." He braced his hands on the kitchen table and hunched over, eyes closed, breathing deep and even. When he looked at her again, his face had softened. "I don't know. I feel like I'm losing everything. I lost my brother. I'm losing my career. I guess I'm afraid I'll lose you, too."

No. Those sad eyes would not draw her in again. He was feeling lost, didn't know what he wanted—he'd admitted it. And she could not be his remedy, his distraction. "You can't lose something you never had," she said, going to get her purse. "We don't have a relationship, Mateo. Sex is not a relationship. Swooping in to save the day and be the hero does not entitle you to a relationship."

"I'm not a hero." He sank to the couch, shoulders hunched, body deflated, and damn it if the sight of his dejection didn't topple her resolve.

"You don't have to be a hero." Hadn't anyone told him that? "You're a good man. You take good care of your family. You're loyal and you're strong." She almost went to sit with him on the couch. Almost. But he didn't want what she wanted. The give and take, the painstaking effort it required to build a bond that could withstand anything. When she loved someone, she went all in. She would give everything, but not to someone who couldn't do the same. So she stayed right where she was, near the front door, clutching her purse. "Thank you for watching out for me." Emotion overpowered her voice. "I'm sorry I made you worry." She dug out her keys and went for the door. "I think it's best if I stay with Darla tonight."

"Wait." He rose from the couch and caught her shoulder. "I don't know what to do. How to fix everything. What should I do?"

"You don't have to fix anything." Maybe he did for his family, but he didn't have to do that for her. "You just have to give someone else your heart." No matter how risky it felt, no matter how vulnerable. And that was one thing she couldn't teach him.

Chapter Nineteen

What's wrong?" Ana Sofia targeted him with a third-degree glare.

"Nothing." Mateo peered down the hallway that led to Levi and Cassidy's guestrooms, where his mom had disappeared to freshen up before dinner.

Not wanting to go out, he'd put on a pot of chili earlier. Since Levi had gone to the city to stay with Cassidy for a few nights, the three of them had his place to themselves, which would give Mateo the perfect opportunity to tell them both the truth. The problem was, he still didn't know how to say it.

"Don't tell me nothing's wrong," Ana said. "We share DNA. Which means you can't lie to me. I knew something was wrong right when I saw you at the airport, but I didn't want to say anything in front of Mom."

It would be easier if he could only tell Ana about Andres and leave it at that. His little sister was tough. She'd be upset, but his mom would be devastated. "We'll talk about it over dinner." Not that he'd be able to eat anything. He hadn't eaten anything all day.

After Everly had walked out on him again last night, Mateo had called Gunner. He'd asked him the same question he'd asked Everly—what did he have to do? How could he fix what he'd broken? According to his old mentor, Mateo had to start here. With his mom and his sister and his brother. He had to fix the future by going back to the past. He had to accept that it'd damaged him, that it had destroyed his ability to trust anyone, to rely on anyone except himself.

"You found Andres, didn't you?" Ana Sofia's voice had sobered. "You know where he is."

No. He didn't. That would be the hardest part to tell them. Their brother, their mom's son, would never be found. He would be his mom's lost boy forever. "We'll talk about it over dinner," Mateo said again.

"Talk about what?" His mother had somehow snuck up behind them. It wasn't hard for her to do. Florencia Torres was less than five feet tall and had a quiet way about her. It still shocked Mateo that she never seemed to change. Her plump cheeks, smooth olive skin, and quick smile easily took twenty years off her sixty. The thick bun she'd worn every day for years still didn't have one gray hair.

"Mamá…" Once again, instinct tempted him to protect her. That's what he had been doing for years. But Gunner had also told him that wasn't his job. He could comfort her and take care of her, but he couldn't shield her from the truth.

"Mateo has something important to tell us. That's why he brought us all the way out here." Ana's fiery glare prodded him to get on with it. She didn't like being left in the dark, especially by him. They'd always been the closest out of all his siblings. He had decided he could tell his other two sisters the news over the phone, but he knew Ana needed to hear this from him in person.

His mother gazed up at him. "What is it, *mi tesoro*?"

She might never call him her treasure again after she heard the truth. "Why don't we sit down?" He suddenly realized dinner could wait. He had to get this over with.

"I know it's about Andres." Ana marched to the leather sofa and sat. "You found something, and I want to know what it is."

"Andres?" His mom clasped his hand in hers. "You have heard from Andres, too? You know where he is?" The hope expanding in her eyes made his heart wither. Without answering, he led his mom to the couch and then sat in the chair across from them. "I need to start at the beginning." He pulled his wallet out of his back pocket and opened it, carefully unfolding the picture. "Andres was like a father to me." He set the photograph on the coffee table so they could see it.

"My boys." Tears flooded his mom's eyes as she reached out to touch it. "My precious boys."

Ana simply stared down at the picture, her face pale.

"I idolized him," Mateo said, the words choking him up. But he had to do it this way. He had to tell the whole truth, the truth he'd been denying himself all these years. "He taught me everything. How to play soccer." They used to drive their mother crazy kicking the ball around the house. "I hated learning math so he'd make a game out of it." A game show, actually, modeled after reruns of *The Price is Right*. "And he always took me fishing. Just the two of us at a stream close to our house." They never caught much, but they'd pass the hours telling jokes and talking about how someday things would change. Andres wanted to be a soldier. He wanted to fight and protect. He wanted camaraderie. Maybe that was why he'd ended up in a cartel. He'd needed a place to belong. A place where people took care of him instead of the other way around.

"We know, Mateo," Ana said. "We know all of that."

But he had to say these things, to hold onto those memories instead of the one from the day his brother had walked out on him. "Andres never got mad no matter how much I screwed things up." He'd been like a patient dad even though he was only a kid himself. "He taught me how to get odd jobs, too. To make money to help out the family." They'd go down and sell newspapers on the corner so they could give the money to their mom, but Andres would always buy him a piece of candy on their way home. Mateo paused and looked at his mom and sister. Tears rolled down their cheeks as if they, too, were remembering.

"I hated him when he left," Mateo admitted. "I hated him because he chose to leave. I woke up that morning. I caught him sneaking out."

"You saw him?" Ana dried her tears with her sleeve.

"Yes." He looked past them out the windows, craving the wild freedom he felt when he rode, the physical release of the stress, but he forced himself to stay in that chair. "He had his bag packed and I knew where he was going."

"Where?" His mother had clasped her hands tightly, rocking her upper body back and forth. "Where was he going?"

"He was running drugs for a cartel." Pain needled his heart at the horror on his mother's face. "I never found out which one. But they recruited him. Wanted him on full-time. He said he had to go. That it was his only chance to have a life."

He wished he could stop there, but he'd promised himself he would tell them everything. "I know he always watched out for us. Even after he left. He'd leave money in my room sometimes, but I knew where it came from, so I couldn't keep it."

"You never told me any of this!" Ana shot to her feet. "You always pretended to miss him as much as the rest of us."

"I *did* miss him." He wanted to pull her into a hug, but he knew better than to get close when she was this upset. She needed space. "I couldn't tell you. I didn't want you to think of him like that." He'd figured if they didn't know where Andres had gone they could at least imagine better possibilities for him—that he'd crossed the border into the United States to find his dreams, maybe. Mateo wished he hadn't known the truth.

"When I moved to the States, I wrote him off. I didn't want to know what had happened to him." He leaned over the coffee table to address his mom. "But when Ana told me you got the letter, I called in a few favors with Gutierrez."

"You found him?" his mother asked, breathless. "You found Andres?"

Mateo pushed out of the chair and went to kneel in front of her. His throat tightened. Tears burned. He took both of her hands in his, holding them tightly. "Andres is gone." Heartbreak cracked his voice. "He's dead."

"What?" Ana crumbled back to the couch.

"Dead. Andres." His mom moaned the name. "My boy…"

Mateo tightened his hold on her trembling hands. "Gutierrez told me that Andres turned a while ago. He started working as an informant for the police. Someone found out and they killed him. I don't know where he died. Or how. I only know he's gone."

His mom started to collapse, weeping, but he caught her in his arms and held her up.

Next to them his sister pushed to her feet, wobbling. Without a word, she disappeared into the hallway.

"Wait, Ana," he called. Mateo pulled away from his mom and started to rock to his feet, but she rested her hands on his shoulders.

"Let her go, *mijo*," she said between sobs. "You know Ana. She needs to be alone. She will come back when she's ready."

Mateo slumped on the couch next to her. "I'm sorry. I'm sorry I let you wonder all these years. I thought it was better."

"You were only a boy." His mom put her hands on his face and drew it closer to hers. Sorrow blanketed her features. "My boy," she murmured. "What a big burden for you to carry all that time."

"He was only a kid, too." The cartels targeted kids like Andres, kids who lived in poverty, who were just trying to survive. "I should've told you a long time ago." Instead of avoiding reality. "But I didn't want to break your heart."

"You never stop grieving for your child." His mom picked up the picture and studied it. "I've grieved every day since he left." She paused, taking in measured breaths that seemed to calm her. "But I always knew he was good. And he knew it, too. He made it right at the end, Mateo. It's never too late to make it right."

He wanted to believe that, but it was too late to tell Andres anything. He couldn't tell him he was sorry he'd given up on him. He couldn't tell him he was sorry that he'd denied even ever having a brother. He couldn't tell him he was sorry he'd hated him.

"I always knew he would come back to us." His mom pressed the picture against her heart. "He did what was right so he could come back to us. And now he has. He will always be part of our family."

His mom had always amazed him, but never more so than now. Mateo put his arms around her, finally letting himself cry. Andres may have been a lost cause in his eyes, but she still hadn't given up, even after all of these years. She had so much faith. Love wouldn't let her give up.

That was the kind of person he wanted to be.

One of the best things about owning a café was that she got to sit with her friends and have a leisurely brunch at least once a week. Typically, Thursdays were Everly's slowest days, so her friends had developed a habit of coming in to keep her company.

She looked around the table. It was a rare treat to have everyone there, but since word had gotten out that their days of gathering in the café were numbered, they had all made it. Darla, Jessa, Naomi, Kate, and Charity all sat around the table, finishing their cinnamon rolls and the special hazelnut coffee she'd made while they chatted about Kate's upcoming wedding.

Over the last few days, Everly had made an effort to face the impending changes in her life head on, which meant opening her hands to let go of the café and everything it had meant to her. She'd even called that diner Gus had mentioned, and she had an interview next week. But moments like this still made her eyes all misty. Even if she saved enough money to buy some land and start over, it wouldn't be the same as sitting here in this cozy old house-turned-restaurant.

The conversation hit a lull and Jessa clanked a spoon against her coffee mug. "Before we finish our breakfast and go on with our days, I kind of have an announcement to make."

Judging from Naomi's squeal, her sister-in-law already knew what it was. She wasn't the only one. Everly almost laughed. All of the women around her were gasping and clasping hands and tearing up. Jessa didn't need to make a formal announcement.

"As you all know we've been trying IVF..." Her smile bloomed into a beautiful expression of joy. "And...we found out about a month ago that we're having babies!"

"*Babies?*" On the other side of the table, Charity frowned. "As in more than one?"

Jessa nodded, tears streaming down her cheeks. "Triplets."

Murmurs of excited astonishment went around the room. Everly jumped to her feet along with everyone else, waiting for her turn to hug the stuffing out of Jessa. Three babies! Three little miniature Lance and Jessas running around? "Oh my God! You guys are going to be the cutest family!" She threw her arms around her friend, but then eased up so she wouldn't hurt the babies. "And everything is fine? The babies are all healthy?"

"So far." Jessa rested a hand over her tummy and grinned through her tears. "I'm due in May, but triplets usually come early." She shook her head as though she still couldn't believe it. "Triplets. Wow. Guess it's a good thing I have big hips, huh?"

Everly laughed. "You're going to be an incredible mom."

Exactly the kind of mom every child deserved. "And even though I won't have a restaurant, I'll still bring you lots of meals." At least a few a week so she would have an excuse to go over and hold those babies. The thought made it a little easier to think about leaving the café. As long as she had a kitchen, she could still cook. She could still feed people. Maybe she could still even teach a few classes. Not in Darla's small kitchen, but maybe when she found a place of her own. "Oh! And we'll have to plan a shower for you. A huge party—"

The door opened, bringing a momentary lull in the celebration. Everly gave Jessa one last hug, and then quickly went to greet the two women who had walked in.

"Hi there—" *Oh.* "I know you." It was the woman from the Italian restaurant. Mateo's little sister. "Ana Sofia."

She grinned. "And you're Everly."

"Florencia and Ana!" Naomi dodged tables and chairs to hurry over. "Hi! So glad you could make it." She put her arm around Everly. "Flo and Ana are staying at the Hidden Gem for their last few days in Topaz Falls. This morning I was raving about the café while they were enjoying their coffee and I told them it was the perfect place to come for lunch."

"Wow." The shock of seeing Ana face to face again finally started to subside. "Great. It's so nice to officially meet you both."

"Nice to meet you, too." Everly hadn't realized how friendly Ana's smile was. That could've been because she'd left the restaurant too fast to notice anything at all. But seeing her now, she could tell the woman had Mateo's same wit and mischievous nature. And Florencia...She was every bit as lovely as she'd looked in those pictures. Everly could hardly believe she was a day over forty. "What are you two doing in town?"

Some of the light in Ana's eyes faded. "Just here for a visit," she said quickly. Her wavering smile hinted at pain. Mateo had told them about his brother. He must've. Everly wanted to hug Ana, to tell her she was sorry for her loss, but she couldn't. Not in front of all these people.

"You know my son Mateo?" Florencia asked.

Everly glanced at Naomi. Her friend must have neglected to share anything about her history with Mateo.

"She definitely knows Mateo," Ana answered for her. Those dark eyes sparkled again as she leaned closer to her mom. "I think Mateo would like to know her better."

Recognition sparked in Flo's eyes. "Everly! The girl with the ducks. He has talked about you."

"That's because he likes her," Ana said teasingly.

Everly felt her cheeks flame. "I don't know about that." She turned and waved them over to the tables she'd pulled together for their brunch. "Why don't you both come and sit down? I'll bring you menus, and you can choose whatever you'd like. On the house."

She hurried away to clear more space at the table. It would probably be best if they didn't talk about Mateo. Her heart already beat a little faster just thinking about him.

She hadn't seen him for a few days, not since she'd left him at her house to stay at Darla's. Dev had been reassigned as her official shadow when she went out to care for the animals on the farm. She would never admit it to anyone else, but she missed seeing Mateo. Missed his sly grin and his humor and his energy.

"I don't think we need menus," Ana said, pulling out a chair at the end of the table for her mom. "We were told you have the best cinnamon rolls in the entire world."

"And the egg white frittata," Naomi added.

"Definitely," Darla agreed, greeting the women with a warm smile. "Make sure you put the extra frosting on those rolls."

"That all sounds perfect." Ana sat in a chair next to her mom.

"Coming right up." Everly linked arms with Naomi and pulled her back to the kitchen with her. "Does Mateo know you told them to come here?" She prepped the pan for the frittatas and turned on the oven so she could reheat the cinnamon rolls.

"Nope." Her friend smirked. "But I wish I could see his face when he finds out." Naomi pulled out two plates for her. "Wait until his mom hears he kicked you off the farm."

"I don't want them to find out. Not unless he tells them." The last thing she wanted to do was get Mateo in trouble with his mom.

"Fine." Naomi pouted while they prepped the food, but she knew her friend would respect her wishes. When the frittata was steaming and the cinnamon rolls were dripping with frosting, they brought out the plates and set them in front of Flo and Ana.

Mateo's sister stared down at her plate with a look of awe. "That's the biggest cinnamon roll I've ever seen."

"And smell the herbs in these eggs." Flo shook out a napkin and smoothed it across her lap.

"Fresh basil and thyme from the garden." Everly sat down next to them, marveling at how much Mateo looked like his mom.

"Delicious." Flo enjoyed a few bites while Everly's friends traded looks. Naomi must've quietly spread the word that they weren't allowed to talk about the farm. With that topic off limits, no one seemed to know what to say.

"How did you make this frosting?" Ana asked, wiping a smear off her chin. "It's soooo good."

"I always add a little mascarpone cheese." She never minded revealing her baking secrets.

"I can't believe Mateo hadn't brought me here yet." His sister took another bite and closed her eyes, chewing slowly.

"I can't imagine why," Charity said innocently.

Everly gave a subtle shake of her head. "How long will you two be in town?" she asked, steering the conversation away from the farm.

"Only until Monday," Flo said. "It will be sad to leave after staying at the Hidden Gem and meeting all of Mateo's wonderful friends. He has told me a lot about you." She patted Everly's hand. Not Naomi or Jessa's. Only Everly's. All eyes in the room seemed to land on her, including Ana's.

Everly simply smiled at Mateo's mom, wondering how high Hilda had turned up the thermostat that morning.

"You know, it's funny." Darla focused on Everly as she spoke. "Mateo's a *friend* but no one seems to know much about him. Do you have any fun stories to tell? From when he was growing up?"

"Oh, there are so many." Flo sent down her fork.

"So many," Ana echoed, looking like she'd be all too pleased to share them in an effort to embarrass him.

"I will tell you one of my favorites," his mom said, not giving his sister a chance to expand. "It was Christmas, when he was eleven."

"Of course you're telling that one." Ana shook her head. "Come on, Mom. It's not even embarrassing."

Flo ignored her daughter. "We didn't have money. Those were hard times. Mateo knew I couldn't buy presents, but he was determined to have something under the tree."

"He *loves* Christmas," Ana informed them.

For some reason that came as a surprise. Everly wouldn't have guessed that holidays mattered much to him.

"Anyway," Flo went on. "On the morning of Christmas Eve, I walked into his bedroom and all of his furniture was gone. His bed and his dresser. The few toys he had gotten over the years." She laughed softly. "Even his pillows and blankets."

The room had silenced. No one ate. No one seemed to breathe. At least, Everly wasn't breathing. Flo didn't have to finish the story. She already knew what he'd done.

"He'd gone to the market," his mom said, dabbing her eyes with a napkin. "And he'd sold everything he had in his room so he could buy presents."

"He wrapped all of the gifts in old newspapers and hid them in the closet." Even Ana had gotten a little misty-eyed.

Everly had gone way past misty-eyed. Tears rolled down her cheeks and she was powerless to stop them. Powerless to stop that surge of blind love for him, for how he cared for the people he loved. Her heart may have been teetering on the edge before, but that story gave it a final push.

"I still have that scarf he bought me," Flo said. "I hang it on my wall right next to his picture."

"I still have the bracelet, too." Ana held out her wrist, showing off a simple beaded leather band.

The table had turned into a chorus line of sniffles. It seemed even Charity wasn't immune.

"He's a good boy," his mom said fondly.

No one argued with that.

Chapter Twenty

If he could've known how much it would change things, Mateo would've told his mom about Andres a long time ago.

He parked in front of the Hidden Gem Inn, still fired up about the stellar training session he'd had with Amigo that morning. The last few days, everything had seemed different. He felt lighter. Spending time with his mom, reminiscing, and living in the truth had somehow freed up a space inside of him, giving him a capacity for more. More understanding, more contentment, more hope that he hadn't screwed things up beyond repair.

His mom had forgiven him for living a lie. They'd talked a lot about Andres, about what he'd meant to them, and she insisted that she would be the one to tell his older sisters the news when she arrived back in Mexico. But Ana still wouldn't even talk to Mateo. She'd avoided him, opting to read or watch a movie instead whenever he came by. That had to stop. Today.

He pushed out of the truck and strode up the sidewalk
to the Hidden Gem's quaint front porch. Ana couldn't avoid
him forever. He wouldn't let her.

Prepared to tell her so, he bounded up the steps but
stopped when he saw the piece of paper taped to the door.

Hi Mateo—Naomi told us we had to go to the café for
lunch. (And a cinnamon roll. You know how I feel about
pastries.) We were going to wait for you, but we got hungry. Meet us there? Love, A

Mateo crumpled the note in his fist. Well, there went his plan
to take Ana and his mom to the highway diner that was located outside of town for a quiet lunch away from the dirty
looks and muttered insults he'd gotten lately courtesy of random strangers around town.

He lumbered away from the Hidden Gem's main entrance
and climbed back into his truck. Mom and Ana knew nothing about the farm or his plans to develop it. At least they
hadn't known yesterday. They likely knew now, seeing as
how he'd heard that had been the topic of conversation at the
café lately.

He hadn't been anywhere near Everly since the night he'd
called out the search party. He had this idea that when he finally did talk to her, he'd have everything figured out. He'd
be sure that what he had to offer her would be enough—
everything she deserved. But mostly he'd avoided her because he didn't want to watch her walk out on him again. He
couldn't. Then he'd lose hope that she'd see the change in
him. Hope was all he could grasp at right now.

The short drive over to the café didn't boost his confidence. Neither did the sight of the cars in the parking lot—

looked like Darla's, Jessa's, Charity's, Naomi's, his sister's rental, and a few others he didn't recognize. Other members of the book club, most likely, and he was most definitely still on their shit list.

This ought to be fun. He might've turned the truck around and peeled out of there if he didn't want to see Everly so badly. It was time. He might not have things figured out, but everything in him seemed to hum at the prospect of seeing her. There were no doubts about how much he wanted her. He could be what she needed. He *would* be. And if he had to face the fury of her friends, so be it.

The dining room silenced when he walked in, but the only thing he saw was Everly, sitting with his mom and his sister, the three of them smiling like they were old friends. He couldn't take his eyes off of her. She always looked so radiant, the brightest spot in any room.

"You finally made it." His sister patted the empty chair next to her. Mateo walked over feeling the glares of Everly's friends, but he didn't acknowledge them. He kept his eyes on her. Only on her. He loved her hair pulled back that way, loose and carefree. Loved her pink-tinged cheeks and the flicker of passion in her eyes. "Hey," he said, everything in him begging for another kiss.

"Hi." She didn't look away, either. The air between them seemed charged with unspoken words. "Are you hungry?" She stood abruptly. "I could get you something to eat."

He almost said no, but if she got him something to eat, maybe he could talk to her alone. Right now, all he wanted to do was talk to her alone. "Actually, a cinnamon roll would be great."

Everly nodded and tucked some of the stray hair that had escaped her ponytail behind her ear.

He let her get partway across the room and then stood up. "I think I'll give you a hand."

Ana raised her eyebrows at their mother, and Mateo just smiled as he walked away. His sister could read him like no one else. She'd picked up on his feelings at the restaurant weeks ago, before he would even acknowledge them himself.

When he got to the kitchen, Everly appeared rushed. She'd already pulled a tray of cinnamon rolls out of the refrigerator. "I'll heat it up and frost it. It'll only take a few minutes."

A few minutes. That was all she had to give him. And he'd make every one of them count. "I'm surprised your friends didn't launch an offensive when I walked in."

"Oh. They wouldn't." She busied herself with doing a few dishes that sat in the sink. "And no one said anything to your mom and sister about the farm. I don't want you to think we were conspiring against you."

"That's good to know." Mateo grabbed a towel and dried the clean pan she'd set on the counter. "I told them about Andres."

Everly's hands froze. "I wondered." She set down the pan she'd been holding in the sink, and turned to face him. "How'd it go?"

"It was...hard. But good. Freeing." Jesus, he'd spent all this time thinking about what to say and now it was like he'd forgotten how to use words. "It's changed things for me. I know we don't have time to talk right now with everyone else here, but I'd like to tell you about it." When it was only the two of them. When he could sit across the table from her and focus on everything he wanted to say. "Maybe we could hang out sometime."

"Oh. Sure." Everly whirled back to the sink and finished washing the pan. "We can hang out sometime. Probably after the big farewell on Saturday. Things are pretty busy right now getting ready for that."

"Yeah, okay." Was she putting him off? Was this one of those times when she'd say *sure, let's get together* and it would never happen? He couldn't let it be. "I'll give you a call next week so we can set something up." And if she didn't call him back, he'd keep calling.

Her hands stilled. "You're not coming to the farewell?" She looked at him over her shoulder.

"I thought it was best if I didn't." Everyone knew he was the reason for the farewell. "I doubt anyone wants me there."

"I do." One corner of her mouth rose in a shy smile, much like the one she'd flashed when he'd spoken to her in Spanish.

There was his glimpse of hope. "Then I'll be there." Even if the crowd wanted to stone him. He'd be there.

Mateo wolfed down his cinnamon roll without saying one damn word. He knew when to be quiet.

Everly's friends were being polite enough to his family—asking Ana questions about school, and showing a genuine interest in his mother's recipes, but they completely iced him out with their frosty stares. All of them except for Everly, who was more gracious than he deserved.

Mercifully, his mom finally reached over and patted his hand, telling him she was ready to go. Her smile had grown tired. They bid everyone a quick good-bye—him without making eye contact with anyone—and Everly walked them to the door.

"I'm so sorry to run out like this," his mom said to Everly. "I always get tired in the afternoon."

"It's the altitude," Mateo said, giving his mom a stern look. "She doesn't drink enough water. It happens every time she comes for a visit."

"It got me, too, when I first moved here." Everly hurried to the small refrigerator by the cash register and pulled out a water bottle. "Drinking water does help." She handed it to his mom. "And a nap always helped, too."

"Thank you." Mateo's mom hugged Everly. "It was so wonderful to meet you. I hope we will see more of you." She smiled at Mateo, not bothering to disguise her approval.

"I might see more of you tomorrow when I come for another cinnamon roll," Ana said. "I'd have to agree with Naomi. They're the best cinnamon rolls in the entire world."

"Thank you." Everly beamed. "You're welcome to come back anytime." Right as she said it, her bright smile dimmed. "I guess I should start cleaning up. Hope you all have a great afternoon."

She ducked away before Mateo could get a good look at her face, but he'd heard the sadness in her voice. Mom and Ana couldn't come back to the café anytime. The next time they were in town there would be no café. Not if he signed the contract that had been sitting in his inbox for two days. He'd read it multiple times, sent it to a lawyer Levi knew. Everything about it appeared rock solid—a great investment, the lawyer had said.

And yet Mateo hadn't signed it.

He got into his truck and followed Ana and their mother back to the Hidden Gem. Once they arrived, he walked them to the door. "I thought we could take a walk down by the river while Mom goes in to rest," he said to his sister.

Ana narrowed her eyes with suspicion, as though she

knew he had an ulterior motive, but after a second she shrugged. "Sure. I could use a walk."

Once they got their mother situated in her room, he and Ana made their way around to the back of the property. The wide river flowed at the edge of the expansive lawn, bordering the mountain on the other side. With the sun shining, the cloudless sky radiated an unfathomable blue.

"It's beautiful here," Ana said as they walked along the riverbank side by side. "I can see why you're finally putting down some roots."

"It's actually starting to feel like home." He hadn't said that about any place he'd lived since he'd left Mexico. Not even Gunner's place. He'd been so aware that it didn't belong to him, that he was simply passing through on his way somewhere else. But that didn't feel true here.

They walked in silence for a few minutes until they reached a small wooden bench at the bend in the river.

"I'm guessing you didn't invite me to go on a walk so we could talk about the scenery." Ana took a seat, looking up at him expectantly.

Busted. He sat down next to her. "I wanted to talk about Andres. You haven't said much since I told you the news." He'd been giving her space, but she would be accompanying their mom back to Mexico soon, and he couldn't let her go without knowing she was okay. "I just wanted to know what you think about it all. How you're handling it."

Ana stared across the river. "I'm sad. I hate to think about his life ending that way." A guilty look diverted her gaze back to him. "But when I really thought about it, I realized I didn't know him the way you did. I guess I looked at you the way you had looked at him. As the big brother. The protector. The dad we lost." She stared down at her hands. "I was so young when he left. And it didn't matter to me as much because I still had you."

"Aw. Sis." He nudged her shoulder, knowing she wouldn't want him to make a big deal out of the admission. "So you're not mad at me? For keeping it from you?"

"Of course I'm mad at you." Her smile softened the sentiment. "But I get why you didn't say anything."

"Really?"

"Sure." She turned to him, her expression somber. "You and I are a lot alike, Mateo. Obviously. I haven't talked about Andres because I don't want to think about it. We spent our whole childhood in survival mode. It's easier to survive when you don't let things get to you."

"Yeah, well, I guess I'm starting to figure out survival mode isn't enough." It had been until he met Everly, until she'd made him want more.

Ana leaned her head on his shoulder in a rare display of affection. "It gets lonely trying to survive."

He hadn't thought of it that way, but that was exactly how he'd felt for years—isolated, restless, filling his life with women and parties and travels and events, but never really connecting with anything. "Are you lonely, sis?"

"It's gotten better since I went to school. I've made some really good friends up there."

"Then you need to go back." He used his best dad tone.

"I know I do. Now that Mamá knows about Andres, I will. As soon as I get her back home and settled." Ana teased him with a smirk. "I would ask if you're lonely, but I saw Everly's face light up when you walked into the café earlier. I think she likes you."

"I like her, too." Instead of his heart picking up like it usually did when he thought about Everly, it felt weighted. Dull.

"Then I don't understand. Why aren't you two together?" his sister demanded. "She's amazing. Such a warm person. And she makes some freaking delicious pastries."

"Yeah. I think she's pretty much the best woman I've ever met."

Ana widened those sharp dark eyes and raised her hands, demanding an explanation.

"Things got complicated because I bought the land she leases. That's the investment I told you about. I've been talking to the ski resort about building some condos there."

"On Everly's land?" His sister pushed off the bench and stared down at him. "What'll happen to the farm? To her café?"

"It's so run-down. It would take too much to fix it up." All of those arguments had weakened. "Her lease is up soon, and I told her I wouldn't renew it."

"You're *forcing* her out?"

Mateo stood, too. "It was supposed to be an investment property. Something that would give our family long-term security." He paced away from his sister and stared at the swirling river. "I don't know how much longer I'll be able to compete. I wanted to make sure we were set. All of us."

"You *wanted* to." Ana moved in front of him. "But now you're not so sure."

"No. Now I'm not so sure." He'd been holding onto the investment idea so tightly, looking at it as a business decision instead of a personal one. But he couldn't keep denying that it was intensely personal to Everly. "I just keep thinking about Mamá." He slumped back to the bench. "Do you remember how she would always eat last? Sometimes there was nothing left. And she would tell us she wasn't hungry or that she'd eaten earlier."

Ana sighed, nodding. "But she couldn't have eaten earlier because there was never any food."

"Right." To this day, he still wondered if that's why she was so small. All those years of malnourishment while she tried to provide what her kids needed. "I don't want her to have to worry about anything. Ever again. I don't want any of us to worry." That was why he hadn't gone and talked to Blake yet. That was why he'd let the contract sit in his in-box.

"Mateo..." Ana sat back down next to him. "Even though we were poor, we had a good life. We had a lot of love." She rested her hand on his forearm. "I know I didn't take the brunt of feeling responsible for everyone the way you did. But I think you need to let it go. I only have a few years left in school, and I'll get a job. I'll be successful. I can help, too." Determination lit her eyes. "Mamá wouldn't want you to give up a chance to pursue a life with someone who could love you. None of us want you to do that."

"What if she doesn't stay?" What if she decided he wasn't worth sticking around for? He might be on the road to forgiving his brother, but those questions had been part of his life for so long, driving the way he lived, the way he approached every possible relationship. "What if she leaves me and I gave up everything for her?"

"That can't matter." Ana smiled at him as though willing him to be brave. "If you really care about her, you have to do what's best for her, even if it hurts you. Even if it means you give up everything."

Chapter Twenty-One

If there was one thing her friends knew how to do, it was throw a party. Everly snuck away from the dance floor that had been set up underneath a large white canopy tent on her driveway.

For the last hour, she'd been dancing a lively two-step, switching between dancing with Gus and Charlie. They might both have arthritis but they were still surprisingly agile on the dance floor. Gus had even dipped her twice, wearing a sly grin directed at Charlie.

But, wow, her legs ached from the dancing, the mingling, the walking between the animal pens—where all of the kids had gathered—and the food tent—where all of the men seemed to be hanging out—and the gardens, where enthusiasts *oohh*ed and *ahh*ed over her meticulously arranged plots.

And don't get her started on the good old-fashioned kissing booth Charity had set up that was currently being manned by Ty. The line of women wanting to kiss a rodeo star wound all the way around the food tent.

It seemed like the whole town had shown up and then some. People had come from as far away as Glenwood Springs, thanks to Darla's entrepreneur network. In the last three hours, Everly had been surrounded and uplifted and inspired by everyone she loved the most... well, almost everyone.

Making her way back to the chicken yard, she scanned the many groups of people talking and laughing and enjoying some of Darla's finest wines. Everly waved and smiled the way she had all afternoon, but after a full scan of the property her hope deflated. Mateo hadn't come. Even after she'd asked him to. It was true that her friends hadn't been overly welcoming to him at the café the other day, but still. He'd said he would be there.

"What a great party." Kenna met Everly at the fence. She looked adorable in a long knit dress and jean jacket, but the best part about her ensemble was her smile. It seemed bigger and brighter than it had when Everly had dropped by her house.

"This is the best party!" Jake launched himself into Everly's waist and gave her a squeeze. "Mom said maybe we can have chickens someday," he announced, glancing at his mom for assurance.

Kenna's wide eyes seemed a little spooked, if you asked Everly.

"Maybe someday," the woman said noncommittally. "Like in twenty years when you have your own house," she muttered so only Everly could hear.

Everly laughed. "Chickens are a lot more work than you think, buddy, but I'll tell you what. I'll talk to my friends Jessa and Lance about letting you go out to visit the chickens at their place once we move them." Thankfully her friends had offered to let Everly board the animals at the ranch. She'd have to build an enclosure, but at least she wouldn't have to give them up. As ridiculous as it sounded, she loved her animals like they were her children.

"Why are you moving the chickens?" Benny asked, hiding behind his mom's leg.

"We talked about this, sweetie," Kenna said gently. "Miss Everly is moving to a new house soon."

"It's not gonna be as cool as the farm," Jake grumbled.

"Jake!" Obvious embarrassment flooded Kenna's fair cheeks.

"It's okay." Everly gave her arm a squeeze. "That's true. There aren't many houses as cool as the farm. I'm going to miss it, too."

"Then why are you moving?" the boy asked, clearly confused.

"Why don't you go play with the chickens again?" Kenna prodded Jake and Benny toward the gate. "We have to go in a few minutes so make sure you get all of your wiggles out."

"Okay! Get out, wiggles!" The boys took off, flapping their arms as if they were wings.

"I'm sorry about that." Kenna shook her head. "I do try to teach them polite manners. I swear."

Everly waved it off. "They are polite. God, they're such sweet boys. It's refreshing, actually. How honest kids are sometimes." Her smile faded as she glanced at her cozy little farmhouse behind them. "It's funny. When I was a kid I used to dream about living in a huge castle and having servants and fancy dinners and pretty dresses."

"Me too," Kenna said with a humorless laugh. "It was all

those fairy tales we read. The ones that tricked us into thinking Prince Charming really existed."

"Exactly." Oh, how quickly she'd learned Prince Charming was a myth. The whole thing was a myth, actually. That money and princes and pretty things brought happiness and fulfillment. "Who needs Prince Charming anyway?" Everly gazed over at her little house. "I'd rather have something real." Like a damaged but well-meaning lover who made her laugh and dance. And a tiny house surrounded by stunning mountains. "I never thought my dream home would turn into an old two-bedroom farmhouse with peeling paint and flickering lights and toilets that run."

"I'm sorry, Everly." Her friend uttered a helpless sigh. "After everything you do for others, it seems so wrong that this is happening."

"It's okay." For the first time, those words felt true. She watched little Jake and Benny giggle, and the sheer joy on their faces brought a smile. "Over the last few weeks, I've realized it's not necessarily the place that matters. It's the people. And they're not going anywhere." Her book club friends. Charlie and Gus and Hector. Kenna and the boys. And Mateo. Even Mateo. Especially Mateo. She searched for him again, still hoping.

"I wanted to thank you again for bringing those dinners," Kenna said, emotion thick in her voice. "And for letting me fall apart in front of you. I try to hold it together, but you caught me in a weak moment."

"Anytime." She turned fully to her friend, wondering again if she had enough people in her life who mattered, who could get her through. "I know you want to be strong for your boys, but you need a place where it's okay to fall apart, too." She needed a community that could hold her up and help her put the pieces back together. And Everly knew just the people. "In fact, I was talking to some of my book club friends, and we'd all love it if you could join us sometime."

"Really?" Her friend's eyes misted.

"Definitely. I can't tell you how much being a part of it has helped me heal."

"It gives me hope to hear you say that," Kenna murmured. "That you've healed."

"I have." She hadn't realized it until she'd seen Mateo at the café when his mom and sister had come the other morning. But she'd healed enough to love again. At some point it had happened: her heart had chosen him. Maybe at first because he was fun and different and so charismatic, but her feelings had grown deeper when she saw how he took care of the people he loved. How loyal he was to them. That morning, she hadn't been able to fight it anymore. When he'd followed her back to the kitchen, longing had overtaken her. All she'd wanted him to do was pull her against his body and kiss her again. At first it seemed like he'd wanted to, but something had held him back.

"Book club sounds great," Kenna said, watching the boys play. "I could definitely use some adult time. Don't get me wrong, I love my kids—and my students at school—but they can't exactly understand what I'm going through."

"Then it's settled." Shoving aside thoughts of Mateo, Everly put her arm around Kenna's shoulders and directed her toward the food tent, where she knew Darla would welcome her with open arms. "Let me introduce you to a few people while the boys play."

They ambled over to where the air smelled like delicious, tangy barbecue. Darla had hired the food truck from Denver she'd used at a few of her events at the Chocolate Therapist.

"There you are!" Darla flew over to them, as animated as usual. "I've been looking everywhere for you. There's a head chef from a Vail restaurant here. He said he would be very interested in investing in another locally grown food source, like a sustainable farm, perhaps."

Panic fizzled up Everly's throat. "I'm not sure I'm ready for an investor." She loved the simplicity of her farm, of being her own boss, of growing what she wanted when she wanted and deciding what to put on her own menu. "I don't think I would ever go commercial."

"Just talk to him," Darla insisted. "He's sitting right over there with the managers of his restaurant." She pointed to a table where a good-looking man sat with two older women. "I told him I'd send you over. You don't have to sign a contract or anything. But this could be huge if you wanted to start up a business somewhere else."

"All right. Fine." She could at least hear the man out. But first…"Darla, do you know Kenna?"

"We haven't been formally introduced, but you're joining our book club, right?"

Kenna smiled bravely. "I'm thinking about it."

"You totally should. We'd love to have you. We have the best snacks. And wine, of course," Darla said proudly. "While Everly goes and talks to the chef, I'll introduce you to the rest of our friends." The two of them walked away.

Everly would've much rather gone with them, but instead she made her way over to the table Darla had pointed out. If she had to start over again, she might as well open herself to any and all possibilities.

Mateo had to talk to Blake Wilder.

Originally, he'd planned to wait until Monday, until Mom

and Ana were on their way to the airport, but after what he'd seen, he couldn't wait anymore.

It had only been a half hour since he'd struggled to find a parking place near the café. He'd finally ended up all the way down the street. From there, he'd kept to the outskirts of Everly's event, watching all of these people come together to rally for her. He'd never seen anything like it, and as he stood there on the outside looking in, he realized this wasn't where he wanted to be. On the outside. He wanted to be right there. Standing with her. But he hadn't earned the right.

From his hidden spot behind the food tent, he'd watched Everly walk over to a table and sit down across from some polished-looking man and two other women who didn't seem to be nearly as interested. The guy, though? He clearly checked Everly out as they shook hands.

Mateo fought the urge to go over there and interrupt. He couldn't talk to her. Not until he'd made everything official. Not until he told Blake their deal was off. He had to do it now. Before he lost his chance with her for good.

Mateo tore away from the tent and jogged along the driveway. Blake likely wouldn't be working on a Saturday evening, but he'd described where he'd built his house near the lodge. It shouldn't be too hard to find. He'd look for the biggest and most pretentious palace on the street.

When he reached the sidewalk, he went to turn but stopped cold. Dev and Charity stood talking near Dev's cruiser, which just happened to be parked in front of Mateo's truck. Perfect. He'd never get out of here now. Not without an interrogation from Charity, at least. "Hey," he said, casually walking past.

As expected, Charity glared at him. "What're you doing here, Mateo?"

"Actually, I was just on my way out." He didn't look at her.

"Already?" Dev sauntered over, a paper bowl full of barbecued meat in his hands. "Didn't you just get here? Thought I saw your truck pull up right before I did."

"Uh, yeah." He dug the key remote out of his pocket and unlocked the doors. "I haven't been here long, but I have to go." As in, he had no time for small talk.

"Have you tried the barbecue yet?" Dev shoveled in a bite. "It's pretty good. Darla had it brought in all the way from Denver."

"I don't have time to try it." He tried to slip past, but Charity blocked his path.

"What's the matter? You afraid to face everyone now that they all know about your condo resort?"

Yeah, maybe he could stick around a few minutes to defend himself. "No, I'm not afraid to face everyone. I'm going to tell Blake Wilder our deal is off. Okay?"

Charity sized him up as though deciding if she believed him. "Really?"

"Really. I can't do it. I can't take this away from her." Didn't matter if Everly gave him another chance or not. He couldn't take something she loved so much.

Charity still eyed him with suspicion. "So you're going to build the resort but keep the farm, too?"

"I can't. Blake made it pretty clear he wouldn't move forward unless I agreed to demolish the farm." Besides that, Everly had wanted to expand. There wouldn't be room for both. "So no condo resort."

"Oh my God, Mateo!" Charity hugged him. "I knew you weren't a complete jackass."

"Thanks?" He awkwardly patted her back.

She pulled away. "Well, what're you waiting for? Go tell Blake."

Mateo looked back to where Everly sat, still talking to the suit. "Do you think I should tell her first?"

"No," Charity said. "You can't tell her until it's a done deal."

Dev nodded, munching on his barbecued meat. "Blake Wilder's not gonna let that go easily. You'd best break the news to him before you get Everly all excited."

"Right." If he went now, he could get back and catch her after everyone else left. Then it would just be him and her and he could say the things he hadn't been able to put into words before.

He headed to the truck. "Don't worry about doing the rounds with Everly tonight," he called to Dev. "I'll be back in time." He'd make sure.

"Roger that. I doubt we have to worry anyway. With all the noise and people around, I'd guess that cat is long gone."

He still wouldn't take any chances. "I'll be back," he said again, climbing into the driver's seat. "Don't tell her. I want it to be a surprise." He wanted her to hear it from him. He wanted to tell her how much he cared about her. How much she'd changed things for him.

He rehearsed what he'd say to her during the forty-minute drive all the way up the winding mountains, past the ski lodge, and on to where Blake had said his house sat.

It was the only structure on the street. Mateo wouldn't call it a home. It was more like an ultramodern ski chalet— all concrete and glass and wooden beams fit together in squared, clean lines.

He jumped out of the truck and took long purposeful strides up to the massive front door. If he wanted to be back in time to help Everly with the animals, he had to make this quick. The drive had taken him much longer than he'd thought.

While the doorbell chimed, Mateo tapped his foot impatiently.

Finally, Blake answered.

"Mateo." The man stepped out onto the stamped concrete veranda. "This is a surprise."

"I just came to tell you I'm keeping the farm." He didn't have time to sugarcoat it.

"Excuse me?" Blake almost looked amused.

"I'm not developing the land," Mateo said more slowly. "I decided to renew Everly's lease. Which means the farm stays."

Blake seemed to get the idea this wasn't a joke. "We had a verbal agreement."

"I never committed to anything. I never signed the contract." And he knew his rights. "We talked about it. I looked over your proposal. And I decided I don't want to move forward."

"Because of a *woman*?" Blake looked past him as if he needed time to think. "What can I do to change your mind?" His sharklike eyes fixed on Mateo's face. "You want a higher percentage? I can make that happen. I can make anything happen. Tell me what it'll take."

Well, damn. Anything? That could amount to a hell of a lot of money. His conviction wavered. Was he crazy for giving up on an opportunity like this?

Yep. He totally was. He was crazy. And he might've been conflicted on the money part, because... man, that was a lot of money to turn his back on. But he wasn't conflicted about his feelings for Everly.

"It doesn't matter what you offer me," he said firmly. "The deal is off."

Chapter Twenty-Two

Everly walked across the meadow in front of the farm-house, picking up stray cups and plates and napkins. Her friends had taken care of most of the cleanup, but as soon as the sun had started to set, she sent them all on their way.

Jessa had practically fallen asleep at a table when she thought no one was looking. Naomi had already spent hours away from her sweet family setting up and working on all of the details in the days leading up to the farewell. Kate and Jaden had to leave for a weekend trip to visit her parents. And Darla...well, she would've stayed, but truthfully, Everly had wanted to be alone for a while.

In another month, she'd have to give up her evening walks on the farm. Staring out at the rolling hills and soft grass in the meadows, it was impossible for her to imagine what it would look like with a bunch of condos stacked everywhere. But she didn't have to think about that. Not tonight, anyway. She could enjoy the stillness, the fading light of the sunset, the calming breeze.

Breathing it all in, Everly let herself into the chicken yard and shooed the hens and ducks into the coop for the night. Surprisingly, Dev hadn't shown up to escort her around this evening, which was just as well. She'd loved the party, but she was all chatted out.

"Good night, chicks." She locked up the coop and hiked around the back of the property to the goat pens. "Uh-oh." The gate stood wide open, and Tilda, Honey, Trunchbull, and Wormwood were nowhere to be seen. That wasn't good. So many people had been in and out of there during the evening; she should've checked on them earlier.

"Tilda! Honey!" Surely those two would hear her and come running. She scanned the hill, the scrub oak, the stand of aspen trees farther to the west, but there was nothing. They must've wandered off in search of greener grasses to munch. "Come on, you hooligans," she called, trudging up the hill. They couldn't have gotten too far.

When she reached the top, a faint bleat quickened her steps. "Tilda?" She jogged around the gnarly bushes, peering over the tops of them, her heart beating faster. Maybe she should've brought the rifle.

Another bleat came louder, then another. Everly broke through the scrub oak into a clearing. All four goats ran at her, sailing right on past, headed for home.

Relief pounded in her lungs. "Oh, thank—"

The mountain lion emerged from behind a boulder, its eyes trained on the goats.

"No." Adrenaline surged hot and fast, flinging her into action. She snatched a hunk of rock off the ground and threw it in the cat's direction. "Go on!" She checked over her shoulder, but the goats were already out of sight.

The mountain lion paced back and forth not more than twenty feet from where she stood, as though trying to decide if she was a threat.

Everly's mouth went dry. She backed up slowly, not looking away. She had to get to the house. Maybe Dev would come. Maybe he was already there looking for her...

The lion prowled closer, its frightening gaze unrelenting.

"Please, no." Everly stumbled, her knees buckling. Her breath sliced in and out of her lungs like a knife blade. The cat moved so much faster than she could going backward. She had to run or she wouldn't have a chance.

As she turned, Everly picked up a stick and threw it, screaming as loud as she could manage. Then she took off in a sprint, blindly running for the hill. Goliath cat was behind her. She could feel it, hear its breath, its paws thudding into the ground. Nausea burned up her stomach and stung her throat.

She fought the drag of fear in her muscles, fought so hard to keep going, but she already knew she'd never be able to outrun a mountain lion.

"Everly?" Mateo stepped inside the house, hoping like hell she'd answer him. Something felt off. Everything was quiet and dim. No lights, no sounds from the animals.

She'd probably gone out again. Maybe to the Chocolate Therapist with Darla. But if she had, why would her door be unlocked? She wasn't expecting him tonight.

Okay. He tried to shake the worry that had sunk into his gut. She had to be out with the animals. Probably waited around for Dev, and went out to take care of things herself when the deputy didn't show. Mateo bounded outside and down the porch steps, not slowing until he'd reached the chicken coop off the west side of the property. The lock had already been set, and it was silent. No obnoxious honking from Walter. No clucks from the hens putting him in his place. Everything was too still.

Mateo started for the goat pens, but commotion on the hill drew his attention. The four goats came tearing down, bleating and running scared.

Shit. Mateo tore out his phone and dialed Dev. "Get over here," he growled the second the line clicked. "To the farm. Now. I can't find Everly."

"Not this again," the deputy grumbled.

"Get the fuck over here!" Mateo shoved the phone back into his pocket and sprinted into the house. His hands shook too hard to unlatch the lock on the gun safe, so he threw the table over and used the poker from the fireplace to smash it open. He snatched up the rifle and tore back outside, running like hell in the direction the goats had come from.

Halfway up the hill, a scream split his eardrums. "Everly!" Where the fuck was she? "Everly!"

Another scream answered. So close. Mateo raised the rifle and sent a shot into the sky. He thrashed into the scrub oak, trampling branches, fighting his way through. He had to get to her. Jesus, he had to get to her...

Up ahead, a form came into view. The mountain lion. The fucking mountain lion. Steadying his hands, Mateo raised the rifle again and took a shot. The cat yelped and darted away, giving him a clear view of the ground where Everly lay.

"No." He ran, stumbling over rocks and branches, securing the rifle under his arm so he could pull out his phone.

Never taking his eyes off her, he hit the emergency call button.

"Nine-one-one, what's your emergency?"

"Ambulance." He choked on the breaths firing in and out of his lungs. "Mountain lion attack at the farm." He let the phone fall from his hand and dropped to his knees beside her.

There was blood everywhere. On the ground, on her clothes. So much blood. Life flowing out of her. "Everly? Baby? Where do you hurt?" He set the rifle off to the side, keeping it close enough that he could grab it if the lion came back. "Where's the pain?" He ripped off his shirt and tore it into strips.

"Mateo?" Her hand patted the ground until she found his.

"I'm here. Okay? You're okay." She had to be okay. "I'm here." His other hand searched her body, gently turning her so he could find where the blood was coming from. Her left shoulder. Puncture wounds. "I'm so sorry. God, I'm so sorry I didn't get here sooner."

She squeezed his hand harder. "It's not your fault."

But it was. Dev would've been here if he hadn't told him not to come.

"I sh…sh…shouldn't have come up here. The goats were missing…" Everly's body trembled. Tears leaked from her eyes.

Mateo gently wiped them away. "It's okay. You'll be okay." He'd make sure. He carefully rolled her onto her good side. "I have to stop the bleeding." Her sleeve was shredded, and underneath the material the flesh on her upper arm had been torn up. He quickly coiled the strips of his shirt around and around her arm, and then tied it tight over the wounds. "Does it hurt anywhere else?" He smoothed his hands down her hips and legs, watching for any sign of pain.

"N...n...no. Just shoulder."

"The ambulance should be here soon." He grabbed the rifle and switched on the safety. "I'm going to carry you down. Can you hold on to the gun?" They couldn't risk another encounter with the lion without it.

She nodded and lifted her right arm so he could tuck the rifle against her. When it was secure, he shifted her and scooped her into his arms, lifting her easily off the ground.

"I'm s...s...so glad you're here." Her breaths came rapidly through chattering teeth, but she smiled up at him. "B...because I'm in love with you. I d...d...didn't know if I'd get to tell you..."

"Shhh," he whispered over her as he painstakingly navigated the rocky slope. "I love you, too." The words choked him up. "You have my heart. It's all yours. I gave it to you a long time ago." That night. That first night when she had been so brave and fragile, sharing her hurts, telling him about her pain. That first night he'd taught her to dance and kissed her. "I was too afraid. I didn't know how to show you."

But he wouldn't make that mistake again. He would show her now. He would show her for the rest of their lives.

Chapter Twenty-Three

Everly tried to move, but her body was so heavy. Why did she feel so tired? She opened her eyes and the sight of the buzzing fluorescent hospital lights brought everything reeling back—the moment the lion had jumped on her from behind and taken her down, how she'd tried to fight back. And the gunshot. The gunshot that let her know that Mateo had found her, that she'd be okay.

"Mateo?" She tried to sit up, but her left arm was immobilized in a sling. Everything seemed fuzzy.

"Easy." Mateo appeared next to the bed, and she burst into tears at the sight of his face. God, that face. It was the best thing she'd ever seen.

"Everything's okay, baby." He moved her pillows and helped her sit up, but what she really wanted to do was climb into his lap and kiss him as long and as hard as he would let her.

"What happened? How long have you been sitting here?"

She tried to think, but a fog had settled over her mind, making everything past the ambulance ride hazy.

Mateo eased onto the bed, facing her. His eyes were tired. Scared. "You took a little nap when they gave you the pain meds." He gathered her hands in his.

"How long have I slept?" It felt like days. Everything seemed disconnected and out of focus.

"Only about an hour." Mateo brushed his thumbs over her knuckles. "But don't worry. I talked to the doctor, and you get to go home soon."

"Oh God." Her shoulders slumped against the pile of pillows. "Good. I have to get Tilda and Honey and Trunchbull and Wormwood back. They were running. I don't know where they ended up."

"I found them over by the café right before the ambulance left. They're in the stable, all safe and locked up for the night."

"Thank you." Her throat was raw. How could she ever thank him for being there when she needed him?

"That's how I knew where to find you." His voice sounded different. Weighted and quiet. "Those goats. They came tearing down the hill right at me."

"They almost got eaten." The horrible images raced through her mind. The cat's yellowish eyes, its razor-sharp teeth. She shifted to move closer to Mateo, but pain shot through her left shoulder. Wincing, she reached over to touch the bandages.

"Careful. You have forty-three stitches in that shoulder. A few open puncture wounds, too."

"It feels like a lot more than forty-three stitches." The pain made her woozy. She rested her head back on the pillow and reached for Mateo's hand again. She needed that warmth, that strength to fill her. Maybe someday she would stop shaking.

"But there's no other damage," he murmured, moving to sit next to her. "All of your bones and tendons are intact." Emotion laced the words. "You're gonna be fine." He slipped his arms around her and held her close.

She relaxed against him, letting herself lean into his embrace. "I'm sorry I scared you." He still looked pale.

"I'm sorry I wasn't there." He turned her face to his. "I should've been there. It took me longer than I thought it would to get back from Blake's."

"Blake's?" He'd been with Blake? That's why he hadn't made it to the party?

"When I saw you at that event, how happy you were, how many people care about the farm, I couldn't do it. I couldn't take it away from you. So I drove to Blake's house to tell him the deal was off."

She struggled to sit upright so she could get a better look at his face. "What about your family?"

"Ana told me it was time to give up the hero complex." He smiled, but it was only a shadow of his full grin. "She reminded me that she'll be fully capable of getting a job once she's done with school. And after I retire from riding, I'll find something else. Maybe I'll raise broncs for the circuit." He sat taller and moved his face closer to hers. The rims of his eyes were red, as though he'd shed a few tears, too. "I should've given up on the investment a long time ago. When I realized how much you loved the farm. That's all I could think when I saw you lying on the ground. That it was too late. And that I'd taken away what you loved the most."

"No. You didn't." Everly didn't bother to wipe away the steady stream of tears. "I would've understood, Mateo. You have to know that. I love that you want to take care of your mom and your sisters. I love that you're so faithful to them. At the party I realized that I don't love the farm nearly as much as I love my people." She leaned forward to brush a kiss over his lips. "You. My book club girls. My favorite retirees." Everyone who had given her a place to belong when she'd needed it the most. "That's what matters. I can live anywhere, but I can't live without the people I love."

Mateo rested his forehead against hers. "Can you live with one of them right next door?" His smile gained momentum. "I figure I'm gonna have to park my trailer right alongside the house so I can keep an eye on you all the time. No more chasing delinquent goats by yourself at sunset."

Everly stopped just short of kissing his lips again. "If you really want to keep an eye on me, you might have to spend more time in my house than in your trailer." She raised her eyebrows in an effort to entice him. "Especially at night."

"I could get on board with that." He raised his hand to her face, gently drawing her lips to his. Heat swirled through her as she lost herself in his kiss. God, his lips. They dulled the pain.

"Whoa. Sorry to interrupt." Dev stepped into the room, holding his cowboy hat nervously in his hands.

Everly pulled away. "It's okay." Heat danced on her cheeks. "You can come in."

"But make it quick." Mateo still seemed focused on her lips. She gave him a look and mouthed *later,* which brought out his real smile.

Dev walked to the foot of the bed. "Just wanted to swing by and tell you the parks and wildlife guys found the cat. The gunshot hit him in the leg, and they put him down. They said from the looks of things he'd been wounded before.

Maybe in a fight with another cougar. That's likely why he was hanging around the farm. He couldn't hunt like he used to, so he was poaching smaller prey."

A relieved sigh whooshed out of her. "That's good news." Though it would still be a very long time before she'd be able to walk the property by herself without looking over her shoulder.

"Sorry, Everly." Dev's gaze dropped to the floor. "You shouldn't have been out there alone."

"That's my fault," she reminded both men. "I wasn't thinking. I figured the goats would be nearby and I'd bring them right home." It hadn't even occurred to her to worry about the mountain lion until it was too late.

"But we've already decided that she'll have a protective detail from now on," Mateo said with a private, sly wink at her.

Oh, yes. She would welcome that protective detail. Especially during the overnight shift.

"So I'm assuming you told her the news about the farm?" Dev asked.

Everly gaped at Mateo. "Dev knew before I did?"

"Dev and Charity caught me running away from the party."

"Dev and *Charity*?" She shot the deputy an impressed frown. "Wow. That sounds promising."

"We were just talking." Dev's face had turned bright red. "Anyway. I'll let you two get back to ... well ... whatever you were doing. Glad you're gonna be okay, Everly," he called as he hotfooted it out the door.

"Thank you, Dev." Her tone may have teased him. She'd have to remember to ask Charity about her conversation with Dev later.

Right now, though…she braced her shoulder and inched closer to Mateo. "How about you go find that doctor so you can take me home?"

Mateo woke in a cold, heart-pounding sweat. He opened his eyes and breathed until his pulse steadied. The mountain lion was gone and Everly was curled up against him in her bed. He turned on his side and draped his arm over her, savoring the feel of her lying next to him, whole and peaceful and almost fully healed.

Over the last two weeks, he hadn't slept through the night once. Dreams would jar him awake, sometimes of the mountain lion, sometimes of Andres. They weren't always nightmares. Some were only images, pieces of the past his mind was still trying to put into place. It was a process, Everly kept reminding him—fitting the past he'd denied for so long into his present. But it was good, too. Good to tell her stories of his adventures with his brother. Good to remember Andres as a kid who'd been so smart and re-sourceful and tough. Man, had his brother been tough.

Everly had listened to the stories and always asked questions, coaxing him deeper into the memories. She was good at that, at helping him find meaning in those moments, at helping him understand how they'd shaped him.

Mateo raised his head to study her face. Even in her sleep, the woman was stunning. That beautiful mouth, curved delicate cheeks…

Her eyes fluttered open. "What're you doing?" she asked through a yawn.

He traced her lips with his finger. "Just admiring you."

"Admiring me?" Her nose wrinkled. "Oh God. Really? My hair is awful. It's frizzy, isn't it? I can feel it."

"No it's not. It's soft." He ran his hand over it. "I like it this way. All wild and messy." It made her look so free. "I like *you* this way." Half naked up against his body, talking in the hushed tones of the early morning.

"I like you this way, too," she whispered, turning on her side to face him so that her body was pressed to his.

He slid his hand up her hip, underneath the John Deere T-shirt that never failed to turn him on. "I didn't mean to wake you up."

"Well, since I'm awake..." She brought her hands to his chest, skimming her fingers down his abs, his hips...

He couldn't hold it together when her fingers stroked him. Couldn't stay silent, couldn't stay still. Mateo eased her shirt up and over her head, and then rolled onto his back and pulled her on top of him, giving her the control.

"I like us this way," she whispered, wriggling until he was fully inside of her, harder than he'd ever thought possible, aching with anticipation, and completely hers.

Mateo smoothed the hair away from her face so he could see into her eyes, so he could watch her come apart. Sexy little sounds came from her mouth, forced out by her ragged breaths. He loved those sounds, loved how they surged more power through him, how they drove him to tease her and shift his hips to graze her most sensitive spots.

"Oh my God, Mateo," she gasped, tensing all over. He watched the explosion take her, forcing out a cry as she rode him harder and let her head fall back when the tremors gripped her body. The sight loosened his control. He lifted his hips off the mattress, thrusting into her once more to meet that blinding, blood-surging crash that sent him reeling. The release trembled all the way through him, and he held her tighter in the midst of it, wanting her to know how good she made him feel.

Everly collapsed over him in a boneless heap, lifting only her head to peer at his face. Her lips quirked. "You can wake me up anytime you want."

"That might get a little old." Because he wanted her all the time. "I can't seem to get enough of you." His hand lazily stroked her back.

"Did you have another dream?" she asked, resting her cheek on his chest.

"The mountain lion was chasing Andres. And I couldn't catch up. I couldn't help him." It wasn't the cat he feared, though. It was the helplessness. His inability to save him. That would always be at the heart of his nightmares.

Everly propped her chin on her fist and gazed into his eyes. "He knew you loved him, Mateo. He knew or he wouldn't have written that letter. He meant it for you, too."

She'd said it before and somehow she made him believe it. She made him believe in a lot of things. He almost didn't know what to say. How to thank her. How to tell her what a beautiful person she was.

So he let his kiss say everything.

Chapter Twenty-Four

Are you sure you should be carrying that tray?" Gus dropped his crossword puzzle on the table and stood. "Let me take it for you." He shuffled over, his left leg dragging slightly, and muscled the tray of food out of Everly's hands.

Even though it had been three weeks since the attack—and one since she'd gotten the stitches out—she let him take it. "You're so sweet to me." Everyone had been. Kate and Darla had helped Hilda out for a few days while Everly rested. Even when she had come back to the café, it seemed a different friend would show up every morning ready to help refill coffee and carry things around for her.

"All of the food goes over here." She led the way to the tables her friends had pushed together for their Thursday brunch.

Gus proudly carried the tray and set it on a nearby table. He seemed to strut as he passed Darla, Charity, Jessa, and Naomi.

"Thank you." Everly gave the old man a hug. "Now, you'd better get back to your table before Charlie finishes his puzzle first." The two men always made it a competition, with the winner earning bragging rights for the rest of the day.

"I've only got ten left," Charlie announced, still bent over the paper.

"Yeah, well, I had ten left five minutes ago." Gus lumbered back to his seat and got to work.

Smiling, Everly started to hand out the tea and scones her friends had requested. "I made an assortment. Chocolate chunk, lemon meringue, carrot cake, and maple glazed."

"It's a damn good thing Mateo came to his senses." Darla helped herself to one of each flavor. "I'm not sure I could've lived without your scones."

"Or your frittatas," Naomi added.

"Or the cinnamon rolls." Jessa rubbed her belly. "I swear, that's all these babies want. Sugar."

"At least it's unrefined sugar." Everly sat at the head of the table and poured herself a cup of tea.

"Well, I couldn't live without this." Charity gestured to everyone sitting at the table. "All of you. And this place."

"Agreed." Darla lifted her teacup in a toast. "To the café." She grinned. "And to carbs."

"Hear, hear," Jessa said. They all clinked their teacups together.

"So, what're your plans for the place?" Naomi asked.

"I'm not really sure yet." Things had been so crazy since the farewell party. She'd tried to give back all of the donations, but everyone had insisted she keep the money and use it to officially launch her nonprofit. "Mateo's been gone this week." Yes, she was pouting. Her bed felt so empty.

"He went to see a breeder about purchasing a few more broncs." He seemed excited about the prospect of raising them to compete in the sport he loved after he retired next year. "I know he'd like to build a bigger barn to house the animals. And I still want to start the co-op and maybe more cooking classes." But there were so many logistics involved. If she truly wanted to expand, she'd need space, and she didn't even know how to go about making that happen. "We haven't talked through any details yet." Honestly, the thought of all the upgrades this place needed overwhelmed her. She'd much rather deal with getting the programs started.

"And how is Mateo?" Darla asked with a smirk.

"He's good." The dreamy smile couldn't be helped. He'd been so good to her, careful and attentive, and oh-so-fun.

"And you were mad at me for setting you two up."

"'Mad' isn't the right word." She'd been surprised, caught off guard. "But now I am eternally grateful." She'd needed a little push in putting her heart out there again.

"I have to admit…" Charity helped herself to another lemon scone. "I've never seen Mateo like this. He's completely whipped."

"It's true."

Everly gasped and turned. At some point Mateo must've snuck in through the kitchen. "You're back!" She shot out of the chair, tipping it over, and threw her arms around him.

"I missed you." Mateo lifted her feet off the ground and kissed her until her joints started to melt.

"That's adorable." Jessa dabbed at her eyes.

"Look how happy she is," Naomi murmured.

"You'd better keep it that way, young man," Gus called over.

"I intend to." Mateo gave the older man a solemn nod, and then turned his full attention back to Everly. "Do you have a minute?"

"A minute?" Darla teased. "Come on, Mateo. You can do better than a minute."

"He can," Everly confirmed. She knew from personal experience Mateo could do way better than a minute.

He shook his head at Darla. "Right now, I just want to talk to her. In the kitchen."

"Of course I have a minute." Everly took his hand and let him lead her away.

"Don't violate any health codes in there," Charity called. Her friends all laughed. Everly did, too. She couldn't help it.

"I'm not sure I want to know what you and your friends talk about when I'm not around." He closed the door to the kitchen and took her in his arms again.

"Probably not," she agreed. For the last few years, she'd had to listen to everyone else's romantic escapades. Now it was kind of fun to have one of her own. "Did you really want to *talk* to me?" she asked, smoothing her hands over his broad shoulders. "Because we could take more than a minute, if you want."

His darkened gaze moved slowly down her body. "I do want, but first I have some news."

"Oh?" She stepped backward and leaned against the counter, admiring how he looked in those threadbare jeans and that snug T-shirt. Of course, he would look even better out of them.

"I talked to a contractor in Denver. Told him about the farm, about the upgrades we need to make it so you can turn it into a nonprofit."

"Really?" The excitement in his eyes was contagious.

"Really. I told him the house needs a whole new exterior and some foundation upgrades, along with updated wiring. And we may need to change out all of the plumbing, too."

He said it as though those things were no big deal, but that would add up fast. "It sounds like a lot."

Mateo didn't seem to hear her. "Then there's the café. I talked to him about adding an addition—a commercial kitchen where we could set you up to teach bigger cooking classes."

She glanced around the space. It was cramped, way too cramped to ever manage more than a few people at a time. "I'd love that." She'd never dreamed it was even a possibility.

"I thought so." He collected her hands in his and brought her close again. "The contractor thought he could have the work done within a couple of months, but I didn't commit to anything. I wanted to talk to you first."

"It all sounds amazing." And necessary. The roof might not survive another mountain winter. "But I don't know how I would pay for it."

Mateo shrugged. "That's the landlord's responsibility. Levi has a lead on a sponsorship deal with some new energy drink company. And once you get the nonprofit up and running, you can accept donations, start a board of directors..." The idea seemed to energize him as much as it did her. "I'll help out however I can. I mean, obviously you'll be the executive director, but I can help you manage the facilities and inventory and whatever else you don't want to do."

"I love that idea." Everly blinked faster, but a few tears still managed to slip out.

Mateo clasped his hands around her waist, pressing her against him. The heat flowing between their bodies nearly had her peeling off her clothes right there.

"Of course, while they're doing the work on your house, you might have to move into the trailer with me," he murmured, moving his hips against hers.

She did her best to look coy but it was difficult feeling him so hard against her. "I'm not sure about that. I haven't tried out the bed in there yet." He'd only gotten the trailer back last week, and they'd been opting for her queen-sized bed instead. "We'd better go give it a test run before I make any hasty decisions."

Mateo was already slipping his hands up her shirt. "What about your friends?"

"They'll understand." She tugged on his waist until he followed her out the door.

Epilogue

Eight months later...

Get back here, Walter." Everly cornered the duck against the fence and lunged to capture him, but he dodged her and hightailed it to the right, waddling as fast as his webbed feet could go all the way across the pen.

Dante took off after him, barking and yipping his happy song, always thrilled when the duck gave him permission to play chase. Walter hated chase. He toddled back to Everly quacking like his tail feathers were on fire, and allowed himself to be swept up into her arms for protection.

"Good boy, Dante," she crooned, holding the duck securely against her chest.

Mateo let himself in through the gate and sauntered over to join her. "Sometimes it feels like we're running a circus instead of a farm."

"Yes, but it's our circus." She stretched to her tiptoes to give Mateo a kiss, smooshing the duck between them.

"That's why I love it," he murmured, trailing his finger down her cheek. "Because it's ours."

Everly went to kiss him again but Walter squirmed and almost escaped. "Oh no you don't, mister." She tightened her grip.

"You're really going to make him wear this?" Mateo held up the red bowtie she'd made especially for Walter. "The poor duck. He'll never hear the end of it from the hens."

Walker quacked irritably as though agreeing.

"Yes, he has to wear it." She gently fit the bowtie on over the duck's head. "There. It's perfect. You look absolutely adorable," she assured Walter. He had always been something of a mascot for the farm, and he would be the official greeter for their open house.

Adjusting the bowtie, Everly leaned back to take a look. "It's perfect. Don't you think?"

Mateo cracked up. "Red is definitely his color."

Ignoring the sarcasm, Everly set the duck on the ground and Walter took off quacking and flapping his wings. Dante followed behind at a respectable distance, keeping watch over the animals the way Mateo had trained him to.

"I'm just glad you didn't make me wear one of those things." Mateo pulled her close, overwhelming her senses with her favorite smell in the world—that leathery spicy manly essence that never failed to bring her comfort or peace or relief...whatever she needed in the moment.

"You don't need a bowtie to look hot." She eyed his body with a smirk. "But thank you for choosing a shirt with buttons on it. That means a lot to me."

Mateo tugged at the collar as if it annoyed him. "It's the only shirt I own that has to be ironed." He undid the top button. "I'd be happy to take it off for you."

"Mmm." She slid her fingers up to the opening. "You will. Later. Right now we have to get ready to greet our guests." Hordes of people would start arriving at the farm any minute.

For months she'd been focused on developing the programs and plans for crops and animals while Mateo had taken care of the business side of things. Smart man that he was, he'd enlisted Naomi to plan the open house for them. The idea was to showcase the new programs and classes so they could invite the entire community to participate.

Taking Mateo's hand, she led him on one more round to make sure they were all set—first to the food tent to check on Hilda, then over to the goat pens, then past the stables they'd had built for Amigo and two new horses. "I guess we're ready." Nerves fired up in her stomach again as they passed the upgraded farmhouse. It was still the same cozy little place, but now it gleamed with new siding and a fresh coat of paint. They'd picked a metal roof that would keep the snow off in the winter, and had even worked together to reconstruct the rambling front porch.

"Everything is going to be perfect." Mateo gathered her against his side and they ambled along together the same way they did most evenings after dinner.

"I just hope everyone jumps on board." Instead of a party this time, the event was designed to get people involved—to sign up for the co-op and the classes, to learn more about serving on the board, and to commit to volunteering with the kids' programs she planned to start. She'd been working on it all for months, but she still had her doubts that she could do this.

Mateo stopped walking and faced her. "Are you kidding?" He took her elbow, turning her in a slow circle. "Look at what you've built, Everly. It's brilliant and important and life changing. Everyone will want to be part of this."

"*We* built it." She dabbed at her eyes. "And you're not supposed to make me cry before everyone gets here."

"I wanted to make sure I got to say my piece before the craziness." He reached for her hand. "That's not all I wanted to say, either. I—"

Car noise hummed behind her. One by one, trucks and SUVs filed past them, parking in the area they'd marked off in the field beyond the driveway.

"Hello!" Naomi waved as she got out of her car.

Everly waved back before focusing on Mateo again. "What did you want to—"

"Everything looks fabulous." Naomi traipsed over, intruding on their moment. "Do you need me to take care of any last-minute details?"

"I don't think so." That look in Mateo's eyes had her distracted. He seemed so serious.

"Great. Then you and I should start greeting the guests."

Everly offered Mateo an apologetic look. "We can talk later?"

"Yes, *mi amor*. We will talk later." He gave her that smile that never failed to weaken her knees.

"Perfect." Naomi directed Everly toward the gate that guests would walk through to get to the main festivities. "Mateo, why don't you go help with the parking?"

"I'm on it." He gave Everly one last wink before heading in the opposite direction.

Nothing could've prepared Everly for the crowds walking through that gate. They came in groups—friends and acquaintances and people from two towns over she'd never met before.

When she saw a familiar minivan pull up, Everly left her post by the gate to greet Lance and Jessa. Her friend had only recently brought the triplets home from the hospital, and she was touched that they'd made such an effort to come. "You brought the babies!"

"We were dying to get out of the house." Jessa climbed out of the passenger's seat, somehow looking even more radiant than she had before the triplets were born.

"Fair warning," Lance called as he strode to the back of the van. "It could take us a year to unpack the car and get everyone situated in the stroller."

"I'd love to help." Everly opened the door and unlatched the first car seat. "Hello, little Paisley." As the only girl, she was easy to recognize in her cute little pink onesie. "You're looking extra adorable today."

Inside the car, one of the boys started to fuss. Cole, maybe? Or it could've been Declan. She was still working on telling those two apart.

Lance rolled their triple Cadillac stroller around and easily lifted the two boys' car seats to click them into place while Everly took care of Paisley's. She'd already had practice when she'd helped Jessa do the grocery shopping the week before. "Wow. That didn't take any time at all."

"He's a pro." Jessa went to stand by Lance's side, leaning into him. "You should see him. Super dad. These are the luckiest babies in the world."

"I don't doubt that at all." Everly had to dab at her eyes again. It seemed she'd be emotional all day.

"I guess I should get back to my post," she said. Naomi was frantically waving her over. "I'll catch up with you two in a little bit."

Lance and Jessa said a quick good-bye, and then both bent over the stroller to fuss over the babies.

"Sorry," she said when she got back to Naomi. "I can't resist babies." Normally Naomi couldn't, either.

"I think your parents are here." Her friend pointed toward the parking area. "I mean, they said they were your parents, but I didn't know you'd even invited them."

"I did." Everly's eyes went on a frantic search, but she didn't see them anywhere. "I sent them an email telling them about it. But they never responded." She'd figured they were still angry that she'd refused to sign those petition papers to reinstate her license and hire an attorney.

"Don and Sherri, right?" Naomi asked. She seemed to study Everly's face. "You and your mom have a definite resemblance."

Yes, she'd always looked more like her mom. "They're really here?"

"I'm pretty sure." Her friend looked around, too. "Oh! Over there. They're looking at Walter."

Everly turned, and sure enough, her parents strolled around the chicken yard looking completely out of place in their fancy clothes and shiny shoes. But they'd come.

"I'll be back," she whispered, suddenly too full of emotion to find her voice. It had been so long since she'd seen them. Her dad with his regal white hair and tailored suit. Her mom with that golden hair and proud stoic face. That was how Everly used to be, too. Stoic and slightly detached. But not anymore.

She rushed through the yard, clumsy in her cowgirl boots,

dodging people and smiling and crying. "Mom?" She was out of breath by the time she reached them.

"Hi, honey." For once Sherri Brooks looked unsure of herself.

"I never heard back from you. I didn't think you'd come." She hadn't realized how much she'd wanted them here. After the last conversation with her father, she hadn't let herself hope.

"We had to come." Her dad's eyes had softened. Instead of his rigid stare, they were filled with uncertainty, regret. "I'm sorry for the things I said, Evs. I wanted to help. I wanted to make things right for you." Everly had never seen her father cry. Not once. But tears ran down his cheeks as he looked her over. "But if this place makes you happy, we're behind you. We'll support you."

"That's all we want for you, honey." Her mom hugged her tight. "If you're happy here we can be happy for you."

"I *am* happy here. And I'm so happy you came." She brushed away her own tears and kissed her father's cheek— something she used to do all the time. He still smelled like the cologne he wore to disguise the cigar smell from her mom. "I can't believe you're here. I have so many people to introduce you to." The most important one being that man directing traffic on the driveway. She'd mentioned Mateo in her email so her parents wouldn't be shocked if they did decide to make the trip. Well, that, and she wanted them to know about the most important person in her life.

She led her parents over to him, telling them about the farm the whole way. Mateo saw them coming and immediately shirked his responsibilities.

"Hey." He seemed to do a double-take. She'd shown him pictures of her parents, but she doubted he'd expected them to come, either.

"Hi." Everly's voice still wobbled. "My parents are here. Don and Sherri," she said in case he'd forgotten. "They came to see the farm. Dad, Mom, this is Mateo." Her love. Her best friend.

Based on the way his smile grew, he knew what this meant to her. "We're so glad you could make it." He shook her dad's hand and seemed to surprise her mom with a hug.

"You two have built quite the operation here." Everly had seen that proud look on her dad's face before. When she'd graduated. When she'd gotten hired on at the firm. She never thought she'd see it again.

"Everly made it all possible." Mateo eased his arm around her. "She's done a lot for this community. These people love her." His hand squeezed her hip lovingly. "And so do I."

Her mom sniffled, but Everly didn't even bother trying to hold in the happiness that kept welling up in her eyes.

"We heard your parents are here." Darla led the charge of her friends. They all crowded in, showering Don and Sherri with friendliness and introductions.

Continuing the chitchat, the group moved toward the food tent, her friends sweeping her parents along with them. Her mom was already gabbing with the girls like she'd known them for years. Everly started to follow, but Mateo held her back. "I need a minute with you."

"You can have all of the minutes you want." She wrapped her arms around him. "Have I thanked you lately? For all of this?"

"Last night was pretty good." That secret smile rose again. "So was the night before that."

"I'll make tonight even better," she promised.

Mateo suddenly looked shy. His eyes wouldn't quite meet

hers. "What about every night after that? Every night for the rest of our lives?"

Her heart leapt up into her throat. They'd talked about the future. Of course, they'd dreamed about it, but they had so much to do. So many tasks to complete. Any plans or logistics for the two of them building a life together had gotten shoved to the wayside.

"I can't wait anymore." Mateo dropped to one knee right there in the dirt and held up a ring she hadn't realized he'd been holding. A single solitaire diamond set in a gleaming gold band. "I love you, Everly Brooks. These past eight months have only made me admire you more. You're compassionate and patient and understanding. Beautiful. So beautiful. I know I'm just a cowboy, but I want to spend the rest of my life making your dreams come true." He gazed up at her, and the love she saw in his eyes promised everything—strength, support, devotion, passion, and his special brand of fun.

"Yes." Everly tugged on his hand, beckoning him to stand with her. He rose slowly, his expression as earnest as his voice had been when he'd asked her to be his wife. His *wife*. "This is my dream." She held his face in her hands and whispered against his lips. "You and me. Sharing a life together. That's everything."

See how the Rocky Mountain Riders series began!

What would a big-time rodeo star like Lance Cortez
see in a small-town veterinarian like Jessa Mae Love?
She has no idea. But once she's inside this rugged
cowboy's ranch—and has fallen into his strong
cowboy arms—she's too swept away to ask...

An excerpt from *Hometown Cowboy* follows.

Chapter One

Sorry, sir." Jessa Mae Love threw out her arms to block the heavyset man who tried to sit on the stool next to her. "This seat is taken."

He eyed her, the coarseness of his five o'clock shadow giving his face a particularly menacing quality. Still, she held her ground.

"You been sittin' there by yourself for an hour, lady," he pointed out, scratching at his beer belly. "And this is the best spot to watch the game."

"It's true. I have been sitting here for a while." She smiled politely and shimmied her shoulders straighter, lest he think she was intimidated by his bulk. "But my *boyfriend* is meeting me. We have an important date tonight and I know he'll be here any minute." She checked the screen of her cell phone again, the glowing numbers blaring an insult in her face. Seven o'clock. *Seven o'clock?*

Cam was never late. He'd been planning this date for

more than a week. Since she was coming straight from the animal rescue shelter she owned, they'd agreed to meet at the Tumble Inn Bar for a drink before he took her to the new Italian restaurant on Main Street. "He'll be here," she said to the man. "Cam is *very* reliable."

"Whatever," the man grumbled, hunching himself on a stool three down from her.

Signaling to the bartender, she ordered another glass of pinot. "And why don't you go ahead and bring a Bud Light for my boyfriend?" she asked with a squeak of insecurity. But that was silly because Cam would be there. He'd show up and give her a kiss and apologize for being so late because... his car broke down. Or maybe his mother called and he couldn't get off the phone with her.

"He won't let me down," she muttered to cool the heat that rose to her face. He would *never* stand her up in this crowded bar—in front of the whole town.

Everyone considered the Tumble Inn the classiest watering hole in Topaz Falls, Colorado. And that was simply because you weren't allowed to throw peanut shells on the floor. It was nice enough—an old brick auto shop garage that had been converted years ago. They'd restored the original garage doors and in the summer, they opened them to the patio, which was strung with colorful hanging globe lights. Gil Wilson, the owner, had kept up with the times, bringing in modern furniture and decor. He also offered the best happy hour in town, which would explain why it was so crowded on a Wednesday night.

She stole a quick glance over her shoulder. Were people starting to stare?

Plastering on a smile, she called Cam. *Again.*

His voice mail picked up. *Again.*

"Hey, it's me." She lowered her voice. "I'm kind of worried. Maybe I got the time wrong? Did we say we'd meet at six? Or seven? I guess it doesn't matter. I'm here at the bar. Waiting for you…" A deafening silence echoed back in her ear. "Okay. Well, I'm sure you're on your way. I'll see you soon."

She set down the phone and took a long sip of wine. Everything was fine. It was true she hadn't had very good luck with men, but Cam was different.

She drummed her fingers against the bar to keep her hand from trembling. Over the past ten years, she'd been *almost* engaged approximately three times. Approximately, because she wasn't all that sure that a twist tie from the high school cafeteria counted as a betrothal, although her seventeen-year-old heart had thought it to be wildly romantic at the time. Little did she know, one year later, her high school sweetheart—the one who'd gotten down on one knee in the middle of the cafeteria to recite one of Shakespeare's sonnets in front of nearly the whole school (did she mention he was in the drama club?)—would go off to college and meet the Phi Beta Kappa sisters who'd splurged on breast implants instead of fashionable new glasses like Jessa's. Breast implants seemed to get you more bang for your buck in college. Who knew?

She pushed her glasses up on her nose and snuck a glance at the big man who'd tried to steal Cam's seat earlier.

"Still no boyfriend, huh?" he asked as though he suspected she'd made up the whole thing.

"He's on his way." Her voice climbed the ladder of desperation. "He'll be here soon."

"Sure he will." The man went back to nursing his beer and tilted his head to see some football game on the television screen across the room.

She was about to flip him off when an incoming text chimed on her phone. From Cam! "It's him," she called, holding up the phone to prove she wasn't delusional.

"Lucky guy," Big Man muttered, rolling his eyes.

"You got that right." She focused on the screen to read the text.

Jessa, I left this morning to move back to Denver.

Wait. *What?* The words blurred. A typo. It must be a typo. Damn that autocorrect.

"What's the word?" Big Man asked. "He comin' or can I take that seat?"

"Um. Uh..." Fear wedged itself into her throat as she scrolled through the rest of the words.

I didn't see a future for me there. In Topaz Falls or with you. Sorry. I know this would've been better in person, but I couldn't do it. You're too nice. I know you'll find the right person. It's just not me.

Yours,

Cam

"Yours? *Yours?*" Ha. That was laughable. Cam had never been hers. Just like the others. Hadn't mattered how *nice* she'd been. She'd been jilted. *Again.* This time by her animal rescue's largest donor. And, yes, the man she'd been sleeping with...because he'd seemed like a good idea at the time. Women had slim pickings around Topaz Falls, population 2,345.

"Is he coming or not?" Big Man asked, still eyeing the empty stool.

"No. He's not coming." A laugh bubbled out, bordering on hysteria. "He broke up with me! By text!"

A hush came over the bar, but who cared? Let them all stare. Poor Jessa. Dumped again.

"It's not like he's a prize," she said, turning to address them all. "He's a technology consultant, for God's sake. Not Chris Hemsworth." Not that she knew what being a technology consultant meant. But it'd sounded good when she'd met him after she found his stray puggle wandering downtown six months ago. Peabody had pranced right up to her on the street and peed on her leg, the little shit. Now, Jessa was a dog person—an *animal* person—but that puggle had it out for her from day one.

When Cam had come in to retrieve his little beast from the shelter, stars had circled in her eyes. He was the first attractive man she'd seen since all those bull riders had passed through town three months ago. So unfair for those smokin' hot cowboys to gather in town and get the women all revved up only to leave them the next day.

In all honesty, Cam was no cowboy. Though his slight bulk suggested he spent a good portion of every day sitting in front of a computer screen, his soft brown eyes had a kind shimmer that instantly drew you in. He'd been good to her—taking her out to fancy restaurants and buying her flowers just because. Also, because she'd saved his beloved varmint from the potential fate of being mauled by a mountain lion, he'd made monthly donations to the shelter, which had kept them going.

Now he was gone.

"I can't believe this. How could he break up with me?"

Everyone around her had gone back to their own conversations, either unwilling to answer or pretending they didn't hear. So she turned to Big Man. "I guess you're happy about this, huh? Now the seat's all yours."

He didn't even look at her. "Nope. I'm good right where I am, thanks."

Oh, sure. After all that, now he didn't want to sit by her? "Fine. That's fine. It's all fine." Raising the glass to her lips, she drained the rest of her wine in one gulp.

"You know what?" she asked Big Man, not caring one iota that he seemed hell-bent on ignoring her. "I'm done." This had to stop. The falling in love thing. It always started innocently enough. A man would ask her out and they'd go on a few dates. She'd swear that this time she wouldn't get too attached too soon, but before she knew it, she was looking up wedding venues and bridal gowns and honeymoon destinations online. She couldn't help it. Her heart had always been a sucker for romance. Her father had said it was her best quality—that she could love someone so quickly, that she could give her heart to others so easily. He got it because he was the same way. Her mother, of course, labeled it her worst quality. *You're simply in love with the idea of being in love*, her wise mother would say. And it was true. Was that so *wrong*?

"Hey, Jessa."

The gruffness of the quiet voice, aged by years of good cigars, snapped up her head. She turned.

Luis Cortez stood behind her, hunched in his bowlegged stance. Clad in worn jeans and sporting his pro rodeo belt buckle, he looked like he'd just stepped off the set of an old western, face tanned and leathery, white hair tufted after a long ride on his trusty steed.

"Hi there, Luis," she mumbled, trying to hold her head high. Luis was her lone volunteer at the shelter, and he just might be the only one in town who loved animals as much as she did. He'd also been her dad's best friend and since she'd come back to town last year to settle her father's estate, she'd spent a lot of time with the man.

Maybe that was part of her problem with finding the love of her life. She spent most of her free time with a sixty-seven-year-old man...

"You all right?" Luis asked, gimping to the stool next to her. Seeing as how he was a retired bull-riding legend, it was a wonder he could walk at all.

"Uh." That was a complicated question. "Yes." She cleared the tremble out of her voice. "I'm fine. Great." She would be, anyway. As soon as the sting wore off.

"Thought you and Cam had a date tonight." Luis shifted with a wince, as though his arthritis was flaring again. "Where is he anyway? I was hopin' I could talk him into puttin' in his donation early this month. We gotta replace half the roof before the snow comes."

Cam. That name was her newest curse word. *Cam him! Cam it!* Feeling the burn of humiliation pulse across her cheeks, she turned on her phone and pushed it over to him so he could read the text. "Cam broke up with me." Luis had obviously missed the little announcement she'd made earlier.

He held up the phone and squinted, mouthing the words as he read. The older man looked as outraged as she was, bless him. "Man wasn't good enough for you, anyways, Jess. He's a damn fool."

"I have a knack for picking the fools." Just ask her mother. Every time she went through one of these breakups, Carla Roth, DO, would remind her of how bad the odds were for finding true love. Her mother had never married her father. She didn't believe in monogamy. *One person out of six billion?* she'd ask. *That is highly unlikely, Jessa.*

It might be unlikely, but the odds weren't enough to kill the dream. Not for her. Neither was the lack of any significant relationship in her mother's life. Jessa had grown up being shuffled back and forth—summers and Christmas in Topaz Falls with her father and the rest of the year with her college professor mother who didn't believe in love, secretly watching old romantic classics and movies like *Sleepless in Seattle* and *You've Got Mail* with wistful tears stinging in her eyes.

"Don't worry, Jess," Luis said in his kind way. "You'll find someone."

Big Man snorted.

Before she could backhand him, Luis gave her shoulder a pat. "My boys ain't married yet," he reminded her, as if she would *ever* be able to forget the Cortez brothers. Every woman's fantasy.

Lance, the oldest, had followed in his father's footsteps, though rumor had it this would be his last season on the circuit. He trained nonstop and had little time for anything else in his life, considering he left the ranch only about once a month. The thought of him married almost made her laugh. Over the years, he'd built quite the reputation with women, though she had no personal experience. Even with her father being one of his father's best friends, Lance had said maybe five words to her in all the years she'd known him. He seemed to prefer a woman who'd let him off the hook easily, and God knew there were plenty of them following those cowboys around.

Then there was Levi. Oh, hallelujah, Levi. One of God's greatest gifts to women. She'd had a fling with him the summer of their sophomore year, but after that he'd left home to train with some big-shot rodeo mentor and rarely came home.

There was a third Cortez brother, but Luis didn't talk

about him. Lucas, the middle child, had been sent to prison for arson when he was seventeen.

"Sure wish I'd see more of Levi," Luis said wistfully. "He ain't been home in a long time."

Her eyebrows lifted with interest. "So, um..." She pretended to examine a broken nail to prove she didn't care too much. "How is Levi, anyway?"

"That boy needs to get his head out of his ass. He's reckless. He's gonna get himself killed out there."

Jessa doubted that. Levi Cortez was making a name for himself in the rodeo world.

"Lance, now, he's the only one of my boys who's got his head on straight," Luis went on. "He always was a smart kid."

From what she'd seen, the oldest Cortez brother had never been a kid, but she didn't say so. After their mom ditched the family, Lance took over a more parental role. Not that she had any right to analyze him. "He's handsome, too," she offered, because every time she did happen to run into him, his luscious eyes had completely tied up her tongue. Yes, indeedy, Lance happened to be a looker. Though it was in a much different way than his cocky brother. "He looks the most like you," she said with a wink.

Luis's lips puckered in that crotchety, don't-want-to-smile-but-can't-help-it grin she loved to see. Her dad used to have one like that, too.

"Anyway...," the man said, obviously trying to change the subject. "What're we gonna do with Cam gone? I assume he didn't leave any money behind for the shelter."

"Not that I know of." Apparently, he hadn't left anything. Not even the toothbrush she'd kept at his house, Cam it.

"You got any other donors yet?"

"Not yet." She'd been so preoccupied with the most re-

cent love—infatuation—of her life that she hadn't exactly
made time to go trolling for other interested parties. Her dad
had a big heart, but he'd always hated to ask for money, so
when she'd come to take over, the list of benefactors had
been...well...nonexistent. In one year, she'd already used
most of what little money he'd left her to purchase supplies
and complete the critical repairs. She could live off her savings for a couple more months, and at least keep up with the
payroll, but after that things didn't look too promising. She'd
probably have to lay off her night shift guy.

With Cam's generosity, she hadn't been too worried. Until now, of course.

"Don't you worry, Jess. Somethin'll work out." Luis's
confidence almost made her believe it. "You're doin' okay.
You know that? Buzz would be proud."

She smiled a little. Yes, her father definitely would've
been proud to see his old place cleaned up. When she'd finished veterinary school and started on her MBA, he'd been
so excited. He'd owned the rescue for thirty years but had
never taken one business class. Which meant the place never
made any money. He'd barely had enough to live on.

She had planned to change all of that. They'd planned
it together. While she worked her way through business
school, they'd talked on the phone twice a week, discussing
how they could expand the place. Then, a month before she
finished school, her father had a heart attack. He'd been out
on a hike with Luis. Maybe that was why the man felt the
need to take care of her, check in on her, help her fix things
up around the house.

Familiar tears burned. She'd never blame Luis, though.
That was exactly the way her dad would've chosen to go.
Out on the side of a mountain, doing something he loved.

"We'll find a way, Jess." Pure determination turned the man's face statuelike, making him look as pensive as his eldest son. "All we need is some inspiration." Which he always insisted you couldn't find while stuck indoors. "I'm headin' up the mountain tomorrow. You wanna come?"

She brushed a grateful pat across the man's gnarled hand. "I can't, Luis. Thank you."

As much as she'd like to spend the day on the mountain, drowning her sorrows about Cam and the rescue's current financial situation in the fresh mountain air, she had things to do. This breakup had to be the dawn of a new era for her. She was tired of being passed over like yesterday's pastries. To hell with relationships. With romance. She didn't have time for it anyway. She had walls to paint and supplies to purchase and animals to rescue. Which meant she also had generous donors to find.

She shot a quick glance down at her attire. Might be a good idea to invest in herself first. Typically, she used her Visa only for emergencies, but this could be considered disaster prevention, right? She needed a new wardrobe. Something more professional. How could she schmooze potential stakeholders looking like she'd just come from a half-price sale at the New Life Secondhand Store?

"You sure you don't want to come?" Luis prompted.

"I'd love to but I have to go shopping." Right after their book club meeting, she'd enlist her friends to help her reinvent herself so she could reinvent her nonprofit.

By the time she was done, the Helping Paws Animal Rescue and Shelter would be everything her father dreamed it would be.

It would keep the memory of his love alive.

About the Author

Sara Richardson grew up chasing adventure in Colorado's rugged mountains. She's climbed to the top of a 14,000-foot peak at midnight, swum through Class IV rapids, completed her wilderness first-aid certification, and spent seven days at a time tromping through the wilderness with a thirty-pound backpack strapped to her shoulders.

Eventually Sara did the responsible thing and got an education in writing and journalism. After a brief stint in the corporate writing world, she stopped ignoring the voices in her head and started writing fiction. Now she uses her experience as a mountain adventure guide to write stories that incorporate adventure with romance. Sara lives and plays in Colorado, where she still indulges her adventurous spirit, with her saint of a husband and two young sons.

You can learn more at:

SaraRichardson.net

Twitter @SaraR_Books

Facebook.com/SaraRichardsonBooks

Instagram @Sarar_Books

Saved by the Cowboy

A.J. PINE

FOREVER

NEW YORK BOSTON

Chapter One

Sheriff Cash Hawkins sat comfortably in his police-issue Chevy Tahoe. There was a beef brisket sandwich from BBQ on the Bluff cooling in the bag on the passenger seat. He'd just cued up a new audiobook on his phone and connected the Bluetooth. His German shepherd, Dixie, chewed on her rawhide in the back.

A pretty perfect Saturday night if he did say so himself. Well—except for the thick, calligraphied square envelope sticking out from the passenger seat visor. Still unopened.

He unrolled the top of the take-out bag and breathed in the savory aroma of homemade barbecue sauce and locally sourced beef.

"Damn, that Lily Green can cook. Can't she, Dixie girl?" he called back to his companion. But then he remembered that Lily and Tucker Green—the husband and wife duo who'd opened the restaurant together—had just split, Tucker having bought out her portion of the business.

"Still her sauce recipe, right?" he asked aloud. "Tucker wouldn't be fool enough to let the woman go without getting all her secret recipes." And yes, he knew he was talking to the dog. He and Dixie had some of their best conversations on quiet Saturday nights doing traffic patrol. It was why he always insisted on taking the shift, even though as sheriff he sure as hell didn't have to. He *liked* it. Not that he'd let any of the other officers at the station know.

First he set up the radar and positioned it in the direction of oncoming traffic, though he knew there'd be none. There never was. He pressed play on the audiobook, then started removing the foil wrapper from the sandwich, readying himself for that long anticipated first bite, when his teeth sank into the warm, toasted roll and all the good stuff in between.

Except something in the distance caught his eye—a car barreling down the opposite side of the street way too fast for comfort. He didn't need an official readout to tell him it was well over the limit. Still, he sighed, laid the sandwich on top of the bag in the passenger seat, and readied his finger on the trigger of the radar gun.

"Speeding down my street when I'm about to eat some damn good barbecue," he mumbled.

Dixie's ears perked up.

"Sorry, girl," he said. "No tasting the goods until I take care of Speed Racer out there."

He nodded toward the windshield just as a canary yellow Volkswagen Bug zipped by.

"Seventy-two miles per hour?" he said, shaking his head. Then he flipped on the lights, pulled into the all but empty street, and sped off after it.

It didn't take the car long to stop. In fact, as soon as the siren made its first wail, the driver hit the brakes, and he was pulling up behind the offender in a matter of seconds.

Dixie howled. She wasn't used to this much police action on a Saturday night. In the three years since he'd been elected sheriff of Oak Bluff, Cash could count on one hand the number of traffic violations for which he'd written actual tickets, and none of them happened on his Saturday night watch. Not much happened in the way of criminal activity, period, and he was planning on keeping it that way.

He hopped out of the truck and strode toward the yellow Bug but stopped before reaching the window. His brows drew together. Half of some sort of ball gown was hanging out the driver's side door. It was torn and tattered, like it had been dragged along at seventy-two miles per hour for the better part of the afternoon and early evening.

Cash shook his head and approached the window, which was still closed. He rapped on it with his knuckles.

It lowered.

Yep, that was a ball gown, all right. A purple one. And inside the gown was a knockout brunette with soft curls tumbling over her bare shoulders... A knockout brunette who'd just broken the law.

He lowered his aviators down the bridge of his nose.

She gasped. "Wow," she said. "I thought that just happened in the movies."

"Excuse me, ma'am?"

"That!" she said, grinning and nodding toward his glasses, her bright blue eyes glowing in the setting sun. "The whole shades-down-the-nose thing, the instant intimidation. It's so amazingly small town. I love it!"

Cash cleared his throat, trying to ignore how her smile lit up her face or how soft her pink lips looked. He wasn't having a ton of success. "Ma'am, do you have any idea how fast you were driving?"

Her smile fell. "Do I really look like a 'ma'am' to you? I know some people think 'miss' is a little degrading, but I'm all for it. Call me 'miss' 'til I'm gray and old—not that I'll go gray gracefully." She laughed.

"*Ma'am*," Cash said with more force, and the laughing ceased. "You were going seventy-two in a fifty-mile-per-hour zone."

She bit her lip. "That's bad, right?"

He nodded. "It's breaking the law, so yeah. I'd say it's bad."

She sighed, then held both her hands toward him, palms up. "Book me," she said. "Lock me up and throw away the key—as long as I make it to Oak Bluff by ten. That's when the B and B closes for the night."

Cash scratched the back of his head. Then he glanced over at his car—the one that had OAK BLUFF SHERIFF painted on either side. He was a man of the law. Rules and regulations. This was all part of the job, which meant he should not let himself get distracted by her teeth grazing her full bottom lip—or the vulnerability he sensed beneath the brash exterior.

"License and insurance card, please, ma'am."

She smiled again, but something in it seemed forced. It wasn't as if he knew a thing about this strange woman, but he was trained to read people. Despite not flinching at being pulled over and possibly arrested, she radiated a nervous energy he couldn't ignore. He'd venture a guess she was not as brazen as she'd have him believe, and something about that bothered him. Cash didn't get pretense. He might have been a quiet man, but he was a man of meaning—meant what he said and meant what he did. Why couldn't everyone else just do the same?

"Right," she said. "I've got them both right…" She trailed off as she acted like she was rifling through a giant bag when all she'd done was click open what looked like a fancy as hell billfold.

She chuckled. "So…you're going to love this, Officer"—she squinted to read his name badge—"Hawkins."

"Sheriff Hawkins," he corrected her.

Her cheeks flushed, and he had to remind himself that he was here to write this woman a ticket—not find her in any way attractive.

"*Sheriff* Hawkins. So—Sheriff. I wasn't even supposed to be driving tonight. I left everything in the hotel room except for what I needed. That's why I only put my lip gloss, the room key, and my phone in the clutch."

"The what?"

"Clutch," she said, starting to lift the wallet-type contraption.

"Ma'am, please keep your hands on the steering wheel if you're not going to produce the items I'm asking for."

She dropped the clutch, or whatever it was, and placed her hands at ten and two with a self-satisfied grin. "It's a purse that you *clutch* in your hand. Only enough room for the essentials."

He crossed his arms. "Something's not adding up."

She narrowed her eyes. "Look, you can try to find me guilty of speeding—"

"Seventy-two in a fifty."

She rolled her eyes. "But I'm not a liar."

He raised a brow. "The keys?"

"What?"

"The car keys, ma'am. If you only put the essentials in your *clutch*, where'd you get the car keys?"

Her mouth opened, then closed. Finally she blew out a breath. "I keep the key in this little magnet case and hide it behind the back wheel. Just in case."

Good Lord, why did he even ask? He didn't have time for this. Okay. Fine. He had all the time in the world. But all he'd wanted to do was eat his damned sandwich and watch the sunset. He and Dixie would listen to a few hours of a new book, and then they'd go home and have an off-duty beverage or two. Well, Cash would, at least. Dixie would get a fresh bowl of water with two ice cubes—her favorite. But instead his sandwich was getting cold, and he hadn't even heard the opening remarks of the book, let alone gotten to chapter one.

"In case *what?*" he asked. Because how the hell long was it going to take to get to the end of this—this situation?

She shrugged. "In case I need to get the hell outta Dodge on a moment's notice."

He pressed a palm against the doorframe and leaned down to the window so they were eye level with each other. He could smell hints of her perfume—a light citrus that made him think of an orange grove.

"No license, no insurance, and twenty-two miles over the speed limit. Ms. . . . ?"

"Belle," she answered quickly. "Olivia Belle."

"Please step out of the car, Ms. Belle."

She scoffed. "You're not serious, are you? I can pay the ticket. I know my debit card number by heart. And I know you can punch my license plate number into your computer thingy and find me. It's my car, registered in—*shit*. Michael co-signed for the loan, and that damned bank put *his* name on the title. Stupid patriarchy," she mumbled. Then she groaned and opened the door, and the rest of the dress erupted out into the street as she exited the vehicle.

"Lemme get this straight," he said, averting his gaze from how the bodice of the dress fit her curves like it was meant for her body and hers alone. The dip and swell of her hips, the way the cut of the dress made a heart below her collarbone, and how the soft skin above her breasts rose and fell with each measured breath. "You were just driving twenty-two miles over the speed limit with no license or insurance in a car that is registered to a Michael?"

She winced but nodded.

He shook his head. He didn't want to do it like this, but if he brought her in any other way, the whole department would call him on it—tell him he was going soft on his first Saturday night offender in a long time.

Cash pulled the cuffs off his belt and quickly clasped one of them around her left wrist, then the other around her right.

He sighed. "Welcome to Oak Bluff, Ms. Belle. You're under arrest."

Chapter Two

Sheriff Hawkins read Olivia her rights, then nodded toward the SUV. "You lead the way, ma'am."

Olivia groaned.

This was a first. Handcuffs. And not in a sexy way. Sure she was speeding, and *maybe* she'd left before grabbing the necessities like her wallet. And clothes to change into so she wouldn't have to spend eternity in this monster of a dress. But wasn't that the whole idea behind fleeing? You leave. Quickly. Without any thought other than self-preservation.

It only took her two steps to stumble on the hem of her dress, break the heel off her shoe, and twist her ankle.

"Damn it!" she cried, throwing her cuffed wrists into the air to catch her balance, but she was going down. There were no two ways about it. Except before she hit the pavement, a strong, muscular arm wrapped around her midsection, hauling her back up.

She was smack against Sheriff Grumpy Pants's chest now, and hell if he wasn't solid as the trunk of a redwood.

"You all right there, Cinderella?" His warm breath teased the skin on her neck.

"Pardon me?"

He bent down and picked up her broken shoe, dangling the crystal clear stiletto pump in front of her. "Ball gown. Glass slipper. I'd say you walked right out of a fairy tale if you hadn't ruined a perfectly peaceful Saturday night."

Olivia scoffed, then spun to face him, but when her full weight fell on her shoeless foot, pain shot through her like a lightning bolt—hot and fast. She yelped, and this time there was no one to catch her as she toppled backward and fell flat on her already-sore-from-driving-four-hours behind.

The sheriff's eyes widened.

"You're hurt," he said matter-of-factly.

She would have liked to have crossed her arms in defiance, affording herself the tiniest bit of dignity, but—handcuffs. So she settled for a glare.

He said nothing, but simply scooped her up and carried her to the passenger side of the Tahoe.

He held her with one arm—dress and all—and opened the door with the other. Then he moved something out of the way and deposited her onto the leather seat.

"You mean you're not tossing me in the caged-in area in the back?"

"Quiet a second, will you?" he barked, his deep voice tinged with an emotion she couldn't put her finger on. Annoyance for sure, but there was something else.

He dropped to a squat, then pushed back the taffeta and tulle—entirely too much material of any sort for a daytime wedding. But the bride had insisted, and everyone knows the bride is the boss, especially when she's your almost-fiancé's sister.

Emphasis on the *almost*.

Coarse hands gingerly cradled her foot.

"Does this hurt?" he asked.

She fisted her fettered hands in the pile of dress on her thighs, then pressed her lips together as he moved her foot slowly from side to side.

"Mmm-hmm," she squeaked.

"Swelling's not too bad. Looks like just a mild sprain. I can get you some ice at the station."

She huffed out a breath. "Maybe there wouldn't be any sprain if you hadn't arrested me."

He took off his sunglasses and stared at her with eyes so green she forgot for a second that she was even wearing handcuffs.

"And if you hadn't been driving without a license *or* insurance card at twenty-two miles over the speed limit in *my* town, I never would have arrested you."

He stood, pulled the seat belt across her torso and clicked it into place, shoved as much of her dress in the door as he could, then slammed it shut.

Something wet lapped at Olivia's shoulder, and she wasn't sure if she should hold still or scream. You were supposed to play dead with a bear, right? Were there a lot of bears in wine country?

The sheriff climbed into the driver's seat with a swift, fluid movement that told her he and this tank of an automobile were well acquainted.

"Is there a bear in your back seat?" she whispered.

"A what?"

There it was again. Something slobbery and smooth on her skin.

"A *bear*!" she whisper-shouted.

He froze, one hand white-knuckling the wheel. Then the other reached slowly toward the back seat, but Olivia was too scared to watch. He let out a heart-stopping roar.

She screamed as he yanked his hand back, cradling it to his chest as he threw his head against the back of the seat and—*laughed.*

She shifted toward the rear of the vehicle to find a German shepherd sitting behind her, tongue hanging out the side of its mouth and tail wagging.

"You're terrible," she said.

"And you're gullible as hell. You must be a long way from home if you think Oak Bluff is bear country." He scratched under the dog's chin. "Olivia Belle, meet Dixie. The reason I don't need a cage back there."

Olivia swallowed. "But she's sweet, right? That's why she was slobbering all over me?"

Pets weren't really her thing. For one, she lived in an upscale hotel, and it wasn't one of those pet-friendly ones. Then there was the issue of permanency. Committing to a pet was—well—committing. And the fact she was here instead of in San Francisco saying *yes* to a guy she'd left on one knee probably said a thing or two about her staying power.

He put the key in the ignition and the massive engine roared to life.

"She'd rip a man's arm off if I asked her to." He paused for a couple of beats. "Woman's, too." He set his sunglasses in the center console. The sun was setting now, and she guessed he wouldn't need them anymore. Then he shifted into gear and pulled off the shoulder of the road.

She swallowed and decided to sit very still. But then she saw her Bug sitting there as they began to move. "Wait!" she cried. "What about my car?"

He kept his eyes on the road so all she could see was his profile—the strong line of his stubbled jaw, a crooked nose that was somehow perfectly imperfect.

She, however, was just imperfect. At least when it came to relationships. She always found a reason to run. And today she'd run to the one place she thought she could find answers, the tiny town of Oak Bluff.

"I'll send a couple deputies—*licensed* drivers—out to get it after I bring you in."

She let out a relieved breath. At least he wasn't towing it.

She raised her cuffed hands to the visor above her. "What's this?" she asked, fingertips brushing the edge of an envelope. "Looks like a wedding invitation." Seemed like everyone was planning weddings, getting married, or proposing. And she was just flat-out running.

He wrapped a hand around one of her wrists and lowered both hands to her lap. "None of your concern is what it is," he said gruffly.

She groaned. "Are these really even necessary? It's not as if I resisted arrest. And I'm hobbled now, so I can't exactly tuck and roll and make a break for it."

The corner of his mouth twitched, but he held back the grin. It made her think the burst of laughter she'd just seen from him was something rare. Because a man who fought off a smile was a man who liked others to view him a certain way.

He tugged at a small key ring that was attached to his belt with what looked like a retractable cord. Without looking, he inserted the small key into the base of each cuff and released her.

"Thank you," she said softly.

He nodded.

She reached for her swollen ankle and rubbed it gingerly.

"Pain's pretty bad?" he asked.

She shrugged. She'd broken her arm in eighth grade. That had been the most excruciating physical pain she'd ever experienced. But worse was her parents arguing in the ER about whose fault the accident was when it was *their* arguing that had initially caused it. But by that point in her life, her parents had found any reason they could to scream at each other, and they'd long since stopped making sure she wasn't around to hear.

The divorce dragged on for years, finalized just months before she'd left for college. She hadn't lived with either parent since.

"That all depends. You gonna make me sleep in a cell tonight instead of the cozy bed-and-breakfast I booked?"

He sighed. "You got someone who can fax in a copy of your license and insurance?"

Emily was the night manager tonight—and Olivia's closest friend. She had a key to Olivia's room. It would just be a matter of avoiding Michael if he hadn't gotten his own room after her disappearing act this afternoon.

"Yes!" she said, feeling the tiniest bit triumphant. Because, come on—she needed a small win here.

He sighed. "If you can prove you're a licensed driver, that the car is registered with *your* insurance, then I guess that'll just leave the speeding. And making my dinner cold."

They pulled to a stop in front of a small two-story brick building that looked about a hundred years old. Yet it was charming as hell, as was every other shop or restaurant that lined the street.

"Sixteen Oak Bluff Way," she said, remarking on the address that was stenciled on the sign below the more prominent OAK BLUFF SHERIFF'S DEPARTMENT. "So the bed-and-breakfast is—"

"Across the street and two doors down, next to Lucinda's Antiques, which is closed on account of the owner having to go to a funeral."

"The bed-and-breakfast?" she asked.

"Huh?"

"The bed-and-breakfast is closed?"

He shook his head. "Lucinda's. Her third husband passed. He lived about an hour outside of town."

"Oh," she said softly. "How sad. Wait; did you say *third* husband?"

He ran a hand through dark brown hair. It was cropped close, but just long enough that fingers could get partially buried. Not that she was thinking of such things about a total stranger who—up until a few minutes ago—had a laundry list of items to arrest her for. It didn't matter that she'd been with Michael since their last semester of grad school and was now in her first year as event coordinator at Hotel Blue—the hotel his parents owned. She could count on one hand how many times she'd run her fingers through *his* hair in the past six months—or him through hers.

Eighteen months—her longest relationship to date. She'd thought he was going to ask her to move in. She'd privately entertained the thought of not living in the place where she worked. But then she'd be ten miles from the place where she spent ninety percent of her time.

But he hadn't asked her to move in. He'd *proposed*.

"Ms. Belle?" she heard the sheriff say, then realized by his tone it probably wasn't the first time.

"Huh?" she answered. "What?"

He shook his head. "I was explaining how Lucinda's third husband wasn't from Oak Bluff. He wanted to be buried by his parents, and Lucinda respected that. So she's there for a few days, getting his affairs in order."

"Oh," she said absently. "What happened to the other two husbands...if you don't mind me asking?"

He shrugged. "Lost the first one to lung cancer." He paused for a second, and she wasn't sure he was going to say more. But then he continued. "The guy was a stubborn smoker who just couldn't—no, *wouldn't*—quit. Second one got thrown from a horse who got spooked. And Earl? Well, he was older. Had a lot of health issues, but she loved him. And he treated her real good."

She didn't know Lucinda but was already fascinated by a woman who could commit to three different men. Even if they all ended in heartache, she kept on keeping on. Walked down that aisle three times. Buried three men she seemed to have loved.

Olivia let out a bitter laugh. If anything happened to one of her parents, the other would probably show up at the funeral just to dance on the grave.

"What's so funny?" he asked.

"Nothing," she said flatly. "Absolutely nothing about anything is funny."

He raised a brow, then threw open his door and hopped out of the truck. In seconds he was at her side of the car. The door swung open, but then he stood there, hands on hips.

"What?" she asked.

He crossed his arms now. "I'm just puzzling out how it's gonna look when I carry you in there and then throw the book at you."

She rolled her eyes, then slapped on the cuffs. "Does this help?" she asked. "Big bad sheriff worried everyone's gonna think he's a marshmallow?" She wiggled out of her good shoe. "And I can walk just fine," she lied. She swung her legs to the right, then looked down. It was a few feet drop to just hop out. And she'd already screwed herself into losing her balance with her wrists bound again.

"I could help you," he said dryly.

A rogue curl fell over her eyes, and she tried to tuck it behind her ear, but it wasn't so easy to do with the cuffs. She blew it out of the way, but it just fell back over her face. Then she groaned.

"Fine," she relented. "But I'm *walking*."

He said nothing as he grabbed her under each arm and then hoisted her out of the vehicle. He set her down carefully, and she put all of her weight on her good foot to start. Then she tested the waters on her injured one.

She hissed in a breath between her teeth, but she was able to do it.

"You are stubborn as hell, aren't you?" he asked.

She jutted out her chin and squared her shoulders even though she knew she was a sight. Tattered bridesmaid gown, no shoes, handcuffs, and her hair falling every which way.

"Oh God," she said as realization struck. "Am I going to have a mug shot?"

There it was again—the corner of his mouth threatening to tilt up.

"I guess we'll just have to see about that." He reached past her and grabbed a greasy-looking brown paper bag, then opened the back door to let Dixie out. The dog sniffed at Olivia's bare feet, then started licking her wounded ankle as if she knew she was hurt.

"Traitor," he said under his breath.

Olivia narrowed her eyes. "She's not really an attack dog, is she? You were just messing with me again."

He said nothing as he strode a couple steps in front of her to get the door, and her eyes instinctively dropped lower than they should have. His belt hung low on his hips, his gun holstered on one side, that ring of keys on the other. The whole uniform was black—not tan like she would have thought—and those pants fit like an absolute glove over a part of the sheriff she certainly shouldn't be ogling.

"After you," he said once the door was open.

Her head snapped up, and her cheeks flamed. Had she just been caught? If so, he could just add it to her rap sheet.

She limped past him and into what looked more like a small office than a police station. There were a handful of desks, most of them empty. Only two were occupied—one by a woman in uniform and one by a man who looked several years younger than the sheriff.

"Deputies," he said, nodding his head in greeting. "Looks like we've got some paperwork tonight."

Chapter Three

Well, your license checks out. Your insurance checks out, and on account of the fact I don't want either of the deputies to have to spend the night making sure you're *comfortable* and well cared for in our seldom used cell, I'm going to write you your ticket and send you on your way."

She beamed at him, and damn if that smile of hers didn't wake something up inside him he'd thought would never come out of hibernation.

"Oh, I could just hug you!" she said, jumping up from the chair beside his desk. "Ow!" she yelped.

"Right," he said. "The ankle. Wait here a minute."

She sat back down and he strode off to the kitchen, grabbing a cold pack from the freezer and a clean towel from the counter. He rummaged through the cabinets until he found a bottle of ibuprofen, then filled a glass with water from the tap.

What if she would have done it—hugged him?

He shook his head and laughed softly. He'd long considered himself *off* the market. He had enough to fulfill him with the job, taking care of Dixie, and—the job. Did he say the job? Well, it was election year. That would keep him busy enough. Besides, he certainly wasn't setting his designs on a strange woman who was only passing through—and breaking a hell of a lot of laws on her way in.

Cash was a permanent staple in Oak Bluff, and he had no interest in anyone who wasn't.

He handed her the bottle and set the water down on the desk. "A few of those should help take the edge off the pain." He dragged another chair to face hers, then knelt down beside her. "May I?" he asked.

She nodded, and he lifted her foot and rested it on the seat cushion. First he laid the towel over her swollen ankle. Then the pack. He watched as she tossed four of the small red pills into her mouth and washed them down with a sip of water. And then another until she downed the whole glass of water.

"Thirsty, huh?" he asked.

She wiped her forearm across her mouth. "Yeah. It's been a day."

"How long were you driving?"

"I ran out—I mean *left*—at about two p.m. So a little over four hours?"

He checked his watch. It was after seven now. "You must be hungry, too."

She chewed on her bottom lip. "Starved, actually. I didn't even make it to the hors d'oeuvres."

He blew out a breath, then grabbed the brown paper bag from his desk. "It's not hot anymore, but it'll still be the best barbecue you ever had."

Her eyes lit up as he handed it to her. She reached inside

greedily and practically tore the sandwich free. She paused, though, just before sinking her teeth into that perfectly crusty bread.

"This is your dinner," she said with realization.

He waved her off. "I know where to get more." Though he doubted that would be happening tonight. BBQ on the Bluff closed at nine, and by the time he got Olivia settled at the B and B, well, he'd most likely be heading home to a frozen pizza and a six-pack.

His brows furrowed. "You coming from some kind of party? I kind of figured with the dress."

Her mouth was full with his dinner, a drip of barbecue sauce in the corner where her lips met. Her eyes fluttered closed, and she moaned with what he knew was the sheer ecstasy of tasting the best local fare Oak Bluff had to offer.

She swallowed and licked her lips, and there it was again: the hibernating bear waking from its long sleep.

He wanted to brush his thumb across that full bottom lip of hers, which was just about the stupidest thought he'd had since asking Tara to marry him ten years ago.

"A wedding," she finally said.

He raised a brow. "Not yours, I take it. I mean, I know brides wear all sorts of dresses these days—"

"No!" she interrupted. "God, no. Me? Married? Ha! I…" But she cut herself off by taking another gargantuan bite. "This is so good," she said around the mouthful of food.

He guessed the whole marriage conversation was over, which was fine by him. They weren't here to hash out each other's romantic pasts—or lack thereof. In fact, they didn't need to be here any longer once she'd polished off the rest of his dinner. And that only took about three more minutes.

He sat on the edge of his desk and watched her dab at the

corners of her mouth with her thumb. Then she brushed off her hands just as Deputies Adams and Walters walked back through the station door.

"Bug's parked behind the B and B, Cash," Adams said. "Am I clocking out now, or is our guest staying the night?" She nudged Walters with her elbow, and the two deputies glanced from Cash sitting casually on the desk to Olivia stretched out across two chairs. Both of his employees were fighting off grins, which meant they were assuming something they shouldn't be assuming. Because they'd be wrong.

He stood to his full six feet four inches and crossed his arms. "I'll be taking her to the B and B in just a couple minutes, so you can both clock out. Who's on call tonight?"

Adams cleared her throat. "You are, sir."

Shit. That was right. Scratch the six-pack. There'd just be the frozen pizza.

"Right," he said. "I'll see you two in the morning, then."

Both deputies nodded at him and then Olivia. "Night, Cash," they said in unison.

"Good night."

Olivia took the ice pack and towel off her ankle and stood. She looked steadier on her feet. Her bare feet.

"You got an overnight bag?" he asked.

She shook her head. "Do you have a Target around here?"

He groaned. "You don't even have a wallet."

"Right. Shoot. I did *not* think things through."

He pulled his cell phone from his pocket and dialed up Wade at the pharmacy. "You busy? Yeah, I got a customer who needs some of the necessities. Okay if I bring her by in a minute? Thanks, buddy. I owe you."

He looked her up and down and shook his head, the faintest hint of a smile playing at his lips.

"What *are* you doing in Oak Bluff, Olivia Belle?"

She shrugged. "I came here to find true love."

Chapter Four

With Michael's sister's wedding in the books, there were no other major events happening that week at the hotel. Olivia could pencil in a few vacation days. Emily was sending an overnight messenger service with her wallet, some of her own clothes, and toiletries. For now, though, as the sheriff walked her to the B and B, she was dressed in a very trendy Oak Bluff sweatshirt and a pair of drugstore yoga pants, because, yes—those were apparently a thing. Pharmacy owner Wade even had a small selection of flip-flops, which meant she wasn't exactly ready for the cover of *Vogue*, but she wouldn't have to spend the night in a ball gown and one glass slipper.

She laughed.

"Did I miss a joke?" he asked.

She shook her head. "Just remembering you calling my shoes glass slippers." She held up the pharmacy bag that was stuffed with her bridesmaid dress, one-and-a-half shoes, and a toothbrush and toothpaste. "I'm most definitely *not* anything out of a fairy tale."

It was dark out now, but the streetlights lit the hard lines of his face, and she could see that he was trying to puzzle something out.

"Got anything you want to ask me, Sheriff? Or can I call you Cash now that you bought me dinner and this fancy new outfit?" They stopped in front of the B and B, which was aptly called The Oak Bluff B and B. "You know? Something bigger with a little more pizazz might get your little town some more tourist traffic."

He crossed his arms. "Our little town doesn't need big names. We get plenty of traffic. In fact, someone sped right through the outskirts just this afternoon. Coulda gotten into a serious accident if law enforcement hadn't stepped in."

She rolled her eyes.

"And I take it you aren't in town long?" he added. "So we should probably just keep it at *Sheriff* and *Ms. Belle.*"

She smiled her best customer service smile—one of the first things they teach you when you major in hospitality management. He was right. They should keep it formal. Formality kept things distant, and distance was exactly what Olivia needed.

Except this stranger of a man could have really arrested her. He could have let her go hungry and left her in her tattered gown until the messenger got here tomorrow. But he hadn't, and somehow those small gestures felt more intimate than Michael's proposal, which meant she was not succeeding at distance here.

"I shouldn't be here more than a few days," she said. "Just need to find what I came here for."

"Right," he said. "True love. That should only take a few days."

She closed her eyes for a moment and replayed Michael's words in her head.

It had been just after the ceremony—and just before cocktails. All she'd done was ask him why he'd been acting so weird all morning. Then everything had spun out of control.

It's the logical next step, babe. The practice wants a family man as partner. The condo co-op board won't put your name on the deed unless we're married. It just makes sense. Only then had he gotten down on one knee—after likening their relationship to a business maneuver. It wasn't the animosity of her parents' relationship, but it sure as hell wasn't love. Not with Michael and not with anyone who'd come before him. What had she been doing wrong?

Being with him had been safe—their chemistry a slow enough burn to take things at a gradual pace—but it was only now, standing in this ridiculous outfit before a man who'd put her in handcuffs in the first five minutes he'd met her, that she wondered what it would be like to throw caution to the wind.

Spontaneity had never been her thing—at least with men. Sure, she could run off and drive three-plus hours down the coast the second she got spooked *out* of a relationship, but she didn't just jump off the ledge the second a man made her heart go pitter-pat. Or maybe it was that her heart had never reacted like this before, but right now it was pittering and pattering beyond restraint.

Aw, to hell with it. Caution had gotten her nowhere so far, and it wasn't like this guy was proposing marriage. She'd already broken the law. How much more trouble could she really get herself into?

She drew in a deep breath and opened her eyes to find the sheriff unabashedly staring at her, his stoic expression revealing nothing. She dropped the pharmacy bag—and before talking herself out of it—rose up on her tiptoes and kissed the man softly on the lips.

"I'm sorry," she said, when his lips didn't move in the slightest. "I was just testing a theory, and it was the worst judgment ever, and—"

He shoved his fingers into her hair, his lips crashing against hers. The kiss was strong, insistent—and clumsy. Teeth knocked together, and his fingers got caught in her curls. But he pulled her closer, and she him—unable to get enough of someone who up until a few hours ago hadn't even existed as far as she knew.

But he existed now. *They* existed in this inexplicable moment of lips touching and tongues tangling and what the hell was she doing?

She stumbled backward, gasping for breath, and he scrubbed a hand across his jaw.

"Good night, Sheriff." She cleared her throat. "Thank you—uh—for the sandwich. And clothes. And no jail time."

He nodded once. "Good night, Ms. Belle. Try to stay on the right side of the law."

She laughed nervously and backed toward the door, reaching behind her to turn the knob and push it open.

Thank the stars the bed-and-breakfast was still open.

Seconds later the door was closed again, giving her that distance she craved.

Never mind that she could still feel the tingle of his lips on hers—or the scratch of his stubble against her chin. Never mind any of it. She was a twenty-five-year-old woman who'd just fled a marriage proposal—a twenty-five-year-old

woman who had, in one way or another, fled every relationship she'd ever been in the moment she knew she wasn't in
love.

Why couldn't she fall in love? Either she was defective
or she just hadn't learned the secret yet. She liked to think it
was the latter. At least, she hoped it was. Otherwise, caution
or no, she was in big trouble.

This visit obviously wasn't about her own love story. It
was about the only one she knew existed in real life. And if
she could figure out how *they* made it work, then maybe, *just*
maybe, she'd have a chance at one day getting it right herself.

Cash had just given Dixie the last slice of pizza when his cell
phone alerted him to the alarm being tripped at Lucinda's.
Not the shop, but the apartment above.

He picked up his radio from the coffee table. "We got a
four-five-nine at Lucinda's. No request for backup yet but
wanted to see which one of you was still awake *and* sober.
Over."

"Roger, Sheriff. Available for backup," Walters said. "I
do believe Adams is on a date, sir. Over."

"Damn it, Walters. Doesn't mean I'm not available for
backup. Available for backup, sir. Over."

Cash shook his head. "Heading there now. Stand by.
Out."

Breaking and entering? That kind of shit didn't happen in
Oak Bluff. The town wasn't perfect. The Everett boys had
had their share of hell when their drunk of a father had almost killed the oldest one, Jack. But that was over a decade
ago, when Cash was studying criminal justice in college. By
the time he'd come back home, the Everetts had been per-

manently removed from Jack Senior's custody. Now the man was dead and gone, and the three brothers were all running the Crossroads Ranch and soon a new vineyard.

The bottom line was, there were no major threats—domestic or otherwise—in their sleepy little town. And hadn't he dealt with enough on what was supposed to be an uneventful Saturday night?

When he got to Lucinda's, he and Dixie climbed stealthily up the back steps to where they found the door perfectly shut.

Cash gripped the handle and gave it a soft twist to the right, and it opened with ease.

Perfect. Lucinda had set the alarm but hadn't locked the door.

He stepped quietly into the apartment's kitchen—and almost tripped over a pair of pharmacy-purchased flip-flops. In fact, he'd venture to guess these flip-flops were only a few hours old.

That's when he saw Olivia Belle through the open archway into the living room, kneeling on the wood floor with a broken floorboard in her hand.

And she was crying.

"I know," she said, her reddened eyes meeting his. "I'm under arrest."

Dixie ran straight to her and collapsed, resting her head in Olivia's lap.

She laughed through a sob. "This furry ball of love would never rip someone's arm off."

"Betrayed again," Cash mumbled. "She *is* trained to," he said louder. "Just hasn't had much occasion to do so, so she's out of practice." More like she never had the occasion to do so, but that was beside the point.

He made his way through the living room to the digital panel on the wall. He typed in the code to disable the alarm, and the silent alert finally left his cell phone alone.

"The door was unlocked," she said with a sniffle. "I was just going to look for—I didn't know there was an alarm." Her brows pulled together. "Wait. You know Lucinda's alarm code?"

He huffed out a breath. "Lucinda is my mother. And when she gets back, we're going to have a nice long talk about how the alarm doesn't mean shit if she keeps on leaving her door unlocked. Also, who takes off their shoes when making an unlawful entry?"

Olivia's eyes widened as she dropped the floorboard to the ground. "Oh God. I broke into the town sheriff's *mother's* home? And I stepped in a puddle out back. I didn't want to mess the place up—just find something that isn't here."

He sat down on the arm of the couch and pulled the radio off his hip. "False alarm. No backup needed." He waited for Adams and Walters to reply, then set the radio on the coffee table and crossed his arms. "Well, you didn't exactly *break* in. But you did enter private property that isn't yours. You wanna tell me why?"

Olivia scratched Dixie behind the ear and blew out a shuddering breath. Cash had the inexplicable impulse to go to her, to pull this force of nature of a woman into his arms and comfort her.

But Cash Hawkins didn't act on impulse. And he wasn't about to start with a woman who couldn't seem to go five minutes without breaking a law.

Her shoulders slumped. "Guess I have to tell you everything now, huh?"

He shrugged. "Either that or say good-bye to the B and B and hello to a musty cell."

"Fine," she said. "I suppose now that I've interrupted your evening again, I owe you that much."

"I suppose you do," he said. He could just march her back to the B and B and call it a night. But he told himself he wanted to hear her story for legal reasons—to make sure this woman wasn't going to be breaking and entering or committing another traffic violation any time soon. It certainly wasn't because he wanted a few more minutes in her presence. Because that would go against all his self-imposed rules when it came to women. Mainly—he didn't do the whole get-to-know-you thing. But here he was—getting to know her.

Olivia swiped under her eyes and sniffled again. Dixie whimpered, and Olivia went back to scratching behind the non–attack dog's ear. "My grandma lived in Oak Bluff until she was nineteen. She met my grandpa on a weekend trip to San Francisco. They had one magical night—his last night in town before leaving for basic training and then being shipped off to the war in Vietnam. They continued their courtship one hundred percent through letters for *three* years."

"I'm assuming things worked out for them since they are your grandparents and all?"

She nodded. "He proposed to her the day he got home, and they eloped the next weekend."

"Get outta here," Cash said. "One date and some letters, and just like that?"

"Just like that. They're coming up on their forty-eighth anniversary."

Cash blew out a long whistle. "Lemme guess," he said. "You're looking for the letters."

The tears started again. "This used to be her house. I didn't realize it because the address was different and—well—it's an antiques shop now. But I did some googling on my phone. Thank God for the B and B's Wi-Fi, by the way. And it turns out this is the place." She held up the loose floorboard. "See?" She pointed to small carvings in the wood. *J and A. 1967–1970.* "Joseph and Anna."

He scratched the back of his neck. "I don't get it. If these letters are so special, why'd your grandmother leave them here?"

"She didn't mean to at first. But their honeymoon turned into a year of travel. Can you believe that? A *year.* And when they finally made their way back here, her parents had up and sold the place. By that time Gran said she didn't need the letters because she had my grandfather, so she never came looking for them. They ended up settling in San Francisco, had my dad and my uncle. My dad married my mom. They had me. Years later they decided they hated each other, so they divorced and are still living hatefully ever after to this day."

"That was a mouthful," he said, still sort of reeling from the verbal onslaught. Most of his conversations warranted nothing more than a one- or two-word response from him, and he liked it that way.

She secured the plank of wood back into its spot, gave Dixie a pat, then stood up. She dusted her hands off on her Oak Bluff sweatshirt.

"I'm pretty sure I've overstayed my welcome. If you're not going to arrest me—again—I should get going."

"So the true love you came here to find... ?"

"Theirs," she said. "I thought if I could read the letters I could figure out the secret. You know?"

He narrowed his eyes. "Secret to what?"

She threw her hands in the air. "*Love!* How do you find it? How do you make it last? What happened in those letters that got them to almost fifty years of marriage when I can barely make it past fifteen *months* of dating a perfectly nice guy with a perfectly good job and perfect co-op who would love to put me on the deed? Do you know I ran from a man while he was down on one knee? With a ring? Why do I keep running from commitment? How the hell do I fix myself so I can find what they found five decades ago?"

Her chest was heaving.

"Wait. You're getting *married*?"

"No! That's just the point. I'm *not*. And I probably shouldn't. Yet I keep hoping I'll figure it out, and maybe that's my problem."

Her arms were flailing at this point, and her eyes were wild—both signs that he should probably back away. Instead he found himself stepping closer, his hands gently gripping her shoulders in an effort to calm or steady or *something*.

"Hey," he said softly. "I don't know a whole hell of a lot about this stuff, but I'm sure of one thing."

She took a few steadying breaths, then fixed her gaze on him. "What's that?"

"There is no secret," he said plainly.

Her bottom lip trembled, but no more tears fell. "So I'm just—broken?"

He could feel the heat of her skin even beneath the sweatshirt, and it made the tips of his fingers tingle. He tried to rationalize that she was simply new and unexpected, and that was why he couldn't seem to stay away. But it wasn't like he was celibate. He spent his nights and weekends off at his favorite tavern a couple towns over. He'd found plenty of companions over the years who were good with keeping it casual.

Weren't they at one time or another new and unexpected, too?

"Aren't we all sorta broken?" he countered.

"Well, that's a cynical way of looking at things. Hey, wait." She paused. "If Lucinda's your mom, that was your stepdad who just..."

He nodded. "Went to the burial this morning. But a sheriff can't quite take a week off the job. It's kind of a 'round the clock situation."

She sucked in a sharp breath. "And the first husband—the one who died of lung cancer—that was your dad."

His throat tightened. "I was sixteen. He was a good father, but hard-headed as all hell."

"Oh, Cash," she said, cupping his cheek in her palm. He didn't correct her. Didn't give her his damned spiel about *Sheriff Hawkins* and *Ms. Belle* because right now, in this moment, he liked the sound of his name on her lips.

"What if I could help you track down those letters?" he asked.

"You would do that for me?"

He laughed softly. "If it means you stop breaking laws in my town and let me get a night or two of peace."

Her cheeks flushed, and hell if she wasn't beautiful when she was embarrassed.

She held up her right hand. "I solemnly swear to stop breaking laws in Oak Bluff, California."

"Deal," he said.

"I'm sorry about your dad, Cash. And your stepdads. You and Lucinda have lost a lot, huh?"

"We get by just fine."

"And getting by is enough?" she asked.

"Has been." Until now, it seemed. Because this woman was making him think things he shouldn't think. And want things he shouldn't want.

She rested both her palms on his chest, and he could feel his heart hammering against his ribs. Could she feel it, too? And when the hell was the last time a woman had made his heart race?

He wasn't like Lucinda. She loved, lost, and loved again. He didn't know how she did it, and she definitely wasn't the norm. People were lucky enough to find love once in a lifetime, if at all. He'd had his once and wasn't about to go looking for it again when one of two things could happen: he could search and never find it, or he could be that tiny percentage like his mother who found it—and lost it—again. Either way, he set himself up for disappointment or worse. No, thank you.

Yet here was Olivia Belle, her fingertips searing his skin through his shirt, obliterating years of rationalization for why he lived his life the way he did.

This was the worst idea. Period.

"You're not getting married," he said plainly, but it was still a question.

"I'm not."

"Ms. Belle?"

"Sheriff?"

"I'm gonna kiss you again."

She bit her bottom lip, and he wondered if there was anything sexier. "I'm gonna let you."

"Good." He dipped his head.

"But," she interrupted, "let the record show that I am defective. I don't know how to—"

"Olivia."

"Yeah?"

"Stop talking, please."

He brushed his lips tentatively over hers, and when she didn't speak, he let the hunger win. Her lips parted, and his tongue slipped past. He tasted the salt of her tears, the coffee she must have had at the B and B, and something sweet, like cinnamon. She was both delicious and intoxicating, and even though he was still on call, he let himself get drunk on the strangeness and newness of wanting like he hadn't let himself want in a good long time.

Because wanting her was safe. She wouldn't be here long enough to burrow her way into his heart, just long enough to get whatever this was out of his system.

Because she'd already admitted she was a runner, and Cash knew a thing or two about being left on one knee.

Because despite it seeming like she somehow ran to *him*, as soon as they solved the mystery of the letters, she'd be long gone, and everything would go back to the way it had always been.

Chapter Five

Olivia met Cash in the lobby of the B and B at half past ten. She bounded out of the kitchen in her favorite jeans, a green cami and cardigan, and her Chuck Taylors. The messenger Emily sent had arrived a bit past eight, and just having her own stuff made Olivia feel like today, anything was possible. Plus, the swelling in her ankle had gone down significantly, so while it still hurt, walking was no longer an issue. Then there was the big, bad sheriff waiting for her in the small foyer. Only in jeans and a form-fitting gray T-shirt, he didn't look so big and bad. Or sheriff-y. But good Lord did he look—*good*.

"Coffee," she said in greeting, holding out one of the two to-go cups in her hand. "I wasn't sure how you took it, so I made one black and one with cream, sugar, and a dash of cinnamon. Figured I'd drink whichever one you didn't."

He gave her a single nod. "I take it black." He paused for a moment, then added, "Cinnamon, huh?"

She grinned. "Oh, thank goodness. I'd have run back to the kitchen if you said otherwise. I can't do without my cream and sugar. I love almost everything a little sweet."

She pressed the opening of her cup to her lips and hummed as her tongue caught the first taste. There was nothing like the first sip of coffee in the morning.

"I thought I tasted cinnamon when I kissed you," Cash said softly.

Olivia coughed, almost spitting the hot liquid all over the floor.

He took a long, slow sip from his own cup, then let out a satisfied-sounding sigh.

Right. He knew how she tasted—and she him. Who the hell was the Olivia who'd kissed a stranger last night—*twice*—and was now wondering when she'd get to do it again?

They hadn't spoken much after Lucinda's. He'd simply walked her next door and made sure she got back into the B and B okay. They'd decided on ten for this morning and then they'd said good night—with no further lip-locking.

But she was watching him drink his coffee now, and coffee drinking involved lips. She knew her focus today was the letters, but Sheriff Cash Hawkins had a mouth that was very distracting.

"What?" he asked.

"Huh?"

"I ate a donut on the walk over. I got chocolate on my face or something?"

"No!" she blurted. "I mean—wait, the cop-and-donut thing is for real?"

He rolled his eyes. "I like donuts. Who doesn't like donuts? The *people*-and-donut thing is for real." Still no trace of a Sunday morning smile.

She shrugged. "I like donuts."

He lifted a white paper bag she hadn't realized he was holding in his other hand. Probably because she'd been staring at his lips. "Chocolate cake, chocolate frosted. From Baker's Bluff. Best donut you'll ever taste."

She narrowed her gaze. "Here I thought I was taking care of you this morning, but you show up with a donut. I can't beat that."

He scanned the quiet foyer. "Everybody still asleep?"

She shook her head. "There are a few people in the kitchen. A few left already on a wine tour. And then there's me." She grinned, taking in the wood floors, the wainscoting on the walls. "This place is so charming. I'll have to tell Gran and Pop about it. Maybe they'll come back for their anniversary."

He scrubbed a hand across his jaw. "When do they hit forty-eight?"

She grinned because that's what thoughts of her grandparents did. They made her smile. Gave her hope when she thought her well had run dry. "A few months. Just after the new year."

"Hmm," he said, brows pulling together.

"*What?*" She waited while he sipped his coffee, as he seemed to contemplate the best course of action for his response.

"Well...It's just that they're selling." He turned toward the curtained front window and grabbed a sign leaning against the glass—a sign she hadn't noticed last night in the dark. A sign that said FOR SALE.

"Oh." The one word was all she could muster. Because after her inauspicious arrival—after coming up empty-handed at Lucinda's apartment—now there was this perfect place that would soon be no more.

Cash cleared his throat. "I didn't realize the bed-and-breakfast meant so much to you—seeing as how you've been here one night and all."

She groaned and grabbed him by the wrist, pulling him out of the foyer and into the sitting room to the right.

"Look," she said, pointing straight ahead.

"It's a fireplace," he remarked without a hint of emotion.

"And knotted pine floors, and that adorable love seat, and the rocking chair where I came up with the brilliant idea to see if I could get into Lucinda's apartment. I'll have you know that I *did* ring the bell. I don't know what possessed me to try the doorknob. No. I know. It was desperation. But the point is—" She groaned. She didn't know what the hell the point was. She just knew she hated the thought of this place going away before Gran and Pop got to see it.

"I mean, I like the DaSilvas as much as the next guy, but they've been making preparations for retirement for the past few years. Both their kids are grown and ended up in Arizona. As soon as they hand over the deed to the place, they're moving into a condo in Phoenix."

She peeked into the kitchen where the older husband and wife team, Rose and Marcus, had been cooking breakfast alongside two newlyweds. The younger couple was sitting at the breakfast bar eating, while the two owners slow-danced to a country song that was playing from a Bluetooth speaker.

Rose waved. "Olivia! Stay out of trouble today, huh?" Then the woman winked. "Mornin', Sheriff."

Cash smiled in Rose's direction, his eyes crinkling so that Olivia knew the gesture was genuine. She wondered how long a person had to know the man before they elicited the same response. Sure, he'd laughed in the police truck yesterday, but it had been at her expense. That didn't count.

"Mornin', Rose. Marcus." He gave the two a friendly nod. "Any bites on the place yet?"

Rose beamed. "We just got an offer on Friday. Waiting to see if the buyer's loan gets approved."

Olivia swallowed. "We should go," she said, tugging at Cash's wrist again. But this time he didn't budge so easily.

She waved good-bye to the kitchen congregation and sped back toward the foyer and then out the bed-and-breakfast's front door.

She paced the sidewalk, stopping when the breeze sent such a chill through her the only remedy was another sip of coffee.

Cash finally appeared several seconds later.

"You want to explain what that disappearing act was all about, or should we just head to the Everett ranch?"

She thought about answering him. There was no logical spin to put on the idea, but then again, she doubted he saw her as anything close to logical after the way she blew into town, knocking laws over left and right when she'd never so much as gotten a detention in high school, let alone ended up handcuffed inside a police vehicle.

"I just feel like it's all a bunch of signs pointing toward me being too late."

"Too late for what?"

She shrugged. "For finding what I'm looking for. It's like Gran and Pop's story disappeared, you know? Her house isn't her house anymore. The letters are probably gone. And now this amazing bed-and-breakfast that totally captures the charm of Oak Bluff—where they could have celebrated the best love story ever—won't even be a bed-and-breakfast anymore. I just think it was probably a mistake—running here."

She wrapped both hands around her coffee cup and brought it to her lips—both to keep herself from fidgeting and to stop herself from unloading any more of her baggage on a man who gave up a quiet Sunday to help her find what she came looking for.

"Here's the thing, Olivia Belle. I don't believe in signs, only intent. And you *did* run here. The question is, do you intend to go home with those letters?"

She nodded slowly, lips still pressed to the small opening on the to-go lid.

"Then don't you give up before you've even started."

Her eyes widened and she lowered her cup, studying him. "You sound just like her."

Cash drained the rest of his coffee, dropped the cup into a street recycling receptacle, and crossed his arms. "I sound like a *her*? Can't say I've ever been told that before."

"No," she said, shaking her head with a small laugh. "You sound like Gran. After my first couple of failed relationships in college, she started giving me the third degree whenever I began dating someone new. Those were her words when she met Michael."

"The fiancé."

"The *not* fiancé. Look, he's a good guy with a good job, and he was good to me."

He cleared his throat. "That's a hell of a lot of *good*."

She waved him off. "But he's not the right guy. And I'm not even the right woman. It's just that you might be right. I could truly be unfixable."

He brushed a rogue curl out of her eye, his fingertips skimming the length of her face. "I mighta said something about being a little broken, but I sure as hell never told you that you needed fixing, and anyone who ever gave you that idea is a damned fool."

Her breath caught in her throat, and for the first time since they'd met—albeit less than twenty-four hours ago—she was at a loss for words.

"Now, let's go find us some letters," he said, holding out his hand.

She placed her palm in his, and he gave it a reassuring squeeze. And in that instant, Olivia Belle's heart did something it had never done before.

It skipped a whole beat. Either this strange man was getting to her in ways no one had before, or she was in need of medical attention. She wasn't quite sure which scared her more.

Chapter Six

Cash knocked on the screen door, but the main door was open. So when no one answered, he took it upon himself to enter. It wasn't like he was an unexpected guest. He'd texted Jack Everett late last night after he'd caught Olivia breaking and entering, and Jack had been more than happy to help.

"You can just do that, huh?" Olivia asked. "Walk into other people's homes when the door's unlocked and not call it breaking and entering. Is that a sheriff thing?"

He held the screen door for her. "No. It's a friend thing. Last time I checked you and Lucinda weren't friends."

She huffed out a breath. "I didn't realize someone with as pleasant a demeanor as you *had* friends. And I bet if Lucinda met me and got to know me, we'd be BFFs in no time."

His brows furrowed, and she groaned.

"Best friends forever?"

He stared at her absently.

She jutted her chin out as she stepped through the door,

and he had to bite back a grin. Of course he knew what the letters stood for, not that he'd ever uttered them in his life. It sure was fun to mess with her, though. And she was right about Lucinda. She and Olivia would be fast friends if they ever had the chance to meet. Lucinda had a soft spot for things that were strange or different yet still beautiful in their unique way.

That was Olivia Belle. Strange. Different. And absolutely beautiful. He was on dangerous ground, even though it was the same earth he'd traversed for the better part of his life.

"Jack?" he called out as they headed down the short hallway toward the kitchen. "I think I'm a few minutes early, but—"

They both stopped short in front of a kitchen table lined with slices of cake—and a half-dressed Luke Everett—the middle brother—blindfolded, his arm in a sling while he was being fed a forkful by Lily Green.

Cash cleared his throat.

Lily yelped while Luke simply chewed the food that was in his mouth, removed the tie covering his eyes, then gave Cash and Olivia a sly grin.

"Mornin', Sheriff. Who's your friend?" He raised a brow.

"Sheriff!" Lily said, with a little more enthusiasm than he was used to seeing from her. "I was just—I mean, Luke was helping me pick a cake for the wedding."

Cash narrowed his eyes. "You two are getting married?"

"Hell no!" Luke said.

Cash wasn't judging, but Lily and Tucker Green had just finalized their divorce.

Lily narrowed her eyes at Luke, then laughed nervously. "*No*. Luke and I are *not* getting married. But my ex-husband is. To Sara Sugar. From that Food Network show, *Sugar and*

Spice? Right. You don't watch television. Anyway, Tucker's getting married, and I'm happy for him, and I'm sort of catering the wedding."

"What?" Olivia blurted. "I'm sorry. I don't know you, and that was rude of me, but—*what*? You're catering your ex-husband's wedding?"

Lily bit her lip and nodded. "I know it sounds crazy, but I need the job."

"And she agreed to it before she knew whose wedding it was. Not that I didn't try to stop her." Luke put his coffee mug down on the counter and swiped the fork out of Lily's hand. "If you all are going to keep on talking about Lily's excellent decision-making skills, I'm just going to take care of the cake." He dug the fork into the hunk of cake and stuffed it into his mouth.

"You're an asshole sometimes. You know that?" Cash said.

Luke just raised his fork in a gesture of cheers and kept on eating.

"Jack in his office?" Cash asked Lily.

She shook her head. "Is he supposed to be? Ava just went to meet him and Owen for lunch."

Cash pulled his phone out of his pocket to double check his texts, then cursed under his breath.

"What is it?" Olivia asked, and he could hear the doubt seeping into her voice.

"Nothing," he said. "Just missed a text from Jack. He took his son Owen to the park for some pitching practice this morning, and now it looks like they're meeting Owen's mom, Ava, for lunch. He was going to dig up some deed history on your grandma's house since I can't find the record of sale from before Lucinda purchased it. Jack's a contract attorney, and he's got a buddy in real estate who might be able to track it down. He says he's sorry if he put us out and that he'll email me what he finds this afternoon."

Olivia's shoulders sagged.

"Hey," he said gently. "It's not a sign."

He glanced back to Luke and Lily who both looked like they were guilty of something, but of what he wasn't sure.

"Heard about the rodeo last night," Cash said to Luke. "Bull threw you pretty hard."

Luke's devil-may-care grin faded. "I got—distracted," was all he said, and Cash could tell not to press the issue.

"You got any horses need working out since I take it you're out of commission for a bit?"

Luke's jaw tightened. After his brothers, Cash knew riding was the most important thing to Luke Everett. Being benched wouldn't be easy for him.

"Yeah," Luke said. "Cleo and Bella are always good for a workout."

Cash nodded toward Lily. "You make sure he stays put."

"Oh, I'm not here to—I mean, I was supposed to do the cake tasting with Ava." Her face brightened. "Do you two want some cake? I'm sure Luke would love the company."

Luke mumbled something Cash couldn't quite make out. And as good as some of Lily Green's homemade cake sounded right about now, he somehow felt like he and Olivia were intruding.

"We'll take a rain check," Cash said.

"I'm Olivia, by the way," she said.

"Lily," the other woman said. "And this ray of sunshine is Luke. You new in town?"

Olivia shook her head. "I mean, yes. I am new, but not

staying. Just visiting—and trying to stay on the right side of the law. It was nice to meet you both."

"I'll hold you to that rain check, Sheriff!" Lily said as they turned toward the door.

"That's what I'm hoping," he called over his shoulder, and they were out the door a few seconds later.

Cash led her toward the stable. He was going to make sure this morning wasn't a loss as far as Olivia giving up hope. "I know what you're thinking," Cash said when they were a good distance from the ranch.

Olivia's cheeks were pink, and she was smiling. "You mean that there was some *major* sexual tension happening during that *cake tasting*?" She put finger quotes around *cake tasting*.

"You are aware that there was actually cake. And Luke did seem to be tasting it."

She raised her brows. "So you didn't notice it."

"No."

She took a step closer to him, and he could swear the crisp October morning grew warmer with her approach.

"You didn't feel the heat? Or you like to pretend that kind of thing doesn't exist?"

He cleared his throat. He knew that kind of thing existed. He knew damned well. But yeah, he was pretending right now. Real hard. Not with Luke and Lily, though. Whatever was going on there was none of his business. The problem was that whatever heat Olivia had noticed back in that kitchen, it had followed them to the stable. And now it was just him and her.

"We're not here to talk about heat," he said. "And apparently we're not here to talk about the deed to your grandma's house. At least not yet."

She moved in closer, that heat he didn't want to acknowledge melting the space between them, and he knew she felt it, too. "What *are* we here for, Sheriff?"

He could tell she was trying to be coy, but there was a slight tremor in her voice that mirrored the erratic rhythm of his pulse.

He was here to clear his head. That much was true. "We're here so I can show you Oak Bluff the way it's meant to be seen—on the back of a horse."

On the back of a horse? "Whoa there, Sheriff. Slow your roll. I don't ride horses. I'm from San Francisco. I ride trolley cars. Sometimes I even ride Ubers—"

"And sometimes you ride a canary yellow Bug way too fast in a town that moves at a much slower pace."

She narrowed her eyes at him. "Horses don't move at a slow pace."

The corner of his mouth twitched, and she gasped dramatically.

"What now?" he asked.

She stepped closer and was even so bold as to touch that spot where his bottom and top lips joined, inspecting it, eyeing it with scrutiny.

He wrapped his hand around her wrist, but the touch was gentle—not full of the force she knew a man of his stature was capable of.

"I was just seeing if this thing worked," she said. "I mean, other than when you're laughing at my expense."

He rolled his eyes. "I smile."

"Mmm—no. You don't. You're that strong, silent type, so stoic, burying your feelings. I mean, if you have them."

He sighed and lowered her hand, but he didn't let go. "I'm having a feeling right now," he said dryly.

She laughed. "I bug you, don't I?"

"Yes. Because you're stalling. Come on."

He tugged her toward the stable door, and only because he'd now laced his fingers with hers did she not resist.

"Oh!" she said when he opened a stall door to reveal a gorgeous caramel-colored horse. Gorgeous and *huge*. How did anyone even get into the saddle without a ladder?

"Olivia Belle, meet Cleo. Cleo…" He stroked a hand down her mane. "Meet Olivia. You two are going to get to know each other rather well today."

"Cash," she said nervously now. Because this was getting a little too real. "I'm not sure this is a good idea. Maybe I could just watch you ride? I'm quite good at spectating. My dad's a huge Giants fan, and we go to tons of games. I can—"

"Shhh," Cash said, covering Cleo's ears. "Cleo here is Jack Everett's horse, and he's just about the biggest Dodger fan there is. You don't want to spook her with talk of another team, do you?"

She forced a smile but backed away from the stall.

"Hey," he said, his tone shifting from playful to concerned. "What's wrong?"

She fidgeted with the button on the bottom of her cardigan. "So…My parents actually took me riding once when I was in middle school. They were concerned I didn't have a thing, you know?"

"A thing?"

"I wasn't into sports or ballet or playing a musical instrument—by the way, the cello thanked me for quitting. I just hadn't found what made me tick."

He raised a brow. "Fast driving."

She sighed. "*No*. Event planning." He opened his mouth to say something, but she cut him off. "Before you make fun, I'll have you know that I am an excellent party planner, and it all started with my best friend's thirteenth birthday party. It was Harry Potter themed, and all the kids in school were talking about how amazing it was afterward. But that's not my point." She paused, waiting for him to interrupt, but he just stared at her with those gorgeous green eyes all patient and *slower paced*. "My parents took me to this farm that gives you a half-hour lesson and then lets you set off on this trail. So there we were, the three of us on horses, and my parents get into an argument."

His brows furrowed. "About what?"

"You name it. Whether we should walk or trot, go right or left at the fork in the trail even though both routes led back to where we started. Then I think it escalated into whether or not my dad's horse was brown or chestnut. At one point my mom yelled at him so loud that my horse got spooked."

"Shit," he hissed quietly.

Olivia nodded. "Threw me right off. I broke my arm in two different places and had to listen to my parents continue arguing in the ER about whose fault it was. So—yeah. Horses did not end up being my thing."

He followed her out of Cleo's stall and closed the door.

"You don't have to get back on the horse, Olivia."

She laughed at the pun even as the mere thought of the incident made her heart race with the familiar fight-or-flight response that always accompanied one of her parents' shouting matches.

"But," he continued, "if you'll let me, I'll change your memory of horses to one that's far less painful." He pulled her hands from the hem of her sweater where she'd all but torn the bottom button off.

"Are you a cowboy or a sheriff?" she asked, trying to stall her answer.

He shrugged. "Maybe I'm a little bit of both. After my—after Lucinda's first husband passed, that's when she sold our farm—and with it the few horses we owned. She bought the antiques shop, and we moved into the apartment above it, and the rest is history. The Everetts let me ride every now and then—whenever I get to missing it."

"Are you missing it right now?" she asked, already knowing the answer.

"I am." The wistful look in his eyes softened the hard lines of his face.

She sighed. "Why does hearing you talk about horseback riding like that make me want to kiss you?"

And then something wholly unexpected happened. Cash Hawkins grinned.

Her mouth fell open.

He shook his head and chuckled. "You know, I'm not stopping you."

He let go of her hands, and she used her freedom to run the tips of her fingers over his stubbled jaw. "It's sexy lawmen cowboys like you that make it awfully hard to concentrate on my unparalleled equine fear."

He raised a brow. "You talk like we're a dime a dozen."

She snaked her hands around his neck, clasping them there as if she'd never let go.

"No," she said. "I get the feeling they broke the mold when they made you, Sheriff."

"You gonna keep talking?" he asked.

She skimmed her teeth over her bottom lip. It was dangerous how much and how often she wanted to kiss this man after only just meeting him. Yet there was also safety in Oak Bluff—in this seemingly far-off place where what she was running from couldn't catch her.

He dipped his head, and she rose on her toes to meet him the rest of the way. Their mouths met with a soft brush, then a gentle flick of her tongue. His lips parted, and she tasted the bitterness of his black coffee mixed with the sugar of hers.

She let out a hum of pleasure and felt him smile against her.

"Now you're just showing off," she teased.

"I told you I smile," he said, his voice low and sexy. "Just not for everyone."

He kissed her again, his lips firm yet gentle, and his touch—the sheer nearness of him—made her forget how scared she really was.

"Do you promise you'll keep me safe if I ride?" she asked.

He straightened to look at her, his green eyes so damn sure.

"You have my word."

She slid her hands from his neck but left them splayed against his chest.

"Then show me your town, Cash Hawkins. The way it was meant to be seen."

Chapter Seven

Riding was easy when it was on Jack Everett's mare, Cleo. But Cash could still see the tension in Olivia's shoulders, which meant the horse could sense it, too.

"It might help if you breathe," he said. "She's not gonna throw you, but if you want her to trust you, you have to do the same with her."

They were moving at a snail's pace across the pasture and toward the new Everett vineyard, but at least they'd made it past doing guided laps in the small arena.

"How am I supposed to trust someone I just met?" she asked calmly. He guessed she was keeping her voice even so as not to spook the mare. But Cleo didn't spook. She was older and set in her ways, and spooking wasn't one of them.

"That's a good question," he said. Because Cash was wary about most people other than Lucinda and his deputies. It went with his line of work. And—he guessed—his personal life, too. "But you trust me, right?"

She studied his face for a moment and then nodded. "Even though we just met, too. Is it weird that I feel like I've known you longer than a day?"

He shrugged. "Multiple arrests will do that, you know. Bring a cop and a criminal together."

She snorted. "Your job must be really boring if I'm your definition of criminal."

He watched her shoulders relax as she laughed, and Cleo began to move with less trepidation.

"See?" he said, giving Bella a slight nudge with his heels to pick up the pace. "It's all about trust."

They crested a small hill, and Cash pulled on the reins. "Whoa, girl," he said softly, and Olivia did the same. Then she sucked in a sharp breath.

"Not bad, eh?" he asked.

She shook her head, mouth still hanging open.

The Everetts' vineyard sprawled before them at the bottom of the hill, but to the west they could see the main part of town, and thanks to the clear sky, the ocean beyond.

She swiped under her eye.

"Hell," he said. "What's wrong? Tell me I didn't just make you remember something else you'd rather forget."

She laughed, then sniffled. "No. It's not that. It's just—I mean I've seen the ocean before. I grew up in San Francisco. But—"

"It looks different here," he said.

She nodded, and he understood.

"Small-town living isn't for everyone," he said. "But this is one of the many reasons I never really left."

"I don't blame you." She took a deep breath of the crisp air. "But you have been outside the town limits, right?"

He nodded once. "Four years at City University of New York."

Even behind her sunglasses he could see her eyes widen. "Eighteen years in Oak Bluff to New York City?"

He cleared his throat, then turned his gaze just past her and toward the horizon. "They had a good criminal justice program."

"Uh-huh."

He could feel her stare burning a hole straight through him. No one asked him about CUNY anymore, and he didn't exactly bring it up voluntarily. So what the hell was he doing mentioning it now?

"For someone who doesn't seem to like much change in the status quo—who has already expressed that there are many reasons why he stayed in his small town—I find it very interesting you went so far away for school." She gasped. "You followed a girl!"

He squeezed his eyes shut for a moment, grateful they were hidden behind his aviators.

"Oh, come on," she said. "I told you my story. It's only fair I get to hear yours."

He grinned and enjoyed watching her brows raise once more. "Only if you can keep up." He tapped his heels against Bella's flanks, not hard enough to make her gallop but just enough to get her moving a bit faster than before.

"Hey!" she called after him as he started descending the hill. "Not funny, Cash!"

He knew she was safe, though, whether she followed or stayed at the top of that hill until he came back up. But he could hear Cleo's hooves in the grass behind him, so he kept going, just a few paces ahead of her, until he reached the fence that denoted the end of the pasture and the beginning of the vineyard.

He hopped down and tied Bella's reins to a post. By the

time he finished, Olivia was pulling Cleo to a stop beside him.

Her jaw was set, and she was *not* smiling.

He moved to give her a hand dismounting the horse.

"No, thank you," she said, chin raised. "If you're going to leave me to fend for myself, then I'm going to fend for myself."

He stepped back and crossed his arms. Damn, this woman was stubborn. But he already knew that—and kinda liked it. She was strong and not afraid to challenge him. It had been a good long while since someone had.

She swung one leg over Cleo's side so she was balancing in just the one stirrup. She yelped and he rushed to her before she fell flat on her back, catching her in his arms.

"Your ankle," he said. "Shit. I forgot."

She nodded, her face so close to his—lips near enough to kiss. Again. "I guess I forgot, too. It wasn't really bothering me until I put all my weight on it. And here you are again, sheriff in shining armor, catching me before I fall. Maybe one of these days I can swoop in on a horse and rescue *you*."

He chuckled. "What makes you think I need rescuing?" he asked.

She blew out a breath. "Oh no you don't. You don't get to change the subject. You said you'd answer my question if I could keep up. Well, I kept up." She shimmied out of his arms, biting back a wince when she landed, but she stayed standing. "Now you have to tell me about the girl you chased across the country."

He showed her how to tie off the reins, then helped her over the fence and into the vineyard. They walked slowly down a row of vines.

"All this land belongs to the Everetts?" she asked, running the tips of her fingers along the budding vines. "I thought the sign on the property said *Crossroads Ranch.*"

"Mmm-hmm," he said. "And soon they'll add *and Vineyard* to that. It's a long story, but their father passed away recently and left them a failing vineyard in the will. For three guys who grew up knowing nothing but ranching, they've really turned this place around."

She was a few paces ahead of him when she spoke again. "You know, you don't have to tell me about her if you don't want to. I get wanting to leave the past in the past."

He sighed. Because that was exactly where he wanted the past. And he thought he'd left it there until the Saturday morning mail arrived. Now here it was, still lurking in his present.

"Her name was Tara. *Is* Tara. Shit, it's not as if she died." He mumbled that last bit to himself.

Olivia stopped walking, then turned to face him. "High school sweetheart?"

"Yep. But I didn't follow her to New York. Small-town living can get to you when you're younger and don't appreciate it, and I needed to get away to make sure staying was what I wanted. So I researched criminal justice programs on the East Coast. Lucinda had money set aside from the sale of the farm, so when I got in..."

"She followed *you*," Olivia said with realization. Then she pushed her glasses to the top of her head so he could see what he knew was coming. The pity. "You came back, but she didn't." She gasped and covered her mouth. "It was her wedding invitation in your truck!"

He let out a bitter laugh. "I'm that damned obvious, huh?" She opened her mouth, but he cut her off. "I swear, Olivia Belle, if you say *Oh, Cash,* or tilt your head to the side and give me that look..."

She crossed her arms. "What look?"

He raised his glasses, tilted his head to the side, and drew his brows together, mimicking the look of pity everyone gave him when they found out about the post-graduation proposal that got turned down. The look that everyone gave when he rolled back into town on four wheels, an empty tank of gas, and an even emptier heart. The same look Henrietta, the mail carrier, gave him when she walked up the stairs to his apartment and handed him that damned invitation just as he was leaving to take Dixie for her morning walk.

Olivia giggled, and he raised a brow.

"Oh God," she said, laughing harder now. "That *is* a terrible look. I promise not to ever give you that look."

He chuckled, realizing that up until that moment *he'd* been the one pitying himself. But now he was with this woman. *Laughing*. Maybe he balked at Olivia calling him on it, but it was something he rarely did these days.

"Much appreciated," he said. His phone buzzed and he pulled it from his pocket.

"Something wrong?" Olivia asked as his jaw tightened.

He put the phone away and met her gaze. "That was Jack Everett. Wanted to let me know that he tracked down the builder who transformed your grandmother's house into a retail space and apartment. Says anything they found as far as personal effects got dropped at a local Goodwill."

Olivia's expression fell. "They must have thrown the letters out, right? I mean, why would they keep them? To a builder they would have been trash."

A sheen grew over her eyes. Damn it; he didn't want to see her cry again.

"Maybe…" he said, and he knew he was grasping here. "But maybe not."

She sniffed back the threat of tears. "What are you saying?"

"I'm saying that Lucinda sometimes shops the farmer's market for little odds and ends for the store." She gave him a look, and he waved her off. "Not food. There's this woman who sells handmade crafts and stuff like that. But she also deals in found items, and I know Lucinda has picked up some stuff for the store from her before. We can ask her if she's heard anything about the letters."

Olivia sucked in a breath and grinned. "Well, let's go! What are we waiting for?"

He cleared his throat. "That's the thing. The farmer's market is only open on the weekends and only until noon on Sundays. It's a quarter past twelve now. *And* there's also the chance that even if we go to the market, she's not there."

He expected her shoulders to sag, but instead she pursed her lips and narrowed her eyes. "So I'd have to stay here the week," she said. "And then run the risk of still coming up empty handed."

He nodded.

"I have the vacation time," she said. "But what would I do here all week?"

A surprise gust of wind blew her soft curls over her face. He chuckled and pushed them out of the way and behind her ears. And it must have been the brush of his skin against hers—this crackle of whatever was brewing between them—that made him lose all sense of self-preservation.

"I'm on duty the next forty-eight hours," he said. "Off Wednesday. Then back on Thursday and Friday. If you can keep yourself out of trouble for a couple days, I'd like to take you to dinner Wednesday night."

Olivia cleared her throat. "Are you—are you asking me on a date?"

He shrugged. "Figure if we keep kissing like we're doing I could at least buy you a meal. Even though you stole my dinner last night."

"You *offered*!" she scoffed. "And...then you brought me a donut." She scratched the back of her neck. "I kinda feel like I should maybe buy *you* dinner."

He laughed. "My town, my rules. Means I get to not only buy you a meal but continue to give you hell for stealing my last one."

She groaned, but he could tell there was a smile hiding behind her annoyance.

"So...you'll stay the week?" he asked, a little surprised by how much he wanted her to say yes.

She bit her bottom lip and nodded. "Are you gonna kiss me again, Sheriff?"

He dipped his head, his lips a breath away from hers. "Every chance I get, *Ms. Belle.*"

And then he did.

When his lips touched hers he tried not to think about how much he enjoyed it, or how a sudden warmth spread through him, slow but deliberate. He tried not to admit to himself that Tara's wedding was starting to bother him less and less. And he tried to ignore that their date was just a date—that Olivia Belle in Oak Bluff was only temporary.

Because if he didn't try all of these things, he might realize that she was melting his long-frozen heart, which meant he was in danger of the one thing he'd protected himself from for so many years.

Falling in love and getting left again.

Chapter Eight

Cash's forty-eight hours on the job had been busier than he'd expected.

Monday he'd had to fetch Mrs. Middleton's fifteen-pound cat from her oak tree. Twice. And he had the scratches on his neck to prove it. He'd made a note to himself to start forwarding Mrs. Middleton's number to one of his deputy's phones, even if it was their day off.

Just a couple hours ago he'd received a call from The Night Owl, Oak Bluff's one and only tavern, that Walker Everett was drunk and disorderly again. Hell, Cash knew the Everett brothers had a messy past to contend with, but Walker—the youngest of the three—had been *contending* worse and worse these days. Nora, owner of The Night Owl, tried her best to deal with Walker on her own, but sometimes things got out of hand. It had just been one of those nights.

Actually, it had been a day—or two—to say the least. Now, at mere minutes past midnight and the end of his shift, all he wanted to do was collapse into bed, Dixie at his feet. But something felt off.

He'd already let the dog out, so that wasn't it. He'd tossed his uniform into the washer and locked his gun in the safe. Everything was as it should be.

He scratched the back of his head and stared down at his phone charging on the nightstand. The screen lit up with an incoming text. The sender? Cinderella, the name he'd programmed into his contact list for Olivia Belle.

Cinderella: Hope the residents of Oak Bluff obeyed the law better than I did. ;)

Cash laughed out loud. Then, even though he stood on the cold floor in nothing but his boxer briefs, that inexplicable warmth spread through him.

He sat on the side of the bed, picked up the phone, and unlocked the screen.

Cash: Isn't it past your bedtime?

Cinderella: Nah. I like to wait till everyone's sleeping before I try breaking and entering.

He chuckled.

Cash: But I'm the sheriff, and I'm still up. Might be a flaw in your logic.

Cinderella: Wasn't counting on you being awake. Figured

you'd crash as soon as your shift ended, but I'm glad you didn't.

He leaned back against the headboard, and Dixie gave him a knowing look. That was when he realized he was wearing a dopey grin on his face, and he rolled his eyes at himself. He was damn glad Olivia Belle was still awake, too.

Cash: Been thinking about me, huh?

Because he understood, now, the reason something felt off. Missing. As busy as he'd been, thoughts of Olivia had lingered in the back of his mind these past two days. While he'd been saving a cat, what had she been doing? When Walker Everett needed a police escort home—and Cash to be a friend and sneak him into the house without waking Jack, Ava, or their son Owen—where had Olivia been?

Cinderella: A lot, sorta. Is that bad?

Cash: Not at all. Been thinking about you too. You enjoying our little town?

Cinderella: YES! I love that even though you let me have my car back, I can walk anywhere I want to go. Been to the bakery, to that little craft shop where some of Ava Ellis's paintings are. She's really good, btw. And tonight I cooked dinner at the B and B with the other guests. It was so fun! And we made sangria. I had a glass. Or maybe two. Delish!

Cash laughed at her rambling. She texted like she spoke, but he liked it. He liked hearing about her day at the end of his.

"Huh," he said aloud. That was a first—wanting to talk to someone other than Dixie before he went to bed.

Cinderella: Also I ignored texts from my mom, dad, grandmother, and Michael. Basically everyone in my real life. So that was fun. Also I might be buzzed.

Cash's small bubble of whatever he was feeling deflated just a little at the sound of that name. *Michael*. The guy who wanted to marry her.

Cash: Don't you think you should maybe deal with all that?

He regretted hitting send as soon as he did. He was nothing more than a pit stop on her way to who knows where. Who was he to tell her when she should deal with her life?

He watched those three dots hovering where Olivia's next text would appear, his chest tightening as he did.

Cinderella: They all think they know what's best for me. But right now real life isn't best. I want to live in the fairy tale a little longer...with my fairy tale straight and narrow lawman. Is that okay? ;)

He blew out a breath. Yeah, he'd say that was pretty okay. After all, wasn't he living in a fantasy, too? In a few days, they'd be strangers again—she back to her life and he back to his.

Cash: It's okay.

He thought the response maybe merited some sort of emoji to let her know he wasn't going to pry into her life any further, but Cash Hawkins had never used an emoji in his life. He sure as hell wasn't about to start now.

Cinderella: Good. I'm kinda sleepy.

Cash: Sangria? Or because it's past midnight.

Cinderella: Both, I think. But I just wanted to say hi. So . . . hi.

Cash: Hi.

Cinderella: Now I should probs say good-night. Good-night, Sheriff.

Cash: Good night, Cinderella. I'll see you tomorrow.

Cinderella: You think you might kiss me again?

He chuckled.

Cash: I think I just might.

He waited a few minutes, but there was no response. She'd probably fallen asleep. As tired as he was—make that exhausted—he lay in bed, eyes wide open, for a while after that. She'd thought about him...and he her. Correction. He was *still* thinking about her right now.

Dixie let out a long sigh, then nudged his foot with her nose.

"I know, girl. I think we're in trouble, too."

Chapter Nine

Olivia stood in front of the mirror and twisted back and forth. She loved the rich blue color of the dress, the off-the-shoulder style and bell sleeves. But what really topped off the look were the black suede ankle boots.

"You look fantastic."

Olivia startled, then spun to find a familiar-looking blond woman standing just inside the door of the small clothing boutique.

"Lily," she said. "Lily Green? We met at the Everett ranch. I was feeding cake to Luke Everett." She winced as she said Luke's name.

"Oh!" Olivia said. "The brother who got thrown off the bull. And you're catering…"

"My ex-husband's wedding. Yep. That's me."

Yeah. Olivia remembered. She also remembered the tension in that kitchen between Luke and Lily that seemed to have nothing to do with her ex's wedding. "Right." She let out a nervous laugh and then glanced down at the dress. "It's not too much?" she asked.

Lily shook her head. "Why would it be too much?"

Olivia's cheeks flushed. "I don't look like I'm trying to look all cowgirl to impress a sometimes cowboy?"

Lily shrugged. "You look like a woman who's going to blow Sheriff Hawkins's mind when he picks you up tonight." She gasped and threw a hand over her mouth. "Was I not supposed to know about the date?"

Olivia laughed. "How many people live in this town?"

Lily was laughing now, too. "Yeah, okay. The whole town knows about the date. Cash hasn't gone on one—at least not around here—in a long time. We're all kinda rooting for him."

Olivia's heart sped up, but then she remembered waking this morning to a text from Michael asking if she'd reconsidered his proposal and a text from her mother asking if she was crazy passing up a guy who could give her so much more than her dad ever gave to *her*. This afternoon her dad had actually called, and she'd let it go to voicemail just so she wouldn't have to listen to him asking when she was going to grow up and come home to face her problems.

Reality.

"I'm just here for the week," she insisted. "So whatever this is with me and Cash, it's temporary."

Lily nodded with a knowing grin. "Mmm-hmm. That's why you're buying a new dress for a first date with a guy you don't plan on seeing again."

Olivia's mouth fell open, but she had no comeback.

"He's a good guy," Lily said. "If you can get past that gruff exterior, there's a real sweetheart underneath."

Olivia blew out a breath. She'd seen that sweetheart already, not that Cash would admit it. "What about you and the cake-eating rodeo star?" she asked Lily, trying to get the attention off her and Cash.

Lily shook her head. "Luke Everett hasn't been able to stand me ever since Tucker and I started dating. Now that we're divorced, seems I get under his skin even more."

"You know what they say about love and hate," Olivia said. "It's a very thin line."

Lily's cheeks grew pink, and Olivia wondered if they'd already crossed that thin line.

"Do all the Everett brothers look like that?" she asked.

Lily rolled her eyes but nodded. "It's really not fair. Blond-haired, blue-eyed, all that cowboy-rancher swagger with a sun-kissed California vibe. They're like a pack of horseback-riding Hemsworths. Though I'm guessing you prefer the dark-haired brooding type."

Olivia laughed. What she preferred was not worrying about the future because the *What comes next?* was the part that terrified her. All she knew was that kissing Cash Hawkins was as easy as breathing because he had no expectations of her beyond the present. She didn't know how to be anything other than who she was—a runner. That was why she'd run here, to the town where Gran and Pop fell in love through the words written on the page. But for these next few days with Cash, she could just be herself. With him. Until their time ran out.

"Something like that," was all she said.

"Well, I should go." Lily started backing toward the door. "I was just walking by and saw you. I hope it's okay I stopped in to say hello."

"I'm glad you did. I was a little on the fence about the dress, but now my mind's made up." Olivia yanked the tag that was hanging from her sleeve and walked it over to the small checkout counter where the owner was helping another customer. "I'll take it all," she whispered.

"Good choice," Lily said and then waved. "I have a good feeling about you, Olivia."

And then she was out the door.

After a hefty but worthwhile dent on her debit card, Olivia soon was, too.

She checked her phone once she got back to the bed-and-breakfast. She had exactly thirty minutes before Cash was supposed to pick her up, so she decided to head down to the common room and see who was around.

Everyone was around because Wednesday nights were apparently game night, and just about all the guests plus the owners, Rose and Marcus, were seated around the long wooden table setting up Trivial Pursuit.

Olivia bounced on her suede-booted toes and clapped. "I love this game!"

"Come join us!" Marcus said. "We're just getting started."

She worried her bottom lip between her teeth but then grinned. "Okay, maybe just a couple rounds. I—I sort of have plans."

Rose raised a brow. "You mean with the sheriff."

Enthusiastic mumbling broke out among the guests, and Olivia groaned.

"How does *everyone* know?" she asked.

"I saw him at the market this morning in the produce section," Marcus told her. "Cash never shops for fresh produce. I knew he had to be doing something special for *someone* special."

"And I bumped into Carol from the boutique at the bank

who said something about Lily Green and a new customer talking about the sheriff," Rose said. Then she looked Olivia up and down. "New outfit?"

Olivia blushed so hard she thought her face would actually catch fire. "I guess there's no point in my *answering* any of your questions since you seem to know everything already. So there's only one thing left to do."

"What's that?" Marcus asked.

"Kick all your butts in Trivial Pursuit." She sat down at an empty spot on the bench seat, her chin held high. Then she glanced at her opponents, who all seemed to be sitting in pairs. *Couples*, to be exact. "That's okay," she said in response to her own thoughts and most likely what everyone else was thinking. "I can hold my own against teams."

A throat cleared in the open archway of the common room.

A *man's* throat. And hell if Olivia couldn't recognize said man just by that sound. Still, she spun slowly to find Cash Hawkins standing behind her.

"I've played on a team or two," he said.

Rose waved him off. "High school football doesn't count," she teased.

Cash slid into the empty seat beside Olivia, barely giving her time to take in his plaid shirt, the sleeves rolled to reveal his muscular forearms. His dark jeans hugged his hips and—well, speaking of *butts*. Cash Hawkins was a sight to behold. And she was enjoying a long moment of beholding.

Olivia swallowed. "I was running early."

He leaned in close—even with the whole table watching—and whispered in her ear. "So was I."

His breath tickled her skin, and he smelled—*mmm*—she had to fight to keep from sighing.

"Rosemary," she said out loud. "And mint."

"Should we get started?" Rose asked, reminding Olivia that she and Cash were not alone, and oh how she wished they were now.

"Do we still have time?" Olivia asked Cash, hoping he'd tell her they were in some rush to make a reservation. Then her brows drew together as her eyes dipped from his to three small but fresh cuts on his neck. "What happened to you?"

He sighed and shook his head. "Mrs. Middleton's cat. Twice."

Her concern morphed into a giggle. "Please tell me you actually saved a cat from a tree. Twice. That really happens?"

Cash nodded and she noticed a slight tinge of pink spreading over his cheeks. Somehow him blushing made her blush, and she was sure everyone could see. Her heart raced even though she was sitting still, and as much as she'd been looking forward to tonight, something as simple as a first date suddenly felt—dangerous. She'd thought her time in Oak Bluff would be a welcome diversion from the mess that waited for her in San Francisco. But physiological reactions like this were not in her repertoire. Cash Hawkins did more than divert her attention. He captivated it.

The sheriff pulled out his phone and fired off a quick text. To whom she had no idea.

Then Rose handed him the dice, and he rolled. "You're in Oak Bluff now, Ms. Belle," he said. "We've got all the time in the world around here."

A whole ninety minutes later Cash held the door and Olivia exited the bed-and-breakfast out onto the pavement.

"I can't *believe* you knew that Denmark had the oldest

flag design," she said, walking backward so they could continue their conversation.

He raised his brows. "Hey. You got us the sports and leisure piece by being able to name what teams all those NFL coaches coached. Impressive," he said.

She shrugged. "Why? Because I'm a woman?"

He laughed. "No, because they're not current. You'd have had to be a young kid when they were all in their prime."

Her smile faded. "My dad's a huge football fan. Sunday afternoons and Monday nights used to be our thing—until he and my mom started arguing louder than the flat screen with surround sound. Kinda lost my love of football after that." They got to the corner, and she finally turned to face the street they were about to cross. "You were good?" she asked. "In high school?"

He shoved his hands in the front pockets of his jeans as they continued to the other side of the street. "Mighta been able to play in college. But I blew out my knee the week Dad went into hospice."

Her throat tightened. She pulled one of his hands free and laced her fingers through his, giving him a gentle squeeze.

"I'm pretty much the worst, aren't I?" she said.

He tugged her across the street perpendicular to the one they'd just crossed, only answering her when they were on the sidewalk again. "How do you mean?"

"I've been complaining about my parents and their messy divorce pretty much since you met me. And as much as they both drive me to drink—heavily—I can still say that word. *Both.* Because they're both still here, and you've lost—"

"Hey," he said, pulling her close. Then he glanced up and down the street, from shop window to window.

"You worried about who's watching us?" she asked, knowing that just about the whole town probably was.

"I'm not worried about a damned thing," he said. "Especially you thinking your pain is anything less compared to mine. It's not a competition. We all have our baggage—our pasts that shape us. It's what we do with all that shaping that matters."

She narrowed her eyes. "You're talking about me, aren't you? How I run from my baggage?"

He chuckled. "Or how I keep mine sealed up in a really fancy envelope."

She looked over her shoulder, only then realizing where they were standing.

"Sheriff?"

"Ms. Belle?"

"Am I under arrest?"

"You break any laws today?" he asked.

She pretended she was counting her fictional offenses on her fingers. "Nope," she finally said. "Unless you count the liquor store I robbed before breakfast."

He shook his head and chuckled again. "Well, I guess I'm harboring a known criminal. We better get you inside before the rest of the town is onto us."

He grabbed her hand and pulled her toward the department's front door. But once inside, instead of continuing straight into the office, he veered left, to a staircase she hadn't noticed the last time she was here. When she *was* under arrest.

She followed him up the stairs and to a sparse hallway that had one door at the far end.

He opened that one door and ushered her inside. There she found a small apartment, modestly decorated and furnished, with a German shepherd curled on a doggie bed on the floor next to a bookcase. Dixie.

But it wasn't the sweet, non–attack dog who didn't even stir when they entered that caught Olivia's attention. It was the round wooden table set for two, a bottle of red waiting to be uncorked, and the smell of something absolutely delicious.

"You—cooked for me?"

He pushed the door closed behind them. "I figured if we went to eat anywhere in town we'd be dealing more with the stares and whispers than anything else. Thought if I took you somewhere outside of town you'd think I didn't want anyone to know I was taking you out. Decided that if I had the whole day off, I might as well make use of it. So yeah, I cooked for you."

This made her smile. "So you *do* want people to know you're with me tonight?"

"I want my damned privacy," he said. "And to show you a good time. The rest doesn't matter as long as it's you and me tonight."

Dixie barked and looked up from where she was tearing apart a piece of rawhide.

"And your ferocious beast," Olivia said, laughing.

She dropped down to a squat and gave the dog a scratch behind the ears. Dixie responded by rolling onto her back, exposing her belly for additional scratches. The dog wriggled back and forth, and Olivia lost her balance. She yelped with laughter as she collapsed right onto her butt.

"You okay?" Cash said, extending a hand.

She let him help her up, and she brushed off the skirt of her dress. "Yes, but I do seem to have trouble staying on my own two feet when I'm around you, Sheriff."

"Any idea why that is?" he asked.

She looked deep into those green eyes of his, hoping for some sort of logical answer as to how, just a few days ago, she'd run so far and fast from forever that she'd ended up in handcuffs, yet now she was already wondering how in the heck she'd be able to walk away from this man and never look back.

"Guess you just make me weak in the knees," she said, voice shaky.

He wrapped an arm around her waist. "I don't think there's one weak bone in your body, Olivia Belle, but far be it for me to argue with a beautiful woman who knows her obscure trivia."

She wrapped her arms around his neck. "And far be it for *me* to go one more second without kissing a man who cooked me dinner."

Chapter Ten

And just like that, her mouth claimed his.

Cash felt Olivia smile against him as she parted her lips, and somehow that made the kiss even sexier—knowing how much she was enjoying it.

His hands slid up her sides, and she sucked in a breath as his thumb grazed the side of her breast. That was all it took to unleash something in him he hadn't known still existed.

It was more than hunger. More than want. Cash Hawkins *needed* this woman, and he wasn't sure how to wrap his brain around that. He'd let himself believe for so long that he didn't need any*one* or any*thing*. Because needing someone and then losing them? That was something Cash had experienced too often to write off as coincidence.

He'd loved and lost, in more ways than one. And until Olivia Belle blew into town, he'd whittled down that circumference of love to the only two females he'd let past his barriers: Lucinda and Dixie.

Cash's tongue tangled with hers, but he needed to come up for air. So he kissed down the length of her neck, breathing in her sweet citrus scent. He paid equal attention to each of her bare shoulders, lips brushing across skin pebbled with gooseflesh.

But he still couldn't quite catch his breath. He couldn't let go of one, singular thought.

In the span of four days he'd gone from wanting to get Olivia Belle and her disregard for rules and regulations out of his hair to needing her in his bed tonight—and all the nights to come.

The oven timer went off, and he silently thanked the buzzer for a moment of reprieve.

"We should eat," he said, backing away, his voice hoarse.

She straightened out nonexistent wrinkles in her dress and stared at him. "How the heck did you cook me dinner while we were playing Trivial Pursuit at the B and B?"

This, at least, got him to grin. "Walters and Adams have a key to the place. I texted them when to come on up and preheat the oven. I prepared everything and left it all marinating in the fridge. Just had to be thrown in to bake while I was— detained."

She breathed in deep, then closed her eyes and sighed. "Mmm. I'm starving, and whatever you made smells unbelievable." She strode toward the table. "Can I pour you a glass of wine while you're getting everything out of the oven?"

"Sounds perfect."

A bottle of pinot noir later, he watched as Olivia swirled her last bite of steak in the marinade. "Seriously?" she said after she swallowed. "I thought single men subsisted solely on canned beer and frozen pizza."

He coughed on his last sip of wine. He wouldn't confirm how close to the truth she was. It wasn't that he *couldn't* cook. Her empty plate was evidence enough of that. It was that he didn't see the point of putting in so much effort just to eat alone.

"Guess I'm not your typical single man," Cash said.

She polished off the rest of her wine. "I guess you're not," she said. She reached down and rubbed her ankle under the table.

"Still bugging you?" he asked.

She winced slightly. "It wasn't," she said. "But I think walking around in heels mighta made it a little angry."

He stood and offered her his hand. "Come here."

She didn't question him, just placed her palm in his and let him lead her to the couch.

"Sit," he said, and when she gave him a pointed look, he added, "*please.*"

She sat, as did he, a little farther apart than he might have liked. But he had work to do before—well, before anything went further than the couch. *If* it, in fact, did.

He unzipped her boots and pulled off her ankle socks. Then he swung her legs so her feet were in his lap, cherry-red painted toes and all.

"What are you—*oooh*," she said as he started massaging her foot. She sunk into the arm of the couch and hummed. "God, that feels good."

He worked his way up her calf, kneading her tight muscles.

She sighed with what he hoped was pleasure.

"Ever since the knee injury, I see this athletic masseuse every now and then. When the muscles get too tight. The trick is that you gotta take care of the muscles around the injury because when they seize up, it makes it hurt more."

"*Mmm*," she said, eyes falling closed. "Was something hurting me? I can't seem to remember." Then she flexed and pointed her uninjured foot. "I know this one isn't hurt, but I might walk funny if the muscles in this leg are all tight when the other one is soooo relaxed."

He laughed softly and happily turned his attention to the other foot. "We wouldn't want that to happen, now, would we?"

She opened her eyes and shook her head. "I could injure myself so badly I might not be able to drive home in time to get back to work on Monday."

His eyes met hers. "Would that be so bad?"

"Being too injured to drive?"

He shook his head. "Staying longer."

She was silent for a long moment, and he knew he should take the words back—words that were full of pressure to commit, to plant her feet in one place for the long haul. Something she'd made clear she didn't do—and something he had convinced himself he no longer wanted.

"You know what?" he finally said. "Don't answer that."

Her mouth fell open. "What if I want to answer?"

"If you wanted to, you would have. But you don't because you didn't. So let's just take the question off the table."

She yanked her feet from his lap and straightened. "Do you think you know what's best for me?"

"Whoa," he said, hands raised in surrender. "I wasn't—"

"You were deciding what I needed, just like everyone back in my real life who thinks I need to deal with reality."

His jaw tightened. "And you don't see me as reality."

Her hands balled into fists. "I didn't say—"

"But you did."

Now she groaned through gritted teeth. "Cash Hawkins, you are infuriating."

Infuriating? She was going to call *him* infuriating? "Well, you, Olivia Belle, are one-hundred-and-fifty percent *maddening*. Guess we're quite the pair if we're not talking about the real world."

She crossed her arms. "You met me *four* days ago, and you think you know me well enough to want me for longer?"

He straightened as well because two could play at this game. "What I know is that you make my blood damn near boil."

"With anger," she interrupted, but her voice had softened.

He nodded. "And downright irritation."

She scoffed.

"But what I also know," he added, "is that in four days you've made me realize the daily routine that's worked so damn well for me might not be enough."

She sucked in a deep breath, most likely to continue tearing him a new one, but then her shoulders relaxed as she blew it out.

"I make you want more out of your life?" she asked, the momentary anger in her voice fizzling to nothing.

"Yes," he admitted.

"I also make you smile sometimes."

"Yeah," he said, the corner of his mouth turning up. "You do that, too." He slid closer to her, then scooped her into his lap. He figured her wrapping her arms around his neck was a good sign. "I know it's only been a few days, but here's the thing: San Francisco and Oak Bluff—it's not as if the two are on opposite sides of the planet."

"True," she said. "But you already know I'm no good at this. It's not just Michael. I dated three guys when I was an undergrad. Ended it each time one asked me to go home for the weekend to meet his parents or even mentioned the idea of looking at engagement rings. If I can't make it stick with someone I see every day, what makes you think I'd be any better with you?"

He pressed his hand above her heart and felt it race against his palm.

"Can I ask you something?" he said.

She nodded.

"Any of those other guys make your heart do this?"

She shook her head slowly.

He raised a brow. "I have a theory, Ms. Belle. I think you've been so damned scared you'll end up like your parents that you've made sure you never get that far. We're a lot alike, you know. I've kept everyone at arm's length to protect myself from loss while you've surrounded yourself with people you know will keep your heart safe."

"And how do these *people* keep my heart safe?" she asked, though he was pretty sure she knew the answer.

"Because." He shrugged. "You never truly give it to anyone. That way it never gets broken."

She blew out a breath. "*You* could break it."

"And you could destroy mine. I have no doubt about it."

She pulled him closer, resting her forehead on his. "I don't want to destroy your heart, Sheriff."

He laughed softly. "And I sure as hell don't want to break yours."

"So what do we do?" she asked.

He kissed her once, soft and slow, and she hummed a sweet moan against his lips.

"We take these next few days to figure it out."

She nodded.

"Stay with me tonight," he said, deciding to go for broke.

She squeezed him tight, then kissed the line of his jaw all

the way to his ear, her breath against his skin driving him completely mad.

"Okay, Sheriff," she said. "You got yourself a deal."

He stood with her in his arms and strode to the bedroom in ten easy steps, kicking the door shut behind them before lowering her to her feet.

Wordlessly she unzipped the back of her dress and let it pool around her ankles so she stood before him in nothing but a pair of black lace panties.

For a second it was as if all the breath had been sucked from his lungs, and he could barely breathe, let alone speak. Even though Cash was a man of few words, he felt like now would be a good time to say something. To say the *right* thing. But he wasn't quite sure what that was.

"I didn't realize it until now," he said, finally recovering his voice.

"What's that?" she asked.

"Maybe it can happen more than once."

Her brows drew together.

"All these years I've told myself I had my chance and blew it," Cash continued. "I convinced myself that Lucinda finding happiness again and again—even after losing it— was an exception to the rule, but I'm not so sure anymore. Maybe I didn't put my life on hold all these years just to play it safe. Maybe I did it—because I was waiting for you."

"That's a lot of maybes," she said, and he noted the slight tremble in her voice.

"Sure is."

She stepped toward him then and unbuttoned his shirt, pulling it down his arms and letting it fall to the floor. She unbuckled his belt, helped him out of his jeans. Gone went the boxer briefs, too.

"Wow," she said softly.

He raised a brow, then hooked a finger inside the seam of her panties.

"May I?" he asked.

She nodded, and he lowered himself to one knee, carefully sliding the undergarment over her soft skin, the tips of his fingers exploring her as they trailed the length of her perfect legs.

Perfect because the legs belonged to *her.*

"I'm on the pill," she blurted with a slight wince. "In case you were wondering."

He grinned. "I was prepared if things were otherwise."

He pulled her to him, her soft breasts against his torso, and she let out a sweet sigh.

"I forget to breathe around you, sometimes." She kissed his neck.

"I guess that makes two of us. Because you take my damned breath away."

He backed her toward the bed, which he'd actually made to impress her. He realized now there wouldn't be much *looking* at it, though. And he was perfectly okay with that.

He laid her down on her back and just stared at her for a long moment. Then he dipped his head, kissing her soft lips, then her neck and her collarbone until he came to the swell of her breast. Her stomach contracted, and he could tell she was holding her breath. He grinned as he flicked his tongue out, tasting her hardened peak.

She gasped and dug her fingers into his hair, which was all the encouragement he needed to continue kissing, licking, nipping.

"More," she pleaded.

God, he loved that sound in her breathless voice, a sound that echoed everything he couldn't quite put into words.

Need.

Hell yes, he craved her touch, hungered for the taste of her skin on his tongue. But something more than physical was happening here, wasn't it? Did she feel it, too?

"Cash," she said, and he heard it again. That something more. "Please."

"Whatever you want, Ms. Belle." He crawled over her, kissed her, then entered her as her legs fell open, inviting him in.

Every dip and swell of her curves was brand new, unexplored territory. Yet at the same time it was as if he'd known her all his life. They moved to a rhythm that was solely their own. When she kissed him, he didn't taste the bottle of wine they'd polished off with dinner. He tasted *home*. Because hell, that was what this woman was for him.

He brushed his lips against hers, teased them with his tongue, and she gripped him tighter, pulled him closer. Deeper.

"Cash," she said, a breathless plea, and he knew she was close.

"It would be worth it," he said, slowly sliding out and then entering her again.

She gasped and opened her eyes. "What would?"

He rolled to his side, pulling her with him, hooking her leg over his hip.

"You—destroying my heart. It'd be worth it."

Her breathing hitched, and he wasn't sure if it was because he'd just snuck his hand between the place where they joined or if she felt it, too—the falling.

Because it wasn't that he *could* fall for this woman.

He *was* falling. Had possibly already hit the ground with deadly, destructive force. But he didn't care. All that mattered was this moment, showing her how well they actually fit.

Like Cinderella's glass slipper.

He chuckled, but she was too close to the edge to notice, and soon he would be, too.

He fell onto his back, pulling her on top of him and letting her take the wheel for the final moments.

"God, you're gorgeous," he said, staring up at her, her wild curls spilling over her shoulders and a look in her eyes that made it feel like all she could see was him.

She leaned down—he *thought* to kiss him—but instead nipped at his ear.

"And you," she whispered, her breath warm against his already heated skin, "are the most beautiful, wonderful, genuine man I've ever met. If I knew how to give someone my heart, Cash Hawkins, it'd be yours."

And before he could speak the words that were on the tip of his tongue, she kissed him and took them both the rest of the way home.

Hours later, when she was still naked and asleep in the crook of his arm, he realized all the work he'd done protecting himself—*convincing* himself he'd already had his one shot at love—was complete and utter horseshit.

It didn't matter if she was unable to give her heart away. She had his, now, and with it the power to crush it into a million irreparable pieces.

What the hell had he gone and done?

Chapter Eleven

It had been two nights since Olivia had slept in Cash's arms and two whole days since she'd seen him. She'd shopped, hiked, and cuddled in the B and B sitting room with a romance novel she'd found on the bookshelf. Her days had been both pure bliss and pure agony as she ached to see him again, which made no sense. Olivia Belle had never ached for anyone before. Except now she did.

She hoped Cash slept during those forty-eight hours on duty. Maybe that was why he lived above the station. What a solitary existence that seemed to be—just him and Dixie behind a desk or in that small apartment.

Where he'd cooked her dinner and made love to her.

She checked her texts as she swung her feet beneath the sidewalk bench where she waited for Cash's Tahoe to pull up. First she reread the one he'd sent her late last night.

Sheriff: Wish your head was tucked against my shoulder
right now.

It was the only text he'd sent during their separation. She
hadn't seen it until she woke up this morning, which had both
relieved and confused her. She'd left the ball in his court after her texts during their last time apart, and it had been radio
silence. She knew he was the strong and silent type, but the
other night had been—*Wow.* But where in the world did they
go from here? Where *could* they go? So she decided not to
respond, especially since Adams or Walters could be around.
She knew Cash would hit the office even though he had the
day off because that was just what Sheriff Cash Hawkins did.
He took care of things even when he didn't have to.

Michael: The co-op would like an answer. Have you reconsidered?

She groaned. She was more than a name to add to a deed.

Mom: Where the hell are you? Your father thinks it's my fault
you ran away. Says you're just like your mother.

Dad: I blame your mother.

Gran: Am I doing this right? I've never texted on this new
pHone. Oh darn. How do I get rid of that capital h? Sweetheart, are you where I think you are?

Mom: Your grandmother thinks she knows where you are. Can you just answer one of us? Actually, no. Answer me before your father.

She answered none of them. But then she felt bad about Gran. Gran was the reason she was here. She at least owed her the truth.

Me: Yeah, Gran. I'm here. I'm gonna find the letters. Just don't tell Mom and Dad. Please? Luv u.

And because he had impeccable timing, that was exactly when Cash pulled up, effectively rescuing her from the life she still wasn't ready to return to.

He hopped out of the truck and she stood, holding up the cup carrier with two coffees from Baker's Bluff.

"Hey," she said, not sure how she was supposed to greet him after two days.

"Hey yourself," he said, then dipped his head to kiss her—like, *really* kiss her—and yeah, that was exactly how they should greet each other after two days.

"What's with the uniform, Sheriff? Thought you were off until traffic duty tonight."

She looked him up and down, from what she assumed were steel-toed boots all the way to his sheriff's badge and crisp collar.

"Scratch that," she said. "The uniform is hot as hell. You can wear it whenever you want."

He smiled, but his eyes didn't crinkle like they did when he laughed, and she could feel there was something he was holding back. But he'd kissed her like he meant it, and boy, had she meant her part in it, too, so she wouldn't pester him about a smile.

"Wasn't sure if I'd make it back home before it was time for official business, so I figured I'd look—official for the whole day. But it seems to me that you don't mind it much."

She shook her head. "I don't mind it at all. Is Dixie not riding along later tonight? If you need someone to keep you company..."

Ugh. What was she doing? He was being nice and taking her to the farmers market, but he didn't need her with him at work. He'd already told her he'd stop by the B and B when his shift was up so they could spend whatever was left of the night together. Because she'd be heading back to San Francisco tomorrow. She had to. There was a job, and a life to deal with even if she wished she could avoid it for one more day. Or week. Or maybe even the rest of her life.

"Dixie's in the back. She'd never forgive me if I went to the market without her. There's this vendor—Felix—makes the best damned dog treats from scratch. She goes nuts for them."

Olivia laughed. "And you can't just bring some home for her? Man, does she have you wrapped around her paw."

This, at least, elicited a genuine chuckle.

"Yeah," Cash said. "She sure as hell does. You're welcome to join us, though. Tonight, I mean. Traffic duty's *usually* pretty quiet on a Saturday night."

She raised her chin. "I was in a hurry," she said haughtily.

He took the drink carrier from her and opened the passenger side door. "You ready to go find what sent you to Oak Bluff in such a hurry? The answers to true love?" he asked.

"I guess." She wasn't sure what made her more nervous, not finding the letters or finding them and realizing that what her grandparents had was something impossible to replicate. She used to think that if she could just see *how* they fell in love, she'd understand what was missing from her own romantic DNA and would be able to fix it.

But what if Cash was right? What if she kept choosing guys she knew wouldn't be *forever* guys because that was what kept her safe from having to commit and get hurt?

Despite how amazing the other night was—how being with him was unlike being with any other man she'd been with before—wasn't she still doing the same thing by choosing a man she couldn't commit to because he lived over two hundred miles away?

She climbed into the truck, her heart suddenly heavy. Here she thought she was finally doing something different, but despite how she felt about Cash—and *oh*, there were feelings—his life was here, and hers was not.

As soon as she settled in her seat, Dixie gave her a wet kiss on the back of her palm. Olivia laughed hard, and with it some of that weight on her chest dissipated.

"She give you a proper welcome?" Cash asked when he settled into the driver's seat.

Olivia nodded. "I've been properly welcomed by both of you this morning, so thank you very much."

He leaned over and kissed her again. "I plan on welcoming you a few more times today, if that's okay with you."

"*Mmm-hmm*," she said, sneaking one more sweet kiss. "It's very okay with me."

The ride to the farmers market was long enough to warrant turning on the radio, which made Olivia thankful she didn't have to fill the silence with all her talking. For once, she just wanted to be. So she let country music take up the space between them as they got closer and closer to finding the letters.

"You wanna grab lunch first?" he asked.

"Yes!" she answered with a little too much vigor. The truth was, now that they were here, she was terrified of finding what she'd come for—and terrified of the letters being lost for good. Lunch was the perfect distraction.

"Good," he said. "I know the perfect place."

The three of them—Olivia, Cash, *and* Dixie, strolled through the rows of market stalls. Finally Cash pointed up ahead.

"There it is," he said, and she followed his gaze to what was no more than a food cart. A *one*-type-of-food cart.

"Corn dogs?" she asked. Not that she had anything against the popular carnival delicacy. But they were at a farmers market. It seemed—wrong.

"Corn dogs," he confirmed. "The best you ever had, made with cornmeal sourced from a local farm and most likely some sort of illegal secret ingredient that keeps patrons coming back week after week."

She eyed him in his sexy uniform, then narrowed her gaze. "Does a woman work the corn dog cart?" she asked.

He cleared his throat. "I'm not sure. Haven't been in a while. Might be."

Olivia placed her hands on her hips. "Sheriff Cash Hawkins, does the pretty girl at the corn dog cart give you free food because you're a tall, dark, and devastatingly gorgeous officer of the law?"

Dixie barked, and Olivia nodded emphatically.

"See? Even your long-time friend agrees that flirting for food is very unbecoming of a sheriff."

A vendor walked by with a basket of Calla lilies. "Flower for the pretty lady, Sheriff?" he asked Cash.

Olivia blushed and smiled at the young man, who couldn't have been much older than eighteen.

"Sure," Cash said. "How much?"

Olivia waved her hand. "Oh, it's okay. I don't need—"

"For such a beautiful woman," the guy said, "it's on the house. Just—uh—don't tell my employer over there at the florist stand, okay?" He nodded back toward the way they'd come, then pulled a lily from his basket and handed it to Olivia with a wink.

"Thank you," she said as he backed away.

Cash cleared his throat and then smugly raised a brow.

"*What?*" she asked.

Dixie barked.

"Looks like my long-time friend is calling bullshit on you, Olivia Belle."

She groaned. "It's not like I come here weekly to score a free lunch or anything." She squinted toward the corn dog cart. "Wait, speaking of lilies...isn't that Lily Green and Luke Everett?"

Cash turned his head back toward the corn dog cart, and as soon as he did Lily seemed to glance in their direction.

"Hide!" Olivia said, grabbing Cash by the wrist and pulling him behind the side of a tent where a couple was selling soaps and lotions.

Dixie barked again.

"Shh!" Olivia said. "Come here, girl!"

She was more than a little surprised when the dog obeyed, and she grinned with satisfaction.

"What in the hell are we doing?" Cash asked. "Why wouldn't we just go and say hello?"

Olivia shushed him, too, and he raised a brow.

"Oh, stop, Sheriff. I'm not afraid of you." It was only a

half-truth. She wasn't scared of being ticketed, arrested, or possibly thrown in jail. But there was the whole issue of how her heart hadn't quite returned to its regularly scheduled rhythm since Wednesday night. *That* was more frightening than anything she'd experienced to date. Including being thrown from that horse in middle school.

"Remember what I said about the sexual tension between those two?" she asked.

His brows pulled together. "Lily and Luke? I told you. He's her ex-husband's friend. There are certain rules when it comes to that stuff. Plus, they can't stand each other. I've seen 'em go at it—bickering and arguing about who knows what."

She rolled her eyes. "*Yes*, Lily and Luke. I'm telling you there is something going on between those two, and saying hello is not going to do them any favors."

"So we're just going to hide out back here until..."

Olivia tiptoed to the back of the tent where she could sneak a peek at the food cart in order to check her theory.

She gasped.

"What's the matter?" Cash asked, rounding the corner.

"Nothing," she said. "But I rest my case."

She turned Cash's attention to where Luke and Lily were still standing in front of the food cart—doing something that looked an awful lot like kissing.

"Aw, hell," he said. "Nothing good is going to come of that."

Olivia licked her lips, thinking of the last time she'd experienced a kiss as steamy and romantic as the one Luke and Lily were basically broadcasting for all to see. At least it looked steamy and romantic from several yards away. Based on whatever she saw simmering between them in the Everett kitchen, she didn't doubt being right. As far as the last time she'd had a kiss to rival theirs? It had been with Cash.

He wrapped his hand around *her* wrist now, gently tugging her with one hand and Dixie's leash with the other, until they'd made it at least a hundred feet in the other direction.

"What in the hell are we doing now?" she asked, parroting his words.

"That's none of our business," he said. "Whatever's going on between them is none of our damned business—and now I have to find us somewhere else to eat because who knows how long they'll be there doing—what they're doing."

Olivia *was* still hungry. But it was no longer for food. "Do you wish *we* were doing what they're doing?" she asked, giving her lily an innocent sniff.

"Jesus, Olivia," he said.

"What?"

"I thought we came here to find your letters."

She took a step closer. "We did, but I thought you said you'd planned on giving me plenty of proper welcomes today."

He shook his head and chuckled. "I did say that. Didn't I?" Then he slid his fingers under her hair, cradling her neck.

Goose bumps peppered her skin. Her breath quickened, and her heart felt like it was beating double-time. What was it with this man? A week ago she hadn't even known him, and she'd been doing just fine without his presence in her life—if you didn't count fleeing a wedding where you were a bridesmaid and the bride's brother had just proposed to you.

Other than *that,* Olivia Belle was just fine without Cash Hawkins in her life. But what if *just fine* wasn't enough anymore?

The second his mouth touched hers, it was as if her whole
being woke up from a long sleep. She pressed her palms to his
chest and swore his heart was doing the same thing as hers.
When her tongue slipped past his lips, she grabbed on to his
shirt, fingers grappling at his collar as the kiss grew from sweet
to something so much more.

Then as quickly as the kiss began, Cash let her go and
backed away.

"I'm sorry," he said. "I just—"

"You're in uniform," she interrupted. "And we're in public. It's not professional. I'm the one who should apologize."

Dixie tugged at her leash.

"She can see the dog treat stand," he said with a soft
laugh. But Olivia could tell it was forced. Something was up,
and it was more than just professionalism.

"Everything okay, Sheriff?" she asked.

He nodded, then pulled his sunglasses out of his shirt
pocket and threw them on, effectively hiding from her any
trace of emotion.

"Let's get Dixie a treat," he said. "Then we'll find what
we came here for."

He was quiet while Dixie enjoyed her grain-free pumpkin
biscuits and while she gnawed on her sweet potato slices.
Conversation was like pulling teeth when they finally settled
on roasted corn on the cob as their so-called lunch, since neither was too keen on checking out the corn dog stand again.

Dixie lay on the ground beside their picnic table while
she and Cash avoided eye contact as they ate.

Well, *she* kept trying to gain his visual attention, but he
seemed plenty taken by his corn.

"What in the world is going on?" she finally asked.

He stood, dropped his plate and napkin into the trash and the stripped cob into the compost bin.

She rose and did the same, then crossed her arms waiting for him to answer.

"Cash Hawkins," she said. "Is kissing me so terrible that you can't even stand to talk to me anymore?" Because the way she'd seen it, that very first kiss the day he'd arrested her had been the start of something in her she couldn't quite name, so how in the hell could it have been the *end* of something for him?

"It's not terrible at all," he said flatly. "I just think we might be losing sight of the agenda. You came to Oak Bluff to find something, and it wasn't there. So here we are, chasing down your answers, and I think we should stick to the plan, is all." He picked up Dixie's leash from the grass. "Come on, girl."

The dog looked up from where she was still enjoying what was left of her sweet potato treat and whimpered.

"*Dixie...*" he said with a little more force.

She rose slowly, the treat hanging from between her teeth.

"Sure," he said. "Bring it with you."

Her ears perked up.

Olivia grabbed the rest of Dixie's goodies and followed Cash as he started walking.

"Her stall is usually in the second row," he said.

"Cash."

"Just keep in mind it's been a lot of years since the house was remodeled into retail space and apartment. She might not have any clue what in the hell we're talking about."

"*Cash*," she said again.

"What I'm saying is that you should prepare yourself— for whatever we may or may not find."

She was having trouble matching his gait, so she was now a few paces behind. "Damn it, Cash Hawkins, will you shut the hell up about the letters and just *talk* to me?"

He stopped suddenly, turning to face her, and she plowed right into his solid wall of chest.

She groaned. "What the hell has gotten into you?"

"I'm in love with you, Olivia!" he snapped.

Her eyes widened to saucers, and her jaw fell open. Passersby slowed at his very vocal declaration, and Olivia shooed them away.

She pulled his aviators from his face so she could see his eyes. His gaze, always so steady, was now a raging sea of emotions she didn't recognize on him.

"You're...*what*?" was all she could seem to muster.

"I'm in *love* with you, damn it. And I don't need a pile of letters to tell me if what I feel is real or if I'm doing it right. Because there is no right. There's just me fooling myself into thinking I could avoid getting my heart stomped on again and *you,* blowing into town, messing up the status quo, and then leaving."

She swallowed, her throat suddenly dry. "Cash, I—"

"There," he said, pointing. "Cora's Collectibles. That's our spot."

He strode in the direction of the stall, Dixie at his side.

"So you're just going to drop a bomb like that and walk away?" she asked, scrambling to catch up. "Don't you even want to hear what I have to say?"

He stopped and blew out a long breath. He looked so— tired.

"What happened to us getting through this week and figuring it out?" she asked. "Wasn't it you who said that San Francisco and Oak Bluff aren't opposite ends of the earth?"

He scrubbed a hand over his jaw. "You *are* leaving tomorrow, right?"

"Well...yeah. I have to work on Monday."

"And when do you think you'll be headed back this way?"

Her brows furrowed as she flipped through her mental calendar. "Well, I have the Goldman bar mitzvah on Saturday and a baby shower brunch on Sunday...The next weekend there is that small dental convention..."

"That's what I thought," he said.

"Hey," she said. "That's not fair. It's my job." A job she wondered if she'd still have on Monday. After all, she did run out on the hotel owners' son, which—though having nothing to do with her professional qualifications—could possibly cause some friction at work.

"You're right," he said. "I'm sorry. I was out of line. I just—I wasn't counting on you, Olivia. And now I'm not sure how to make heads or tails of all this."

"Cash Hawkins? It *is* you! Get on over here and say hello!"

They both glanced over Cash's shoulders to find an older woman—presumably Cora of Cora's Collectibles—calling him as she stood in front of her stall.

So that was that. The end of their conversation for now, and she still hadn't addressed the elephant in the farmers market.

He *loved* her.

"Mrs. Abbott!" he said with a wave and what she recognized as his "for the public" smile.

Cora scoffed as they walked over. "You're not in high school anymore. I think you can call me Cora." She looked over the frames of her glasses. "And it looks like I need to start calling you Sheriff. Has it really been that long since you came here with Lucinda?"

She reached up to hug him, her short white hair and petite frame reminding Olivia of Gran and of why she'd come to Oak Bluff in the first place. Because she'd been starting to lose focus.

"Been a little more than ten years," he said. "But you still see Lucinda from time to time, don't you?"

"I sure do. About once a month." She frowned. "So sorry to hear about your stepdaddy."

"Thank you," Cash said, then he checked his watch. "I was wondering if I could ask you a business-related question. It's kind of why we're here."

Cora's blue eyes brightened. "You mean you're actually here to see me? Well, that is a treat. What can I do for you two?"

Cash put his hand on the small of Olivia's back, and she sucked in a breath.

"This is Olivia Belle. Olivia—Cora Abbott of Cora's Collectibles."

Olivia extended her hand to shake, but Cora just pulled her into a hug, too.

"Oh!" Olivia said, then laughed. "It's—nice to meet you."

She cupped Olivia's cheeks in her palms. "Aren't you a pretty one. And where do I know that name—Belle?"

"My grandfather," Olivia said, her voice suddenly a bit shaky. She wasn't sure why, but she felt like she was on the verge of something. "He wasn't from around here. My gran was, though. Oak Bluff, actually."

Cora slapped her knee. "Anna Moretti!" she exclaimed. "Married that boy who went off to war. His name was Belle."

"Holy hell," Cash said.

"Oh my God," Olivia added. "I didn't expect you to *know* them. I just thought you might have their letters."

Cora laughed. "*Know* them, sweetie? Your gran and I were in school together. Lost touch after she and your grandpa ran off and got married, though. And letters? What letters?"

Olivia's heart had just begun soaring to new heights when four words—*four* words—sent her heart and her hope on a collision course with the ground.

Her throat tightened, and her eyes started to burn.

"Damn it," Cash said under his breath. "I'm sorry, Olivia."

Cora put her hand on Olivia's arm. "What letters, dear?"

Olivia drew in a shaky breath. "Their whole courtship was letters," she explained. "They had this one magical night together before he left for the war. But he courted her for years via his letters, and she gave him something to come home to with hers. When he got home, he gave her back the letters she'd written that he'd been able to save, and she kept them safe beneath a floorboard in her bedroom when they eloped."

Cora's eyes widened. "And then she never went back for them?"

"Said she didn't need to once she had *him*." Olivia shook her head and swiped at a tear. "I know it's silly to react like this over something that was never mine to begin with, but…"

Cora gave her a reassuring squeeze. "I bet it would be a great love story for you to read. But if I'd have come across that sort of treasure, I never would have sold it. Though I'm not sure I'd have read them, either."

"Why not?" Olivia asked with a sniffle.

Cora opened her mouth to respond, but Cash cut her off.

"Because it's *their* story," he said. "It's theirs and no one else's, which means whatever worked for them in their time and place could have only ever worked for them."

His voice was gentle, but Olivia's sense of loss was slowly morphing into anger. Because who was Cash Hawkins to tell *her* there were no answers in those letters?

"Thank you, Cora," she said, taking the woman's hand. "It was really nice to meet you, but I think we should probably get going."

Cora patted the top of her palm. "I hope you find what you're looking for, honey."

Olivia forced a smile and then started for the car. She only slowed her gait when she realized it was Cash's car toward which she was heading. She supposed she wouldn't get very far without him.

"You're mad," Cash said from behind her, and she spun to face him.

"*Yes,* I'm mad," she admitted. "You just discounted my whole reason for coming here. Do you have any idea how that made me feel?"

His jaw tightened. "Do you have any idea how it feels to tell a woman you love her and have her unable to respond without having the definitive answer of what love is from a relationship that originated decades ago?" He ran a hand over his close-cropped hair. "Damn it, Olivia. I know you told me you're a runner, but hell if there isn't something real right here in front of you, and you're still running."

She placed her hands on her hips and huffed out a breath. "I am *not* running," she said. "I'm standing *right* here telling you that you made me feel like shit back there. Has this whole week just been you silently judging me for why I came here? *Oh that silly Olivia, thinking she'll find the answers in some stupid letters.*"

"That's not what I said."

"But it's what you implied." Her shoulders slumped. Because even if that wasn't what Cash had been thinking, had *she*?

Olivia had come here on a whim, but up until today she'd all but forgotten why. Now that the letters—or lack thereof—were staring her in the face, what had really been the point?

"Can you just—take me back to the B and B?" she asked, her heart sinking as she thought about saying good-bye to Rose and Marcus. Would she get a chance to see Lily Green again before she left? Olivia guessed she had her hands full with planning her ex's wedding and figuring things out with Luke.

She hadn't found her grandparents' letters in Oak Bluff. But she'd found—*something*.

"Olivia..." he said softly.

Dixie, ever the intuitive dog, whimpered.

Olivia squatted in front of her and gave the German shepherd a scratch behind her ears.

"I'll miss you, too," she said. Then she straightened, meeting Cash's gaze. "Please," was all she said.

"Yeah. Okay."

They rode in silence until they hit the outskirts of Oak Bluff. This was it—the street where they'd met.

Olivia laughed mirthlessly. How had she gotten herself into such a mess in the span of only seven days?

"Aw, hell," Cash said, looking in his rearview mirror.

In a flash he pulled onto the shoulder of the road, grabbed his radar gun, and pointed it at the window.

Seconds later a black sedan flew by—a sedan she recognized all too well.

Cash clocked the car at eighty miles per hour. Then he threw on his lights and put the Tahoe in drive.

"Aw, hell," Olivia mumbled, parroting his words.

The car pulled over as quickly as it had passed, and Cash slowed to a stop.

"So," she said. "When is it a good time to tell you that's my father?"

Cash let his head thud against his seatback. "Of course it is."

Chapter Twelve

Olivia's father would have been enough, but when Cash approached the driver's side window, he could hear the crescendo of voices with the glass still up.

He knocked, but the driver's back was to him as he engaged in a heated argument with the woman next to him.

"Oh my God," Olivia said, coming up next to him.

"This is official police business," he said. "It's safer if you stay in the car with Dixie."

She let out a bitter laugh. "Yeah? Well, that's *both* my parents in there." She pressed her nose to the glass. "And Gran, too! Good Lord, they sent the cavalry after me!"

Cash pounded on the window with a little more force, and this seemed to get the occupants' attention.

The glass lowered, and the car fell silent—until Olivia poked her head over his shoulder.

"Livvy!" her mom yelled from the passenger seat. "Oh, sweetie, I was so worried. I told your stubborn father to slow down, but does he listen? Even his own mother told him he was driving too fast, and—"

"Elizabeth!" Olivia's father yelled. "There's a damn sheriff at the window!"

"I can *see* the sheriff, George. He's standing right next to our daughter, the reason we're *here*." She rolled her eyes.

Jesus. This was what Olivia had grown up with?

Olivia's grandmother met her gaze and Cash watched her mouth, *I'm sorry.*

"Just remember that I *let* you ride with us," her father continued. "Even with a GPS you still would have ended up halfway to Vegas before you'd realized you made a wrong turn."

"Oh, yes," the woman responded. "Thank the heavens I came with you so you could endanger us all with your daredevil driving and then get arrested." She turned her attention to Cash. People usually did this a lot sooner in the whole pulled-over-for-speeding scenario. "You are going to arrest him, aren't you?"

"Enough!" Olivia yelled.

Cash crossed his arms and took a step back.

"What are you even doing here? All of you?" she asked. "I didn't ask you to come. I'm a *grown* woman. I should be allowed to take some time for myself."

Her father threw up his hands. "You didn't answer any of our texts. Is that something a grown woman does? We were worried!"

Olivia shook her head, then pointed an accusing finger toward the back seat. "You promised, Gran. I trusted you."

The old woman's eyes narrowed, but instead of responding from where she sat, she opened the door and got out, standing to face her granddaughter.

The two women were the same height and even had the same slender build. But where Olivia's wild brown curls whipped around her face in the breeze, her grandmother's white hair was short and straight. But they both had the same fire in their brown eyes, and for a second Cash's mind flashed forward fifty years. He imagined himself in his early eighties, Olivia looking much like her grandmother did now, and the thought knocked the wind clear out of his lungs.

"Anna," the older Belle woman said, holding out her hand to Cash but still staring straight at her granddaughter.

"Cash," he said, giving her a firm shake. "It's nice to meet you, Anna. I've heard a lot about you."

This got her attention, and she looked up at him. "Let me guess," she said. "The letters?"

"The letters."

"Can't say I had any clue about *your* existence," she added. "Unless, of course, you've only just met my granddaughter because you've arrested her for whatever reason."

He chuckled. "No, ma'am. That was last Saturday."

Anna shook her head and laughed, too.

Olivia waved a hand between them.

"Um...*hello*? Remember me—the person you're talking about as if she's not even here?"

"Sheriff, may I have a word alone with my granddaughter?"

"Am I getting a ticket?" Olivia's father said, still sitting in the car.

"Yes!" Cash, Anna, and Olivia's mother said in unison.

Cash pressed his hand to the top of the car and leaned down to the window. "And if I hear any more arguing between you two, I'll write you both up for disturbing the peace."

This effectively shut them both up.

He nodded to Anna and Olivia, a silent *I'll take it from here*, and the two women set off a bit down the road where they found a slice of privacy in a bus depot.

It wasn't his business what they were talking about, but that didn't mean he wasn't curious, so he kept himself busy by heading back to his truck and writing a ticket to the second San Francisco Belle he'd met this week.

"Mr. Belle," he said, handing the man the citation. "You were close to thirty miles over the speed limit. I'm letting you off easy by giving you a ticket that says only half as much. This way you don't have to go to traffic court in Oak Bluff."

The man let out a relieved breath. "Thank you, Sheriff."

Cash shook his head. "That's not the end of our bargain. I'm gonna need your word on something—both of you—and I hope there's honor to that word, sir. Ma'am."

Olivia's parents both nodded.

"I've known your daughter for a week, which isn't long. And I don't pretend to have learned the entirety of her family history in that time, so I know what I'm about to say may be overstepping, but I'm going to say it anyway.

"I don't reckon the end of a marriage is easy, and it gets even more complicated when children are involved. But I think Olivia's been hurting for a lot of years, and maybe it's time you two put your differences aside long enough to ask her why."

Elizabeth Belle's jaw tightened, and she narrowed her eyes. "You got a lot of nerve, Sheriff. You don't know anything about our family, about Olivia."

"You're right," he said. "I have a hell of a lot of nerve, but it's only because I'm in love with your daughter and want to see her happy—even if it's over two hundred miles from here." He handed Mr. Belle his ticket. "I do apologize for any disrespect, but I hope we have an understanding here."

He straightened just in time to see Olivia and her grandmother approaching, hand in hand. Both women's eyes were damp. Anna let Olivia's hand go when they got to the car.

"It was a pleasure meeting you, Sheriff," the older woman said. Then she shook his hand and got back in the car. "Close the window and turn on some music, George. Let's let these two have a moment."

George Belle seemed none too happy to give Cash a moment alone with his daughter, but thankfully, it looked like Anna's word was gold.

Olivia worried her bottom lip between her teeth.

"You're going home," he said. It wasn't a question.

She nodded. "I can't keep hiding," she said. "I have to go back, face the mess I made, and try to clean it up."

He'd known this was his last day with her, but somehow it hadn't fully registered until now.

"Time to turn back into a pumpkin, huh?" he asked, forcing a smile.

She laughed, and a tear leaked out the corner of one eye. "It always was. Maybe I should have answered their texts so you didn't have to deal with all this."

He shrugged. "It's all part of the job."

"See?" she said. "I'm not a fairy-tale princess. Just a woman who needs to stop pretending. Though I did enjoy playing make-believe with you."

His chest felt like it was caving in, but he wouldn't put that weight on her. She *had* to go. Even if he somehow convinced her to stay in Oak Bluff, how would that be fair to her and figuring out what she really wanted?

"I'm sorry for diminishing your reason for coming here," he said. "I was frustrated, and it was a shit thing to do."

"Is that really what you believe? That I ran here for some silly letters that don't mean anything?"

He shook his head. "I think you ran here hoping the letters were the answer, and I get that. I really do. I just hope, now that you know they're gone, you can still find what you're looking for."

"What about you?" she asked. "You gonna go to your ex's wedding?"

He raised a brow. "I was sort of hoping you forgot about that."

She nudged his shoulder with hers. "Hey. If I have to face my future, don't you think it's about time you faced your past?"

He laughed. "We're quite a pair, aren't we?"

She smiled, and he realized how much he'd miss seeing her do that for him.

"The sheriff and the reckless driver?"

He shook his head. "I think we're a little more than that."

He waited a beat, letting this moment—their parting—be her call.

She stepped toward him—thank the stars—and splayed her hands on his chest. "We're *so* much more than that." Then she rose on her toes and pressed her lips to his.

He didn't care that they had an audience or that said audience was almost her entire family. Cash Hawkins kissed Olivia Belle with everything he had. He didn't hold back. He didn't worry about self-preservation. He just kissed her like it was the last time he ever would.

Because it probably was.

She melted into him, and for this one tiny pocket of time,

he let himself forget there was anything other than her, right now, in his arms.

Only when they both needed air did they part, though oxygen couldn't compare to how much he realized he needed *her*.

"I have something for you," he said, letting his forehead rest against hers.

"What?"

He led her to the back of the Tahoe, where he opened the door and removed a shoe box. "I'm not good with gifts or good-byes, so just do me a favor and open it when I'm not around, okay?"

"Okay," she said. "But—I feel like this is too quick. I need to tell you—"

"No," he said. "You don't. I think this will be easier if we leave—certain *things*—unsaid from here on out."

She narrowed her eyes at him. "Easier for whom?"

Him. Which he knew was selfish. But she already knew how he felt. Knowing her feelings either way wouldn't change the fact that this was good-bye.

"It's okay," she said. "How about you don't answer my question and I don't say anything else. Not even good—"

He kissed her again.

She was right. They shouldn't say good-bye. Because the truth was, he couldn't.

Cash waited until Olivia's father pulled back onto the road, and then he watched the car fade into the distance as they headed into town. When he climbed into the driver's seat, he pulled the fancy cardstock envelope from the passenger visor and fished out the response card. Then he grabbed the pen from his shirt pocket, clicked it open, and checked off the box next to where it said *Will attend.* He even added a little note.

Tara—
   So happy for you and Tim. Congratulations.
   All my best,
   Cash

   He stuck the card in the envelope and sealed it shut, closing the door on past heartache just in time to open a new one for Olivia Belle.

Chapter Thirteen

It didn't take long to pack up her stuff. When you were used to living with one foot out the door, packing became second nature. But when Olivia opened the small closet in her room at the bed-and-breakfast, her breath caught in her throat when she stared head-on at that giant, poofy dress.

"Nope," she said aloud. "No one wears a bridesmaid dress twice. Plus, first step in facing my life is facing the fact that I'm not a part of Michael's family anymore." Which meant leaving the dress behind and telling him—in person— why she ran.

She didn't love him, not the way she was supposed to. But he didn't love her either, and they'd both ignored the truth for far too long.

She slid the closet door shut but then threw it open again, checking the floor. Then she looked under the bed, *around* the bed, in her small bathroom, to no avail. Nowhere in the room were the shoes—those gorgeous, clear, four-inch heeled pumps. It didn't matter that she'd almost broken her ankle in them *and* had broken the shoe. They could be repaired, and it wasn't as if she planned on getting arrested in them again. If worn and used properly, those shoes were spectacular. And they were gone.

Then something caught her attention out of the corner of her eye. On the striped upholstered chair in the corner of the room sat the still-unopened box from Cash. A *shoe* box.

She sucked in a breath as she approached it, then picked it up and hugged it to her chest. The shoes were in there. She knew they were, but she couldn't bring herself to open the lid, not while she was still here. Because if she confirmed her suspicions, she might never leave Oak Bluff.

She let out something between a laugh and a sob. Because didn't that just take the cake—Olivia Belle having wild and crazy thoughts of staying put.

Instead she tucked the box under her arm and threw her weekender bag over her shoulder. Rose and Marcus were waiting at the foot of the stairs to help her to her car.

"Thanks," she said, a little teary. "But this is all I have."

Rose took the bag and the box from her anyway, then set it on the floor. "But how am I supposed to hug you with all of that in your arms?"

Olivia laughed as the woman drew her into a warm embrace while Marcus quietly picked up her things and brought them out to her car.

"When do you close on the offer?" she asked.

Rose sighed. "The buyer has had some trouble getting a loan, but we're hoping to finalize everything soon."

"What if the new owners don't want to leave it a B and B?" Olivia asked. "Can you make it part of the sales agreement that this has to be a place for tourists to have a home away from home? Or that Trivial Pursuit on Wednesdays is a must or no deal? What about group dinner prep—or using fresh blueberries in the waffles?"

Rose laughed. "Those are all very important stipulations, but I'm not sure we can make the sale contingent on those requests."

Olivia sighed. "Okay," she said reluctantly. "But maybe just say you'll think about it so I can sleep better tonight."

Rose grabbed her hand and gave it a soft squeeze. "I'll think about it."

It was well past dark when she hit the outskirts of San Francisco. And though the first thing on tomorrow's agenda was to face Michael, his family, and whatever came after that, tonight she just needed quiet—which was how she ended up in Gran and Pop's spare room.

Olivia sat in bed, a cup of tea on the nightstand, and the box from Cash beside her, staring at her, *waiting* for her to finally make a move.

A knock sounded on the door.

"Come in."

She'd expected Gran, but it was Pop. He sat down on the edge of her bed. He was a contradiction of a man just to look at him—in his worn jeans and flannel shirt hanging open over an old T-shirt, he looked more like a teen than a man of seventy-four. But then there was his tan but weathered skin and the thick salt-and-pepper hair that always seemed to need a trim.

"Sounds like I missed one hell of a trip to your grandma's hometown. Sorry I had to work this weekend, but you know...if the garage closes, people take their business elsewhere."

She laughed. "I know. And you're the best mechanic, Pop, but when's it gonna be time to retire?"

He grinned. "When I stop loving what I do or when your grandmother tells me I have to. Whichever comes first. Now, let's get back to this little trip of yours. I've heard a lot about it from Gran, but I think I'd like to hear your take on it."

He patted her feet, which were snuggled under the duvet.

She shrugged. "Michael proposed, and I panicked."

"He proposed to you at his sister's wedding?"

She nodded. "I know. But he'd just heard from the co-op board that he could add a fiancée to the deed, and he was really excited." She winced. It didn't matter how many times she said it out loud or what kind of spin she tried to put on it, the proposal never got any better. But the truth of it was that she hadn't wanted it to be better. She hadn't wanted it to happen at all, and she wasn't too sure Michael had either. "A little tacky, right? I mean, if I had said yes, that would have totally stolen the bride's thunder."

Pop laughed. "I think your little disappearing act might have done that anyway."

She sipped her tea, then hugged a pillow to her chest. "I wanted to find the letters. Yours and Gran's. I thought if I read them I could learn your secret."

This time Pop's laugh was loud, straight from the belly. "Oh, darlin', why in the hell would you want to see those? I was an idiot teenager who had no *idea* how to talk to girls. Hand me a wrench and pop the hood of any vehicle in existence, and I could talk for days. But I'm lucky your gran even answered my first letter let alone married me when I got back."

Olivia rolled her eyes. "I think you're downplaying a great romance, Pop. But it doesn't matter. The letters are gone."

"Look, I get that you've grown up with what looks like two extremes—your gran and me"—he groaned—"and then your dad and mom. Sometimes relationships work, and sometimes they implode so damned badly that you wonder how two people ever could have loved each other in the first place."

Her throat tightened. "Did Dad love Mom when he married her?"

"Oh, sweetheart." Pop's face lit up. "I never saw your daddy so head over heels for a girl before your mom *or* after. And she with him. But they expected it to always be easy."

"But it was easy for you and Gran." Olivia had never seen her grandparents fight. Not once. When it came to her parents, she couldn't remember them *not* fighting.

Pop shook his head. Then he leaned over and kissed her on the cheek. "Do you want to know the real secret that you'll never find in some lovesick teenage boy's letters home from the war?"

Olivia nodded, tears in her eyes. "God, yes. I really do."

"Falling in love is easy. Staying in love is work, *hard* work. When you find the man who makes you fall, then makes you want to do everything in your power to keep on falling, that's how you'll know." He raised a brow, grinned, and then left the room.

She thought about the past week—Cash catching her when she tripped in those ridiculous but sexy-as-hell shoes only so she could fall ass over elbow in the middle of the street seconds later. He caught her again when her ankle gave out on their horseback riding adventure. Then she collapsed right onto her behind while petting Dixie the night Cash had made her dinner.

In one week's time, Olivia had *fallen* for Cash Hawkins not once, not twice, but *three* times.

Her heart sped up as she tore the top from the shoe box to find what she'd known was there all along—her glass pumps, the broken heel repaired.

But it wasn't the shoes that stole her breath. It was the envelope on the bottom of the box.

Cash had written her a letter.

Dear Olivia,

Well, now you know why I didn't want you opening the box while I was around. It's bad enough that words aren't really my thing, but having to watch you read those words? Well, it would have been torture—almost as much torture as letting you go.

I let myself believe that not getting my heart stomped on again was better than risking it, so I closed myself off to even the possibility of love a long time ago. I wasn't counting on some wild-haired beauty to speed through my quiet little corner of the earth and turn it way the hell upside down. But damn it if you didn't do just that. Now I can't seem to put everything back just like it was. Funny thing is, though, that I don't think I want to.

I wasn't lying when I said you destroying my heart would be worth it. But the real truth is, you didn't destroy a thing.

I watched Lucinda love and lose in the worst possible way three times. And I kept wondering how she did it—how she could take risks like that again and again. But I think I get it now.

You saved me, Olivia. Falling in love with you might hurt like hell right now, but you know what would be worse? Never having let myself do it.

I'm going to give you your space to get things back on track, but I'll be here if you ever speed into town again.

So, here are your glass slippers, Cinderella. Good as new. I hope you enjoyed the ball.

I love you.

~Cash

Chapter Fourteen

Two Months Later

Cash still didn't know how to fill his nights off, now that heading to crosstown taverns and pubs didn't have the same appeal. Tonight was warm for early December, so he'd decided to take Dixie for a walk up and down Oak Bluff Way.

Things were uneventful until he happened by the bed-and-breakfast and saw something peculiar—a missing FOR SALE sign.

He pushed right through the front door without a second thought.

It was Wednesday, so he found everyone in the common room playing Trivial Pursuit.

"Sheriff!" Rose said. "We were wondering when you'd join us for another game!"

He'd loved playing the one time he did, but he hadn't been able to bring himself to do it since Olivia left. Half the fun had been watching how much she'd enjoyed it. The other half had been—well—*her*.

"The sign," he said. "The *For Sale* sign. Where is it?"

Marcus grinned. "We got a new offer, just last week! The buyer was approved for the mortgage today." He held up a glass of red wine. "We're celebrating if you want to join us."

Before he could answer, his phone sounded with an alert—one he'd heard at least two other times this month.

He radioed the station.

"Walters, it's Hawkins. I'm off duty, but there's a B and E at Lucinda's. I'm next door, so I'll take care of it. She probably just forgot she armed it again. This weekend I'm installing one with an ear-splitting siren. Maybe that'll help."

"Roger that," Walters said with a chuckle. "Here if you need backup, boss."

He groaned. What he needed was for Lucinda to remember when she armed the alarm.

"Come on, girl," he said to Dixie. Then he turned his attention back to Marcus and Rose. "I think I'll take you up on that glass of wine in a few. Let me just check next door."

Rose bit back a grin. "See you soon, Sheriff."

He and Dixie were up Lucinda's back steps and at the apartment door in less than ninety seconds. The main door was ajar, the screen door shut. When he entered, he nearly stumbled over a pair of women's hiking boots.

"Damn it, Lucinda, how many times do I have to remind you to *disarm* the alarm when you walk in the door? And since when do you wear hiking boots?"

His mother appeared in the archway between the kitchen and living room, her long gray hair pulled into a braid that hung over one shoulder.

"I think I need an alarm that makes noise," she said, echoing his thoughts. "And the boots aren't mine."

His brows furrowed.

"Cash, did I ever tell you about the letters I found beneath the floorboard in the living room?"

His stomach dropped.

He hadn't told her about the letters. *Or* Olivia. The truth was, despite what he'd said to Olivia in his letter, the hurt was still too fresh, and Lucinda had been dealing with a far greater loss. He wanted to be strong for her when she needed him most. When she was through the worst of it, he'd planned to tell her what she'd missed the week she'd been gone.

"No," he said. He cleared his throat.

"It was right when we moved in. I was cleaning before the furniture came, and one of the boards sorta jiggled when I was vacuuming. I pulled it out to inspect. It was the edge of a yellow ribbon that caught my eye. The letters must have shifted from just beneath the board during a quake or something, but the light caught the ribbon, so I stuck my hand in there to grab it, and there they were. A stack of letters with postage marks that were older than you."

His hand gripped Dixie's leash so hard he thought the leather might slice straight through his palm.

"What did you do with the letters?" he asked, trying to keep his voice calm.

That was when his mother stepped out of the archway to reveal the woman standing behind her.

"She gave them to me," Olivia said, voice shaking.

Dixie barked, and her tail started wagging.

"Oh, come here, you," Lucinda said. "Let's go take a walk and give these two a few minutes to themselves."

She grabbed the leash from Cash, then whispered, "I really like her, son. Don't mess this up."

He let out a nervous laugh as his mother and Dixie headed back down the steps.

Olivia fidgeted with the stack of envelopes in her hands. "I drove down to deliver some paperwork, and I realized I never got to peek inside Lucinda's shop. We got to talking, and I told her about the letters, how you tried to help me find them, how I realized I didn't want to live and work in a hotel where I was really good at my job but not in love with it, how I fell in love with Oak Bluff *and* her son and decided to use all the money I'd put away not paying rent to put a down payment on the bed-and-breakfast, and—"

"W-w-*wait*," Cash said. "Back the hell up, Speed Racer, and say that again."

She bit her lip. "I used my savings to put a down payment on the B and B."

He shook his head. "Back up further."

"I...fell in love with Oak Bluff?"

He narrowed his eyes. "*Olivia*..."

"I fell in love with *you*, Cash Hawkins. And you let me leave here without ever telling you."

"Wasn't the right time," he said. "You needed to figure out you, and I wasn't about to mess with that."

But she'd just said she'd fallen in love with him, right? And she was buying the bed-and-breakfast. Did that mean she was still in love with him?

He braced a palm on the kitchen counter. "I think I need to sit down."

"What's wrong?" she asked, concern lacing her words.

He shook his head. "Not sure. This has never happened before. My knees..."

She threw a hand over her mouth, then dropped the letters on the kitchen table. She approached him slowly.

"Sheriff? Is that your old football injury, or do I make you—weak in the knees?"

He straightened and blew out a shaky breath. "Hell yes, you do, Ms. Belle. You gonna catch me if I fall?"

She threw her arms around his neck, that beautiful smile knocking the air from his lungs like only her smile could.

"You're way too heavy," she said. "I'd fall right with you."

He raised a brow. "Some knight in shining armor you are."

She laughed. "Cash Hawkins, I want to fall for you and with you as many times as you'll let me. And when things get hard and messy, I want to work at it so we get right back to this place."

"And what place is that?"

She rose on her toes, her lips a breath away from his. "The place where I tell you I know there is no secret to getting it right. The place where I admit that I'll always be afraid we'll end up like my parents. The place where I remind you every time it gets too hard that I love you, and that's why I'm not running anymore."

"I love you, too, Olivia Belle." Then he asked, "Are you gonna read those letters?"

She shook her head. "I'm gonna give them to Gran and Pop for their anniversary. I already read the only letter I need."

His letter.

He dipped his head to kiss her, but she backed away.

"Wait!" she cried.

"What?"

She grabbed one of her hiking boots from in front of the door and handed it to him. "Try it on me!" she insisted.

"What the hell are you talking about?"

She groaned. "Put the boot on my foot and see if it fits."

His brows pinched together. "It's *your* boot. Of course it fits."

"It's a *metaphor*!" She shoved the boot into his hand. "Cinderella?"

He rolled his eyes but laughed, then he knelt down on one knee, boot in hand.

She lifted one foot in the air, balancing on the other. As soon as he tried to slide the boot on, she fell backward onto her rear end.

Cash barked out a laugh, and Olivia swept her foot beneath his, sending him off balance and onto his own ass as well.

He crawled to her side and leaned over her.

"Is this what you meant by falling for me and with me?"

She winced. "Maybe not quite so literally, but then, I never could stay on my own two feet around you, Sheriff."

He shrugged. "Works for me."

And then her arms were around his neck again as she pulled him to her, their mouths colliding to seal the deal.

"You're gonna have to start driving slower," he said. He kissed her again—lips touching lips, then along the line of her jaw, down her neck...

"How else am I supposed to get the attention of the town's sexy sheriff?" she asked.

He rose to his knees and scooped her into his arms. "You got a room at that B and B?"

She grinned. "I sure do."

"Well then, Ms. Belle, consider yourself in police custody for the rest of the night."

She pressed her forehead to his. "You mean yours, right? Would now be a bad time to tell you about the speeding ticket I got on my way into town tonight?"

He stood, set her down on her feet, then held out his palm.

She reached into her pocket and pulled out her car keys, handing them over without protest.

"You're not headed anywhere. At the rate you're going your license will be suspended by the new year."

She shrugged. "Keep 'em. No reason to run off in a hurry anymore. I'm right where I belong." They kissed once more, her knees buckling against his, ready to fall and save each other again and again.

Ready for more cowboys?
Don't miss these other great Forever romances.

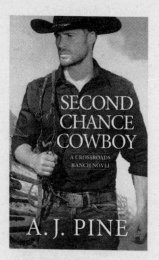

Second Chance Cowboy
By A. J. Pine

Once a cowboy, always a cowboy! Jack Everett can handle work on the ranch, but turning around the failing vineyard he's also inherited? That requires working with the woman he never expected to see again.

Cowboy Bold
By Carolyn Brown

Down on her luck, Retta Palmer is thrilled to find an opening for a counselor position at Longhorn Canyon Ranch, but she's not as thrilled to meet her new boss. With a couple of lovable kids and two elderly folks playing matchmaker, Retta finds herself falling for this real-life cowboy.

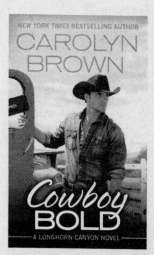

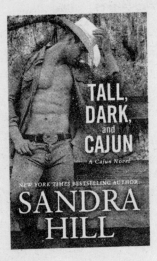

Be sure to follow the conversation using
#ReadForever and #CowboyoftheMonth!

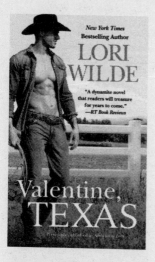

Valentine, Texas
By Lori Wilde

Can a girl have her cake and her cowboy, too? Rachael Henderson has sworn off men, but when she finds herself hauled up against the taut, rippling body of her first crush, she wonders if taking a chance on love is worth the risk.

True-Blue Cowboy
By Sara Richardson

Everly Brooks wants nothing to do with her sexy new landlord, but, when he comes to her with a deal she can't refuse, staying away from him is not as easy as it seems.

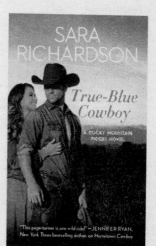